MOONS' DREAMING

MOONS' DREAMING

THE CHILDREN OF THE ROCK
VOLUME 1

Marguerite Krause
and
Susan Sizemore

Five Star • Waterville, Maine

Published in 2004 in conjunction with Tekno Books and Ed Gorman.

Set in 11 pt. Plantin by Minnie B. Raven.

Printed in the United States on permanent paper.

Library of Congress Cataloging-in-Publication Data

Krause, Marguerite.
　　Moons' dreaming / by Marguerite Krause and Susan Sizemore
　　　　p. cm.—(The children of the rock ; v. 1)
　　　　ISBN 1-59414-062-6 (hc : alk. paper)
　　　　ISBN 1-4104-0191-X (sc : alk. paper)
　　　　I. Sizemore, Susan.　II. Title.
　　PS3611.R377M66 2003
　　813'.6—dc22　　　　　　　　　　　　　　　　2003049286

To our first fan, Miriam

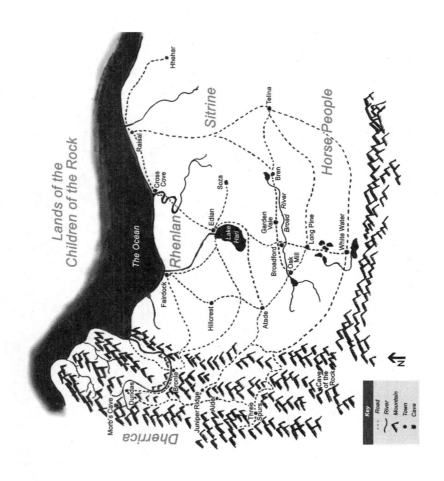

PART I

CHAPTER 1

"There's no other choice. We'll have to kill her."

From his position by the door in the small audience chamber, Dael, captain of the Rhenlan guard, looked on helplessly as King Hion made his pronouncement. Now he understood why this meeting of the king's council had been convened here, rather than the more public space of the great hall of Edian Castle. Better to announce this decision in comparative privacy, and let the public spectacle wait for the death itself.

Light streamed in through the tall windows on the southern and eastern walls, drawing unexpected glints and sparkles from the king's jeweled belt and the silver inlay in his son Damon's dagger hilt. Ledo, Hion's brother, wore so much gold thread that his sleeves glowed in the sunshine. In contrast, Vissa's black gown was enlivened only by its red sash and the embroidered patterns on sleeves and hem that indicated her rank as first among the Redmothers of Rhenlan. The Brownmother beside her wore a brown-marked robe far less elaborate than that of the court Redmother, but her manner conveyed similar dignity. Next to the stately women, the three men looked like bright-hued butterflies.

Not one of the king's councilors spoke up to protest Hion's decision.

Dael swallowed, his mouth dry even though he had no right to be surprised. He had seen this tragedy coming. He had also been fool enough to hope that somehow the situation would change, or that someone on the council would make the effort to find a way to avoid this logical, but heartless, solution.

Prince Damon fixed his steady gaze on the king. "You realize, Father, that she's hardly more than a child."

"She's a Shaper, the daughter of a ruling house." Hion leaned forward in the oaken chair that served as this chamber's throne, and rested his hands on his knees. "If her mother had taught her the first thing about responsibility and loyalty, we wouldn't be facing this crisis." His gaze traveled the circle of his advisors; first Damon, then Ledo, Brownmother Thena, and finally Vissa. "Isn't that so, Redmother? According to tradition?"

"It is a very new tradition, Your Majesty," the old woman replied, her expression pinched with disapproval. "But technically, you are correct."

"No one asked how old the law was. It's a law. That's all that matters," Damon said. "Surely there are precedents."

"There is no precedent in my memory." Given the perfection of a Redmother's trained memory, the statement was inarguable, and Damon fell silent.

In spite of himself, Dael felt a faint stirring of hope. Prince Damon inevitably supported his father's policies; any protest he made would, in the end, only clarify and bolster Hion's original intentions. Duke Ledo rarely said a word in council meetings, for fear of losing favor with his brother or nephew. Brownmother Thena clearly felt out of her depth in this discussion; her areas of expertise and responsibility were the health and welfare of the citizens of the town, not the fate of foreign princesses. Dael himself was not an official member of the king's council, so his opinion would not be welcome in this discussion. He attended the meetings only to provide information when requested, and because it was the most efficient way for Hion and Damon to keep him informed of decisions that he, as captain of the guard, would have to enforce.

Redmother Vissa, however, possessed the wisdom, and perhaps the strength of will, to change Hion's mind.

"Before the fire bear plague, this situation would never have occurred," Vissa said, her mouth a thin, bitter line. "Before the plague, Keepers were content to keep their lands and herds, and Shaper families were honored to

10

govern their own small kingdoms. No one argued over ownership of land!"

Ledo's eyes widened at the tone of Vissa's critical words. Dael's brief surge of hope faded into despair once more. He agreed with the Redmother—life had been safer and saner, a person's duty to the gods clearer and easier, before the plague. Unfortunately, Dael had observed over the years that appeals to tradition rarely worked with Hion. Vissa had never learned that lesson. Perhaps she couldn't. Her life was devoted to maintaining the continuity of their culture; to her, old ways were, by definition, always better than new.

"We live after the plague," Hion replied, "not before it. New situations require new traditions. Redmother Vissa, you are old enough to remember the villages that had to be abandoned, the chaos that threatened until the Eighteen Kingdoms were consolidated into three larger, more manageable tracts. We must not allow that chaos to threaten again. Recite the terms of the law."

The Redmother grew still, her expression blank as she searched her mind for the words the king sought.

"In the event of a border dispute," Vissa recited at last, "in the absence of a high king or queen, and to avoid disrupting the lives of the Keepers of either kingdom, the Shaper families concerned will either exchange goods for land, exchange land for land, cede the territory in question to an adjacent neighbor, or arrange a union of their families in marriage and bequeath the territory to the offspring of that couple. If either side proves false to its vows in this matter, both land and life are forfeit."

Damon shook his head. To Dael, his expression seemed sincerely regretful. "If only Queen Dea had been reasonable."

Hion scowled. "She's not fit to rule. Anyone can see she'll never make proper use of that forest. We made a more than generous offer, and how were we repaid? With treachery."

Ledo cleared his throat. "Are we quite convinced that Princess Emlie was part of the plot?"

"Tell him, Captain," Damon commanded.

Dael braced himself and took a single step forward, away from his unobtrusive post by the doorway. Leave it to Ledo to ask that question, one for which Hion had already determined the answer. In the spring, a pair of merchants from a tiny village in Dherrica, only a stone's throw across the border from Rhenlan, came to Edian to ask for assistance in driving off a band of Abstainers. Hion sent two guard patrols to take care of the matter, a generous and sensible response to a common threat. What Dael hadn't expected was that Hion would then claim the village and its surrounding lands for Rhenlan, on the grounds that he was obviously better able to protect the population. Dea obviously hadn't expected it, either. She sent Princess Emlie with arguments to counter Hion's demands, and for a while, a peaceful settlement, perhaps marriage for the two heirs, had seemed imminent. Then negotiations had broken down, and Dael had been forced to deal with the results.

"Several men in the force that attacked our patrol were members of the princess's escort," Dael told Ledo. "When I confronted her, she admitted that she had sent them to the border, to secure a way for her to leave Rhenlan."

"Without our knowledge," Damon said, "and in spite of our efforts to negotiate a reasonable settlement of our differences."

Dael nodded. He did not believe that the young princess had a malicious intent to deceive Hion and Damon; she had simply been overwhelmed by an impossible situation, and sought to escape her responsibilities. However, to say that Emlie hadn't meant any harm did nothing to change the consequences of her decisions.

"There's no denying two of our guards are dead," Hion said bluntly, and dismissed Dael to his post with a wave of his hand.

"A clear breach of the truce," Damon agreed. "We must respond accordingly."

"It will accomplish nothing." Vissa turned away from the young prince and appealed directly to Hion. "If Emlie dies, how will you ever reach an agreement with Dea? Once there is blood between you—"

"There already is," Hion snapped.

Dael clenched his fists at his side, torn between his loyalty to Hion, and his conviction that, in this instance, his king was making a mistake. Hion had dedicated his life to protecting all of his people, from the lowest guard to the richest merchant, and held all ruling Shapers to the same high standard. Dea had failed to defend the villagers, and Emlie had failed to properly exercise her authority over the guards under her command. Queen and princess both had, however briefly, forsaken their vows. When vows failed, only law could provide a semblance of justice—but Dea and Emlie, in their refusal to accept any of Rhenlan's offered terms, had turned their backs on the law, too.

However you looked at it, Dea and Emlie were at fault. For Hion and Damon to ignore that fact would be a betrayal of their vows to the people.

Dael understood that, but he still couldn't believe that this was the only appropriate response to the crisis.

"What else can we do?" Damon asked the Redmother, his words an uncanny echo of Dael's tortured thoughts. "As her mother's representative in Rhenlan she has full authority over her people. With authority comes responsibility."

"It is wrong to shed blood over a question of jurisdiction."

"The forest was never the issue."

"Sometimes it's necessary to prove a point," Hion said. "How we designate territory as the charge of one royal house or another is part of our Shapers' responsibility. Such decisions must be reached through reason and compromise, and the decision-making process cannot be abandoned on a whim, or replaced by a show of force. Dea may continue to refuse us the forest for now, but the princess's death will remind her that the law cannot be ignored."

The council recognized that the king's decision was final. Hion leaned back in his chair. "There is nothing more to say. You are dismissed."

Dael stepped aside to let Brownmother Thena pass. Damon approached the doorway more slowly, one hand on his uncle's arm, speaking into Ledo's ear with great intensity. As they reached the door, the prince looked at Dael and smiled. "My father and I appreciate your support, Captain."

"Thank you, Highness." Dael bowed his head in respect, and because he did not want the prince to see the doubt in his eyes. It was his job to support his king's decisions, but he wasn't very happy with this one.

Damon and Ledo swept past him and departed. Dael remained where he was until he felt eyes on him once more. He looked up to find the Redmother standing in the doorway, her old face filled with hatred.

"This situation is despicable." Despite her anger, she kept her voice low. "Emlie never plotted against anyone in her life."

Dael glanced past her at the silent figure on the throne. Hion, lost in thought, either couldn't hear them or wasn't bothering to listen. "The evidence, Redmother, suggests otherwise. His Majesty has no other choice."

"This court should be concerned less with evidence and more with justice."

There was no answer Dael could give. Vissa passed him and stalked away, her black skirts swirling around her ankles. Dael waited until her footsteps faded away before addressing the throne. "Orders, Your Majesty?"

"See Damon."

"Yes, Your Majesty."

Vray could not hold anything in her memory this morning. She couldn't even remember from moment to moment whether the sky outside the study room window was cloudy or clear. Trying to commit the family histories of every person in the city of Edian to some storehouse in her head was impossible. Her tutor's voice buzzed like a fly, and made as little sense. Study and work held no meaning for the young princess. All she could think of was her father's council meeting.

The tower walls of the castle seemed to dissolve around Vray as anxious speculation, instead of family records, filled her head. What could they decide? She knew what Damon wanted, and why. Nothing mattered to him more than the prestige and security of the kingdom of Rhenlan. Whatever best served Rhenlan—a border war to prove who had jurisdiction over a border village, marriage with an unwilling bride to cement an alliance with Dherrica, a public execution—was the course of action he would pursue with all of his energy. Yet, how could he? How could Father allow it? No show of power was worth the price of the princess's life.

Was it?

She wished her mother was in Edian Castle. *Mother is never here,* a bitter voice far in the back of her mind reminded her. Vray kept that angry little girl with her red braids and tear-stained face very deep inside her, usually. Her mother never listened to her, and rarely involved herself in the affairs of the kingdom. Vray was used to taking care of herself. Everyone said she was very mature for a fourteen-year-old.

Parents were supposed to make everything all right. But Queen Dea had sent her daughter into an enemy's castle, while Queen Gallia of Rhenlan cared more for her purebred horses than for her duties as wife and mother. Vray had learned that lesson well early in life. The nurses and teachers had quietly whispered it to each other, as if she, with her sharp ears and talent for observing, hadn't been just across the room when the servants gathered to gossip. No, it was only to be expected that Mother would be absent from Edian during this maddening crisis. Even if she were here, she would probably do nothing to interfere with Damon. Vray clenched her fists in frustration. Mother never interfered with Damon. She just smiled, as if his self-indulgence was amusing.

And I'm not just a jealous little sister.

Father—and Dael—insisted that it was not her place to

15

question Damon's decisions as heir. Dael told her to stay out of Damon's way, while Father told her to be a dutiful princess. But the things her teachers told her about duty contradicted everything Damon did. They were ruling Shapers, sworn to protect and guide their people. Damon was only too happy to give orders. He did not, in Vray's opinion, care how his decisions affected the people he led; all he cared about was being obeyed.

Well, she was a dutiful princess. As was poor Emlie. Vray squirmed restlessly in her chair, checking the weather outside the diamond-paned window once more. She saw only clear blue sky, and a flight of birds in the distance, rising from one of the fields beyond the outskirts of Edian.

Vray's stomach tightened with worry, and the ache in her head grew worse. If she was so afraid, how must Emlie be feeling?

"I have to talk to Emlie," she said. The words came out as a dry rasp, and she heard a gasp from her tutor, Danta. Vray realized that she had been talking to herself. She looked at the startled Redmother and was surprised to see that Danta's fleshy, wrinkled face had gone pale. Vray's anxiety for Emlie transformed to anger at the thought that Danta might forbid her from seeing the jailed princess.

"You don't think it's wise?" Vray demanded.

Danta's gaze dropped. She bowed her head, her plump fingers fidgeting with the black material of her skirt, but she made no answer.

Sometimes I think I can be as scary as Damon, Vray thought as she rose from her chair. She patted Danta affectionately on the shoulder but didn't pause long enough to apologize for being harsh with her. Danta was in no danger. It was Emlie who needed a kind word while the ruling Shapers downstairs debated her fate.

Vray rushed down the tower stairs, her blue skirts hitched up and red hair flying. As she reached the bottom, Dael's familiar voice bellowed, "By the great crumbling Rock!" For once, he wasn't chastising her. If Dael had left the audience chamber, then the council meeting was over.

She followed the sound of the curse around the corner and saw him, already halfway across the stone-flagged courtyard, probably on his way to the guard barracks. She ran to intercept her friend.

"Not now, Kitten," the guard captain said as she planted herself squarely in his path. When she didn't move, Dael gave a most perfunctory bow, then straightened, swinging his long golden braid back over his shoulder. He tried to step around her, adding, in a voice dull as unpolished pewter, "Please, Highness."

His eyes, blue as the deep lake beyond the town, avoided hers, his face an impassive mask. Vray recognized the look. He was hungry for some comfort but too angry with himself to ask. Her hands automatically came up to clasp his upper arms.

"What's happened?" she asked him.

Dael closed his eyes and swallowed, clamping down hard on whatever had torn that curse from his lips. Her brother, probably. Dael trusted her, but he also tried not to rouse her quick temper where Damon was concerned.

"It's no use, Kitten," he said. "The law is the law, and there's nothing anyone can do to stop it now."

"Tell me."

He took a deep breath. "Princess Emlie must be held accountable for the actions of the guards in her service."

"That sounds like one of Damon's arguments," she said angrily. "I've heard them all before." She began to turn away, and it was Dael's turn to grab her.

"Don't, Kitten."

She stood stiffly in his grasp and glared at him. "She's barely two years older than me. She still likes to play in the garden with the kitchen cats!" Then the implication of his words struck her. "Execution?"

He nodded.

"They're going to kill her?"

He nodded again. She tried to pull her arm from his grasp, but he held her easily, looking around in case there were servants or guards about to see them. She was fourteen, gangling and thin, and he was captain of the king's guard, no giant but big and strong enough to hold one stubborn girl. She knew that it embarrassed him when their arguments escalated into public shouting matches, or when he had to physically restrain her from doing something he didn't consider wise. He would not let her rush off to confront her brother; not unless she could convince him that she knew what she was doing. Dael worried more about her impetuous behavior than she did.

"King Hion has decided to take firm action in the matter."

"King Hion decides nothing!" she snapped back.

"Hush," he warned, shaking her. "Think—and keep still, Kitten." He'd given her the pet name during the years he'd helped raise her. He hardly ever used it now, not since she'd discovered the sport that was possible between men and women and decided that he would be an ideal partner. The fact that he used the name now showed how distracted he was. He would never admit it in so many words, but she was dear to him, and he didn't want to see her do anything foolish.

"How can I keep still?" she demanded. "Someone has to speak up against this. You know it all comes back to my brother's pure, blind ambition!"

"Your father doesn't see Damon the way you do."

"Then I have to show him!"

"There's a glint of battle in those eyes of yours." He shook his head, fluffing out the hair surrounding his face. "No. There's nothing you can do."

"Am I not even permitted to try?"

He thought for a moment before answering carefully. "You're a princess. Hion's daughter. Damon's opposite. Perhaps you can be of some influence on the king. More likely not, but who am I to keep you from trying?" He released her and stepped aside. "Go to your father," he told her. "He was still in the audience chamber when I left. Go, if you must. I have work."

She let him by and watched him hurry out of sight, through the door to the guard barracks. He had a great deal

18

to organize if the execution was to take place without any difficulties. An execution that he would have to oversee.

Vray's heart tightened with anguish.

"No," she whispered hoarsely. She ran for the audience chamber.

I've been dying for years now, Hion of Rhenlan thought as he slumped in his seat, letting the pain have its way with him for a few minutes, using it to take his mind off his latest decision. He was alone, as he liked to be, his son and counselors gone about the business of concluding the matter. *A long time dying for any man,* he complained to the silence. He would have to make it swift and painless for that poor lamb Dea sent him. Foolish, stubborn woman. He hunched forward, resting his head in his hands. The pain was very bad today. He had barely been able to make it through the meeting without showing his weakness.

He had been a heroic king once, a proud and conscientious Shaper, responsible for freeing his country from the ravages of the last of the fire bears. Fire-bear wounds were poisonous, a cumulative poison. Hion had been wounded more than once in his combats with the creatures. The last time had been fatal, a slow fatality that even Greenmother Jenil could not prevent. She could only slow his dying, coming to Edian every year or so to perform what healing magic she could. Her talent kept the pain damped down to something he could live with. She always apologized because there was no cure for him, and wondered, solicitous in her silly Dreamer way, that he lived at all.

Jenil couldn't cure him, but at least the Greenmother's magic kept his heavily-muscled body from turning into barrel-chested fat. She masked the ravages of the pain, keeping his blond hair from going white too quickly, his blue eyes alert instead of dulled from pain-numbing herbs.

"I'm a stubborn man," he had told Jenil more than once, and repeated the words into his hands now. *Have to be stubborn, have to live until Damon learns enough to take my place.*

"Father?"

Hion jerked upright, and found Vray on her knees before his chair. Her cat-eyed face was full of worry.

"What are you doing here?" he asked gruffly, more annoyed than usual at the girl's resemblance to her mother, whose slender grace and feline features he'd once found so attractive.

Vray sat back on her heels, looking up at him anxiously. "Are you ill?"

Gathering his strength about him, Hion sat up straight, squaring his shoulders and masking his face with a scowl. "Silly child."

Odd how neither of his children resembled him. Damon looked more like Hion's sister, pale-skinned and raven-haired. Vray was the image of Gallia and her whole red-maned family. The guardsman Dael, blond and blue-eyed, looked more like him than his own flesh.

Thinking of Dael and looking at Vray reminded Hion of something. "What's this I hear about you at the Golden Owl?"

Vray blushed. "It's a perfectly respectable inn."

"Where my guard captain spends much of his off duty time. Leave the man alone, child. If I hear of him dragging you home once more—"

"That's not important now," she cut him off, and got to her feet. Before he could gather enough air into his lungs to thunder at her disrespect she hurried on. "I have to talk to you about Emlie. You can't kill her, Father."

Vray was a stubborn, difficult child, and he had neither strength nor inclination to fight with her now. Nothing held her attention for long; he would answer her questions, and she would go away and forget the whole unpleasant incident. "It's the law, girl. The dispute's not been settled within any of the precepts the law allows. Dea delegated her authority to her daughter, and now the girl must pay. I'm only trying to prevent more deaths."

She stared at him. "Prevent death by killing? How, Father?"

"It's no affair of yours, Vray. Go to your studies." She

20

stubbornly remained where she was, her expression pleading, and let the silence build between them. Hion finally grew uncomfortable enough to growl, "Well?"

She cupped her elbows in her hands, pressing her arms close to her body. "Father, there is no honor in this."

"And what do you know about it?" Hion demanded. Before the fire bears came, the world had been full of honor, and laughter and security and magic and all the other frivolities of those prosperous, untroubled times. By the time Hion became king, honor and tradition were luxuries that took time and energy away from the immediate fight for survival. Damon understood the sacrifices demanded by necessity, but his daughter never would.

"You're training me to be a Redmother," she reminded him angrily. "Damon's Redmother . . . not that he'll ever listen to anything I have to say. Not that you listen to me."

"Your childish arguments have no place in the council chamber."

"I'm fourteen. Emlie's just sixteen, unmarried. Doesn't that make her a child, too? Will you kill a child?"

"She plotted treachery against me! Against our people!"

"I don't believe that." She walked away into the shadows near the hearth, then paced back to confront him once more, chin up, eyes glaring. "I don't think Damon believes it, either. The girl is a poor negotiator, that's all, and Damon's pride was hurt when she refused to marry him. That's the real reason he wants her dead!"

"Your brother's only concern is the welfare of our people. You would do well to learn from his example."

"What about Emlie's welfare? What about Queen Dea?"

"Enough! I've made my decision." He could no longer concentrate on her naive, jealous accusations. The pain was consuming him. He wanted to go to his chambers where he could be alone to scream the agony away. He wanted even more to be rid of this hornet and her stinging words.

"Be gone, Vray. Now."

"You've made a mistake." Her words held the tone of a Dreamer's prophecy. Light fell on her from the room's high windows, turning her hair to flames, hurting his eyes. "You can stop it, or we can all suffer for it."

Hion clutched the chair arms and heaved himself to his feet. Tottering unsteadily he lunged at his daughter, open palm striking her across the face.

"I said, be gone!" he roared.

She whimpered and collapsed into a blue heap before him, silenced. For now. Hion gazed down at her. Her huddled figure roused a dim, guilty memory of the laughing three-year-old daughter who had enticed him into games of hide-and-seek, and clambered into his lap in search of affection. He remembered the first time her innocent exuberance pained one of his old wounds, and her tears at his anger when he sent her away.

He shook his head to banish the memory. An explanation or excuse would have been useless then, and would be useless now. Dear Gallia had taught him that.

The girl raised her head and touched a cut one of his rings had made in her fine-skinned cheek.

"Be gone," he repeated once more, and slumped back into his chair.

Shame and sadness mingled in her whispered, "Yes, Sire." Without looking at him, she pulled herself to her feet and fled from the room.

CHAPTER 2

"Look out behind you!"

Pirse, prince of Dherrica, didn't waste time looking. He swung his sword wildly over his head, threw himself to the left, and half ran, half slipped between the sturdy trunks of two towering trees.

The dragon tried to follow. Its frustrated roar mixed with the creaking and groaning of splitting wood as it struggled to thrust its huge body after its prey. Leaves, insects, and pieces of shaggy bark showered down on Pirse. The jungle shook with the sounds of the monster's fury and the alarmed screams of birds and animals.

Flipping hair and sweat out of his eyes, Pirse ducked away from the splintering trees and charged uphill, right under the belly of the rearing dragon. He sucked in great gasps of air, driving his tired body forward, legs quivering with the strain of keeping in constant motion on uneven terrain. The dry, acrid smell of sun-drenched dragon skin was everywhere.

He brushed past the tip of the monster's tail and was clear. "Chelam!" he yelled, whirling to face back toward the dragon. "By the Rock, where are you?"

For answer an arrow whizzed past his shoulder and bounced off the dragon's rump. Pirse back-pedaled up the hill, sword held ready in both hands. The dragon, its heavy head, sinuous neck, and powerful forelegs still entangled in the upper branches of the trees, bellowed again and began a ponderous turn to its right. Another arrow arched over Pirse's head and caught the dragon below the curve of its double-hinged jaw. Outraged, it flung its head back and almost lost its balance.

"Gods, you're a slow one," Pirse panted, gazing up and up and up at the creature. Monster. Dragon. Whatever name it wore, this particular beast was three times the size of a horse. Not particularly large for a land dragon, which was fine with Pirse.

Arching its neck to peer down at the jungle, the dragon took a deliberate step forward. The ravaged trees, which had collapsed against it, tottered and fell. Turning his head, Pirse spotted the cottage-sized boulder he'd chosen at the beginning of the battle, and began easing toward it. The slower this monster moved, the better.

"Chelam, what are you waiting for?"

With a wild neigh of terror, a packhorse burst out of the brush a dozen yards above Pirse and careened across the slope, nostrils flaring. Despite the wide blindfold carefully secured to his halter the gelding was well aware of the nearby dragon, and his frantic, plunging strides proved he had no intention of believing a single word of the reassurances Chelam had bestowed on the decoy before sending him on his way.

The dragon forgot about the fight and swung its huge head in the direction of a good meal. Pirse clambered to the top of the boulder. The dragon got its feet straightened out and flipped its tail behind it, cracking branches off yet another tree. The horse pushed desperately through a thicket of low vegetation, angling back up the hill as fast as his legs would carry him. The dragon collected itself, muscles bunching under the mottled hide, head questing forward on long neck, huge, pleated ears fluttering in the hot afternoon air. Pirse waited.

In deadly silence the dragon launched itself forward, jaws gaping wide, the abrupt burst of perfectly controlled speed all the more terrifying in comparison to its usual clumsiness. Pirse, having seen the same phenomenon more times than he could remember, was ready for the dragon's move. More, he was counting on it. He timed his leap to the dragon's smooth rush, throwing one leg over the wide neck as it shot past the boulder. With one gloved hand he grasped the rough scales, and with the other thrust his sword high and true into the base of the dragon's throat.

24

Gray-white fluid geysered out around the blade, soaking Pirse's hand and arm and splashing in a shining arc across the hillside as the dragon twisted and writhed. Pirse hung on grimly, swinging halfway under the flailing neck to push his sword even deeper into the monster's flesh. The result was another gush of the unnatural lifeblood. The dragon's roar became a choking gurgle. Still moving uphill with the force of its initial lunge, it staggered, its legs crumpling.

Pirse jerked his sword free and flung himself clear just before the dead dragon crashed into the ground.

For a few heartbeats the jungle was very quiet. Pirse rolled onto his back and drew in a long, shuddery breath, then let it out with a relieved whoosh. As if in answer the packhorse, somewhere in the brush on the slope above him, snorted loudly. From the direction of the smashed trees several birds called, tentatively at first, then with enough confidence that others joined in.

A shadow fell across Pirse. Shading his eyes with his clean hand, he gave Chelam a quick visual inspection. "You all right?"

"Fine now, Highness."

Pirse accepted his corporal's offered hand and pulled himself to his feet. The dragon was a mound of motionless carrion a few yards to his left, steam already rising from its glistening back. "Was I imagining things, or did that dragon step on you?"

"Not on me, exactly, Highness. On the rocks next to me."

"It was not a reassuring sight, Chelam."

"No, Highness."

Pirse walked toward the dragon, the corporal at his side. "What happened?"

"My foot slipped."

They reached the almost rectangular head, stepping over the glistening trail of ooze that was all that remained of its lolling tongue. Clouds of insects swarmed uncertainly on and over the glistening body, attracted by the unmistakable odor of ripe decay, repulsed by a process of decomposition that could advance with such mind-numbing speed. Chelam took careful hold of the skull and tilted it at just the right angle.

Pirse raised his sword. Even in direct sunlight he could make out the blue flicker of magic that glinted along its eternally sharp edge. He picked up one flaccid dragon ear, feeling it still dry and cool between his fingers. He carefully slipped his blade beneath the fragile membrane and with a swift, smooth motion detached the ear from the head.

The ear stiffened in his hand, changing color from mottled gray to dull brown in the blink of an eye. Pirse dropped it behind him and shifted his position as Chelam twisted the dragon's head to bring the other ear into view.

"Not many people can do what you do," Pirse observed. "Follow orders, however unpleasant, improvise when things go wrong, and face rampaging nightmares like this one with unruffled calm." He snicked off the second ear and thoughtfully watched it harden.

Chelam let the head fall. It squelched when it hit the ground. The corporal grinned with deep satisfaction.

"Nothing better than watching a nightmare die, Highness."

"This one almost watched you die, Corporal."

Immediately contrite, Chelam dropped his gaze and muttered, "Yes, Highness."

"I don't want to have to train a new assistant, Chelam."

"No, Highness."

"You have to be more careful."

"Yes, Highness."

Relenting, Pirse clapped the man affectionately on the shoulder. Pirse was hot, sticky with sweat and tree sap and dragon blood, and overwhelmingly grateful to have survived another fight. Even the horses had survived!

"Come on, Chelam. Let's find a campsite. I need a bath. And you don't have to say, 'Yes, Highness.' "

Chelam picked up the dragon ear that Pirse had dropped, a smile curling the corner of his mouth. "Wasn't even thinking it." He held out the ear, now leather hard. "I'll fetch the horses."

"Thank you."

"Because if you try to get near 'em, your stink will scare them away."

Sword in one hand and dried ears in other, Pirse could only growl under his breath as Chelam made a quick, strategic withdrawal.

Palle of Dherrica was often annoyed he had not been born before his sister Dea. Since he had not had that good fortune, he tried to content himself with the role of advisor to the queen of Dherrica. Although he had to admit that Dea was generally rather good about taking his advice, today she was being difficult.

"They can't be serious. I sent them Emlie in good faith that we would engage in reasoned negotiation. The next step is supposed to be compromise. An equitable solution for both parties. All Hion has done is repeat his original demands!"

Dea paced back and forth across the raised dais of her throne room, fists clenched angrily at her sides. The long, stone-flagged great hall had been diplomatically deserted by the court for several days now. There were servants about, and guards at the tall double doors at the end farthest from the throne, but they were just Keepers. Only the queen's loyal, dependable, selfless younger brother remained by her side. Palle stood by the throne, one hand resting on the back of the tall chair, his gaze following Dea.

She's gotten a few more gray strands in her curls in the last several days, he noted. And her so vain of the family's black hair. He touched his own waist-length mane with satisfaction, trying to keep his smirk at his own vanity to himself. *Concentrate, Palle. This is supposed to be a solemn conversation, and you pride yourself on being the stable member of the family.*

"Hion will have the forest, sister. It's inevitable."

She stopped pacing long enough to face him and proclaim, "It's ridiculous! Hion's family has been expanding

Rhenlan for forty-five years. They'll not do it at the cost of my holdings!"

"Don't think of it that way," he soothed. "Think of this as an opportunity."

"To lose a forest? Why did I let you talk me into going through with this nonsense?"

"I thought you wanted time while you thought the matter over. Emlie's safe enough. In Edian. With Damon."

She waited for him to continue. He waited for her prompt. "And?" she prompted.

"It's a perfect opportunity."

Dea turned her back on him. "Not that again."

"I don't see what you've got against the boy." Palle assumed his most cajoling tone. "The alliance would be perfect for Dherrica and Rhenlan. You know Hion wants Shaper marriage partners for his children."

"No. Vray for Pirse, perhaps. That would be an alliance I could use. Rhenlan with my heir. Not Pirse threatened by Damon's children."

Palle crossed the dais and put a comforting hand on the Queen's shoulder. She stiffened but did not turn. "Why not both? You'd see the sense in what I'm saying if you weren't so worried about the child."

"You heard Hion's threat."

"Rhetoric, nothing more. He wants a quick resolution to this."

"Not rhetoric. Law. Should I have let his time limit pass? What else could I do? I have to think of my country first." She turned abruptly, and dropped her head on his shoulder. "I'm so worried I can hardly think at all. I can't sleep. I wish Pirse were here."

"There, there," Palle comforted automatically, hand patting the white-clad back. *Fool*, he thought inwardly. *You could have linked our family to the next king of Rhenlan, but you've missed your chance.*

The coast of Dherrica stank. Prince Chasa of Sitrine wrinkled his nose as his ship drew closer to the sandy shore.

Too much moisture, that was the problem. He didn't mind the heat. His own Sitrine was just as warm in its northern reaches, but it was arid country, especially around the capital city where he'd grown up. This part of Dherrica always seemed so chaotic: cluttered and choked with vegetation and wildlife, much of it dead and rotting by the smell. Not at all a comfortable place. Pirse was either stronger than he was, or stranger, to spend so much of his time up here.

Maybe both, Chasa thought as his friend came more clearly into view. At least he had the common courtesy to sweat. Pirse's black hair was plastered to his forehead and his sea-green tunic showed dark blotches of perspiration under his arms and down the front of his chest. Pirse shifted his weight from one long leg to the other and absently patted his horse's steaming neck. The shouted commands of the sailors on Chasa's ship seemed to unsettle the animal, as if it had never seen ship and sail before. Then again, considering Pirse's habits, maybe it hadn't. Pirse liked his solitude. He wasn't going to like Chasa's message.

Chasa reached behind his neck to tighten the thong holding his pale, shoulder-length hair back from his face. He wasn't happy about having to deal with an unhappy Pirse. Sea monsters were easier to face. Safer.

The ship shuddered once as its keel touched sand. One sailor threw the anchor overboard while another put the coracle over the side. Chasa waved his thanks and clambered in; a few strokes of his paddle sent the light-weight shell skimming across the last few yards of water that separated him from the shoreline.

He grounded the flat-bottomed coracle far enough up the beach to enable him to step directly onto dry sand. Pirse's horse nervously tossed its head.

"You're a long way from home," Pirse called across to him.

Chasa drew his boat entirely out of the water before crossing the beach to the other prince. "Ivey told me you were killing dragons. I thought you might like some help."

Pirse smiled, managing to look charming despite the

29

state of his clothes and the dirt smudged across his face. "You'd sail across three kingdoms on the word of a self-admitted storyteller?"

"The stories Ivey tells are true. Besides, it was only two countries. I met him in Rhenlan. Cross Cove."

Pirse grew instantly serious. "The Rhenlaners haven't been fool enough to start trouble with your father, have they?"

"There is no official quarrel between Rhenlan and Sitrine," Chasa said. "In fact, some of the Rhenlan Keepers sent out their fishing boats to help us snare a sea monster that ate two of our merchant ships last winter. That's what brought me to Cross Cove."

"One monster wasn't enough for you, is that it?" Pirse asked.

"I like to make myself useful."

Pirse beckoned him closer, then stood aside to give Chasa his first clear view of what was lashed behind the horse's saddle. Not one, but two sets of dragon ears lay dull and leathery across the horse's rump. "You wasted your voyage, my friend."

"I hope not," Chasa said.

Pirse looked at him sharply.

"I wasn't exactly planning on helping you," Chasa continued. "I was planning on replacing you. You're needed at home."

Pirse tensed. "What's happened?"

"Hion's set his greedy eyes on one of your mother's southeastern forests. Word has it they might come to battle over it."

"What? That's madness!"

"I'm just telling you what I heard." Chasa kept his voice steady, not that it would help. Pirse's stormy reaction would get worse no matter how reasonable Chasa tried to be. With good cause, this time.

"So now I'm expected to go back and negotiate to keep our lawful lands?"

"Your mother already sent a negotiator."

The Shapers of Dherrica had been mountain dwellers for more generations of Dreamers than anyone could remember. The cool heights, shrouded in mists or clouds for much of the year, bred the lightest complexioned people of all the Children of the Rock. Pirse's naturally pale face drained to the color of the hot white sand beneath their feet and his fist slammed down on his saddle. The horse backed a step, but Pirse held it still.

"She couldn't, not Emlie!"

"Ivey thought you'd want to know."

"I've got to get back!" Pirse eyed his horse, then the ship that bobbed placidly on the water, visibly trying to calm himself. "How long would it take you to get me to Bronle?"

"Against the wind? Twelve days if we're lucky. Twenty if we run into a storm. You know how changeable the coastal currents are."

"I'll ride." Pirse turned to his saddle and began unlashing bundles.

Chasa watched his friend worriedly. "You'll need supplies."

"I'll take the relay trail, travel light. I can eat when I stop to change horses." He lifted the dragon ears and dumped them unceremoniously in Chasa's arms. "Do me a favor and look after these. Gods willing, I'll meet you on the quay at Bronle and take them off your hands again."

Chasa awkwardly hefted the dragon ears to one shoulder. Pirse tightened the girth of the now nearly empty saddle, then flung himself up onto his mount's back. Only his sword in its scabbard and a small bag of food added their negligible weight to the load the horse carried.

"Be careful," Chasa said.

Pirse stood briefly in his stirrups. "Corporal Chelam is in the forest, hunting. Tell him I'll see him at home."

He leaned forward and the horse sprang away, galloping eastward along the stretch of hard sand between the foliage and the water's edge. After a hundred yards horse and rider veered into an opening in the wall of trees and disappeared from view.

Chasa trudged back to the shore. He dumped the dragon ears into the bottom of the coracle, then returned to wait for the corporal.

It wasn't much, but it was the least he could do to help the prince of Dherrica.

CHAPTER 3

Aage drew in a lung-full of warm, humid air and gazed up the hill. No matter how often he came here, the sub-tropical forest of northern Dherrica always took some getting used to. He shrugged off his robe, which had been comfortable attire in the early morning chill in Sitrine, and folded it over his arm. Wearing only his light under-tunic and boots, he began to climb.

Near the top of the hill, an old man sat on a rock, holding the universe at bay. The wizard Morb didn't look particularly old, but Aage knew he had been born in the generation of Dreamers before his own, hundreds of Shaper and Keeper years ago. The people in the nearest village probably thought of him as a middle-aged hermit, one of their own kind who chose to live up here above the roof of the jungle. They would never guess how he spent his days. If they did guess, they wouldn't understand it. *Rock and Pool,* Aage thought, *I hardly understand it, and I can do it myself.*

Aage reached a ledge twenty feet below the wizard's perch. The rock where Morb sat was a round-topped boulder jutting out from the side of the hill, its surface so smooth and hard that not even the tenacious sucker-vines had been able to find a root hold. The hill was the highest point on this side of the valley, part of a modest range that ran between the Great River and the true mountains to the west. Those peaks rose sheer from the waters of the sea and marched southward without pause, to vanish into the endless ice and snow at the bottom of the world. In Morb's youth, a kingdom of fisher-folk had lived to the west of the mountains. Only the sea, and a few icy passes, had connected them with the rest of the world, but they had been self-sufficient people, served by a wizard and Greenmother of their own.

33

The plague had finished all that. Now, in all the world only two Greenmothers with their life-giving magic still survived. There were fewer Mothers of the other colors, too, but fewer were needed since death had claimed so many of the Children of the Rock.

Morb shifted his grip on the power, and Aage hurried up the path toward him. The older wizard remained seated, legs folded, hands palm upward in his lap, cradling a largish bowl of water, in the center of which rested a round stone. Morb's open eyes were fixed on his miniature rock and pool, his expression placid. All this registered on Aage's outward senses, but his inner sense, his Dreamer's sense, his sense of the power of the gods which filled the world and interlaced itself through most of its creatures, detected more. Morb was putting aside his task of holding the universe at bay.

As Aage came level with Morb's boulder, the wizard's cave came into view. From the outside it was merely a black, semi-circular opening in the side of the hill framed with orchids, its precise outline blurred by trailing leaves and creepers. Inside were the bare necessities of physical life; a bed, a fire pit, and a little rivulet of water that emerged from the back recesses of the cave, formed a pool in a stony basin conveniently near to Morb's hearth, then vanished down a crack between wall and floor.

The lines of power that focused on the seated Dreamer shifted yet again, causing Aage to flinch. Morb's gift sometimes awed him with its intensity. The Keepers in the nearby village would laugh at the thought of anyone being awed by Morb. They had no idea that a great slayer of monsters, dedicated to the protection of the Children of the Rock, lived a half-day's walk from their doors. Keepers and Shapers judged by the evidence of their senses. They believed in the ship-eating monsters of the sea, the dragons of the north, the phantom cats of the plains, the once-deadly fire bears of the highlands, and the wind demons that swept out of the eastern desert.

The monsters Morb fought did not share the same world

with the Children of the Rock. Only benders of power—the Dreamers and, presumably, the gods who had begun it all—could sense the threat from Outside. Not monsters who devoured children or blew down entire villages or ravaged herds. Gray-haired, bandy-legged, round-faced Morb fought off the sort of monsters that could rip the world to pieces.

Just an old man, Aage thought, his throat dry. Sitting on a rock, holding the universe at bay. Who, when he needs a nineday or two of rest, calls on me to take his place.

The sensation of imminent threat receded somewhat as Morb completed his disengagement. The wizard lifted his eyes and smiled at Aage. "There you are." He plucked his stone out of the bowl and drank off most of the water. Then he got to his feet. His crooked legs and short torso made him a good head shorter than Aage, but he jumped agilely enough from the top of the boulder to the path. "Well, what news of the world?"

"Gavea died." Aage unslung his pack from his shoulder and set it on the ground beside the boulder. He pulled out his handsomely carved cherrywood bowl and dug in an inner pocket for his favorite stone.

"I felt her go. She was so very old. Saw four generations of Dreamers," Morb said. "Five generations, if we count the youngsters growing up in your king's country."

Aage found his stone, a water-smoothed ovoid liberally speckled with reds and oranges. "We can't count either of them. We'll see no hint of their gifts for years yet."

"Four generations then. It's still a long time. Gavea deserves her rest."

"I think she gave up on us. I think she saw the end coming and couldn't bear to be here when it happens."

Morb didn't argue with him. Together they walked along the path and into the cave, where Aage filled his bowl from the pool. Not until they were outside once more did Morb speak.

"You're losing your sense of perspective again," he said. "You knew Gavea well enough to know she never gave up.

35

She stayed with us as long as she could. She simply wore out. None of us can bend the power indefinitely. Besides, it's not as bad as you think. The world will survive."

"How can it, without us? We've dwindled to a mere handful. The Shapers' numbers are diminishing as well, and the way they're behaving they're going to drag the Keepers down with them."

"The Keepers are too numerous for that."

Aage set his bowl on the boulder for a moment. "Numerous enough to be feeling more secure than they should. No one understands the danger. They could all be killed! That's what worries me."

Morb stroked a thumb down his bulbous nose. "It's their ignoring your prophecy that bothers you, lad." His dark eyes twinkled. "Lack of attention always makes prophets a bit touchy."

Aage's fair skin warmed with more than the day's rising heat. He would have protested, but he sensed the regathering of forces that had been driven back by Morb's last onslaught. Aage seated himself carefully on the boulder and placed his bowl of water in his lap. He took his stone in his other hand and centered it gently in the bowl. The fundamental figure of rock and pool instantly focused his attention and energies. Rock and Pool, the source of life, the source of his people, mother to the Firstmother. With his decades of experience, Aage could sink through the layers of meditation almost instantaneously, mind clearing, body relaxing. He abandoned hearing, sight, touch, smell, taste, as he became attuned to his other senses. Inner senses? Outer senses? There were no words for what he did now. Words were part of the world of Shapers and Keepers, animals and plants, mountains and lakes. Aage turned inside himself in order to face the Outside, the other worlds, the monsters searching for a way to invade his home.

The lacy web encircling the world was such a tenuous, fragile barrier. Aage sensed the approaching Other, an essence of hunger and burning need. Formlessly it pulsed forward and touched his defenses, seeking an opening, straining to reach past him. Sometimes one of the Others slipped through. In the prosaic world of Keepers and Shapers it might become a dragon or phantom cat or shrieking storm, hunger coalesced as ripping, slashing, violent death. The animal shapes were unstoppable except by magic-forged steel. The less tangible manifestations Aage could eliminate himself, but only at a great expense of energy. Far better if he stopped them here, now, where his magic was strongest, the effort less costly.

Where innocent lives were not at risk.

Aage bent the power and began to fight.

The King of Sitrine rubbed a hand over his balding head and sighed. His daughter wasn't looking at him, but she tsked at him nonetheless. Sene's frown lessened slightly as he continued to study the map spread out on the table in front of them. The parchment showed the three kingdoms of the Children of the Rock, and the plains of the horse people to the southeast.

It was a new map; none of the dead kingdoms' names appeared on the parchment. He traced a forefinger across the diagonal marks that indicated cultivation, wondering if he should have the map redrawn.

Only a few ninedays ago, Dea and Hion had been squabbling over a forest village. This morning, shortly after Aage had departed for Dherrica, more troubling news had arrived, this time from Rhenlan's side of the border. A fishing village, Gleneven, had been attacked by a large band of Abstainers. By now, help must have arrived from Hion or Dea, but it could be days before Sene heard how the affair had ended. He did not want to wait days. He wanted to know now.

"Do we have any messengers left?"

It was Jeyn's turn to sigh. "No," she said, with just an edge of impatience in her amused voice. "Should you want me to saddle Silvy, I will, and ride off to wherever you like. But you can't know everything every moment. Not even Aage knows everything."

"We can forget Aage for now." He tapped his finger on the upper left-hand portion of the parchment. "He completely loses track of time when he's off with old Morb."

"He always says he's fishing," Jeyn muttered.

Sene glanced sideways at his daughter and smiled. "He saves his tales for you."

"I nag."

"What he's doing is important," Sene said more to himself than to Jeyn. "But I need him. I need his ability to find out what's happening in the west."

Jeyn ran her finger across and southwest from the mark indicating their location in Raisal, on the north coast of the continent, to the centrally located capital of Rhenlan. "You'll have a report by midday tomorrow."

"It will contain old news." Before Jeyn could nag him in his wizard's absence, he quickly added, "Which is the best I can hope for. I'm an impatient old man." He was forty, and in perfect health.

Jeyn did not respond to his teasing. She scowled at the map and asked, "What is Hion thinking?"

"The situation has gone too far," Sene agreed. "Rhenlan's gone too far."

"Hion's gone too far," Jeyn corrected him. "And I'm not marrying his son."

"Of course you're not."

"He did send an offer."

"And I sent it back, didn't I?"

That won him a predatory smile from his heir. Maybe the way to deal with Rhenlan was to let Jeyn take a hand in its future. No. The Dreamer problem was more important in the long run than any of Hion's warped ambitions. Jeyn and her twin Chasa would marry the sensible Keepers he had picked out for them. That reminded him that Chasa's betrothed was still with the Brownmothers in Rhenlan. Rhenlan. Not his land to rule. He didn't want to rule any land except Sitrine. Unfortunately, by its location and the policies of its rulers, Rhenlan was becoming the center of everything important to the survival of the Children of the Rock.

"There used to be more than three kingdoms," he said aloud.

"I know that, Father."

"And why are you being so formal?" he demanded, turning his back on the map to look down at the girl. She smiled once again, brown eyes warm with teasing. She and her brother looked remarkably like their pale-haired mother, slender of build rather than big and square like him—but they had inherited his eyes.

"You're being very regal yourself today. Thought you might like formality for a change. Respect from your humble subject."

"Maybe I ought to marry you to Damon."

Jeyn made a face. Sene turned reluctantly back to the map. Beyond the table, the low windows of the terrace opened onto a view of the estate's north pasture, which sloped down to the sea a half-mile away. The bright spring sun was not too strong. A gallop down to the beach would be nice, followed by a leisurely swim. Worrying about the squabble between the kingdoms of Dherrica and Rhenlan was occupying far too much of his time.

"I want to know if Dea took action to aid Gleneven. And I want to know if Hion's deliberating tempting her, or if he was honestly unaware of Gleneven's need."

He looked up to find Jeyn nodding her agreement. As much as she liked to tease him, she was as concerned as he was. She and Chasa understood what it meant to be Shapers.

"Is there anything we can do while we wait?"

"Let's saddle the horses."

"We're going to Edian?" she asked, surprised.

"No," he teased her, "we're going for a swim."

Greenmother Jenil paused in the doorway of the inn. Another illness defeated by her skill. Another child who would live and, if the gods willed, someday have children of her own.

And what of my children?

Jenil stepped down into the darkness of the inn's stable yard, trying to decide whether to walk the miles home to Garden Vale, or transport herself magically to her destination. The walk would give her time to think, to prepare what she had to say. Another child awaited her attention, a girl critically important to the future of the Children of the Rock.

One day soon, Filanora would have to sacrifice everything she'd grown to know and love in order to build that future, but Jenil could not let that fact influence either of them. Coming to the dirt road that wound through the center of the small village, Jenil stood in the humped middle of the track and weighed the value of procrastination against the reality of aching feet.

Her feet won. She closed her eyes and bent herself sideways and forward through the power surrounding the world, leaving behind a puff of smoke and arriving elsewhere with a fluttering in her stomach.

Jenil gazed around her chamber at Garden Vale. It was a pleasant room, full of books and jars of healing herbs, lit by the soft gold light of many candles. Slipping out of her cloak, she said, "Hello, Filanora," to the girl leaning over the embroidery stand. "I'm glad you're still working on that hanging."

Filanora came forward. For once, the girl who much preferred to be called Feather did not make a sour face at the sound of her real name. Instead, her delicate features twisted in an expression of dismay.

"Oh, Greenmother, we've had the saddest news! Gavea the Great has died!"

Jenil took the chair Feather had occupied, and gently brushed back a few of the wisps of black hair that framed the girl's heart-shaped face. "I know, child. I felt her go."

"Aren't you sad?"

"It was her time." She was not sad. The word did no justice to her emotions. Stricken. Devastated. Terrified. The web of power had vibrated all day with the reactions of the remaining Dreamers. *So few of us, and now further diminished.*

Jenil gazed intently at the pretty child in front of her. "Do you remember Gavea?"

"No. We never met." A tiny frown puckered the smooth skin between her eyes. "Did we?"

"It was Mother Gavea who found you in one of your father's lemon groves. You were very young and very frightened. Your family had just died of the plague. It was a small outbreak."

Small. After what the plague had done to the Children, she and Gavea had been grateful that, in this instance, only one village perished. A very brave village. The people had posted guards along all the roads and allowed no one to come near, to prevent the plague's spread.

In a soft, shaking voice, Feather repeated, "Lemon groves. What was this village called?"

"Telina. You are Filanora, daughter of Rish and Alonora. Alonora was a bee-keeper. Her honey was famous all over Sitrine."

"I—I remember her honey. On the floor. She fell, in the kitchen, and the jar shattered . . . flies came." A slow horror spread over Feather's face, and she raised her hands to her mouth, as if that would stop the awful words. "They were everywhere, on her mouth, her eyes, I couldn't—"

"Hush." Jenil grabbed the girl's fragile hands and held them tight. With a deftness born of too much practice, she bent the power and slipped into Feather's mind. "No, you never met Gavea," Jenil said, and into her spoken words she entwined all of her healer's power. "You are Filanora, my ward, and when you are older, perhaps you will become a Brownmother. You have lived here in Garden Vale all your life, and your past is nothing but pleasant memories of berry-picking outings and the embroidery we design together."

The horror faded from Feather's eyes. Jenil sighed. No, she was not ready yet. How long would the healing take? The world desperately needed a new generation of Dreamers—but nothing would be accomplished by driving this child into insanity. Jenil had no choice. She would con-

41

tinue to protect Feather from her memories. Surely, as she grew older she would become better able to deal with them.

Carefully, Jenil withdrew from the girl's mind, and released her hold on the gods' power. "No, you never met Gavea," she repeated, nothing in her voice but the fatigue Feather was used to hearing at the end of the day.

The child blinked. "No. I didn't."

"It's too bad. You would have liked her. She loved to sew, just as you do. Come." Jenil turned in her chair. "Show me what you accomplished on your tapestry today."

Chapter 4

Too many people, Dael thought, making his way as carefully as he could toward the pool enclosure. He looked alertly around him as he shoved and shuffled his way along the perimeter of the courtyard, determined to get close enough to see Vray, but not wanting to use his authority just now. He didn't want to be the one to make a disturbance in the solemn crowd.

This was not a happy gathering, no Festival day bringing people to the castle to listen to Redmother tales. This many people didn't show up for a Redmother's tales anymore. The bright summer colors of tunics, flowing skirts, and light-weight trousers were the same as appeared at mid-summer Festival. But the mood on this day was far different. Sad faces. Angry, some of them. Confused. Some bitter.

This should not be happening. Not a public Remembering. He wished Damon had ordered him to stop it. The girl's death this morning had not been public. Dael didn't want to think about it but it was hard to get the sight out of his mind. He remembered how Emlie's fine black hair clung to the executioner's hands as he tightened the strangling cord. Tears dampened the white yoke of her dress, but the princess died in silence, big pale eyes full of terror, then pain. Dael had witnessed it, but it wasn't a memory he was going to be able to bring himself to share.

He reached the wall to the left of the pool. A number of people still stood between him and Vray, but his height permitted him to see clearly over their bowed heads. Vray stood beside the pool, her black robes trimmed in the red of her order, her head tilted thoughtfully, eyes closed, listening carefully to the voices that spoke, one by one, from the crowd. She looked more solemn than any of those who chose to give her their memories of the dead young woman. *Why are you doing this, Kitten?* That wasn't a fair question. He knew why she had to do it. She'd explained it to him quite emphatically when he'd tried to talk her out of it.

"It's my duty." She'd been crying as she spoke, facing him in the corridor connecting the courtyard with the great hall, minutes after the princess's death. She hadn't cried during the execution. She'd witnessed it in stony silence with the other Red and Brownmothers of the court. When he caught up with her, tears dripped from her sharply pointed chin and clouded her gray-green eyes.

"It's dangerous," he had insisted. "Your father will be furious."

"I'm used to that," she'd argued back, touching a bruise on her cheek.

"Do you have to make it a public Remembering? Wouldn't it be better if—"

"No!" she had snapped. "That would be hiding the truth. All Rhenlan knew she was here. All Rhenlan must know what happened to her. She was my family's guest, and I am our Redmother. She will be Remembered!"

Dael covered his eyes with one hand, shutting out the vivid memories as well as the chilling present. People were speaking, but he didn't want to hear them. Hion wanted the death ignored. He had made his point to Dea. The Remembering ceremony would make an entirely different point to the citizens of Rhenlan. Hion wanted the approval of his people, and had it, usually. If Vray's actions today detracted in any way from the respect and obedience that the people accorded to their king, Hion would never forgive her.

So much misery, all because two Shaper families couldn't reach a compromise. To dwell on the tragedy could spark unrest in Edian, and only make matters worse. Why couldn't Vray see that?

He'd thought she was intelligent enough not to challenge her father and brother. He'd hoped, anyway. *Hion's going to react, Kitten. You're showing you can be a threat to his au-*

thority. You know it, too. Shaper games. I've tried to teach you better than that!

As Dael stared at her, his anger began to slip away. She was so still, so attentive. So beautiful. Despite the Redmother's robes, there was no question that she was a princess. She had brought this crowd together, and now controlled them. *A Shaper shapes,* Dael thought. *They can mold our emotions as easily as Dad fashions an ornament from a lump of soft gold.* Vray was born to rule. She would do it well and properly and fearlessly if she were heir instead of Damon.

Just look at her! He wanted to shout the words at the citizens of Edian, the visiting merchants and countryfolk, his people watching from the walls. This colt of a girl was the soul of Hion's line, maybe more so than Damon. Despite grief, despite the danger of defying her father and angering her brother, she was doing her duty. This was a queen.

I'm scared, Dael admitted silently. He didn't know if she was going to get away with this. He couldn't believe she'd be allowed to get away with it. But by the First Mother, he was proud of her today.

Edian was the king's town. It took in food and raw materials from the countryside all around, and produced nothing. Nothing, that is, except guards. So Tob's father said.

Tob stared around the large central square of the town, and decided that his father was right. At least as far as the guards were concerned. In all his eleven years he'd never seen so many guards in one place at one time. The armed men and women stood in small clumps between craft stalls along the edge of the square. Half a dozen others were mounted near the entrance to the open green, their horses stamping their feet in impatience at standing for so long. Tob swallowed nervously, then broke into a trot as his father continued his passage across the center of the square.

The day's weather had been good for trading. Puffy clouds dotted the blue skies, and a cool breeze rippled gently against the multicolored awnings on the craft stalls. But half of the stalls had been empty and silent all day. Now, although it was only midafternoon, most of the other stall owners were closing down. Tob imagined that he could feel the guards' eyes on them as he and his father left the square and climbed the steep road leading toward the king's castle. With an effort he resisted turning around to look to see if any of them were following. The road was far from empty. Jordy the carter was not the only man in Edian interested in what had happened at the castle.

Tob heard a voice calling his father's name. Jordy paused, then stepped to the side of the road to exchange a few words with a merchant. The pause gave Tob opportunity to catch up. As he reached him Jordy said gruffly, "Stay close, lad. I don't want to lose you in the crowd."

Tob had a fleeting desire to ask if he could hold his father's hand, but he bit back the words. He was no longer that much of a child. For as long as he could remember, he'd looked forward to this, his first summer of traveling as his father's assistant on the summer trading route. He'd enjoyed the hard work of helping Jordy set up camps and load and unload the wagon. Mastering the carter's special skill of memorizing customers and their orders was more difficult, but Jordy had accepted his honest effort with respect. Tob was not going to ruin his position now by giving in to his fears. He compared the worried expressions on the faces around them with Jordy's tight-lipped anger. No. Tob would not be afraid.

"I'm right behind you," he answered his father.

Jordy nodded, turned, and led off once again. This time Tob kept up easily. He was a head shorter than Jordy, but during the ninedays they'd been traveling the roads of the kingdom he'd learned to keep pace with his father's ground-eating stride. He made himself fall into step with Jordy now and kept his eyes firmly fixed on the back of the familiar embroidered tunic.

As they reached the low entrance to the castle courtyard they slowed, other people pressing close as everyone prepared to pass through the narrow gateway. There were guards here, too.

Three hundred people had crowded into the castle courtyard, and more were coming all the time. Despite this, or because of it, the silence was eerie. Jordy reached back and rested a wiry arm over his son's shoulders, drawing the boy up beside him. Tob glanced at him quickly from under thick black lashes, concerned. Jordy shook his head, motioning for silence.

Although the Rock Pool was hidden beyond the heads of the people in front of them, Jordy could just hear the rise and fall of single voices uttering their remembrances. A young woman's voice was saying, ". . . a very gentle way with the kitchen cat. The princess said she had a favorite cat at home and spoke of going back to visit it. I remember a woman who knew kindness."

Around them heads nodded solemnly. After a suitable pause another, masculine, voice was raised. "The princess's favorite color was rose. She asked for a rose bed cover when she first arrived at the castle. I remember going down to a woolen stall to buy one. I remember the princess with the color rose."

Again silence. Jordy waited a few seconds, then took a deep breath and spoke.

"I remember her arrival in Edian." His voice carried clearly to every corner of the courtyard, turning a few heads. He'd lived in Rhenlan for many years but his Dherrican accent had never blurred. "She arrived with royal escort, official envoy between her kingdom and ours. Remember her as her mother's child, called to fill an impossible role."

Beside him, Tob stiffened uncomfortably. Jordy returned the sharp glances of his neighbors, not bothering to mask his anger. Let them hear the truth! Let them remember! Wasn't that what they had come for?

A voice close to the Rock Pool began to speak. Jordy listened long enough to be certain that he had sparked some remembrances of more serious aspects of the princess's life and death. Then he dropped his hand to Tob's elbow and pressed the boy toward the gate once more. People made way for them so they in turn could press closer to the Pool and its ceremony. Jordy doubted that every one of these people had a personal remembrance of the princess to contribute, but whether they contributed or merely came to witness, the important thing was that they had come.

Movement atop the courtyard wall drew Jordy's eye upward. Standing between two bowmen was a slender figure, his black hair cropped just below his ears. Prince Damon. He was paying no attention to the mass of people crowding the courtyard. Instead he was gazing toward the Pool and, Jordy realized, his sister. So, she did not have His Highness's approval for the ceremony? Damon couldn't have expected to avoid a Remembering. According to the word that had spread through Edian, the king had killed the poor girl with all proper pomp and ceremony. A Remembering was the next logical step. You couldn't just bury a body without remembering the person's life. However, a private ceremony restricted to the inhabitants of the castle might have been more to the king's liking.

Jordy glanced briefly over his shoulder. He never had caught a glimpse of Prince Damon's younger sister, the princess who had initiated the ceremony. For the first time, Jordy wondered just how dangerous her position was. Officially, traditionally, she had done the right thing, paying homage to a person who had been a guest, however unwilling, of her family.

But doing the correct thing according to protocol and doing the correct thing for the convenience of King Hion were two separate matters entirely. Neither the king nor his son had reputations for tolerance among the Keepers outside Edian. Jordy hoped fervently that Damon's sister knew what she was doing. He had no use for Shapers and their increasingly high-handed ways, but he had to give his grudging respect to the girl. She at least knew what she was supposed to do—and did it.

An eddy in the crowd propelled them suddenly through

the gate and onto the road next to the castle walls. As soon as they were outside Tob said, "So many people to remember one woman."

"Not just any woman, lad. An innocent playing piece in a game not many understand."

They started down the hill side by side, turning away from the road that would have led them to the town square, making instead for the pasture where they had left the horse and wagon.

"Do you understand it, Dad?" Tob asked in a quiet voice.

"Yes and no," Jordy replied after a long moment. "What I do understand, I don't like."

To his relief, the boy dropped the painful subject. Jordy enjoyed answering his son's questions—when he had answers.

Today he had none.

The final relay station west of Bronle was a lonely farm perched on the side of a hill. The Keeper and his family expressed neither gratitude nor resentment at being chosen to stable a pair of the queen's horses for the use of passing messengers. At least not in Pirse's hearing. Pirse only used the relay stations occasionally. He preferred his usual mount, an experienced animal who would carry him willingly against their enemies and back again with hardy endurance and a canny instinct for dragon fighting. But this mad a dash would have killed him—the animal would have galloped without complaint until his heart burst. Pirse had chosen instead to make for the messenger relay trail and leave his favorite horse, winded but still whole, at one of the stables.

His eighth horse galloped valiantly into the cramped farmyard. The overcast sky, milky-white overlaid with ragged-edged clumps of gray cloud, hung low and menacing overhead, shifting with erratic gusts of wind. The horse shuddered as he reined it in in front of the barn. The farmer, gray-bearded and stocky, swung open the doors as Pirse slid down to the ground.

"I'm Prince Pirse. I require a fresh horse for Bronle."

As the farmer saddled a long-legged gray, Pirse wolfed down the last of his supplies. The man offered no conversation. Pirse chewed hard cheese and harder bread, concentrating on that rather than on morbid imaginings. There was nothing threatening in the man's silence. He probably just disapproved of anyone who arrived on an ill-used animal. Only a fool would read more into the farmer's troubled expression than that.

Except that he'd passed a shepherd girl just before noon with much the same look on her face. A pack of children weeding a field in the valley below had stopped to stare and point at him.

That was not unusual. But none had waved. He was their prince. Whatever the failings of other Shapers, in his own family or elsewhere, he had always kept his vows. He was used to friendliness from those under his protection, not aversion. There was no excuse for the dread which had been following him all day. No excuse for the silent and closed faces.

No excuse, at least among the Keepers. Perhaps they were only reflecting his own disgust—or he was reflecting it in what he thought he saw—with Hion's maneuverings. Perhaps they worried about queen's guards skirmishing on borders, when they should have been protecting roads from Abstainer bands. Perhaps they shared his impatience with his mother for succumbing to Rhenlan's view of needing to have borders to fight across in the first place.

The farmer led the gray out of the barn. Pirse transferred his sword to the fresh horse. Without trying to meet the farmer's eye he threw himself into the saddle and rode away.

CHAPTER 5

"The citizens are starting to gather in the great hall, Captain." The messenger stood in front of the battered old table in Dael's private room above the guard quarters. Dael's predecessor had used the table for a knife-throwing target. Dael looked down at the wood, absently counting the scars as he half-listened to each messenger's report.

Another heavy-booted youngster pushed through the doorway. "Sentries are posted as you ordered, sir," the teenage girl said. "We're putting merchants' horses just outside the wall."

"Very good." Without looking up, he recognized the step of the next lad. "Is Redmother Vissa coming?"

"Yes, sir."

"Good. Go to your posts." They hesitated, and he remembered to look up. "Thank you." They were used to him showing his appreciation of their efforts. He didn't offer them a smile, but they filed out obediently after his words, apparently not troubled by the lapse.

As the room emptied, the report of the night sergeant, the news with which he'd begun his day, ran through his thoughts again. Trying to ignore it wasn't working. Trying not to worry wasn't working. He sensed danger, though he had no solid reason for his fear.

The sergeant's words had not been particularly alarming. A carriage, accompanied by a half-troop of guards, had left the castle yard shortly after midnight. Nothing too unusual in that. Some of the king's relatives were known to come and go from Edian at odd hours. Dael had assumed that some cousin had decided to leave for the family holdings, and thought no more about the report.

Until Vray failed to appear for archery practice.

The girl never missed archery practice. Or any other

51

chance to pester him. After five years of his training, she was good with a bow. She had to be. She knew he wouldn't put up with her if she didn't take the work seriously. In the last year she'd used the lessons as an excuse to try to seduce him. Actually, she used almost every opportunity to try to seduce him. But she'd also continued to improve her skill, so he'd had no cause to send her away. Besides, he enjoyed her company, even when he had to dodge her inexperienced advances.

When she didn't come down to the archery range at the usual time, he began coaching his other students anyway. He thought her annoyance at missing a few moments of his awesome wisdom would be punishment enough.

It was a few minutes before it occurred to him that she might still be grieving for Emlie. The gods knew that the dead girl was still on his mind. He had been hoping to pretend everything was the same as the day before the execution. When Vray didn't appear, he realized it was a vain hope. He left his students to practice on their own and went in search of his princess.

Her maid told him she was gone. The girl couldn't say where. Sometime in the night they'd been awakened, the princess had been taken to a waiting coach, and the maid had just managed to throw a few things into a bag and convince a guard to take it down before the party left.

Dael stood and paced away from the table. Perhaps she'd been sent to her mother's estate. Perhaps to Garden Vale, or to some relative on one of the many outlying Shaper estates. It was best for the king to have the symbol of tradition out of the way, out of hearing, when Damon made his speech. If Vray wasn't in Edian, she could not remind the citizens of yesterday's Remembering. Hion had no love for his daughter. Dael had tended bruises inflicted by the king's hand more than once in the last six years. Hion was astute, and the girl was an inconvenience.

She'll be back in a day or two, Dael reasoned. *A nineday at most. She'll be livid at having been shuffled out of the way, but perfectly safe.*

Another messenger appeared in the doorway. "The

Prince is on his way down."

Dael adjusted his sword belt over his best blue tunic.
"Fine. I'll be right there."

Prosperous merchants and landholders filled the great hall,
a very different group than had gathered in the courtyard the
day before. Again the clothing was bright, but this time it was
of silk instead of linen, and gold and jewels flashed in the sunlight. Yesterday had been for everyone, a traditional ritual.
Today Damon held court with a more select group.

Dael saw the rangy figure of his father in the crowd. Loras
the goldsmith looked as puzzled as many of his neighbors.
Others, the especially wealthy whom Dael recognized as frequent visitors to Damon's wing of the castle, talked quietly
together, giving an impression of proud self-satisfaction.

Dael automatically checked the locations of the few
guards in attendance, then took his usual place, leaning
against the back wall of the hall, arms crossed.

The prince of Rhenlan stepped up onto the dais at the
front of the hall. He chose the exact spot that his father always favored when speaking to the people. A nice touch,
Dael thought, although few in Damon's audience would
consciously appreciate it. They were more likely to be noticing his well-cut silver and blue brocade tunic. Damon
was a handsome man, blessed as well with charm and an
admirable force of character. He could smile at a counselor
or a pretty girl, dark eyes caressing, and the effect would always be much the same: Damon got his way. Usually, with
little more work than that smile.

Nine years ago, Dael, a frightened and grieving seven-
teen-year-old, had felt the prince's intense interest turned
on him. Damon had decided to have a bit of sport on a dull
autumn afternoon, and Dael had ended the day as a guard,
instead of as a condemned criminal. For a long time after
that fateful day, he'd been too grateful just to be alive and
leading an honorable life to recognize that the prince had
acted out of boredom rather than compassion. Resentment
followed the realization, though by then he'd grown too so-

phisticated in the ways of Hion's court to show his anger. Besides, he forgave the prince almost instantly. He'd profited from the prince's actions, whatever his motivation, hadn't he?

It was a long time before Dael began to see other hints that Damon was not entirely the generous, noble person he pretended to be. The prince had a talent for manipulating things—law, custom, emotions—to suit his own purposes. Given time, he seemed to exert an insidious influence on everyone he touched. Except Vray. For whatever reason, Vray remained immune to her brother's charm.

Part of it had to be sibling rivalry. The king and queen of Rhenlan were not easy parents to please, and Vray's behavior often seemed willfully designed to do the opposite. Damon, in contrast, served his father without question or complaint. No wonder Vray resented him!

No, that wasn't fair. Some of Vray's criticisms were valid. Damon was not perfect. But then, who was? Dael had sworn a vow to serve King Hion faithfully, and he served Prince Damon with equal loyalty. He could hardly resign every time he disagreed with a fine point of the ruling Shapers' policies, or to satisfy a princess's whim. Besides, with his background, if he left the guard, where else could he go?

Dael's lips twisted in an impatient sneer at his melancholy cynicism. *You're supposed to be working, Captain. Pay attention.* The crowd had focused its attention on the man beside the throne. Damon bent his head solemnly, dark hair obscuring his features. Then he looked up and swept his glance around the large room, drawing them all in, holding them as he spoke.

"We of Rhenlan obey the laws. Laws of ancient custom, based on the records kept for us in the books of the law readers and committed to the memories of the Redmothers. We live by law. Law holds us together. Laws that are the same for all of the Children of the Rock.

"There has been a dispute over a forest. A bit of land. No one should die for a bit of land. But Queen Dea sent her guards to control the forest before any decision was made concerning the claims we made against her. My father responded by sending guards to watch on our side of the border while we waited for the decision of the law readers. We were not the first to send guards, and no hostility was meant. Princess Emlie said that her mother's guards might fight to keep the forest for their queen. We did not give up our claim at this threat. It was not for us to give up. It was for the law to decide.

"The situation between the border guards grew tense. The possibility of fighting grew each day. We did not want there to be bloodshed. But two guards did die. So we turned to the law, law that provides an answer to unnecessary deaths, and a just conclusion to difficult negotiations.

"Queen Dea knows the law as well as we do. It is possible she will refuse to accept the just decision of the law readers. If so, the tragedy will be ours as well as hers."

A few voices murmured somewhere in the crowd. Dael turned his head. People were scowling. He caught a word here and there, enough to tell that Damon's explanation was working. They were angry, not at Hion, but at the actions of the distant queen.

"Dea chose a piece of land over the preciousness of life. I don't understand how she could ignore the consequences of the law, but she did. King Hion could not ignore the law, though it was the hardest decision he has ever made.

"Princess Emlie was executed in answer to the demands of the law. One life in exchange for the lives of many guards."

Again Damon's audience stirred unhappily. The prince held up his hands, palms outward, keeping his command over his listeners with effortless skill.

"It seems cruel. It was cruel," he said, voice heavy with sorrow. "It was also necessary. It was the only choice the King had. Yesterday a Remembering was held for a tragically misguided young woman. Because of her death, many other such services may be avoided. The death of her daughter might finally convince Queen Dea that she is responsible to the law. It is a pity anyone died, but perhaps these deaths served a purpose. We must not resort to fighting over the possession of land."

Damon lowered his head again, then stepped down into the silent crowd. He touched a shoulder here and there in passing, exchanging a few quiet words with those who spoke to him. As he made his way out of the hall, he beckoned for Dael to accompany him.

They passed through the wide double doors into the relative privacy of the corridor. "Captain, I have a message for you from my father. We both appreciate how considerate you've been in your dealings with Princess Vray these last few years, and how sorely her antics must have tried your patience."

The unexpected subject surprised Dael into blunt honesty. "At times, Your Highness. But she always means well."

"Indeed. I have the highest respect for my sister's good intentions. However, she is young, and impulsive. Our father is aware, for instance, of her recent escapade at the Golden Owl."

Dael blushed at the memory. "No harm was done, Highness."

"Generous of you to say so. However, Vray is old enough to take responsibility for her actions. She proved that yesterday. King Hion was impressed by how well she led the Remembering. She is well on her way to becoming a truly gifted Redmother, if only she concentrates on completing her training. Therefore our father suggested, and Vray agreed, that it would be best if she continue her studies away from Edian for a while."

Damon placed a hand on Dael's shoulder and gave him a rueful smile. "To be blunt, Captain, you are too tempting a distraction for my impressionable sister."

Dael felt another rush of embarrassment, and the first tingle of a new emotion: relief. "Your Highness, please believe me—I tried to discourage Vray's interest in me. Nothing worked."

"Don't worry, I understand." Damon's smile broadened. "Her Redmother training will keep her busy until she's had time to get over you."

"Thank you for explaining the situation, Your Highness. I admit I've been concerned about the princess."

"Not at all, Captain. The king and I are well aware of your diligence, and we trust you to keep the matter confidential. No one wants details of a childish infatuation spread all over town."

"Indeed not, Your Highness."

With a knowing wink, Damon clapped Dael on the shoulder and walked away. Dael's heart felt lighter than it had in days. That explained why Vray had gone away without saying good-bye. Dael had been so caught up in his own concerns—the possibility of further border fighting with Dherrican troops, his bitter grief over the execution of Emlie—that he'd failed to fully appreciate anyone else's point of view.

Yes, he'd been embarrassed by Vray's unceasing affection. But, to be honest, he'd also rather enjoyed it. Maybe it was for the best—her best, and his, not just the convenience of the king—that she spend some time away from Edian. He would miss her, but the important thing was that now he knew what had happened, and why. By the time she came back, maybe they could settle down to just being friends.

Smiling to himself, Dael returned to his duties.

The first person who recognized Pirse as he led his horse up the steep road toward the castle burst into tears. So did the second. Pirse's heart began to pound, and not with the exertion of leading his exhausted mount. Fortunately the guards on duty saw their approach, and had the gate open as they arrived at the courtyard.

Pirse handed the animal's reins to the first willing pair of hands. Few lights were lit in the courtyard or the windows around it, despite the deepening gloom of the evening. A harsh wind from the mountains above Bronle caught at the courtyard torches, giving their light an erratic, dangerous glow. The familiar voice of Cratt, captain of the guards, drifted from the direction of the barracks, its cadences unfamiliarly querulous. Pirse ignored it and everyone else, too aware of the eyes that wouldn't lift to meet his. He took the shortest route possible to the great hall, a sense of warning and desperation growing as he passed through empty corridors on his way to the hall. Where was everyone? What had happened here?

He had to pause when he reached the doorway into the great hall to catch his breath and still the trembling of his legs. The room appeared to have doubled in length since he'd last been home. His mother was a dim, distant figure at its far end, sitting motionless on her throne. Alone. None of her women, no guard, not even Uncle Palle, ever-present and carefully watchful of his elder sister, were to be seen in the darkened room. Pirse pushed himself away from the wall, squared his shoulders, and walked the length of the shadowy room.

The queen looked up when he mounted the two steps of her dais and stood beside her seat.

"What's happened to Emlie?" Pirse hardly recognized the harsh voice as his own. It was simply a voice, asking the question which had been haunting him all afternoon. All that mattered now was the answer.

"I sent her to Hion in Rhenlan." His mother's expression was completely bland, her voice calm as it fell on the emptiness and space between them. "I knew exactly what I was doing."

"But something's gone wrong," Pirse insisted. "I haven't met anyone on the road who would face me. What have you done? Abdicated to Hion? Agreed to have Emlie marry Damon?"

Her continuing mild stare maddened him. He took her by the shoulders and gave her a furious shake, and got no more response than if he hadn't touched her. She seemed to still be alone, her words not answers to his question, but merely thoughts spoken aloud to herself.

"Mother, let me help."

"Shapers should stay to their own lands. Hion has no business in Dherrica. I told him that."

Fear, an acid bite at the back of his mouth, began to burn into his mind as well. "Mother, when is Emlie coming home?"

"She's dead."

Pirse stared, appalled, into gray eyes the mirror of his own. The mirror of Emlie's. He tightened his grip on his mother's shoulders, clenching his fingers with what he knew was bruising force, but she remained oblivious to him.

"No," he croaked. It was a lie. If he left this madwoman to her empty throne room he'd find Emlie in her quarters. She'd smile, happy to see him as always. He'd tell her about killing dragons and she'd show him a new kitten. She used to cry about the death of dragons.

"Yes, she is," the queen's insistent words cut into his thoughts, shattering and scattering them. "The messenger came this morning. I never believed Hion would go to such lengths. But it hardly matters, does it? She's dead."

"No," Pirse repeated more insistently. "Not that beautiful, innocent child. Who could harm Emlie?"

Who would send a little girl into such a dangerous situation? How could this woman he was holding have done such a thing?

She was still speaking. "They held a perfectly formal execution. They took her into a public courtyard, read the sentence, and the executioner strangled her. They executed my baby. She died like a common criminal. The messenger from Rhenlan said she cried, but didn't make any real fuss. How like her to die quietly. Such a gentle thing."

"Shut up!" The cry tore itself out of Pirse. "Stop it!"

"How will the Redmothers remember it?" the Queen droned on, gray eyes focused, but not focused, on something in the middle distance beyond Pirse's shoulder. "I can't stop thinking that because she obeyed me, she's dead."

"No." Pirse didn't shout the word this time. It came out as a whisper, barely audible in his own ears, ignored by his mother, who was lost in her own horror-filled thoughts.

Pirse dropped his hands and stepped back, those simple actions almost beyond his strength. All the energy that had driven him on the long road home, all the tension that had wound through him these past hours, evaporated like a dead dragon in the sun. Dead. Emlie, his pretty, sweet sister, was dead.

Pirse turned his back on the queen and walked away. At the entrance to the great hall he turned randomly to his left, his mother's monotonous voice following him along the corridor. Emlie was dead. He knew he should feel something, say something, but what? How? Denial hadn't helped, and comfort was beyond him, for himself or for Dea. What was the point? Emlie was dead.

He lifted the latch on the first door he came to, and stepped into a black, windowless room. He didn't know where he was, didn't care. Emlie was dead. The trembling returned to his aching legs and back. He was aware of tears on his face, and the empty hollow of his grief where his heart had once been. He sank down on the stone floor, curled into a miserable ball, and let exhaustion carry him into the welcome dark.

CHAPTER 6

Pirse woke with a crick in his neck and, for one blessed moment, no idea where he was. Then the memories came to crush him: Chasa's warning, the long ride home, Dea shattered with grief, Emlie dead.

Groaning, Pirse got to his feet and fumbled in the darkness until he found the door. Light from the wall sconce in the corridor outside answered his first question. He had taken refuge in a storage room, its walls lined with dusty shelves and a heap of wall tapestries.

He doubted that the answer to his next question would come so easily. Emlie was dead. *Gods help me, what do I do now?*

All right, maybe that answer was easy, too. Pirse brushed at his dusty clothing and started back down the corridor toward the great hall. It didn't matter that he was furious, hurt, disappointed, and grieving. He had to talk to his mother. He blamed her as much as Hion for Emlie's death, but probably not as bitterly as she blamed herself. Blame wouldn't bring Emlie back. They had to decide what to do next, how to respond to Rhenlan's barbarity.

By the time he approached the throne, Pirse had ordered his thoughts and started to run down the list of urgent actions to be taken. Check the status of the border guards, of course. He opened his mouth to address his mother, and only then wondered at her silence. She sat on the throne, watching his approach. No, not watching him. He stepped onto the dais, but her eyes continued to stare sightlessly past him.

The front of her gown was dark with blood.

Pirse's legs buckled. He reached for Dea's hand, and at his touch her body slid off the throne and crumpled into an untidy heap on the tiles.

"Rock and Pool, boy, what have you done?"

Pirse turned, still on his knees. Captain Cratt strode down the center of the great hall, Uncle Palle at his side. They stopped at the foot of the dais and Palle pointed an accusing finger at Pirse.

"What did I tell you? He shirks his real duties, he profanes his sacred trust, and now he thinks to claim the throne!"

Cratt's bald head gleamed in the torch light. "You can't do it, Your Highness. Best to hand over your sword, and trust the Law Readers to judge fairly."

"My sword?" Pirse repeated. "Law Readers? Cratt, what happened here?"

"The queen is dead," Palle proclaimed loudly. "And I, for one, will not stand by and see her murderer profit by it."

"Her murderer?" Pirse's voice rose in outrage as he surged to his feet. "You accuse me? Cratt, you can't possibly believe—"

"I've already examined her," the captain interrupted him. "Anyone who has fought with you will confirm it. There's no mistaking the marks of a dragon sword, and no question that you're the only man in Dherrica to wield one." He put one foot on the lowest step of the dais, hands spread in entreaty. A spasm of pain twisted his face. "You were seen, Highness. The last person to enter the hall before . . . before she was found. Firstmother help us, the queen is dead. Your sister's dead. Shaper killing Shaper. No more, Highness, I beg you."

The snick of Palle's sword sliding out of its sheath broke through Pirse's stunned disbelief. A drawn weapon, the sense of danger—these things he understood.

His fingers found the hilt of his sword. Palle's sneering face was the snarling visage of a dragon. Training and experience took over. Pirse dodged under his uncle's first lunge, swung the heel of his free hand against the side of the man's head with bone-numbing force, leapt past Cratt's lunging grab, and ran from the hall.

* * * * *

Palle rolled groggily to his hands and knees in time to see the prince disappear through the doorway at the far end of the great hall, Cratt three paces behind him. Palle staggered to his feet, groped for his sword where it had fallen at the edge of the dais, and ran after the pair.

He caught up with Cratt halfway down the corridor, where the guard captain lay doubled-up on the floor. Head throbbing furiously, Palle shoved his boot under the man and flipped him over. Cratt clutched his ribs, breathing in broken gasps, but the only blood visible came from a gash on his forehead.

"Idiot! Why didn't you stop him?" Palle demanded.

Cratt wouldn't, or couldn't, answer. Palle cursed him and hurried on. Perhaps it was for the best to have the guard captain out of the way. Palle gingerly touched the aching spot on his own skull. He found no blood, but it still hurt. One more score to settle with his beloved nephew.

Lights guttered around the courtyard, and several guards were milling about near the entrance to the stables.

"Nerri!" Palle shouted as he hurried down the stairs. The man he'd singled out turned an inquiring face toward him.

"Have you seen Prince Pirse?"

Nerri indicated the stable door. "Yes, sir, he's just getting a horse."

Palle reached the bottom of the stairs. "Stop him!" he shouted. Heads turned in his direction, eyes widening at the sight of the naked blade in his hand. A clattering of hooves was clearly audible from the stone-flagged central aisle of the stable. Palle ran forward. "Do you hear me? Stop the prince. He's murdered our queen!"

On the other side of the courtyard one of the watching kitchen maids began to wail. The guards nearest the stable scattered as a horse and rider burst into the open. Pirse was astride Captain Cratt's huge roan. Sword in his hand, the prince gave a wordless yell and kicked the mare toward the gate.

Two guards sprang forward to close the courtyard doors,

but they were too slow. One was knocked aside by the horse's shoulder. The other would have been trampled outright had the animal not given a small leap as she knocked him down. Then Pirse was gone, no more than a shadow bending low over the horse's neck.

Palle screamed, "After him!"

More guards came streaming out of the barracks, aroused by the commotion. Cratt's second-in-command, Onarga, ran toward him. "A full patrol, sir?" she asked.

"Yes, yes! And saddle my horse."

Onarga was not very imaginative, but she was well disciplined. Within a few moments, a groom had brought out Palle's horse, and an armed and mounted troop was assembled in front of the gate.

Palle swung into his saddle. "Corporal Onarga, you will remain here, in command of the castle, until I return."

"Captain Cratt?"

"Inside," Palle snapped. "Prostrated with grief. I do not have time to wait for him to recover. I want riders sent out in all directions. They are to inform every village of Prince Pirse's betrayal. Send special messengers to Kings Hion and Sene with the same news. Due to the tragic circumstances, I must assume responsibility for ruling Dherrica."

Onarga listened to his orders with a concerned frown. "Sir? Wouldn't it be safer for you to stay here?"

"Do not delay me with foolish questions!" Palle could not argue with her, because she was right. The last thing he wanted to do was ride in pursuit of Pirse. However, he had no choice. If Pirse surrendered peacefully and started proclaiming his innocence, there were too many people who might be inclined to believe him. Only by leading the hunt could Palle be sure that his nephew would be killed trying to evade capture. Palle needed Pirse dead. Then no one would question Palle's right to be king, or wonder if Dea's wounds could have been caused by something other than a dragon sword.

"Dispatch the messengers," Palle continued relentlessly, "then see that all of the Queen's councilors are made aware of what has happened. One of them can deal with my sister's body."

Palle signaled the guards and spurred his horse forward. Although his nephew had a few minutes' lead, it wouldn't be difficult to find him. The sight of Prince Pirse galloping madly through the night would arouse enough curiosity to insure an easy trail. Besides, Palle knew of only two places he might go. Depending on his frame of mind, Pirse could head toward Rhenlan, intent on revenge against Hion. Of course, crossing the border was out of the question, and within a day all of Dherrica would be turned against him. Therefore, if the boy was thinking clearly, he'd take the road toward the one place where no troop of guards could easily follow—into the northern jungles.

Palle sent two of the swiftest riders ahead of the main body of the troop. They would close the gap separating them from the prince, and likely discover his intentions within a few miles.

After that, all they had to do was catch up with him.

One nineday after Princess Emlie's execution passed, and then another. Dael personally escorted the Dherrican messenger to the king's audience chamber, and stood by as Hion received the news of Dea's tragic death at the hands of her mad son. Palle's first act as King of Dherrica was to gift the contested river valley and forest to Rhenlan. Dael accompanied Damon on a tour of the border region, a show of strength and promise of protection for the battle-weary populace.

Vray did not return. No one spoke of her at court, and few in Edian itself gave a second thought to her absence. On the rare occasions that Dael heard her name mentioned in town, the curiosity was always mild and short-lived. Princess Vray was in training to be the kingdom's Redmother, after all. People considered her wise to look beyond Edian, to get to know the other towns and villages and study with Red and Brownmothers throughout the kingdom. Perhaps she would even visit Sitrine or Dherrica. Didn't both of Rhenlan's powerful neighbors have Shaper princes of a marriageable age?

Dael heard all the good-natured speculation, and said nothing. Duty filled his days, and most of his nights. He adjusted patrol routes to include the newly-acquired territory, oversaw the training of new guards, and dealt with all the petty squabbles that ebbed and flowed in a busy capital like Edian.

Vray did not return.

Pirse took the path because it was narrow and appeared infrequently used. He had no idea where it led. That didn't matter, of course, because he didn't know where he was to begin with. He hardly remembered who he was. All that was important was that he keep moving. He didn't remember why it was so important, but he had something to do, and he wouldn't be able to do it if they caught him.

The path wound across the valley floor, crossed the wide river at an ankle-deep ford, and climbed the side of a hill. He watched his feet moving forward, first one, then the other. When the swarm of insects buzzing around his blood-matted hair became too thick to see through, he summoned up the energy to wave them away with his right hand. His left hand and arm he kept firmly pressed over the gash in his side. Despite his efforts, every other step jarred the wound. But the dull pain had been with him for so long now that it hardly registered on his over-stressed senses.

The forest teemed with life, undisturbed by the passage of one Child of the Rock. He knew how to pass through the forest without alerting its inhabitants. His pursuers did not. They would never be able to approach him undetected here. That was why he had come. He could trust the forest to hide him.

He rounded a bend in the path and stopped, swaying. Was his bleary vision failing? Staring down at the path, he thought he saw four feet, two his own dust-covered hunting boots, the other two clad in soft hide shoes. He waved feebly at the cloud of gnats and flies in front of his face, but the extra set of feet didn't disappear.

"You don't look at all well."

Somehow he took a step back and raised his head. The owner of the voice, and the feet, was a short man with bent legs and a round, pleasantly ugly face.

"Stay back," he croaked hoarsely.

"Watch where you're—"

His next backward step fell on the crumbling edge of the path. Below him was nothing but vertical hillside. He flailed with his right arm. The man paused in mid-sentence, grabbed Pirse's arm, and hauled him forward to safety.

"—going," the man concluded. "You'd better come inside."

He was short but very strong. After a few moments of unfocused and totally ineffectual resistance, Pirse found himself in the back of a cool cave, drinking from a cup of water held to his lips by the man.

"Now I know who you are. You're Pirse, the Dherrican prince. You've been very helpful, you know."

Hearing his name after so many days of solitude was a jolt. Pirse pushed the cup away. "What do you mean? Who are you?"

"We're both dragon slayers." The man put the cup aside and began unlacing the front of Pirse's tunic. "You only kill the small physical ones, of course. But every little bit helps."

"Small?" Pirse protested automatically.

The man pried Pirse's arm gently away from his side, then tsked in disapproval. "I don't like the look of that. You need a Greenmother. Perhaps Savyea will come." He stood. "I'll go get her."

"Who are you?"

"Morb."

Pirse stared at him. "Grandfather's wizard?"

"Not anymore," Morb replied. "Don't move now." With that final admonition the wizard closed his eyes and vanished in a puff of greenish smoke.

Pirse closed his eyes. A wizard. He'd fallen into the hands of a wizard. Wild coincidence to have met anyone.

Except that he didn't believe in coincidence. Not where magic was concerned. His steps must have been guided by the gods—the callous, capricious, useless gods. Since he was a boy he'd been appalled by his mother's lack of belief. She, and the rest of Dherrica's Shapers, refused their responsibility to parent a new generation of Dreamers. He had expected King Sene of Sitrine, who had made sure his brother and sister married Keepers according to tradition, to prosper and triumph over his neighbors. But were the gods just? No. Rhenlan gained in strength and prestige, not Sitrine. The gods did nothing.

The cave smelled suddenly of mown grass and clover. A hand touched his forehead, too close to the tender skin of the knife gash there.

"Ow!" He snarled and opened his eyes.

Morb stood at his feet, holding a large leather bag. The hand which left Pirse's forehead to gingerly lift aside the torn shoulder of his tunic belonged to a plump, pink-cheeked woman whose unbelted black robe and peach under-tunic seemed stiffly formal next to Morb's bare chest and black loincloth. She had hair the color of ripe oats, cut short like a child's, and she clucked over him exactly as his nursemaid had done long ago, when his biggest fears were of thunderstorms and bee stings.

"There, there, don't worry about a thing. You're safe now." Her smile was a delicate curving of lips framed by dimples. "I am Savyea. You haven't been chasing dragons this far south, have you?"

If only it were so simple! "No."

"Well, you've certainly made a mess of yourself. Water, please." She took her bag from Morb and set it on the ground next to Pirse. When she lifted the flap of the bag, a spicy, nose-tingling scent filled the air. The Greenmother brought out an earthenware mug, squat and red as a tomato, which she dipped into the large bowl of water Morb set beside her.

"Now," Savyea said, hands busily unfolding small cloth squares, each containing a different powder or leaf or seed.

"Help me heal you. Tell me what happened."

Pirse turned his face away from her sharp, inquiring, black eyes. "Some things don't heal."

Morb's voice startled him. "He grieves," the wizard explained.

"For your sister, poor boy? I understand."

Before he could stop himself, Pirse corrected her. "For my mother." After that he had no choice but to tell them the rest. It didn't take long. Savyea seemed less interested in the ramifications of Dea's murder than in hearing a precise account of when and where he had received his various injuries.

He'd only had two engagements with Palle's guards. One had come at dawn on the first day of the chase, which had resulted in an arrow graze on the left arm for him and a dead archer for Palle. The other had taken place a nineday and six later, in which he had gone sword and knife against four guards and come away with a gash on his forehead and his side sliced open from waist to breastbone.

Days—two? three?—had passed since then. He felt more rational in the presence of the Dreamers than he had since he'd first fled Bronle. He could remember his initial impulse to seek blood debt against Hion, as well as his later, bitter realization that he would have to survive his uncle's pursuit first. Neither of the Dreamers, however, expressed an opinion regarding guilt, fault, or consequences. Instead, they discussed insects. Morb knew which sorts lived in the valleys and swamps Pirse had traveled. Of those, Savyea knew which carried disease. Pirse marveled that they could be so knowledgeable about such petty details, yet completely naive about the disaster that threatened the entire kingdom.

Savyea lit a tiny fire on the sandy floor, composed entirely of twigs and crumbled leaves removed from her bag. Scent rose from it, soaking into Pirse's skin as effortlessly as it entered his lungs. The flames were blue. They produced neither heat nor smoke.

Savyea said, "It is time to rest, my dear. You're going to

have to be very patient. I wouldn't bend the power to heal you if it wasn't absolutely necessary. I'm afraid it won't save you any of the discomforts of convalescence, though. A body always needs time to recover lost strength. Trust me."

She cocked her head slightly to one side to give him a serene, if slightly apologetic smile. Huge invisible hands engulfed his heart, folded around his lungs, blotted out sound, covered his eyes with darkness. He would have stiffened in terror if he'd retained the tiniest control over his body.

Like a stream over a precipice, his consciousness flowed away.

CHAPTER 7

Aage came forth from the realms of magic as he always did; mouth dry, skin clammy, head splitting. He opened his eyes a slit. Sunlight lingered on the peaks facing him from across the valley, and a glow behind the mountains suggested one or more of the moons rising. His brain was too tired to calculate the date. Morb would tell him how many days he'd been gone.

He turned his head from side to side, muscles responding sluggishly until his body remembered it was capable of movement. The path and the mouth to the cave swam into clearer focus. Where was Morb? The old wizard was usually eager to get back to bending the power.

Aage's fatigue intensified as he got to his feet. He pocketed his rock and drank the water in his bowl in a few long swallows. Morb came out of the cave, his round face wearing so uncharacteristic an expression that for a few seconds Aage couldn't identify it.

"Aage, are you strong enough to run an errand?" the wizard asked.

Worry, that was it. Morb, defender of the Children, slayer of nightmares, was worried. Aage's knees went weak.

"What is it? What's happened?"

"A badly injured boy. Savyea healed the worst of it, but when he wakes someone must be here to care for him."

"Who is it?"

Morb's expression grew more melancholy. "My dragon slayer. The Dherrican boy."

"Pirse?" Aage's dismay increased. Any Shaper who fought the world's physical monsters was important, of course, but in the larger scheme of things this particular prince had an even larger role than that to play! "He's going to be all right, isn't he?"

"If we care for him. I can't stay, and neither can you. Savyea wants you to find someone who will take him away and keep him safe. That's your errand." The older wizard stepped past Aage and settled down onto the boulder. In the dimness Aage heard more than saw the clunk of Morb's rock settling into its bowl of water.

"Why not send him home to Bronle?" The capital was only five days' easy ride to the southeast. Aage felt the power beginning to bend around Morb's seated figure and opened his mouth to repeat his question.

"He can't go there. Savyea was quite insistent on that. Palle would kill him." Morb's expression grew placid as his voice faded. "Savyea says Doron in Juniper Ridge will guard the boy against his uncle."

"Palle? He's not dangerous."

Morb did not answer. The power began to play like invisible lightning around his brown, weathered body, and Aage backed away. He'd get no further answers from Morb now.

In the cave, the prince was thoroughly unconscious. Savyea sat next to him, knitting. It was too hot to knit. The woman never could keep her climates straight. She smiled up at Aage.

"Hello, dear." She pointed one needle at the sleeping man. "Morb told you about the boy?"

"He told me nothing." Aage dropped tiredly beside the Greenmother and leaned against her. She was nearly as drained of strength as he was. "Why is Dea allowing her brother to threaten her son?"

"Morb really didn't tell you anything. Dea's dead." She looked sadly at Pirse. "Somehow, Palle laid the blame on the boy. Something to do with his dragon sword."

Aage twisted his head against Savyea's soft shoulder to take a second, closer look at the prince. "Only Pirse can wield that sword. Could Palle be right?"

"Of course not. That would be Abstainer madness, and this child is no Abstainer. We'll talk about it when you come back. Morb did tell you what we need?"

"A Keeper. Yes, but—"

"Later, dear. Go."

Aage allowed himself an exasperated sigh, but obediently got to his feet. There was no discussing anything with Savyea except in her own good time. If she said Juniper Ridge was the place for the prince, then to Juniper Ridge he must go.

Unfortunately, Aage's options were limited. He was too drained to flit limitlessly from one kingdom to another. He could transport himself to Raisal and confer with his king, or go to the nearest village in hopes of finding a suitable Keeper there. But he would have to make a choice. It usually took days to recover his strength after fighting in Morb's place. Bending the power now, so soon after leaving the battle with the Others, would not be easy.

A responsible Keeper. That was easy enough. As unpredictable as many of the Shaper families had become, the Keepers, for the most part, still took their vows seriously. He needed a Keeper responsible enough to be trusted, but atypical enough to be willing to leave home for a few days.

Aage stepped out of the cave. Keyn was a great lopsided ball hovering above the peaks to the east, her light washing out all but the brightest stars. He closed his eyes and sought within himself for the power he needed. A mental twist applied just so opened the path to the nearest sizable village, Live Oak. The power wove dizzily around him for a long instant, then faded to leave him standing close beside the low-hanging branches of a huge old oak tree in front of the village inn. He left its shelter, dry leaves crackling under his feet, and mounted the stairs.

A short conversation revealed that Live Oak's carter was not in town, and not likely to return in the near future. The few townspeople present in the inn's common room encouraged Aage, however, with the news that a Rhenlan carter had passed through Live Oak that very day, and would surely be able to help him. Aage expressed proper gratitude for the information. Inwardly, he groaned. The gods always provided. Unfortunately, what they provided was seldom exactly what their Children expected.

Aage knew the Broadford carter. Stubborn, opinionated, and generally annoying, but more than responsible enough for the task. If he'd been too far away to be of any use—Eastern Sitrine, preferably—Aage could have ignored the suggestion to go see him. As it was, he had no choice. He fixed the location in his mind, then bent the power to transport himself to the soon-to-be-indignant carter.

Tob was sound asleep by the time Jordy got up to extinguish their campfire and make his own bed for the night. He got the boy's blanket down from the wagon and spread it on the ground beside him. Tob rolled onto the blanket and covered himself with only a slight prodding from Jordy, and without ever really waking up. Jordy tucked the blanket in around the boy's shoulders, then got to his feet and stretched tiredly.

They were camped in the lush river valley three days north and a day west of Juniper Ridge. The smell of thick vegetation was not unpleasant, but the increasing proliferation of insect life as they moved into a warmer, wetter climate was less to Jordy's liking.

Only one log still flickered with flames in the banked fire. It cast insufficient light to reveal the warning wisp of vapor that preceded the arrival of a Dreamer, so that Jordy started and jumped to protect Tob before recognizing the form that materialized in the darkness next to the wagon.

"Aage!" he exclaimed. "Stones, man, don't sneak up on a man like that!"

The wizard's pale yellow hair shown dimly in Keyn's just-past-full light. "My apologies," he said with no sincerity whatsoever, and stepped closer to the fire. "We need your services, carter."

Jordy moved away from his sleeping son, more wary than ever at the wizard's unexpected pronouncement. "We?" he asked.

"We are all Children of the Rock," Aage said impatiently. "If we do not guard the world, all of us together, we are doomed. I'm well aware of your opinion of most Shapers and Dreamers, but I think you have some respect for Prince Pirse?"

Jordy crossed his arms. "What do you want?"

"He's been injured. You must transport him to a place of safety where he can recover. He needs to be protected from his uncle."

"So I've heard." Palle had been a threat to those closest to him for years. Jordy had no doubt there was more to the tale of the queen's death than Palle's guards were telling. However, he did not relish the thought of getting involved in the problems of the Dherrican ruling house. "You don't expect me to smuggle him into Rhenlan?"

Aage looked annoyed. "You'd never cross the border."

"Where then?"

"Juniper Ridge. There's someone there called Doron who can keep him hidden for a few ninedays, or so Greenmother Savyea insists."

"I know Doron." Jordy was also familiar with the prince. The lad had long-since proved his bravery and his commitment to a Shaper's vow by his tireless campaign against the northern dragons. But the danger of the rescue Aage was suggesting—to the prince himself, not to mention to Jordy, Tob, Doron, and the entire population of Juniper Ridge— made Jordy's skin crawl.

"Where is he now?"

"In the hills, a half-day north of Dundas."

"North?" Jordy complained. "There are no cart tracks north of Dundas."

"The horse can be ridden, can't she?" Aage replied with an irritable jerk of his head in the direction of the hobbled Stockings. "You'll manage something."

"I see I'll have to."

The wizard accepted this as acquiescence on Jordy's part. "I'll tell them to expect you."

With no further comment he vanished into thin air.

A stray breeze blew the resulting wisp of fruit-scented

smoke into Jordy's face. He coughed reflexively, then spat to clear the strong taste from the back of his mouth.

"Dundas," he muttered unhappily under his breath. "I've agreed to go to Dundas. I've agreed to go north of Dundas. In mid-summer, too. I must be mad. Why do I let them talk me into such nonsense?"

Still muttering, he fetched his bedroll from the wagon and spread it across the fire from Tob. He lay there for a long time, as the flames died to faint embers, then to ash.

It was nearly Keyn-set before he slept.

Eyes. Dark eyes accusing him. No, laughing at him. Laughing at her. Don't laugh at her! She didn't ask for this.

She should've been more careful.

Darkness around him. Shadows in the room, face in the shadows. Faces watching him. Unvoiced laughter ripped at him from behind the throne.

Pirse's eyes opened to darkness. Humid heat and the smell of orchids had not been part of the dream. He remembered Morb's cave, and separated it with difficulty from his memory of the high stone castle.

Palle had been in the throne room.

Pirse stared across the empty cave. This wasn't a fever dream, even if he was feverish. It was a memory. Palle had been there when he arrived home and learned of Emlie's death. Palle was witness to the fact that he had not harmed his mother.

Palle had not accused him out of ignorance. He had known the truth, and lied. Why?

Because Palle knew how Dea really died.

Gradually Pirse's breathing steadied. Outside the cave it was night. Rain fell, gushing steadily along the rock face of the hill. Fatigue was going to drag him back to sleep, but he wasn't ready. Not because of the nightmares. He had to think this through. Had to think about his uncle.

Father never liked Palle. Tolerated him for Mother's sake. Servants still told stories about the arguments that went on between the three of them. Father wanted a brother-in-law who would fight dragons with him, care for the best interests of the kingdom, be of some use. Palle preferred to stay close to the throne, advising and helping his sister. Help Mother never needed. *Father knew that, so did I, but Mother doubted herself and trusted her brother.*

Pirse stared into the darkness. All those years, and no one guessed Palle wanted to be king. Mother was in his way. *I'm in his way. He cares nothing for the Law. Gods, how did he do it? Dea did not die by my sword, yet the evidence deceived Cratt. How? A wizard or Greenmother would have seen through the trick, proved my innocence, but Mother allowed no Dreamers in Bronle.*

How could he prove his innocence now? Go back to the castle, present himself to the law reader, and hope for understanding and compassion and a judgment that would serve the best interests of all Dherrica?

He could not return to Bronle as long as Palle's guard was hunting him. Not with everyone in Dherrica convinced that he was a mother-killing Abstainer.

Pirse closed his eyes. *Gods, what do I do?*

The news from Edian and Bronle was worse than anything Sene had dared to imagine. Emlie killed, Dea killed, Pirse a fugitive, and now an Abstainer attack on one of Rhenlan's coastal villages. The market and docks of Raisal buzzed with outrage and pessimistic speculation. Merchants, shipmasters, artisans, and the senior Brownmothers of the town came to Sene's house at once to consult with their king.

After sunset a breeze began to pick up. Sene emerged from the last of his meetings and went out to the north terrace. He strode past the still-empty dinner table to stand at the railing and gaze into the night. It had been a difficult day. Another in a series of difficult days of waiting to see how other rulers' decisions were going to effect his people.

Sene gripped the terrace railing and leaned back, stretching the kinks out of his shoulders. A half-mile away, the sea sparkled and danced with the light of all three moons. Dreyn glittered low in the west, its crescent too small to be discernible. In another ten or twelve days, Sene judged, it would be rising and setting with the sun, invisible to watching eyes until it reappeared in the morning sky at the end of the summer. Sheyn was a third of the way up the sky from the vanished sun, twice its own diameter from the location it had occupied at this same time the night before. Larger Keyn, almost full, had just risen in the east. He studied the three orbs. So dependable, passing across the sky in their intricate dance, waxing and waning, now lost in the sunlight, now dominating the night sky. *The gods set paths for us, just as they did for the moons. Why can we not see the patterns laid out so clearly before our eyes?*

"You're brooding, Dad."

Sene turned at the sound of Jeyn's accusing voice. "I wasn't. I was admiring the sky."

"You were scowling at it."

"All right." He linked his arm through hers and allowed her to lead him to the table. "But I was thinking, not brooding."

"About what?"

He gestured vaguely with his free hand. "About all of us. Wondering why we always complicate our lives."

Jeyn sensibly made no reply. They took their places at the table, and Jeyn picked up the bell and rang for the servants. She said, "It's still hard to believe that they destroyed a whole village. I remember docking there with Chasa on our way to visit Dherrica the summer before last."

"I know. Gleneven was a beautiful place. But the greatest tragedy of these past ninedays was losing Gavea."

"How can you say that? Dherrica in Palle's hands, and we don't even know how many people the Abstainers killed at Gleneven, how many children with their whole lives ahead of them. Gavea was over four hundred years old."

"Exactly. We'll never know the potential of the Keepers killed at Gleneven. On the other hand, I'm painfully aware of how much experience, how much sheer wisdom Gavea brought us. She was our last living link with the time before the plague."

"It's not as if we'll forget those days. Any of the Dreamers can remember anything, no matter how long past."

"Any of the Dreamers? And how many are left? All of Morb's time and attention is devoted to the realms of magic. Savyea takes things to the other extreme—thinks the answer to all our problems is for people to have more babies. As for Jenil, she's only willing to act as a healer." Sene emphatically tapped one finger on the table. "From Gavea, I could expect not only information, but interpretation as well, and advice on how I might best take action."

"You haven't mentioned Aage. You're not discounting him in his absence, I hope?"

Sene hid his amusement at his daughter's staunch defense of her best friend as servants arrived with their meal. Her face was all right, and her hands were neatly folded in her lap, but her brown eyes were doing their best to burn holes wherever her gaze came to rest, which was mostly in the center of her father, the king's, forehead.

When the servants had gone back inside, Sene rubbed his brow and said, "Aage does his best. Unfortunately, I can never be sure he'll be here at a moment of crisis. The power bends him to its will, I sometimes think, more often than he bends it. With Gavea there was never any doubt of which was in control."

Jeyn passed him a bowl of cool fruit soup and a slice of sweet bread. "Aage says that everything's connected. That all of the problems the Children of the Rock have struggled against since before the plague are only reflections of troubles in the magical places he and Morb visit."

"I imagine there is some correlation between the Outside monsters and our dragons and phantom cats." He stirred his soup with his spoon. "You know, that's a nasty thought. Magic working through any of us, against the benders of power."

Jeyn frowned. "I'm not sure that's exactly what Aage meant."

The door behind them opened and Jeyn turned, the legs of her chair scraping harshly on the terrace's stone floor. "Chasa!"

Sene gave his children time to embrace one another. Jeyn stepped back from the hug first, wrinkling her nose and winning a grudging smile from her twin. The odor of horse sweat had drifted onto the terrace with Chasa, temporarily blotting out the scent of night-blooming flowers. His scarlet silk tunic stuck to his sweaty back, and his yellow hair hung limply around his square face.

"I see I'm not too late."

"Of course not. Come, sit." Jeyn gestured him toward a chair.

Chasa glanced without interest at their interrupted meal. "I wasn't talking about dinner. Dad, I came back as soon as I could."

"Sooner than I expected," Sene assured his earnest son. "What happened? Eighteen is getting too old to be homesick. After all, it's your third year of monster-hunting without me."

"Haven't you heard about Dea?"

"I heard."

"Pirse?"

"Accused of murder."

"Gleneven?"

"Attacked by Abstainers, its people driven off before any help could come up from Edian. Yes. All tragic events."

Chasa pushed a strand of hair out of his eyes. "Well? What are we going to do?"

"Finish supper."

"Dad!"

Sene hitched his chair closer to the table and lifted his spoon, then regarded his open-mouthed children levelly. "It's been a long day. Chasa, will you eat something now or would you prefer to wash up first?"

"I'd prefer discussing what we're going to do!"

"Nothing. What would you have me do? Gather our troops of guards and march west? To do what? Help Palle in his hunt for Pirse? Defend Rhenlan's villages from Rhenlan's Abstainers?" Sene challenged first Chasa, then Jeyn. Both lowered their eyes. "Not that Hion wants our help, or could make use of it even if we offered. Have you considered that? What happened to Gleneven may not have been Hion's fault. You know how isolated some of those coastal villages are."

"You can't believe he didn't know of the danger—" Jeyn began.

"I refuse to hold Hion blameless—" Chasa said at the same moment.

Sene cut them both off. "I don't believe anything. Yet. Let me finish. Say we hear of another threatened village and decide to send Sitrinian help. We'd have to cross much or all of Rhenlan to get there, but maybe Hion wouldn't notice. Not such a good idea? We could go by sea. It would mean commandeering the fishing fleet and impoverishing all our coastal towns, but we might slip a few dozen guards ashore. Then all we'd have to do is engage a rampaging Abstainer band in battle before Hion—lawfully—sends his guards to fight the dangerous invaders. Us."

"Since when does Hion respect the law?" Chasa growled.

"We respect it." Sene tapped the handle of his spoon on the table for emphasis. "And because we respect it, we'll find a way to use it. The answer to chaos isn't more chaos. Remember that. You're too impatient, son. Too used to instant gratification. Chasing sea monsters has spoiled you. Not every problem can be eliminated by a few thrusts of a javelin."

"What do we do, then?" Chasa asked.

"Collect information," Jeyn suggested. With a wry smile she quoted one of Sene's favorite axioms. "Wait and watch, listen and learn."

"Exactly. Meanwhile we do have our own kingdom to run." Sene smiled. "Agreed?"

Chasa sighed and pulled up a chair. "Pass the bread, please, Jeyn."

CHAPTER 8

Sene's bedroom, like his throne room, his council room,
and his study, opened onto the long terrace that faced the
gardens and the sea. A cool breeze stirred the curtains,
which he had pulled back from his open doorway to admit
Keyn's mellow light. Sene could never live in a castle. His
residence was a home, not a palace, and he made sure that
it was easily accessible to his people, even though the other
Shapers of his generation thought him eccentric because of
his peculiar ideas. He admitted that Bronle needed its high
walls and stone towers, a sensible precaution against
dragons. The castle in Edian also had been built for defense, several generations of Dreamers ago when the horse
people first made incursions far into Rhenlan. Besides,
Hion's family had always had a touch of pretension in its
nature, a trait which wasn't diminishing with the passage of
time.

It had never seemed to occur to Hion or Dea that he
thought they were the eccentric ones. Other than coveting
his orchards, he doubted that they thought of him at all.
Maybe that was just as well. They would not appreciate the
way he monitored their arguments and the movements of
their border guards. He also knew the chief merchants of
their cities, the prices of trade goods, and the state of the
roads. He knew the size of village harvests and herds, listened to news of marriages and Rememberings, and took
note of the number of children presented at Spring and Fall
Festivals.

Sene added his map of Rhenlan to a pile of other scrolls
and books stacked randomly on the bedside table, next to
the tray that held what remained of his evening tea and a
now-empty pastry plate. Then he rubbed the bridge of his
nose and tried to focus his thoughts on his own capital and

the building projects underway there. He had intended to study the spidery drawings Daav had made for a new Mother house in Raisal, but of course he'd ended up reading another report from Edian instead.

It had been a welcome change, after days of worrying about events outside his kingdom, to devote an afternoon in Raisal to Daav, Jeyn's betrothed and Sitrine's most respected builder. Sene had spent several hours discussing renovations to some of the older areas of Raisal with the taciturn young man. Daav wasn't normally taciturn, but he and Jeyn had been fighting again.

Sene sighed and glanced at his bed, the covers turned invitingly back. Still too restless to sleep, he got up and walked onto the terrace. He drank in the light of stars and moons, and filled his lungs with the strong scent of night-blooming flowers and ripe pears.

Pears? The king sniffed again, then caught a glimpse of silver and deeper black amid the darkness between the terrace and the orchard. "Aage?"

The slender wizard stepped out of the garden shadows, face and hair pale in the moons' light.

Sene took the silent Dreamer's arm. "We've missed you. Come inside."

Aage seated himself on the king's bed and helped himself to some cool tea. "I've been busy."

"With Morb, in Dherrica. So you said before you left."

Aage ran the back of his hand across his high forehead. "Where we go, yes, I suppose it is in Dherrica. The power is stronger there than anywhere, except at the Cave of the Rock. Stronger and weaker at once. A place where monsters and evil come into our world. It's in need of constant defense, Majesty."

"So you keep reminding me."

Aage gave a tired shrug. "Dherrica has fewer Shapers than any other kingdom, and it needs them more. Perhaps it's the closeness to the edge of the world." He shook his head. "I know, you think it's a fool's theory. It probably is."

Aage had long suspected that beings from the worlds beyond their own sought to influence the thoughts and actions of the Children of the Rock. He'd even suggested that the plague was sent by would-be invaders from beyond the Dreamer-defended walls of power.

"I won't judge something I can't comprehend," Sene replied. "I do know it's good to have you back."

"What have you heard from Dherrica?"

"Dea dead. Pirse hunted like an Abstainer."

"He didn't do it."

"I never thought he did." Sene heaved a great sigh. "Still, it's good to hear you say so. Is the boy all right?"

"He is now."

Sene folded his arms and listened silently as Aage related what he had learned from Pirse, then described his own efforts on behalf of the Dherrican prince. When he finished, Sene said, "According to Palle's official proclamation, Dea was killed by a dragon sword. Does Palle own a dragon sword?"

"To my knowledge, no."

"Then Palle is in error, or lying."

"Easy to say. Less easy to prove."

"You're not much help, wizard."

Aage smiled. "You don't need much help, king."

"Go to your bed, Aage. I'd like mine back." Aage tossed the empty cup to him. Sene snaked it out of mid-air as the wizard got to his feet. "And don't go off in a puff of smoke. My grandmother always said you had no trouble finding the door when she was young and pretty and this room was hers."

"Ah, what a woman," Aage agreed, a fond glint in his eyes. "She was right. I do know how to walk out."

"Then do so. Good night."

"Juniper Ridge," Tob announced as they approached the cluster of buildings that straddled the road. Even if Pirse had been sleeping, and he had slept a great deal during his days of travel with the carter and his son, he would already have been roused by the unmistakable sounds of a blacksmith's hammer, the cluck of chickens, and children's voices that rose to meet them as they drew near to the village. However, there was no need to spoil the boy's enthusiasm.

"I've heard of it," Pirse answered simply, and leaned sideways in the wagon to peer around the curve of the steep mountain road. Jordy walked ahead, guiding the horse close to the inner side of the track. Juniper Ridge was of typical Dherrican design, its buildings scattered up the hillside in no particular order except for that dictated by the terrain. A swift, narrow stream defined the northern edge of the village. Beyond the houses, higher up the slope, several flocks of sheep and goats were visible in a rocky meadow.

"Tob," Jordy called. "Take Stockings. I'm going ahead to find Doron."

As soon as Tob reached the horse's head, the carter lengthened his stride and quickly outdistanced the horse and wagon to disappear around the next bend.

"It's a nice village," Tob said. "I like the air here."

"High summer in the mountains," Pirse answered absently. The air did smell especially sweet, thanks no doubt to a nearby cluster of the trees from which the village took its name.

"It's not as nice as home," Tob went on.

"Home's always best."

"Dad says that, too."

"He would." Jordy struck Pirse as a hearth-loving man. How he'd chosen his profession was a complete mystery.

"Have you traveled a lot?" Tob asked over his shoulder.

"Mostly in Dherrica. Why?"

"Do you know what's beyond the mountains?"

"I haven't gone that far west. No one has, not for generations of Dreamers. But I know a story of someone who traveled there."

Tob turned to walk sideways beside the plodding horse, eyes bright with anticipation. During their journey south, Tob had been an attentive, helpful companion, and Pirse had paid him with the only coin he had: his knowledge.

"Centuries of centuries ago," Pirse began, "there lived a Greenmother named Larkspur. Her special skill as a Dreamer was weather magic. Her home was the village of Hhehar, which is now part of Sitrine. Hhehar was a very nice place except for three problems. It was near the edge of the desert, and it attracted both phantom cats and wind demons."

"Big problems."

"Not in those days. The Shaper families of the village were very good about controlling the phantom cats. At the proper times of the year, Larkspur would bend her power and produce sufficient rain for the crops. And she was so watchful that no wind demon came within twenty miles of the village. Still, Larkspur wasn't satisfied. She wanted a way to eliminate the wind demons—destroy them utterly— just as Shapers destroy phantom cats and dragons.

"A new generation of Dreamers was born and came of age, and one skilled in weather magic came to live in Hhehar. Larkspur left her village in the new wizard's care and transported herself to the Cave of the Rock. There she vowed before the Firstmother that she would find a way to rid the world of wind demons once and for all.

"She traveled all over the world in search of a way to keep her vow. For a Dreamer, it's only a single step from the port of Raisal to the heights of the Dherrican Mountains, or from the shores of Lake Hari to the horse peoples' steppes. None of the Children of the Rock, the Keepers with their wisdom or the Shapers with their plans or the Dreamers with their gifts, knew of a way to eliminate the wind demons. Therefore, Larkspur sought an answer in lands unvisited by the Children.

"She went into the northeast, beyond Sitrine, and followed the desert all the way to the sea. In the southeast, she traveled beyond the steppes of the horse people, where she found rolling hills and tumbled mountains, some covered with snow, some full of smoke and fiery rocks, covered with forest on their eastern flanks and dropping almost immediately into the sea. Then she went into the hills south of

Rhenlan. She found lakes and forests and a river valley running from the hills toward the west. Beyond the river the land was dry and cold. In the far south, winter covered the sea with ice.

"Larkspur traveled west beyond Dherrica. In the southwest she found only cold, rocky shores. In the northwest, the forests continued after the mountains had flattened out and became jungles, where the winter never comes."

Tob shot Pirse a skeptical look. "Never?"

"Never. The sun is always high in the sky, and the days hardly vary in length from one Festival to the next. Food grows all year round, and strange animals and insects more numerous than I can name abound. Larkspur found villages of Keepers and Shapers on a few of the beaches where the fishing was especially good. They were familiar with dragons and sea serpents, but they couldn't advise Larkspur about wind demons.

"She bent the power to cross the ocean, and found the breeding grounds of the sea serpents. In the northern half of the world she found mountains and steppes and marshes and forests, animals and birds, but no Children of the Rock—and no inspiration.

"Once each year, at the time of the Fall Festival, she transported herself back to Hhehar to tell what she had seen. And the wind demons continued to dance around the village as they'd always done."

Pirse paused. Ahead of them, Jordy turned into a gated yard and entered the wide door of the house. Tob guided Stockings and the wagon around a hole, then looked back at Pirse. "Go on."

"Things went on in that fashion for eighty-six years. At the eighty-seventh Fall Festival—" He spread his hands. "No Larkspur. She was never seen again."

When Pirse fell silent, Tob protested, "That can't be the end of the story!"

"I'm afraid it is. Hhehar was abandoned during the plague. When a village dies, its stories often die with it."

"Where did you learn it, then?"

"I used to study the maps at the king's estate in Sitrine, when I was a boy learning about dragon slaying from Gavea. I asked her just what you asked me: What lies beyond the mountains? Her answer was that story."

"Lands with no winter, and mountains of fiery rock."

Pirse grinned at the skepticism in the boy's voice. "Sorry you asked?"

Tob looked back at him and grudgingly returned his smile. "I guess not."

Doron sang quietly to herself as she worked, one of her husband's favorite melodies. Her dead husband's favorite melodies. The familiar tightness filled her throat. Gods, how she missed him. They had been married only six years, but every hour of the day and night, every village path and building, contained memories of their life together.

She lifted another skein of wool from the vat. *Too much yellow,* she thought critically. Not unattractive, but not what she'd planned. She laid the skein across the drying rack, then wiped her hands on her apron. Perhaps it was best to quit for the day, and go home and fix something to eat.

Betajj used to have supper ready for her when she came home in the evening. On some days, when he knew that she was having difficulty with a dye, he would come down from their cottage to escort her home. But Betajj was gone. She had feared for him when he failed to return from the Bronle fall market, but not until her wandering brother brought a full report of the accident on the river did she know that her husband was half-a-year dead.

A distinctive creaking and rattling drifted up the hill from the direction of the valley. Doron peered down the road, and a smile tugged at her mouth as the familiar, white-stockinged bay mare came into view. The black-haired boy at her head had to be Tob. Last year Jordy had mentioned that his son was eager to accompany him on the road. A black-haired man sat in the wagon. Doron did not recognize him.

Tob seemed to have already learned some of his father's skills. As the road curved he tugged on the mare's halter, drawing her into a tighter turn than she'd seemed inclined to make. Doron shook her head ruefully. The most slow-witted horse in three kingdoms. Jordy deserved better.

Jordy himself was already at her gate. The setting sun brought out a hint of red in his pale hair.

He lifted the gate latch and entered the yard. "Doron. I was hoping we'd catch you here."

She found herself returning the man's ready smile. "A few minutes more and you wouldn't have. Come inside while I clean up." She opened the door of the shop and led Jordy inside. Glancing at him over her shoulder, she said, "We were beginning to think you weren't coming this summer. No trouble on the road, I hope?"

"Actually, there was—and I need your help."

They reached the gate through which Jordy had passed and Tob turned in, the horse trailing dutifully behind him. Another delivery made, Pirse thought, and about time, too. I'm tired of being one more parcel in the back of a wagon.

"What do you mean!" a woman's angry voice interrupted Pirse's thoughts. He cocked his head toward the small building in the center of the yard. Each outburst from the woman was followed by the low mutter of Jordy's voice. "I'll do no such thing! What need have I for a man about the place? I've done well enough on my own. A wizard? How would a wizard know my name? Will this be Ivey's doing, then?"

"Calm yourself!" Jordy's stern roar carried through the closed door.

"Calm, is it? I'm as calm as I need to be!"

"The man's sick. I can't take him all over three kingdoms with me!"

"Am I a Brownmother? They're the ones to nurse the homeless."

"Dherrica hasn't had a Brownmother settlement since before you were born."

"That still doesn't explain a Dreamer picking me out for this honor."

The door slammed open. Pirse knew that his potential guardian was a dyer and a widow. No one had mentioned that she was also young and handsome. And tall. She had several inches on the carter, who followed her out into the yard, a scowl accentuating the lines on his face.

"I don't explain Dreamer motives. I don't pretend they have any. As far as I'm concerned, the wizard made a lucky guess. You are the most responsible person to look after this particular man between here and Garden Vale. And," Jordy continued before the woman could interrupt, "no, I cannot take him to Garden Vale."

Her square jaw was already angrily set as she confronted the wagon. Blue eyes, Pirse noted. They were probably pretty when they weren't crackling with rage. "Do you have any say in this, invalid?"

It was Pirse's turn to wince. "Not really, ma'am. I tried to convince Jordy not to bother."

"You didn't do a very good job, did you?"

"No, ma'am."

Jordy stood fearlessly at Doron's elbow. "You'll admit he's polite."

"He knows lots of stories," Tob piped up from the relative safety of Stockings's shadow.

"I've a polite storyteller of my own," she answered.

"Ivey's hardly ever here," Jordy shot back.

A new voice entered the conversation. "He is today."

Even in the deepening dusk, Doron had no trouble recognizing the mane of curly hair on the man who entered the yard. Her brother was several years her junior and a good half a head shorter, but then, Doron was the tallest woman in Juniper Ridge. "Ivey!"

Ivey wrapped her in a hug, then acknowledged Jordy with a nod. "Let's finish this conversation at Doron's cottage. You know the way, I think."

"Aye." Jordy took the horse's lead rope from his son's

hand. "We'll meet you there."

"Just a minute!" Doron protested. "Ivey, you don't know—"

"Yes," he interrupted her. "I do."

The man in the wagon said nothing, but he and Ivey exchanged a glance that made Doron close her mouth. Her brother and Jordy had known one another for years, thanks to the wide travel required by their professions. Was the stranger also one of her brother's friends, a trader or a minstrel, to have earned such a knowing look from Ivey? Maybe instead of yelling at Jordy she should have saved her anger for her brother.

"Go," Ivey told the carter. "We'll catch up."

The wagon started up the road, and Doron and Ivey turned down the footpath that led toward her home. She let her temper cool before she spoke. "You're looking well. That blue tunic matches your eyes."

His teeth flashed white in the dusk. "A gift from a lady."

"Of course."

"I've a piece for you at the house, too."

"Are you going to tell me what this is all about?"

"Over dinner." He squeezed her hand. "I've been cooking all afternoon. Thought I'd surprise you."

"You have. So has Jordy, with his wounded passenger in search of a refuge."

"Did Jordy tell you the name of this friend of his?"

"No, not yet. But you obviously know him."

They reached the cottage. Ivey pushed the door open and beckoned Doron inside. "Over dinner," he repeated, and went to the hearth to attend the steaming kettle.

A few minutes later the room seemed to grow smaller as Jordy, his son, and the stranger entered with their bedrolls. Ivey lifted the kettle off the hook over the fire and placed it with a thump on the thick mat in the center of the table. "Dori, reach down the bowls, there's a good lass."

Doron passed round bowls and utensils and took a seat at one end of the table, opposite Ivey. As the men began to eat, Doron studied Jordy's unnamed passenger. His good looks were marred by a half-healed scar on his forehead, and a pallor that supported Jordy's claim that he was ill. His clothing did not quite fit, borrowed perhaps from the shorter carter.

Jordy cleared his throat and turned to Ivey. "What news, minstrel? Have you been in Edian?"

"I've just come from there. I know about the princess."

His tone of voice alarmed Doron. "Which princess? What happened?"

"Our princess. She's dead. She failed to successfully mediate a border dispute between Rhenlan and Dherrica."

Doron scowled. "Shapers!"

"Aye." The carter's growl echoed Doron's opinion perfectly.

"Where did you hear about it?" Ivey asked Jordy.

"We were in Edian the day they killed her. A senseless thing. The Shapers are getting worse, if you ask me."

Ivey set his spoon in his half-empty bowl. "Do you also know what happened in Bronle?"

Doron stared at her brother in alarm. Light-hearted Ivey was almost never solemn, and too cynical to be caught unprepared by random surprises from the gods. Or so she had always thought.

"Aye. The queen is dead," Jordy replied. "It's said by Pirse's hand."

"Nonsense!" Doron said sharply. "She was his mother!"

For the first time, the stranger spoke. "Thank you."

Silence fell over the table. At last, Ivey said, "The news in Bronle is that you haven't been seen since the day after the queen died. I can see I've been questioning the wrong people."

Doron ignored her brother to stare at the stranger beside him. "You're Pirse?"

The man—the prince, the rightful ruler of her country, if Queen Dea was truly dead—nodded. "I thought Jordy told you."

"She didn't give me a chance," Jordy said.

"You believe that he's innocent?" Ivey asked Jordy.

"Aye. Don't you? He's no vowless Abstainer. Anyone can see that. Even your friend Aage vouches for him."

Doron held her tongue and let the argument flow around her. It was her house, and ultimately her decision. Before she chose, she needed all the facts. Her sweet-tongued brother might try to persuade her to do something she didn't like, but only if he truly believed it was necessary. As for the carter, years of trade and travel had honed to razor sharpness his ability to assess situations and individuals. He might be stubborn as stone, but he had reasons for every opinion he held.

Ivey faced the prince. "If you didn't kill the queen, who did?"

"A guess is worthless without proof."

"Palle is calling himself king of Dherrica."

Jordy said, "It doesn't need Dreamers' sight to know how the lad would fare if he's captured by that vowless uncle of his."

Doron looked sharply at the carter. "These are the troubles you bring to my doorstep?"

"Aye."

"I am trouble," Pirse agreed. "But I'll be gone soon enough. My word on that, Doron of Juniper Ridge."

"A few ninedays," Jordy coaxed. "This is really the only place he can go."

"You know what will happen if he's discovered."

"Aye. That's why I can't keep him. A village can hide him. A wagon on the road can't."

"And a village discovered hiding him? What will Palle do to us?"

Pirse said, "Would it help if I tell you that I won't be captured alive in your village? If the situation becomes dangerous, I'll accept your counsel and make for the forest."

She pushed a loosened strand of hair back from her face. As hard as she tried, she detected no hint of deception in the prince's voice or manner. "You would, wouldn't you?"

"Do you think Dherrica will prosper with Palle as undisputed king?" Jordy asked.

"You know I don't," she snapped. "That's not the point."

"No. The point is, I've a sick man on my hands, you've a safe haven for him, and time's wasting discussing it."

"The point is," Doron insisted through clenched teeth, "I'm used to my privacy."

"He'll be inconspicuous," Ivey said.

"I'll be inconspicuous," Pirse promised. "Quiet as a mouse."

"He knows how to cook," Tob contributed helpfully.

"I'm really quite self-sufficient. In a day or two I'm sure I'll be able to fetch water or chop wood—"

"Or kill dragons?" Doron suggested.

"If you like."

She glared at Jordy and Ivey. "Oh, all right. He can stay. Until he's healed. Not a day longer."

"Not a day," agreed the prince.

CHAPTER 9

I'm the captain of the king's guard. I don't have time for this.
Dael hurried along the dark street, following the innkeeper who'd run to the guard post outside the castle.
There was a brawl in her tap room and she wanted it
stopped. Dael had called to Peanal and Nocca, the nearest
pair of his guards, and set off for the inn. Not because a
common bar fight needed the attention of the captain of the
guard, but with the hope that duty would distract him from
his thoughts.

Unfortunately, it wasn't working.

Where was Vray? Sent to be among the Brownmothers,
yes, but that was little help. There were Brownmothers in
every town and village. As more and more ninedays passed,
he'd started to make subtle inquiries everywhere he dared,
but no one had seen the princess.

The brawl had gotten to the furniture-breaking stage by
the time they reached the inn. Dael waded through the
noisy crowd blocking the doorway, Peanal and Nocca following.

"Stop it right now!" he bellowed at the top of his lungs.

The onlookers nearby stopped whatever they were doing
and stared nervously at the advancing guards. The four
combatants, still concentrating on damaging each other
with the inn's tables, chairs, and crockery, didn't notice the
uniforms or the sudden silence in the room.

Dael's little brother Nocca, six and half feet tall and very
strong, plucked one of the thick-necked drunks out of the
melee. The drunk's friend turned with an inarticulate growl
and reached for the guard. He never saw Peanal step behind
him, her truncheon raised. She smiled wolfishly as he went
down. Dael nodded his approval at her. It was nice to see
one of his lightly built students remembering his lessons in

fighting dirty. Nocca dropped his drunk in one corner and put his boot on the man's beer-splattered tunic. The third fighter raised his hands and retreated toward the wall.

The fourth man, red-faced with fury and drink, pulled a knife and dove straight for Dael. The crowd gave a collective gasp. Dael heard someone shout, "Fool! Not the captain! He's a killer!"

"Nonsense!" Nocca returned loudly. Dael appreciated his brother's vote of confidence, but would have preferred an offer of help.

The angry drunk's only interest was seeing blood. His knife whisked toward Dael's face.

Dael's reaction was automatic. He stepped, turned, grabbed, and heard the satisfying crack of his assailant's arm breaking. It was all very simple, hardly a killing situation, regardless of his reputation. The expressions of stunned surprise on the faces in the crowd reminded him that in Edian his skills were legendary.

"Did you see that?" someone muttered in the awed silence.

"See what? I didn't even see him move!"

Dael felt himself redden as he lowered the unconscious man to the floor. Nocca laughed with satisfaction.

"You can clean up the mess," Dael growled at his large little brother. He turned to the innkeeper. "The law reader will make arrangements for these four to work off the damages."

She nodded and grumbled her thanks, carefully not looking him in the eye. Dael frowned at her reaction, but it was no surprise after all his years in the guards. People came to him to solve their problems. They didn't necessarily appreciate his solutions.

Before he could maneuver toward the doorway, a delicate hand touched his arm.

"Dael," a familiar sweet contralto murmured.

Oh, gods. I don't have time for this, either. Aloud he said, "Not now. I'm on duty."

The brown-haired, heart-faced girl leaned on his arm.

"That's never stopped you before," she sighed at him.

He removed her and gently put her aside. "Another day," he promised. *When I don't have so much to worry about.*

This time the crowd let him through. Out on the street he took a few deep breaths of fragrant summer evening air. A nearby herb garden and a pen full of sheep helped scent the night, although many people would have had another word for the aroma the animals contributed to the evening air. Besides, anything was better than the combined stenches of drink and sweat and fear that had surrounded him inside.

Vray enjoys Edian, too, a nagging voice in the back of his mind taunted.

"You make it look so easy."

Dael stopped and turned, annoyed at the further interruption of his thoughts. At least the owner of the light baritone voice was not likely to be bringing him another problem to be solved. "Ivey," he acknowledged the younger man curtly. "I didn't see you inside."

"I wasn't inside. Watching people watching you tells the tale well enough for someone who knows you."

"Was it an entertaining tale, minstrel?"

"Sarcasm? So that's how it is." Ivey came up beside Dael, curly head tilted to one side in solemn contemplation. The effect was diminished somewhat by the presence of the dappled gray pack pony trailing patiently at the minstrel's heels. "Actually, I have used your exploits as entertainment from time to time. I hope you don't mind."

"You wouldn't stop if I did." He couldn't see much of the other man in the gloom of the street, but he knew the smells of dust and horse sweat and what they meant. "When did you arrive?"

"At sunset. I've been in the market square."

"Let's walk."

Ivey and his pony followed without comment as Dael led them downhill, away from the castle. Far ahead of them, a young couple strolled arm in arm, heads bent toward one another in intimate conversation. The rest of the street was quiet and empty.

"They say Emlie died quickly," Ivey offered.

"It was quick, as merciful as an unnecessary death can be." Dael rotated his shoulders, the muscles stiff with a tension that had nothing to do with his brief flurry of activity at the inn.

The pony snorted loudly, a fitting comment as far as Dael was concerned. Ivey said, "I know you, Captain. You tried to save the princess, but couldn't. And now you're judging yourself too harshly."

Dael almost let the misconception stand. Once Ivey believed he understood the root of something, be it a conflict between kingdoms or a man's mood, he would let the matter rest and go on to the next challenge. The gods knew there were enough challenges in the world to keep the minstrel busy. He didn't need to hear Dael's formless fears. Even as the thought flicked through his mind and slid away, Dael heard himself say, "Vray's gone."

The controlled breathing of the minstrel didn't change. "When?" he asked quietly.

Dael looked at him accusingly. "You already knew."

"No. I had no idea. But it explains the feeling I've had for the past few minutes."

After a suitable pause Dael prompted, "What feeling?"

"The feeling that if I said the wrong thing you'd run away from me exactly as you ran away from the inn."

"I didn't run . . . All right. I am running. In circles. She held a Remembering."

"So I heard."

"The next morning she was gone, sent abroad in Rhenlan to study as a young princess should, and it's partly my fault."

"Oh?"

Grateful that the darkness hid his embarrassment, Dael described Vray's growing infatuation with him, and Prince Damon's practical solution. Ivey sensibly refrained from any ribald remarks and allowed Dael to finish his story without interruption.

"I don't see why you're worried," the minstrel said as they turned the corner into another quiet street. "You know why she's gone, and what she's probably doing."

"She hasn't been seen, Ivey."

"How far have you looked?" Ivey asked. "For that matter, how far should you look, given that her absence is with the knowledge and approval of the king?"

"It's just that I miss the girl, Ivey."

"I'm sure she misses you, too. And she'll probably be kept away from Edian until she stops missing you." They reached the goldsmith's lamp-lit windows and turned down the path to the back door. "Your parents are going to think I don't like Edian's inns. I stay with them too often."

"They like you."

"They like my singing."

"They like being the first to hear your news."

"I've a lot to tell." Ivey stopped Dael before they reached the door. "Don't worry about Princess Vray. If I hear anything, I'll send word to you."

Dael draped his arm over the minstrel's shoulders. "Thank you." He pushed the kitchen door open. "Dad! Mom! Company!"

Hot nights in the mountains didn't happen very often. The heat contributed to Pirse's being unable to sleep. The heat and the memories. He lay in the darkened main room of Doron's small house and willed himself to stop sweating. A nineday before he would have blamed it on fever, but the fever hadn't bothered him for some time now. It was just a still midsummer night. Too still. Too quiet. He could hear his thoughts too clearly. He could see his memories more vividly than the shadows the sickness had made of them. Lying here in the dyer's house, all he could think of was his mother's great hall, all he could hear was Cratt's despair, all he could see was the accusation in his uncle's dark eyes. Accusation and triumph.

Pirse sat up abruptly, unable to stand his own dark silence any longer. The cot creaked beneath him. He heaved himself to his feet and clutched his aching head with one hand, fighting nausea. The door to the porch was open, a rectangle of bluish light crossed with the motionless shadows of tree branches overhead. He moved hastily outside, bare feet silent. Since his intrusion into her life, Doron often appeared at his bedside when he was restless, day or night, to offer her brusque sympathy and see to the little details of nursing him back to health. Health he didn't deserve. Health that meant facing up to the future.

He crossed to the porch steps and sank down, dropping his head into his hands. An owl hooted somewhere in the forest to the north. He always noticed hunters. He was a hunter, much good it had done him. *How many of the castle guards died in the lawful hunt for me? I don't even remember. Why didn't I let them take me? I should never have left Bronle. I'm no good to anyone out here.*

"What are you doing awake?"

Pirse jerked upright. Doron stood in front of him, at the bottom of the stairs. "How did you get there?"

She planted her large fists on her hips and scowled up at him. "I've a right to be in my own yard."

"I thought you were asleep in the house."

"You were wrong. And you should be resting. To bed with you." She made a shooing motion with her hands. It made Pirse feel like a hen being chased back into a chicken coop. He assumed it was that image which almost made him smile.

"I can't sleep," he answered her, and made the effort to be polite, even if it was the middle of the night. "Does the heat disturb you, too?"

The moonlight shone over her shoulder, leaving her face in shadow. She turned and sat beside him, revealing a sad expression on her strong features. Staring across the yard, she seemed to forget his presence for a time.

She was really quite pretty, he decided, in a raw-boned, square-jawed sort of way. A woman of character, of strength. That's what his mother would have said. She believed in finding something complimentary to say about all people.

Mother. What am I going to do?

Sheyn was bright tonight. His blue light positively glistened on the woman's face. Pirse blinked and looked more closely at Doron. It wasn't moonslight. A slender trail of tears marked her cheek.

Without thinking, he touched her shoulder. "Doron? Are you all right? Is it something to do with me?"

She shook him off. "Shapers." Her low voice was roughened with emotion, but not so rough that he missed the underlying contempt. "You're not the center of the world, man. I had a life before you came to Juniper Ridge. Had." A deep sigh shook her. "Go to bed, will you?"

He bit back his first proud retort and answered with forced patience. "There's no sleep for either of us. I'm only trying to be of use. I know I'm not much help in a village, but I do know how to listen if you need to talk."

"You don't know me, Shaper, nor I you. What makes you think you can help where family and friends have failed? I had a man. He's dead. Talking or listening can't help that."

"I had a mother and sister," he retorted before he could stop himself. "They're dead. I hurt tonight. Advise me, Doron. If talking doesn't help the grief, what does?"

"Rock and Pool," she whispered. "I wish I knew." Suddenly she was facing him, the tears rolling more freely, her mouth twisting with despair. "I don't know what to do!"

He swallowed uncomfortably. "Doron . . ." His voice didn't respond as he'd expected it to. Instead, his vision blurred and his hands went to her shoulders again, this time without rebuff. She moved into his offered embrace, her head burrowing into his shoulder. He tried to take a deep breath, but the inhalation became a sob. He buried his face in the softness of her hair and the tight control he'd kept over his emotions shattered.

"I told myself, no tears," he said when he was done with his crying. Said it not to Doron, but to himself. "Tears wash away grief. I don't deserve that."

"Oh hush," was the unsympathetic retort from the woman. "Tears come. They solve nothing. They just come." He pushed her gently upright. "Fine pair, aren't we?"

"Pair? That we are not." She stood and walked back into her yard. "Go to bed. Go to sleep. That also solves nothing, but it passes the time."

She disappeared beneath the shadows of the trees. Pirse levered himself to his feet. "Passing the time? Maybe that's enough for you." Fatigue caught up with him as he spoke. A yawn took the place of whatever else he was going to say, and drove the words right out of his mind. He made it back into the house with barely enough energy to find his cot. If he wasn't good for anything else, he thought as his eyes closed, at least he could play the obedient lad for the dyer of Juniper Ridge. *That's the trouble with Dherricans. We all think we know what's best for everyone else.*

We just can't decide what's best for ourselves.

The pain grew during the night, ebbing near dawn. It was a frequent pattern and Hion had learned to live with it, but it exhausted him, eating away at Jenil's healing magic.

"Magic," Hion snorted, and dragged himself from beneath the sweat-soaked sheets. He stumbled across the room and opened the curtains to let in the dawn light. Behind him, the door opened, and he heard the familiar sounds of his servant preparing his bath. He settled heavily into the chair by the window and watched the light grow over the fields and buildings of his city. He loved the view from his room. His view alone. It had been years since he'd shared quarters with the queen. Gallia was hardly ever in Edian. When she was, she certainly didn't come near the king's chambers. She hadn't shared his bed since the night the girl was conceived. Not that Hion particularly cared. The red-haired woman's presence wasn't missed.

He shared his bed with the pain, which was all the company he could bear. Hion was glad to have no meddling woman about to question him. His room was the only refuge he had. Here, he could be weak. If he showed weakness in the castle, in the council chamber and great hall, on his rounds of the city, there would be talk. If there was talk, a delegation of Shapers would follow, to challenge his right to rule them—and Gallia would lead the delegation.

He had given his life in defense of Rhenlan. He had no intention of retiring to some estate to quietly nurse his failing strength. He was not yet fifty years old! Every moment he still ruled—some worse than others—reminded him of the rewards of his Shaper's duty.

Hion sighed. He was feeling particularly bitter this morning. It had been a bad night, and now he had a council meeting to prepare for. He moved to the tub of hot water that his servant had filled. She was the only person he allowed in his rooms. Hion didn't think they'd exchanged more than a few words in all the years she'd served him, but she understood his habits and never got in the way. She'd been young and pretty once. Gallia had been jealous.

Gallia had liked to pretend, in the early days, that she loved her husband. She'd given up the pretense after Damon's birth, doting on the baby for a while. Eventually she lost interest in their son and went back to the horses she loved. She still spoiled Damon when she came to court. Fortunately, the castle was no more to her than a place to stay during the annual horse fair, so Damon was spared her smothering attention all but a few days of the year.

Hion eased himself into the steaming water and leaned his head back against the wooden edge of the tub. He closed his eyes, paying no attention as the servant went through the familiar ritual of bathing and shaving him.

Poor Damon. The boy had had poor luck with his parents, and poor luck with the times he lived in. A Shaper needed challenges, things to struggle against. Since the plague, the monsters that still afflicted Dherrica and Sitrine had been absent from Rhenlan. Hion had seen to the last of the fire bears himself. Though they kept patrols on the southern border, the horse people had been quiet for a dozen years or so.

It might have been better for the boy if he'd been able to set his mind and strength against some tangible threat. Damon had grown up a brilliant administrator, but he lacked compassion. At twenty-six, he showed no more understanding of the basic needs of Shaper and Keeper than he had shown at sixteen, or six. Hion was grateful for all the help his son gave, but worried as well. Although he allowed Damon to oversee more and more of the business of running the kingdom, his son was not yet qualified to assume the full responsibilities of kingship. He had not yet told the council, or Damon, how soon he might have to relinquish the throne to his son. Only Jenil, who had sense enough to keep her Dreamer's nose out of the business of government, knew that the king spent much of his time lost in pain.

The hot, pine-scented water soothed Hion's aching body. *That's something else the kingdom owes me. Rhenlan stole my life. Worse, it has stolen my boy's childhood. I've used him, turned him into my deputy, but he's not ready.*

Hion grunted and heaved himself out of the water. Time to start the long, hard day. The serving woman handed him a towel and he went back to his bedroom to dress in the clothing she'd laid out while he soaked.

The morning was growing older and he had the council to think of. His eyes sought the window and the long view over the countryside. He was a fool to keep trudging up the many flights of steps to the privacy of this tower chamber year after weakening year. He could sleep nearer to the ground, but he had no intention of giving up the privilege of the dawn.

He turned his thoughts to the council and what they needed to discuss today. Ah, yes. The message from Palle, and Captain Dael's request for guards.

Dael will ask that the guards now on the border be put to use hunting down Abstainers. Best to talk to Dael before the meeting. No need to discuss Abstainers in front of Damon. Dael's a good lad, responsible, but Damon's my son. It was hard on the boy when his uncle, Gallia's brother, renounced his vows and ran off to the abandoned lands rather than live among civi-

lized people. Soen's mad, always was. Still, Damon cared deeply for him. Now he's afraid that every Abstainer executed will be his dear uncle. He'll have to deal with Abstainers when he's king, but I'll manage that problem for now. Tell Dael myself we can't spare any more guards.

What else? Hion waved the question away and got to his feet. Never mind. He'd find out soon enough.

CHAPTER 10

I wish I had time to get drunk, Dael thought as he mounted the steps of the law reader's house. Good and drunk. A days and days long drunk. Several people followed him through the wide doors. The petitioners were stopped by the porter to ask their names and business while Dael continued on into the cool interior of the old wooden building. He headed up two flights of stairs to the top floor, turned left, and entered the room of the senior law reader, an old Shaper named Oskin.

"Dael. Good. I want to have a word with you."

Dael approached the tall, carved oak table. The white-haired man behind it put down his quill. Dael gave the book one disinterested glance. He didn't really understand Shapers' need for recording things with pigment and parchment. All he knew was that most Shapers couldn't recall what they'd had for breakfast unless a Redmother was there to remember for them, or they marked it down in a book or scroll. Oskin probably had a hundred books lining the shelves behind him. Vray said she liked to read the old records. Liked to read, though she didn't really need to with her memory training. Personally, Dael preferred to listen to a storyteller, or a minstrel's songs.

"I need a favor, Oskin."

The old man glowered at him. "I need more guards. Maybe we can help one another."

"For the cells? You know I don't have any people to spare."

"Well, without guards we can't hold prisoners. You'll have no labor at all for the roads if every malicious offender is executed because there's no one to oversee the labor crews."

Dael grimaced. "That's why I'm here. You'll receive a

106

delegation from Hillcrest today. They want a road repaired.
You have to tell them to do their best without any help from
Edian."

"This can't go on."

"It will go on as long as guards are needed at the borders. We have to make do with what we have."

A knock on the door interrupted them. "What is it?"
Oskin called.

The porter stuck his head in. "Will you hear a blood
debt settlement, sir?"

"Now? It's an hour before my witness arrives. Can't they
come back later?"

"The woman's with the midwife now, sir. They weren't
expecting the baby this early."

"I'll witness as long as I can," Dael offered. "I have to
see the king in an hour."

"Oh, very well," Oskin agreed. "Send them up."

Because of the gentle rain which had been misting down
all day, Doron did not expect to hear the sound of voices
outside her dye shop. For that reason, and because she was
concentrating so closely on the pigments she was grinding,
she missed the beginning of the conversation. The first
words that came clearly through the open window were in
Prince Pirse's good-natured voice.

"Fine day for it, Tamik!"

Doron raised her eyes from her mortar. Fine day for
what? The voice of Tamik, an old shepherd who lived with
his wife on the south edge of the village, sounded faintly
through the rain. "Aye. It is that."

"Is that Star, then?"

The gate leading into the yard swung against the fence
with its characteristic boom. "Nay, laddie. This is Myrtle.
Star has the brown marking on her back."

"I'll try to remember that."

Shapers can't remember anything, Doron thought sourly.
Then the nagging question returned: Fine day for what?

Tamik said, "You have a neat hand with that."

107

"Plenty of experience, I'm afraid."

That does it. How can I concentrate with people talking in riddles outside my window? Doron dropped her pestle into the mound of blue powder and stalked to the window. *When I'm alone no one interrupts me. Why did I ever think I didn't like living alone?*

Tamik said, "Perhaps you'd have time another day to come by my house? I've one or two blades could use proper attention."

"Gladly."

Doron leaned one forearm on the windowsill. Blades. She might've known. Since Pirse had begun feeling stronger he'd been badgering her for useful things to do. He'd reset several stones in the hearth at her house, replaced half the fence at the east end of the yard, patched the roof of the storage shed in the dye shop yard, pulled weeds in the garden behind her house, and during the past nineday had begun the task of filling her woodshed for the winter. She admitted, at least privately, that he was a handy man to have around the place. She did not, however, recall giving him permission to get into her cutlery.

She stuck her head out the window. "Fine day for what? Good day, Tamik," she added with an effort at friendliness. "Fine day to stay indoors, if you ask me."

Pirse straightened. His soft black hair was even curlier than usual, thanks to the damp weather. He was seated on one of her three-legged stools in the shelter of the over-hanging eaves, an oblong block of oiled stone nestled in the palm of one hand, her best carving knife in the other. In a basket beside him were the rest of her cooking knives, as well as two pairs of shears from the dye tool shed and the small sewing scissors she kept on the chest at the foot of her bed.

"Tamik's going fishing," Pirse told her.

"Trout will be active, this weather."

Yes, of course. Trout. Silly of me to even ask. The shepherd had a long pole balanced over his shoulder and a woven basket hanging against his back. Water rolled in tiny droplets off the dog Myrtle's long-haired coat. She was looking larger every day.

"When are the puppies due?" Doron asked.

"Oh, not for a few ninedays."

Pirse looked closely at the dog. "Ah. Definitely not Star. Careless of me to have forgotten."

His echo of her earlier thought made Doron shiver. The Shaper did that too often for her liking. Tamik, meanwhile, had picked one of the knives from the basket and was examining the edge.

"Nice work. Though not the quality of steel you're accustomed to."

"Betajj brought that knife back from Bronle for me," Doron huffed in automatic defense.

"Perfectly suitable for the use it's put to," Pirse agreed. She wasn't entirely certain that was a compliment, but he continued before she could make a reply. "I could stop by after supper, if that's convenient."

"Aye, do that." Tamik nodded pleasantly to Doron. "You're welcome as well, dyer. Karalie and I haven't seen much of you this summer."

That's because an irate widow is poor company, Doron thought, but all she said was, "My thanks, Tamik. Perhaps another day. I've no time tonight."

"No time?" Pirse regarded her with undisguised disapproval. "Don't be absurd! Would do you good to get out and visit your friends." To Tamik he added, "We'll come."

"He'll come," Doron corrected sharply. The prince raised his eyebrows innocently at her. "If I have to kick you down the hill."

"You wouldn't." He tried his dazzling smile on her. "You might enjoy the attempt. Far be it for our staid and serious Doron to enjoy anything."

"Well, I'll be going." Tamik backed away from the shop. "Karalie and I will be expecting you." He diplomatically left open the question of how many guests they'd be expecting. Diplomacy, or cowardice.

As soon as the shepherd was through the gate she

reached down and rapped Pirse on the top of the head. He yelped. She said, "I enjoyed that."

"Bully," he complained.

"So I am. I'll thank you not to organize my life for me."

"You're not doing very well on your own, are you?"

She stepped back inside, and just avoided hitting her head on the top of the window by a hairsbreadth. Insufferable man! The sooner he was fully recovered and out of the village, out of her life, the better she would like it.

"You're drunk."

"Am I?" *Must be drunk,* Dael thought. *Didn't hear Nocca approach. And, little brother, you are not a quiet one.*

He turned, somehow avoiding the big hand that tried to fall on his shoulder. He looked up at his brother's broad, handsome, concerned features. Dael wasn't a small man, but Nocca, eight years younger and in his first year in the guard, was half a head taller. He had the family's gold hair, worn long in the style of the guard. A style Dael had started. He wasn't happy to have a brother follow him into the guard. It wasn't as though he'd chosen this life, or wanted to inspire anyone to be like him. It left only Ruudy at home to learn the goldsmith's trade from their father. At least Ruudy'd brought home a wife with some skill at gem carving. Not that anyone could replace their dead sister, Milla.

He felt his eyes begin to mist with tears and knew he really was drunk. Milla would be the last to appreciate his being maudlin.

"What do you want?" he asked his very big little brother.

Nocca shook his head. "Three days, Captain." He looked around at the dimly lit inn with disapproval. The big room was nearly empty this early in the day. A pair of farmers sat in one corner, nursing mugs of ale. Dael had woken up behind the bar, on a pallet supplied by a pretty girl. He could remember her face and kindness, but not her name.

"Three days?" he repeated.

"You've been here three days." Nocca tugged on his sleeve. "Come home. You can drink yourself into a stupor there. Or in your own quarters."

"Can't drink myself into a stupor," Dael answered. "I've tried." He lifted his mug and downed the ale in a few gulps. Putting it carefully on the counter before him, he said, "There's a wine from Sitrine I've been meaning to try. It might do the trick."

"Come home." Nocca put his hands on his hips and looked insistent. Or tried. To Dael he just looked like a big, long-haired puppy with their father's eyes.

"I think they water the ale here," Dael continued. "But they're good to me, so I won't report it to myself. I'm very good at not telling myself things."

"You promised Father ninedays ago to travel with him to White Water when you could get leave."

"So I did."

"Have you asked the king?"

Clattering noises came from behind the curtain strung across the opening behind the bar. Perhaps the pretty girl was up and working. Dael smiled at the thought of her. The thought didn't go any further. He really was drunk. Drunk and incapable. "Ruin my disgusting reputation." He looked at his brother. "Why would a princess want me?"

Nocca wrinkled his long nose. "No one would want you now."

"Just as well, then."

"Have you asked the king?"

Stubborn child. Dael turned and leaned back against the bar. "Not yet."

"Why not?"

"I've been getting drunk. Why must I always state the obvious to everyone?" He was beginning to get annoyed. It wasn't safe for him to be annoyed. Dangerous things tended to happen. So he stopped being annoyed, and sighed. "What am I supposed to ask the king?"

"About traveling with father," Nocca answered with the patience one used to speak to the simpleminded.

Dael suddenly remembered what Nocca was talking about. After the king had refused to let him take a troop or two to clean out the bands of Abstainers reported along the roads to White Water, Dael had thought of something clever. His father had valuable cargo to transport. If Abstainers heard of a goldsmith traveling with some of his wares, he was sure to be attacked. Which was what Dael wanted, since he planned to accompany Loras's wagon with a troop of his best people. The king couldn't object to a training exercise, couldn't object to Dael being a dutiful son. A perfectly good plan. Of course, he'd have to sober up to put it into effect.

"How'd I get here?" he asked, abruptly annoyed, with himself and his brother and the king, and others he was probably too drunk to think of, for wasting time.

"You walked," his brother answered dryly. "You gave command to Sergeant Hamer and told him to leave you alone. He's left you alone."

Dael nodded. It made him dizzy. He swallowed. "I've lost the mood for keeping order in Rhenlan."

"Well, you'd better get it back."

He stood up and put his hands on his brother's shoulders. "It's because of Vray, you see. She constantly annoys the king. She would make him give me the guards I need to serve the kingdom. Gods, I miss her."

Nocca removed Dael's hands from his shoulders. "Is that what this is about? The princess?"

"No. Of course not. It's no business of mine. I'm just the captain of the guard. Why should I care for a girl I raised?"

Nocca looked thoughtful. "Father said she's taken Milla's place for you. Please come home, Dael."

Nocca wouldn't remember their dead sister very well. Besides, it wasn't true. Vray was herself. Too much. Headstrong child. Dael rubbed his forehead. His head hurt—probably the result of trying to use it. "I'm going to be sick."

"Good. Maybe then you'll sober up."

Once he was sober he'd start thinking again, and he wasn't sure that was what he wanted. Unfortunately, it seemed he no longer had a choice.

"Take me home," he said, and let Nocca guide him out into the bright day.

CHAPTER 11

Doron's house was too small. Given the time and energy Pirse would happily have rebuilt it, beginning by doubling the size of the foundation. But as a recovering invalid he'd had to content himself with minor items such as chimney repair and window caulking; now with the return of his strength, time had run out. The house would have to remain as it was.

Pirse sighed and pulled off his shirt as he stepped into the steamy heat of the bath house, a low-ceilinged structure attached by a doorway to the main building in a manner common to the mountain villages. Inside were wooden tubs of appropriate sizes for washing people or their clothing, and a few shelves for soap, wash paddles, and brushes. The squat water tank atop its iron-enclosed fire dominated the room. He chose a tub and slid it into place over the drain set in the smooth wooden floor, then opened the spigot from the tank. Perhaps it wasn't a matter of the house being too small. What was important was that it was adequate for the woman's needs, safe and comfortable. Too comfortable. He'd been entirely too self-indulgent lately. He'd allowed himself to begin to like it here.

He kicked off his trousers and reached across the tub to turn off the water. A cool breeze touched his naked back just before Doron's voice said, "Pirse."

He turned. One hand on the half-open door, the other balled into a fist at her side, Doron glared at him. "Since when does anyone take a bath in the middle of the afternoon?"

"I've earned it. I split the last of the firewood. Would you mind closing the door? There's a bit of a draft."

To his surprise she stepped further into the room before swinging the door shut. She was wearing a simple, long-skirted dress of pale green with no sleeves, stained here and there by the products of her shop, in spite of the apron tied at her waist. He noticed that her face was flushed. The warmth of the room, or perhaps the exertion of her climb up the road from the dye shop.

"Since when do you come home before sunset?" he counter-challenged.

"The village of Alder has been attacked by Abstainers. One of their people has arrived, looking for advice. We're gathering in Tamik's barn to talk to her."

"Alder. That's the other side of the range, isn't it?"

"Aye. Four days travel when the roads are clear."

"On foot. That would be less than one day by horse."

"You don't own a horse."

"I'll borrow the potter's."

They stared at one another. She said, "Why do we bother to argue when each of us knows what the other is going to say?"

"Do we?" he asked. "If you know how I feel about Abstainers and don't want me to leave, why were you so eager to tell about Alder?"

"The woman has come for advice, not a swordsman."

"But my advice when facing Abstainers is a swordsman. Several, if you can find them."

He stepped impulsively forward and kissed her on the cheek. He intended it as a gesture of gratitude and acknowledgment of the care she'd shown an unwelcome stranger. He was also not without hope that such an act of effrontery would end the discussion, and quite possibly their relationship, very neatly. But she did not flinch away. She didn't even slap him.

Her face beneath his lips felt hot. He was the one to pull back, startled, abruptly reminded that only a few layers of thin summer linen separated them, none of it his. She had one hand on his chest, but not to push him away. With his breath quickening, he kissed her again, properly this time, his hands finding her hips and pulling her close.

Once her dress was off and added to the mound of his clothes, he could barely feel the hard wooden floor beneath them.

★ ★ ★ ★ ★

Sweaty. Sex in the bath house was always sweaty. Doron stuck out her lower jaw and blew a sharp puff of breath upward, fanning the damp hair away from her forehead. Pirse, sprawled on his back beside her, opened one eye. "A bit warm?" he asked.

"We shouldn't have done this."

He rolled onto one elbow, facing her, all suggestion of lassitude gone. "By the mothers, why not? If it's your dead husband you're thinking of . . ."

Mention of Betajj brought only a distant sweet ache. She reached up and tugged at his ear. "I was thinking of the fact that we haven't time to bathe. We'll be missed."

A puff of daffodil yellow smoke near Pirse's feet coalesced into a black-robed woman, her pink face fringed with short, oat-brown hair. She smiled fondly down at them while they scrambled for their clothes. "Oh, good. I told Morb you should be feeling better by now."

Pirse got quickly to his feet. The pleasant haze induced by their love-making gave Doron a last impression of the young prince's physical grace and poise, even looking embarrassed and slightly put out; then cold reality smashed down on her and she saw only a muscular but too-thin, too-pale lad with too many smooth white scars marring his skin. "Don't Dreamers respect privacy?" she snapped.

"No, they don't," Pirse answered for the woman. "Doron, this is Savyea."

To Doron's discomfort the Greenmother beamed at her. "Oh, I know Doron. A fine, strong family. Normally I wouldn't dream of intruding, children, but I told Morb better me than Aage."

"Morb is in need of me?" Pirse accepted the trousers Doron held up toward him, his puzzled gaze never leaving Savyea's face.

"He's grown far too used to your work. Sene's son could manage a dragon or two for a change."

"Dragons? Where?"

The black cloak rustled as Savyea made a soothing ges-

116

ture with both hands. "Now, dear, don't get excited. Morb dwells too much on monster-slaying in my opinion. But I won't say he's not practical about it. That's why he's asking after you now, so that you'll have plenty of warning."

"Greenmother," Pirse paused in the lacing of his tunic. "Is there or isn't there a dragon?"

"There are always dragons," Savyea returned with equal patience. "At present Morb thinks you'll be concerned about one that is moving along the coast. He asked me specifically to tell you that it will be hunting on the shore due north of Dundas in three ninedays, if unopposed."

Doron dressed, berating herself for a fool. Dragons and Dreamers marked the boundaries of Pirse's existence. Admittedly, he'd extended himself a bit since arriving in Juniper Ridge, but only because he was a dutiful Shaper. The villagers—Keepers throughout Dherrica—were right to respect him. That didn't mean they should presume to love him.

For the past few days, Doron had been intending to remind him that he had better things to do with his time than to mend fences and chop wood. A little fun on the bath house floor didn't change that. Certainly there was no reason to resent a man being true to his vows. She said, "Don't forget the Abstainers."

Pirse glanced at her, all brisk efficiency. "Plenty of time. Trust me."

"Well, if there's no hurry," Savyea said brightly, "don't mind me. Just go on with what you were doing. Priorities are everything, you know."

A scent of sun-warmed earth and cut clover lingered in the air after the Dreamer disappeared. Doron found herself sharing a bemused, somewhat embarrassed look with the prince. Then she remembered he was leaving. "I'll go ahead to Tamik's," she said, turning away. "Tell them you're coming."

"Doron." He grabbed her upper arm and tried to peer into her face. "What's wrong?"

"Don't, Your Highness." She gazed levelly at him. "I've done my part. You're well again."

117

"There's more between us than that."

She pulled firmly out of his grasp. "I'm no innocent girl to need pretty words and well-meaning reassurances. You've work to do. Let that be the end of it."

Once more she started for the door. His voice behind her was cool, determined. "I'll be back."

"The villagers will welcome you, I'm sure."

"See that you do," was his parting remark as she escaped from the room.

There was no evidence of sheep in Tamik's barn, for his flocks had been out on the mountain all summer. Instead, the large structure smelled primarily of the hay stored in its upper reaches and the vegetables in the root cellar below. During the winter, the entire village would be fed out of the surplus put aside in the shepherd's barn. When Pirse entered, a fair number of the Keepers were already present, standing in a loose circle on the bare clay floor, most talking quietly with the people nearest them. In the center of the circle stood Tamik, Doron, and a woman with long, dusty-brown braids who could only be the stranger from Alder.

Pirse tried to slip into the circle, but a few determined hands propelled him into the center beside the barn's owner.

Doron said, "Jonna, I think this is everyone. Will you tell us what happened?"

"Six Abstainers," the woman replied immediately. "We missed a few goats a nineday ago, but Corl thought it was wolves. Then seven days ago the storage cave at the head of the valley was ransacked. Some items stolen, but most destroyed, trampled, casks smashed open. The next day we saw them for the first time. Four men and two women, we think. They fired both farms on the south bank of the creek. You know where I mean, Hanig," she added, directly addressing one of the Juniper Ridge women. Hanig nodded grimly.

"Was anyone hurt?" Tamik asked.

"Aussol was burned trying to save his chickens. I don't know how serious it is. I left first thing in the morning. That was five days ago. Who knows what's happened since?" She looked past Tamik. "We're a small village, Highness. Seventeen families scattered the length of a valley."

"I know the place," Pirse replied. "I visited five years ago with Captain Cratt and a troop of the Queen's guards."

Jonna's expression grew, if anything, more serious. "I remember the captain, though I don't remember you. They were following up a report of Abstainers to the south."

"I'm afraid we never found them. It's conceivable this is the same group. Or part of that group."

"You have experience with these people." The statement from Tamik was accompanied by one of the shepherd's judicious scowls.

Somewhere in the ring of listening villagers a voice said, "If you can call them people."

Pirse said solemnly, "There has been some discussion on that very point. We say we are all Children of the Rock."

"But they deny that," another voice muttered darkly.

"They make no vows," Hanig agreed. "They recognize no system of cooperation between individuals, since even the simplest cooperation requires the making and keeping of agreements."

"Whatever they are," Jonna interrupted, "they have to be stopped."

"Seventeen families," Doron said. "Even spread out as Alder is, that's a lot of people for six Abstainers to face. Perhaps they'll have already moved on."

"Possible, but not likely. Once they make a successful raid on a given community they keep coming back until there's nothing left. There have been Abstainers at least as far back as Redmother memories and Shaper records go, and we've yet to find an answer to their violence."

"Short of death," Jonna said softly.

"Short of death," Pirse agreed. The villagers stirred restlessly. He looked at them, once more feeling out of place. Keepers' vows centered on sustaining and maintaining the fabric of the world. Death as part of the natural cycle they accepted without question or discomfort. To consciously choose the death of another person, even so dubious a person as an Abstainer, was almost inconceivable to them. Fortunately, Shapers had a different way of looking at things.

"I will go to Alder," he continued. "I have my sword, but I'll need a horse, and the names of anyone in Alder who might be able to help me. Former guards, perhaps?"

"There are a few," Jonna said.

The potter raised his voice. "My horse is the closest you'll find to saddle-trained between here and Bronle. Take her, and welcome."

Pirse smiled his thanks. "I'll send her back as soon as I'm able."

"Send her back?" Tamik asked. "You're leaving us, then?"

"I'm afraid so."

The silence which followed his statement was thoughtful. "You're not returning to Bronle," Tamik said, the words more statement than question. If anyone in Juniper Ridge intended to betray Pirse to his uncle, they had not done so yet. Most of the villagers had accepted Pirse without question, on the recommendation of Jordy and Ivey, who were known and respected—unlike Palle, the man behind a growing number of unpopular edicts and proclamations that had come south from the capital in the ninedays since Dea's death.

"No. Not yet."

Tamik gave a curt nod. "Good."

"What about you, Jonna?" Pirse asked. "Palle is king, and he has commanded that I stand before the law readers. Do you think I should obey?"

"He may be king, but he hasn't kept the Abstainers from our doors."

"No, he hasn't. But I will. Alder needs its prince. After that, there are dragons in the north. That's where my duty lies."

"Go to keep your vows, and the gods go with you." The old platitude, uttered in Hanig's reedy voice, seemed to provide a satisfactory conclusion to the meeting as far as the Keepers were concerned, and they began to leave the barn. Those who had gotten to know Pirse stopped to wish him well and offer their support should he ever return to their village. Tamik urged Pirse to gather his horse and any supplies he needed promptly if he intended to get on the road before nightfall. Pirse looked around for Doron. He wanted her with him, just in case she might have some final, useful advice to add before he left.

But she was gone.

Summer had turned toward autumn. Jordy leaned against the back rest of his wagon's driver's seat. One hand on the reins and a fraction of his attention were sufficient to keep Stockings moving along at her usual steady pace. Most of his thoughts were occupied with how best to use the remaining days of the trading season.

He watched the passing scenery. This was lake country, the terrain flat for the most part, heavily forested from their present position all the way back to the village of White Water, three days' journey to the south. With the exception of an occasional shepherd or two, no one lived in the mountains beyond White Water anymore. Very few people dwelt anywhere in the region, although Jordy thought it must once have been a beautiful place to live. Every few miles there was a lake, sometimes large, sometimes little more than a pond, always deep and full of fish. After so many ninedays of living on what game Jordy could procure with rock or bow, Tob was enthusiastic about lake fish dinners.

A break in the trees on the eastern side of the road gave Jordy a brief glimpse of flashing sunlight on the lake where he intended to camp on this particular night. Another day's travel and they would reach the small village of Long Pine. If the weather held and they continued north, six more days would bring them straight to Broadford; six days of fallow fields, abandoned farm sites, and lonely, empty village

121

squares whose names even the Redmothers had forgotten. Or, they could take the road that led east out of Long Pine and cross the Broad River just before it fell into the marshes that separated Sitrine from the land of the horse people. He had good customers in Sitrine, and the villages were only one or two days' apart. They could work profitably all the way north to Raisal, then back into Rhenlan along the coast. The only drawback was that it would take ninedays to complete that route. By then it would be well into autumn, and they would be lucky to reach home before snow closed the roads for the winter.

Besides, he wanted to see his wife.

In the back of the wagon, Tob sat up. "Dad? What's that noise?"

Jordy listened. The wind was out of the southeast, strong enough to produce a great rustling and sighing in the trees along both sides of the road. Stockings's harness jingled and the wagon creaked rhythmically. The wind quieted for a moment, and Jordy caught a snatch of something on or near the road ahead of them before the wind returned, covering the sound. He pulled back on the reins.

"Dad?"

"Hush." In the comparative silence that fell after the horse and wagon came to a halt, the sighing of the trees seemed louder than ever. Then the wind paused once more and the noises became clearly audible. Distant shouts intermixed with the long, high neigh of a distressed horse, and the unmistakable ring of steel against steel.

"Get my bow," he commanded. Tob obeyed without comment. Jordy climbed down from his seat. Taking Stockings by the halter, he led her a few yards along the road until he found a space between two trees large enough to admit horse and wagon. He coaxed the mare into the underbrush, careful not to guide the wagon over anything too large to bend before its weight. Only when the patch of light that marked the location of the road was nearly invisible behind them did Jordy stop and tie Stockings's lead rope securely to a low tree branch.

Tob, his eyes round and solemn, jumped down from the wagon, Jordy's bow in one hand and his quiver of arrows in the other. "You think it's Abstainers," he whispered.

"I think it's someone in trouble. I'm going to take a look." Jordy took the bow and strung it before slinging the quiver over his shoulder. He didn't want to frighten the boy, but he wasn't going to lie to him either. "You know what to do."

"Stay here, stay quiet, and wait," Tob recited, obviously unhappy but not, thank the Mother, rebellious.

"How long do you wait?"

"Until you come back." Under Jordy's patient stare he continued reluctantly. "If they are Abstainers and they continue past here without seeing me and you haven't come back, I'm to go on to the next village. If they do find the wagon, I hide in the forest and let them take it."

"Good boy." Jordy put his hand on Tob's shoulder and smiled. With his other hand he pushed a wisp of black hair out of the lad's midnight-blue eyes. "I'll be as quick as I can."

Most of the brush that had been flattened by the wagon's passage had already begun to spring back by the time Jordy returned to examine it. He snapped off a few telltale, dangling branches and used them to sweep away the wheel marks that led into the forest. That done, he hurried silently along the road. As he walked, he fitted an arrow to the string of his bow. The noises of battle grew more distinct. It was a battle, not just Keepers against wolves. Wolves did not wield swords. Nor, however, did it sound like a few unfortunate travelers fighting a band of Abstainers. The lawless ones were not known for waging protracted battles. They preferred to take their victims by surprise, winning without ever really having to fight. Any sign of competent resistance—a drawn and well-aimed bow, for instance—was usually enough to send them away to await a less difficult target. The continuing sounds of struggle increased Jordy's unease.

The road curved into the square of an abandoned village

fifty yards from the shore of the lake. The village was abandoned. The square was not. Jordy slipped into the shadows next to a half-fallen wall. Abstainers they were, both men and women. Five of the would-be thieves were scattered lifelessly across the trampled grass. The other six continued to fight, outnumbered and outmatched by the nine travelers they had attacked. The travelers had a wagon similar to Jordy's own in size and overall design, except that this wagon was drawn by a matched team of black horses, their harnesses studded with silver. The driver's seat was shaded by a blue and red canopy and the wagon bed was completely enclosed by wooden walls and a peaked roof.

Jordy lowered his bow. He wasn't needed. Four of the travelers stood shoulder to shoulder next to the wagon, knives drawn, but as far as Jordy could see, unbloodied. The other five were king's guards.

One of the mounted guards exchanged a brief flurry of sword strokes with a loudly swearing Abstainer woman before he found his opening and decapitated her. Two of the Abstainers tried to flee, but another guard spurred her horse after them, trampling one and impaling the other. The third mounted guard was engaged in the difficult task of recapturing several loose horses. The archer of their group was trying to get a clear shot at two Abstainers mostly hidden within another of the village's ruined buildings.

The final guard had dismounted and was fighting on foot, sword to sword. The Abstainer slashed wildly at his enemy, matted hair and beard flying. The guard, a tall, strongly built young man with long golden hair worn braided down his back, evaded the stroke and eased left, all of his concentration on his opponent.

As the swordsmen circled one another, one of the partially hidden Abstainers balanced a knife in his hand. Either the guard-archer did not see the threat, or he had no clear shot at his target. Jordy's arrow was still nocked. He lifted his bow, aimed quickly, and fired. His arrow sped just in front of the Abstainer with the knife, who jerked back, startled. Able to see his target at last the guard-archer shot. The Abstainer cried out as he died, which distracted his companion with the sword, who fell in turn. The last Abstainer panicked and leapt out of his hiding place, only to be caught by another of the guard-archer's well-placed shafts.

"Captain!" one of the riders called. "Did you see that other arrow?"

"It came from that direction." The archer nocked another arrow and used it to point toward Jordy's location.

"Shooting at them or us?" their captain, the blond swordsman, asked quickly.

"At them," Jordy called. Nine suspicious pairs of eyes fixed on him as he stepped away from the wall, carefully showing his empty bow.

The captain came toward him. "Name yourself."

"Jordy of Broadford. I heard the fighting from my wagon. I left it in the forest back there." He indicated the southern road with a jerk of his head. "I'm surprised to find king's guards so far from Edian."

At a sharp gesture from the captain, the other guards lowered their weapons and moved away. The captain stopped a few feet in front of Jordy. "The king's guard has always been responsible for the safety of the roads."

"I see you take your responsibilities seriously."

The younger man responded to the challenge in Jordy's voice. "I do my duty."

Jordy gave a dismissive shrug. "Well, many are interpreting their vows oddly these days. Makes life uncertain for the rest of us." He glanced significantly at the dead Abstainers being piled in the center of the square. "Not everyone knows how to recognize an unkept vow."

One of the traders came up as Jordy was speaking. He was a few years older than Jordy, lean and wiry with a weather-beaten face, pale hair, and shrewd blue eyes. "Did I hear you say you left a wagon down the road? Are you a merchant?"

"A carter."

"Local?"

"I was in Cross Cove in the spring for their first harvest. Since then I've been through Edian, Dundas, a few other places. At the moment I'm carrying wool from White Water."

A grin grew on the trader's face during Jordy's casual recitation. "Not local. My name is Loras. A goldsmith. Quite frankly, this is the farthest I've been from Edian in fifteen years." He clapped the captain of the guards on the shoulder affectionately. "My eldest son needed a lure for his quarry."

"Dael," the captain identified himself as he slammed his still-bloody sword back into its sheath. Jordy, watching the younger man, concluded it was best not to point out that this was no way to treat good steel.

Loras looked around the square. "None of us will be traveling much farther this afternoon. Would you care to camp with us, carter Jordy?"

Jordy braced his bow against his boot and unstrung it. "That might be interesting," he agreed.

Captain Dael pulled out of his father's grasp and strode away from them without a backward glance.

CHAPTER 12

Killing was easy. It had always been easy for him. Dael didn't know why, it just was. He hadn't meant to make it his profession, but it was the only thing he was good at. It was the only thing he'd done since he was seventeen. He'd been told often enough that that wasn't true, but he knew what he was. Captain of the guards or Abstainer—he could have been either. Did Abstainers feel sick when all the violence was over? He killed efficiently, with no qualms while he was in the fight. To be ruthless and efficient meant staying alive. Abstainers were supposed to be violent and ruthless for the joy of it. Dael felt no joy. In fact, he felt nothing during a fight. The horror at his own capacity for violence always came after the battle.

He used to think he would go mad, until Greenmother Jenil instructed him to make a ritual of brooding. She'd told him to take himself somewhere away from the deaths, not to take his stone or bowl, but to immerse himself in the normal, to observe the world around him until he was ready to return to it, as a way of contemplating the necessity of what he did. He supposed it was true Dreamer wisdom. At least it worked well enough to keep him whole. His men had gotten used to his taking himself out of the way as soon as his work was done. They knew it to be to their own advantage. Certainly Captain Dael was not a friendly sort just after a battle. The last thing he had needed today was questioning from a suspicious carter. The stranger had been lucky not to have his head taken off. Perhaps if Loras hadn't been there he might have.

It seemed to Dael that the carter asked a lot of questions about who worked for whom. Guards guarded. Why should it matter to a traveling Keeper who kept the roads safe, as long as he was able to get his goods from one village to the next? He hadn't appreciated being quizzed on his loyalties, even if the carter had just saved his life. Not when his nerves were beginning to shriek, covered as he was in other people's blood, the echoes of their dying still ringing in his mind.

Dael hurried off to save his sanity. Presently, just as Jenil had taught, he regained his interest in the world around him. He pulled out his sword and set about cleaning the blade. The setting sun tinted the lake a glowing orange that gradually faded to purple. Sounds from the woods and the voices of guards and traders slowly changed from grating noise to pleasant reassurance.

Dael left his people to their work of stacking the Abstainer bodies for cremation while he followed his father and their wagon to a campsite on the lake shore, upwind and well away from the village. Dael sat on a fallen tree trunk and concentrated on putting himself in order. The carter fetched his wagon into camp. With the wagon came a lad of about twelve who Jordy introduced to Loras as his son, Tob. The boy'd been left down the road, hiding in the loaded wagon, waiting for his father's return. During the introductions, the carter threw a look of rebuke toward Dael, but a moment later Loras draped his lean arm across Jordy's shoulder and turned him away, no doubt explaining that Dael needed some privacy to make himself civilized after a battle. At least Dael assumed that was the center of the conversation, because the next look he got from the carter had more sympathy in it.

As camp was made and the evening meal began to cook, Dael watched the wiry-framed carter and his dark-haired boy as they moved purposely and efficiently about their work. He found he liked the obvious affection between the pair, restrained though it seemed to be on Jordy's part. It reminded him of his own father's treatment of his children, though Loras was more open with showing his love to Nocca, Ruudy, and Dael himself. Tob had a look of the horse people about him. It would seem this Jordy had a foreign wife, and upon reflection, Dael decided that the carter also had a Dherrican accent. A man who traveled and knew the world from several sides of the Shapers' borders might very well be a questioning sort.

Dael gradually relaxed. Calm and control covered his natural ferocity once more. He stood and went to rejoin the others. With the world back in place, he began to think that perhaps there might be a question or two he could ask the carter.

Sunset was long past, but the fire burning in the abandoned village put its own reddish tint to the western sky. Abstainer bodies did not go into the ground. In life, Abstainers rejected the gods, as well as all that the gods expected of the Children. There was no reason to return their bodies to the source of life. Nocca and two of the other guards stayed to watch the cremation fire in the empty square. Little was left of the bodies, but the embers would not die down completely before dawn.

Loras's wagon sat beneath a pair of old oak trees, its tailboard within a few inches of the carter's wagon. The horses were tethered in the open space beyond the wagons, just visible in the flickering light of the camp fire. A few occupied bedrolls were scattered within the angle formed by the parked wagons. Dael stepped over one snoring guard, and ignored the obvious noises coming from a couple out of sight behind a pile of driftwood on the beach. At least the carter's son was already asleep. Dael wasn't sure if the boy was of an age to be embarrassed in the presence of lovemaking.

Jordy and Loras were still seated beside the fire. The carter nodded agreeably as Dael came to sit beside Loras on the upwind side of the fire. During his solitary sojourn on the edge of the camp he'd overheard enough to know that his father and Jordy had taken a liking to each other. They had mutual acquaintances in Edian and several other of the larger towns in Rhenlan and Sitrine. Dael plucked a heel of bread from his father's plate. "I'm still growing," he said in reaction to Loras's indignant stare.

"Just don't grow as much as Nocca," Loras answered.

"We've got to get that boy married. There's no room for him in the house anymore." Loras looked at the carter. "You have any more besides young Tob?"

"Two girls."

Loras sat forward. Dael suspected most of the eagerness was feigned. Most. "And how old are your lovely daughters, good carter?"

"Too young." A smile softened the brusqueness of the words. "And I doubt they'll ever grow large enough for your strapping lad."

"That's what all the fathers say," Loras sighed. "Nocca's been trying out the girls of Edian for some years now." He gave Dael a mildly disapproving look. "Takes after his older brother here, that way."

The captain of the king's guard hung his head. "Yes, Dad. I'm sorry, Dad."

"A few grandchildren," Loras continued. "Is that too much to ask?"

Jordy chuckled. "I have a few years before I have to worry about Tob's interest in that area." He glanced over his shoulder to where the boy slept underneath their wagon. "I hope."

"So," Loras said, putting his empty plate on the ground beside him, "tell Dael what you were telling me about the roads west of Long Pine."

"You came directly south?" Jordy asked, facing Dael.

"That's right."

"So you haven't been to Oak Mill recently?"

"The town west of Long Pine?" Dael said with sudden understanding. "Actually, no. I spend most of my time in Edian these days. One of the troops patrolling the Dherrican border is responsible for checking on Oak Mill when they can."

The lines in the carter's craggy face deepened with his scowl. "They don't visit often, from what I'm told, and when they do they come in from the north. I come in from the east. There were three places last year, between Long Pine and Oak Mill, where spring rains had washed out part of the road. This year there were seven."

Loras grunted. "Not easy on a wagon."

"Not easy on the carter, either. Spent five days on a trip I used to make in two, and that with my son's help. Without him I might have lost a nineday. What does the king think of that, Captain?"

Dael rubbed the bridge of his nose. He wondered himself, and the wondering gave him a headache. He knew how he wanted to answer the carter's question. He was less sure what sort of diplomatic answer the king's representative should make. He sighed and ended up answering for himself. "You're probably right. I suspect no one in the king's service has seen that particular road for years. Too many other demands on our time."

"Too many demands that have little to do with the Shapers' proper duties."

"The borders need protecting," Dael said. "It almost came to bloodshed with Dherrica this summer. We have to keep watch."

"If all three rulers would recall their guards we could all forget this border nonsense," Loras commented.

"Dad." It was almost a whine, but Dael controlled it. "The Shapers are doing their best to govern unusually large regions. We have to expect some uncertainty in establishing borders."

Loras grimaced. "Uncertainty, maybe. It's the fighting I don't understand."

"The bloodshed." Jordy's voice was bitter. "I was present for the bloodshed in Edian."

Dael was on his feet before he realized he'd moved. "I was a witness, carter," he rasped, not knowing why Jordy's few words hurt him so terribly. "I saw the princess die. I was told it was for a good reason." He wanted to stop the words, but they came out anyway. "I know what it is to lose a loved child to Shaper duty. I remember Emlie."

Jordy looked up at him, undisturbed by Dael's threatening stance. "Continue to remember her, lad. She's the clearest example we've had of how far the Shapers have come from fulfilling their responsibilities."

"Sit down, son," Loras said.

Dael sat. He couldn't argue with the carter. He didn't want to argue. He didn't want to feel helpless, either. That was the worst feeling he'd ever known. Worse than loss or grief or the aftershock of killing. He'd been working for Hion for eight years now, long enough to be painfully aware of the decline that had afflicted the kingdom. He didn't like his part in it. He didn't know what to do about it. His own sense of duty kept him immobilized, kept him moving almost blindly from day to day. Duty was supposed to be the basis of one's life. But duty left him empty. What was wrong? Something was lacking. Was it in him—or in what he was being ordered to do?

"You might bring the subject of that road to the king's notice once you're home," Jordy suggested. "There's a nineday's work there for a troop or two. And it will only get worse if something isn't done."

"I'll report it," Dael said.

"You cleared this road of Abstainers. That should please people. Pleases me," his father told him.

The carter nodded. "Aye. That's the proper work for guards. Part of the proper work."

Dael smiled in spite of himself as he made the carter's point for him. "The other part is fixing roads."

Loras got to his feet and stretched. "That's agreed, then. I'm going to sleep." He patted Dael's shoulder and sauntered toward the roofed wagon.

Dael and Jordy also rose. "You'll continue south with your father?"

"And back to Edian again, yes. Will we see you there? Perhaps at the Fall Festival?"

"If not then, some other time." Jordy nodded at the fire. "My thanks for the hospitality."

"My thanks for your help."

"They were Abstainers. It had to be done."

Jordy went to his wagon. Dael settled back by the fire, staring thoughtfully into the flames.

★ ★ ★ ★ ★

"Aage."

The princess had been standing pensively just inside the study doorway for several minutes. Aage was aware of her presence and her mood, but continued to ignore her as he scratched words onto stiff paper with even stiffer fingers. Writing was an easy task for Shapers but it came hard to Dreamers. It took all his concentration when he sat down to record his memories of new dangers encountered during his duty between worlds. It was important to get the description and defense just right, reference for those who would follow him. Such records had been kept in Raisal through five generations of Dreamers. Aage inherited the task, along with his rooms in the king's house, from Disani. She'd been friend and teacher and only thirty years older than he. She'd died in his arms during the plague, a very young death for a Dreamer. He sporadically dusted her shelves of books, and added his words to journals she had begun.

He waited until he'd finished writing before answering Jeyn. "You're moody, love. What is it?"

She sighed loudly and came forward to throw herself into the chair beside his. Peering down at what he'd written, she said, "You can't spell, Aage."

He frowned, and closed the heavy leather-bound book. Dust flew up from the cover and he rubbed his nose to keep from sneezing. "I know what the words mean." He turned his chair to face hers. She gave him a teasing smile, and he found himself smiling back. Her forlorn attitude had vanished as soon as he acknowledged her presence. "I spoil you."

She nodded eagerly. "No more than I deserve, oh great bender of power. And I spoil you."

She was Chasa's twin, but her resemblance to Aage was strong as well. Aage was related to Sene's children on both sides. The three of them had the same fine-boned features, light hair, and shape to the eyes. In color Jeyn's eyes were like her father's, a rich brown. It was her one physical resemblance to Sene.

133

You could be my child, but for your eyes. It was a very strange thought. He dismissed it immediately. Putting the book aside, he pulled another one forward.

Jeyn slapped his hand. "Talk to me."

He was happy enough to do that. "Would you like to go for a walk?"

"No," she said quickly. She glanced furtively out the window. "Daav's working on the pasture wall. I don't want to see him today."

"He's a good boy," Aage said mildly. *Dull,* he added to himself. *Steady.* "Your father is fond of him."

"My father isn't going to have to live with him for the rest of his life. This is all your fault, wizard." He wondered if she realized how bitter she sounded. "If you didn't go around talking to the gods, I wouldn't have to marry Daav."

"The gods talked to me," Aage corrected. "When only two Dreamers were born to your parents' generation, the gods granted us another chance. You are among the Shapers chosen to marry Keepers and help save the world. You should feel privileged, love. Besides, Daav's big, strong, handsome, and intelligent. Savyea approves of him."

"I have a horse that's big, strong, handsome, and intelligent. I want . . ." Jeyn waved her hands expansively. "I don't know what I want."

"You're too young to know."

"Do you know what you want, oh ancient wise one?"

"Most of the time."

Her eyes narrowed. "Why does it have to be Daav?"

"Your father chose him when you were children."

"I've known him for ten years and I still don't like him." She nodded emphatically. "If I'm to fulfill this prophecy then you should have a say in the matter."

"What matter?" he asked with practiced innocence.

"Who I marry. After all, we're going to have Dreamer children—your children."

"What is it you don't like about him, love?"

"I think he thinks we're already married," she answered. "He's jealous."

"Oh, really," Aage smiled, folding his arms. "Of who?"

"Do you know the minstrel? The one who works for father?"

"Everyone knows Ivey."

She looked annoyed. "I don't. I've seen him, spoken to him a few times. But Daav says I flirt with him."

"Do you?"

"No! I've never thought about the man. He has nice hair though, doesn't he?" she added, contradicting herself at once. "All those long brown curls. And such bright blue eyes. Of course, he's a minstrel. Minstrels are supposed to be handsome, and they're supposed to be looked at. Daav just wants something to complain about because I don't want to get married yet."

She wasn't ready for marriage, Aage agreed with that. "I'll speak to Daav for you. That is what you want me to do, isn't it?"

She nodded. "Have you eaten anything yet today?" she asked, concerned for him now that she'd gotten her business over with. "No, I didn't think so."

"Don't fuss."

"You like it when I fuss. Shall I ring for a servant?" She stood up, gathering his books off the table and taking them to the shelf next to the window. He might be the one who dusted in here when he remembered the task, but it was Jeyn who kept the place in order. "Or should I fetch you something myself?"

He stood, shaking out his black robe. She giggled. "What?" he asked sharply.

"I know why you became a wizard," she announced.

He came forward, taking her hand in his. "I was born a Dreamer," he said, knowing from the twinkle in her warm eyes that she expected his serious answer and intended to contradict it.

"No, that's not it."

He waited for her to continue.

"It's because you look so good in black."

Aage lifted his head haughtily, and his stomach rumbled.

He ignored it, and her grin. "I see. Vanity is the whole reason for my existence."

She tugged him toward the door. He let her lead him toward the terrace, smiling at her response to his teasing without really hearing whatever she was saying. He needed this. Needed her, her friendship, the laughter she brought. So much was going wrong. Amid so many tragedies she was the one affirmation that life was supposed to contain joy. *I am hungry. I want to rest. I want to be with people who care for one another. I don't want to think about children dying, and children still unborn. So few of us left. I can't think about that now, either. I have to replenish my energy. That's my duty. Jeyn is full of energy, and to spare. She's what I need right now.*

PART II

CHAPTER 13

"What news, minstrel Ivey?"

"That's what I was about to ask you."

Ivey pulled a tall stool close to the bar and sat down. Bronle's oldest and, to Ivey's mind, most attractive innkeeper brought him a mug of ale as he removed his backpack and lowered it to rest on the floor at his feet. The short, thick curls of Elbere's white hair formed a soft cloud around her face.

She waited until he had finished his first thirsty swallow of the ale. "Cratt is dead."

"Oh, gods," Ivey groaned. "When?"

"A nineday and two ago." Elbere leaned against her side of the bar. "No one from the court attended his Remembering."

"He was guard captain for twenty years. He slew fire bears side by side with the kings!"

All other conversation in the room died. Elbere ignored the uncomfortable silence. "King Palle cares nothing for history, or tradition. Or maybe you hadn't noticed—you've spent little enough time in Bronle these past three years."

"Then my opinion hardly matters. What do the people of Bronle think of the king?"

"What does the rest of Dherrica think of Prince Pirse?" the innkeeper countered.

Ivey sipped at his ale before answering. "People respect a man who helps them defend their homes and loved ones."

"Then the rumors are true? He still lives?"

Ivey chose his next words carefully. "I have not heard that King Palle's troops have recovered his body."

Elbere's expressive mouth thinned with disapproval. "Now and then a patrol claims to have seen him."

"They lie." A man in the uniform of the Dherrican

guard, brown hair carelessly braided, came up beside Ivey. "Pirse knows the mountains and rain forest too well. He comes out of hiding long enough to slay dragons and Abstainers, then disappears, and no one in the villages knows a thing about it."

"Karn. I didn't see you when I came in. Elbere just told me about Cratt. I'll remember him."

"Everyone remembers my father. Everyone except Palle." The young man rested his elbows on the bar and turned his head to meet and hold Ivey's gaze. "Ironic, isn't it? Cratt grieved for Palle's family more than Palle himself did. First the princess, then the queen—it broke his heart."

"Cratt was a loyal man."

"He loved the prince, too. Never doubt that." Karn clenched his fists. "We sent to Dundas. They still have a Redmother, although she doesn't call herself that in front of strangers. She'll remember my father, if no one else will."

"So, Captain Cratt forgave Prince Pirse for what he did?" Ivey asked.

Karn straightened with a sigh. "I don't know. The evidence was clear. Even Chelam, who hunted dragons at the prince's side for years, testified that only a sword forged with magic could have caused the queen's wounds. Painful as it was, my father accepted the truth. Or so I believed."

"What happened?"

"I don't know!" Karn repeated. "I just got the impression, from a few things Dad said these past ninedays, that he had begun to have doubts."

The innkeeper took Ivey's mug and refilled it. "All I know is, His Highness is better off hiding than facing his uncle."

"Why, Elbere?"

Elbere replaced Ivey's mug on the bar more firmly than was necessary. "Because His Majesty's first interest isn't justice, that's why." She produced a rag and took a few swipes at the ale she'd spilled. "Don't expect too much of our royal Shaper, Karn. You'll be disappointed—as your father was, in the end."

Ivey rescued his mug before Elbere could joggle it again. "You're remaining in the guard, then?"

"I can't just quit. Onarga's been made captain. I respect her." Karn half-shrugged. "She would have been Dad's choice."

Ivey glanced over his shoulder at the other occupants of the inn's common room. They'd listened quietly to the conversation, their attentiveness a tacit signal of approval and agreement. *All anyone wants,* Ivey thought, *is to live in peace.* Why was that simple goal so difficult to achieve?

"Quit?" he said to Karn. "No. None of us can do that."

A flock of long-legged gray birds strutted through a bed of dry reeds at the edge of the lake. Greenmother Jenil took no notice of them, or they of her, as she moved down to the water's edge. The wind coming up from the south stirred her robes and long, graying red braids as she stooped to gaze into the rippling surface of the salt lake. It was nearly spring, time for the warm northern winds and their precious gift of rain. She dipped her hands into the brackish brown water, said one word, then gulped down the newly sweet liquid. Even that minor act of magic gave her a twinge of pain. She scrubbed her face with her still-damp hands. Tired. Very tired. It had been a long day. A long day and night since Mojil had first become ill. Even with all Jenil's healer's skill, the Dreamer-child had nearly died. But she was resting now, peacefully asleep, free of the dangerous fever. The Brown and Redmothers of Bren had gathered in the courtyard of the Brownmother house to offer thankful prayers to the gods.

Jenil could not make herself join them. Jenil did not feel safe in the hands of the gods just now. She was too worried, too frightened. One of her children, the only type of child she would ever have, had nearly died. If Mojil had gone, half of the future would have gone with her.

She scrubbed at her face again, wiping tears away with the water.

"I'm afraid," she said to a brownish reflection of herself.

141

"We count on them for everything. No two children should bear such a burden. It's not fair to anyone. Not them, not us, not the world."

She stood, fear turning to anger. The birds, startled, thundered into the air on a hundred wings. The clatter of their wings seemed to accuse her. "I have not been ignoring the problem," Jenil told the now empty landscape.

A pulse of power bent the air next to Jenil, and Savyea stepped onto the grass. "Yes, you have, dear," she said.

Jenil scowled at the older woman. "You were eavesdropping."

"Your were very loud. I just looked in on Mojil. You did well with her."

"What if I had failed?"

"The world needs more Dreamers."

"As you've been saying for years."

"You know it, too. You simply have not wanted to accept how desperate our situation will be, if we do not act."

"I am not you, Savyea, to wander the world and nag people to make babies."

"Nor am I you, Jenil. Each of us has our own tasks to perform. Come."

Despite her weariness, Jenil followed Savyea into the web of power. They puffed into being just outside the Dherrican cave occupied by the world's oldest wizard. Plump Savyea immediately unbelted her robe and fanned her hand in front of her face. "I prefer snow on my mountains," she murmured with the faintest hint of disapproval.

Morb emerged from his cave. "You used to like it here."

"We were younger then, dear, and not interested in the weather."

"You didn't come to reminisce, my love," the bandy-legged wizard observed. "Do we need the youngster?"

"Yes," Savyea said, and glanced at the top of Aage's silvery-blond head. "If he can be spared."

"I'll check." Morb closed his eyes for a moment. Savyea strolled down the path, stopping to examine the delicate bloom of an orchid that hung near the mouth of the cave.

142

The power bent and wavered around them, sending an unpleasant quiver along Jenil's magic senses. She wanted nothing to do with the monsters the wizards faced. Healing was hard work, but she was glad she'd been born with that gift and not theirs.

Aage straightened his back. Morb opened his eyes and gestured toward the cave. "Let's get you out of the sun," he said to Jenil, "before you freckle."

"What's happened?" Aage of Sitrine struggled somewhat clumsily to his feet. Jenil met the younger wizard's eyes for just a moment, and thought, *there is snow, or at least ice, on Morb's mountain after all.* She looked away and hurried into the coolness of the cave.

"Make it short," Morb said as he dropped cross-legged onto a floor mat. "He's only got a few minutes."

"It's about the children," Savyea said. "We need children."

Aage threw himself down beside Morb. "Don't you ever say anything else?"

"Not as long as it needs to be said." Savyea thumped Aage on the top of the head. "You of all people know how important it is." He winced, then grinned at the elder Dreamer. She nodded and settled regally next to him. "You're such a pretty boy."

"Not now," Jenil said as she sat in front of the other three. She twisted her hands in her skirts. "Mojil was ill last night. If I hadn't been visiting Bren, she might have died. No message could have reached me in Garden Vale in time. We would have lost her."

Savyea said. "It's time the Children gave us babies again. It's your prophecy, Aage. Those princes and princesses are certainly old enough by now."

"King Sene chose Keepers for the twins years ago!" Aage protested.

"Well, they aren't married yet, are they?"

"Chasa's busy. And Jeyn's not ready for a husband."

Savyea waved his excuses away. "Oh, nonsense."

"Yes," Jenil agreed. "Nonsense."

"You can take care of those two easily enough," Morb said. "But what about Hion? His boy won't agree, and the girl hasn't been seen in three years. You won't marry her off that way."

"That's why I need your help. It's time we got involved. Today. This instant."

"She's feeling a bit urgent," Savyea told the wizards.

Aage jumped to his feet. "I must get back," he told them. At the cave entrance he turned. "King Sene has ways of finding out things. He might be able to locate Hion's daughter."

Jenil nodded. "After we find the girl," she said, "I know a Keeper we can trust who will take her in. His village has plenty of eligible lads."

"Fine." Aage ducked beneath the orchid vine and hurried back to his work of protecting the world of the Children from the things that constantly tried to invade it.

Jenil sat back and nodded at Savyea and Morb. "King Sene. It's past time I have a word with him."

Savyea did not look completely satisfied. "Remember, it must be the right Shaper and Keeper couples."

"There isn't just one choice," Morb argued.

"Perhaps not, but there is a best choice."

"I don't care about choices," Jenil told them. "All I ask is a chance."

"The gods have given us that," Morb said. "If we stop wasting it, we can make the prophecy come true."

Jenil's interview with Sene took less than an hour. As Aage had suggested, the Sitrinian king was perfectly willing, even eager, to locate Hion's daughter for her. Discussion of the princess led inexorably to the subject of Sene's children and their readiness for marriage. This time, Sene's cooperative response put the burden for action back in Jenil's lap.

The sun hung low in the west when Jenil stepped through the web and took solid form in the front garden of her home. Feather rose quickly from the herb bed, clippers in hand, and brushed the dirt off the front of her skirt.

"Greenmother! I wasn't expecting you!"

No excuse to put the announcement off for even a night. "Come inside, child. We need to talk."

Feather's eyebrows arched upward, but she followed Jenil to their shared rooms without argument. Jenil loosened the belt of her robe and sank gratefully into a chair, glad to be off her feet, glad that the girl had been here waiting for her. How many times had she begun this conversation, over the years, only to have to stop because of the child's distress? Well, Feather was older now, stronger—and there was no more time to waste.

Feather went to a side table and poured water from a glazed earthenware jug into a cup. Jenil studied the girl. *What is she now, fifteen, or sixteen? I'm no Redmother to remember every little detail of every life I encounter. Sixteen, I think, though she hasn't grown a bit since she was ten. A lively, pretty child she always was, too. Full of vinegar, and too clever by half, with a tongue like a razor. A little thing like her shouldn't be such a handful. Imagine, she thinks she wants to spend her life surrounded by the peace and unchanging atmosphere of Garden Vale. A quiet life doesn't suit you, my Feather, whatever you might believe.* Jenil accepted the water from her ward and drank, eyes lowered to gather her thoughts. *Feathers are supposed to be soft and pliable. By that definition, my girl, you'll never live down to your name.*

After handing back the empty cup, Jenil folded her hands in her lap and met Feather's gaze. "Your parents were from Sitrine, you know. They died of the plague when you were four."

The girl's dark eyes grew wide. "No, I didn't know." She sat cross-legged at Jenil's feet, her expression a mixture of curiosity and wariness. "Sitrine?"

"In the village of Telina. Your parents were Rish and Alonora. Plague struck the village, and they died. Everyone died."

Feather listened carefully, head tilted to one side. "I was four? Shouldn't I remember some of this if I was that old?"

"There's a very good reason you don't remember." Jenil controlled her dread as memories of the rotting bodies and empty homes of Telina rose in her mind. "You were the only one left alive when King Sene, Gavea, and I arrived. One very young, very frightened, child. You used to have terrible nightmares. The older you grew the worse they became. Eventually you refused to sleep. So I thought it best to take the memories away. The dreams stopped. I suspect some of the memories will come back when you return to Sitrine."

"Ah." The girl's eyes narrowed with suspicion. She showed no sign of recognizing any personal significance in Jenil's tale. Considering what awaited her in Raisal, an objective reaction might serve her better than the terror that had once paralyzed her at the mere mention of her parents' names. "And why should I return to Sitrine, Greenmother?"

"I'm getting to it, child." Jenil leaned forward and ran one soothing hand over the girl's fine hair. It wasn't necessary for Filanora to have grown up pretty, but Jenil was glad she had. "When word of the plague reached Raisal, King Sene decided he couldn't abandon your village to its fate. He risked catching the plague himself to try to bring your people some help. Gavea and I went the way of Dreamers, and he followed, driving a great wagon full of supplies. We were too late. I had already gone by the time he arrived. But Gavea had stayed, with one frightened but healthy little girl. The king took you home, to live with him." Later, Sene had confided wryly that it was an interesting journey. "Once in Raisal, you took a liking to Gavea and Aage, got along very well with the king's twins, and followed Sene everywhere. But the dreams kept getting worse and worse. You were ten years old when I brought you here to heal you. You said you wanted to become a Brown or Redmother, so here you've stayed. It's a wonder Sene hasn't asked for your return before now. He was always fond of you."

Feather looked skeptical. "A Shaper fond of an orphan Keeper child? What's this really about, Jenil?"

"You are betrothed to Prince Chasa. You have been since you were both very young. You are to fulfill Aage's prophecy."

"Oh, nonsense," Feather shot back angrily. She sprang to her feet and began to pace, her shadow on the wall far larger than she was. After a few quick turns around Jenil's cluttered room she turned back to the Greenmother. When she spoke her voice held as much sadness as it did anger. "The dreaming's over. Yours is the last generation. The Shapers won't allow you to exist anymore. If I've learned anything from all those times you've dragged me to Edian, it's that Shapers rule, Keepers do as we're told . . . and Dreamers die. That's the world we live in. It's the world the plague gave us. I have no intention of mating with any king's son for the sake of a dead dream."

Jenil flew to her feet without bothering to let her muscles do the work of standing. Feather blinked and backed a step as the Greenmother glared at her with all the power the gods had given her in the look. "We're not done yet, girl," she declared. "We are the life of this world! King Sene, and Gavea the Great—and I—chose you to be a mother of Dreamers. You've been honored, and don't you forget it!"

Even as she spoke, Jenil knew her outburst was useless. She resumed her seat as rebellion hardened in her student's black eyes. Feather was not going to be ordered, bullied, or awed into anything. Of course not. She wouldn't be Feather—Sene's Feather—without a strong mind and will of her own.

It was going to be another interesting journey.

CHAPTER 14

"Spring Festival will be here before we know it." King Sene rubbed his hands together. "I can hardly wait."

"You've said that every year since you were a boy," Aage replied. He leaned against the verandah railing, elbows back, legs stretched out before him, one ankle crossed lazily over the other.

"So I have, Great-Great Uncle," Sene agreed. He went from rubbing his hands to rubbing his bald head. "Why is it I've lost my hair, while an old man like you just gets more of it?"

"Because he's vain," Jeyn answered for the Dreamer. She leaned beside Aage; a gentle breeze tugged at their matching tow-colored locks.

"I see. What about my vanity?" Sene demanded of Aage. "Can't you use a bit of dragon ear powder on my head?"

"Only if you really want it to shrink, Nephew."

Jeyn giggled. Sene abandoned his mock-scowl and joined them at the railing. "I hope we'll have fine weather for Festival. You're magic's good enough for that, I trust?"

"Jeyn wouldn't let me into the feast if it wasn't."

"You'd deserve to stand out in the rain, wouldn't you?" Jeyn teased him. She turned her head and sniffed loudly. "Cinnamon."

Sene watched the pair of them. As much as Jeyn had tried the patience of many of her tutors over the years, she never seemed to annoy the wizard—and the wizard never seemed to annoy her. Aage annoyed almost everyone else. Despite appearances, he was very old, and had lived his long life during unpleasant times. He was a good counselor when Sene needed a counselor, and always took care of wind demons or other weather matters promptly. But few Keepers in Sitrine knew him, and Sene's relatives couldn't

stand him. Most of Sene's relatives. His daughter appreciated Aage. Between Aage and Jeyn, the appreciation had
long since mellowed into something more. With Jeyn, Aage
became relaxed. Happy. In fact, a rather nice person.

"What?" the rather nice person demanded, staring
haughtily down at her impish face.

"Cinnamon," she repeated. "You smell of apple. I'm always tempted to sprinkle you with cinnamon."

"Don't," he suggested.

"There is a feast coming," she reminded him. "You can
be dessert if it rains."

"Threats, dragon-bait?"

Sene sniffed the fresh breeze from the sea. To his surprise,
he detected the aroma of roses. It was too early for roses.

"Jenil," Aage said, and Sene turned as the smoke of the
Greenmother's arrival spread out on the wind.

Jenil stepped from the smoke as a person sheds a cloak.
"Sene," she said, her expression irritable. "The girl is your
problem from now on."

"Girl?" Jeyn asked.

"Girl?" Aage repeated.

"Feather," Sene said.

Aage pushed himself upright and looked sharply from
Sene to the Greenmother. "What about Feather? Is anything wrong?"

"On the contrary," Sene said. "Jenil has decided that it's
time to bring Feather home. I sent horses and escort to
fetch her."

"Does Chasa know?" Jeyn asked.

"He's looking forward to seeing her again."

"He didn't mention it to me."

"He's a bit nervous."

Aage gave a knowing nod. "You're nervous too, aren't
you?"

"Of course not."

"She hasn't been part of the family for years. Hasn't seen
Chasa for years."

"They're old enough to marry."

"I'm sure Chasa's willing enough. The question remains, is the girl willing?"

"That's one question." Jenil folded her hands in front of her. "I hope you get the chance to ask it."

Sene gave a patient sigh. "Where is she?"

"She didn't want to leave Garden Vale at all. If you hadn't sent that big corporal and the horses, I'd probably have had to drag her by the hand the whole way. She's a very stubborn child."

"I remember." Sene smiled. "How is she?"

"Stubborn," Jenil said shortly. "The question isn't how she is, it's where she is."

"Not here," Jeyn prompted helpfully. Aage nudged her to silence with his elbow. Fortunately, the aggravated Greenmother did not notice their exchange.

"You said she's my problem." Sene did his best to sound like a king asking for a report. "Could you be more specific?"

"She took one of the horses and ran away."

Sene nodded sagely. "Efficient of her."

"Sene!" Jenil shouted. "I hate the way this family gets giddy before a Festival. Just because it's spring doesn't mean you have to act like children!"

"They are children," Aage reminded her.

"You stay out of this!"

Jeyn buried her face against Aage's shoulder, but her cackling laugh wasn't muffled very much.

Sene kept his expression serious. "I assume the child's not in any danger. You wouldn't have left her if she were." His soothing, kingly tone did not, however, have its customary effect. Jenil's expression grew even more exasperated.

"She's quite safe. Your guard is with her. But I can't escort them every step of the way from Garden Vale to Raisal! I have another princess to worry about."

"I understand." Sene's good cheer evaporated. Thoughts of Rhenlan always had that effect. Jenil had convinced him to use his resources to locate Hion's daughter, with the promise that she would deal with the consequences. Sene could not refuse, especially after he heard the initial reports of his spies and realized that the situation was even more serious than Jenil had implied. He would have offered further assistance, but once he gave Jenil the name of the town, she insisted that she could manage better alone, and Sene reluctantly agreed. If Hion learned that the Greenmother was interfering in his affairs, he would be furious. They could not allow him to suspect that the King of Sitrine was also involved.

"I have no idea how you are ever going to convince Feather to do her duty," Jenil continued. "I don't even know how you're going to get her to Raisal."

"Drag her by the hand," Jeyn sniggered.

"Hush," Sene ordered before Jenil could respond. He took the Greenmother by the arm and led her toward the garden. "Feather is my responsibility," he agreed. "Thank you for all your help. I'll take over now. Where is the child?"

"Telina. According to your guard, she started asking about it the moment they entered Sitrine. I don't think she really believed it existed—or if it existed, that it would still be abandoned."

"I'll take care of her," Sene promised.

"See that you do."

"Wake up, laddie."

A warm hand gripped his shoulder. Tob squirmed away from it, yawned mightily, and opened his eyes. He had burrowed under the blanket in his sleep. Only faint daylight filtered through from the outside. He was sprawled against several bales of cloth, one leg draped over the crate of oranges his father had found back at Fairdock. The sweet, tangy scent of the fruit lent an exotic newness to the otherwise familiar smells of straw and damp wool that permeated the old wagon bed.

Tob reached up and batted the edge of the blanket away from his face. "Right," he mumbled, blinking against the brightness. "I'm awake, Dad."

"Ready to stretch your legs? We're almost home."

With a grunt, Tob gathered together his ungainly limbs and pulled himself upright. His father was walking along the edge of the road, hands deep in the pockets of his loose-fitting trousers. Tob rubbed his hand over his eyes and blinked.

The landscape was definitely familiar. They were nearly at the top of the north ridge. Behind them lay five miles of the lightly forested, rolling hills that rose gradually but steadily until they leveled out in the grasslands of the Atowa Plateau. This far from the village, the road was a hard-packed dirt track just broad enough for two wagons to pass one another without either of them tipping into the brush that straggled up to its edge. Stockings toiled steadily up the center of the road. Jordy complained that the mare had less sense than all of their friend Herri's barnyard geese put together. As fond as Tob was of Stockings, he had to agree. She was stupid enough to walk straight into a tree if her driver didn't guide her around it.

Fortunately, the road was empty here and Jordy allowed her to make her own way. Tob put one hand on the side of the lurching wagon and got to his feet. It was mid-morning. They had made good time from their camp at the edge of the plateau. He sniffed experimentally.

"Going to rain?" he asked his father.

Jordy glanced at the eastern sky. The thin gray clouds showed no change from the overcast to which they'd wakened. "Not before sunset," he replied. Then he tilted a half smile at Tob. "We hope."

Tob grinned back. They crested the top of the ridge and Jordy called a stern, "Ho," to Stockings. After a discernible delay, the horse came to a halt, blowing hard from the long climb. This left the wagon itself comfortably perched on the short stretch of level ground before the road began its descent into the river valley.

Tob swung over the side of the wagon and landed lightly on the ground. His father went forward to Stockings and ran a practiced hand along her harness, checking for hints of strain or slippage. Tob did the same for the wagon, paying special attention to the wheels and the lashing of the load.

Everything was secure. As always, Tob thought smugly. His father knew his business. He couldn't remember anyone ever claiming damaged goods from one of Jordy's runs. Tob finished checking the right side of the wagon. Stockings flicked her ears nervously as he reached the front of the wagon, so he stepped well away from her onto a ledge of rock at the side of the road. The ground below him fell away sharply, in places almost vertical, until it met the surface of the road where it twisted back on itself on its way into the valley.

They'd be home in time for supper. From this vantage point, Tob could see most of Broadford spread out along the north bank of the river. The inn was invisible, hidden behind the trees of an orchard, but Tob could place it accurately enough by the thread of smoke from the smithy next door. The northern edge of the ford was similarly obscured by trees, their spring foliage still pale green. Toward the center of the river, a line of ripples showed white against the gray of the water, marking the downstream limit of the ford's shallows. On the far southern bank, the road emerged from a sandy beach and disappeared after a quarter mile into the trees of the forest.

Jordy straightened from his inspection of Stockings's hoofs, and beckoned to Tob. "Take the reins, son. Remember to hold her steady on the first downslope."

"I will." Tob climbed eagerly onto the driver's seat and picked up the reins. Stockings lifted her head slightly, ears laid back in resentment. Tob told himself not to take her tempers personally. Concentrating, he gave a flick to the reins just before he used his left foot to raise the brake lever. To his secret surprise, it worked. Stockings leaned into her harness as the slight slope of the road started the freed wheels rolling. He guided Stockings into the curve, then turned to look to his father for instructions.

Jordy walked with one hand resting on the side of the

wagon. "It's a dry road, you can trot her," he informed Tob. He allowed the wagon to move ahead of him, then caught hold of the tailboard and vaulted neatly aboard.

Tob faced forward again. With a click of his tongue he urged Stockings to quicken her pace. The wagon rocked a little as they picked up speed, and Tob shifted slightly in his seat, bracing one knee against the side support for security. Behind him he could hear his father moving among the bundles and crates, humming under his breath. Tob smiled. It was good to be home.

After what seemed to Tob far too short a time, Jordy ordered him to slow Stockings to a walk once more. When they reached the first sharp turn a few minutes later, Stockings tried to continue straight on. The low hedge that bordered the road apparently did not register in what passed for her brain. Tob pulled her head sharply to the right. She slowed, but resisted turning.

Jordy came to the front of the wagon and rested his elbows on the back of the driver's seat. His watchful eyes studied first the horse, then the boy. Tob grimly ignored the scrutiny. He was not going to let Stockings take advantage of him. Foolish beast! Foolish, but not unaware of who was driving her. She almost never tried her tricks on Jordy. Three years before, when Tob had first started traveling the summer trade route with his father, he had understood her lack of respect for him. As a twelve-year-old he'd lacked the weight and strength necessary to force his will on an obstinate horse. But he'd grown since then.

As though reading his mind, his father said in his ear, "You'll never impress her with your strength, lad. I've told you more than once, in a contest of brute strength, the horse wins every time. Don't wrestle with her. Intimidate her. Take charge."

Tob took a deep breath, and unleashed his frustration. "By the Rock, I'll come up there and twist your ears off!" he shouted. Stockings, startled, began to turn her head to look back at him. "Now, gee!" he concluded with a final sharp tug on the reins.

154

It worked. Stockings danced nervously to the right, almost shying from the hedge as though it had just that moment sprung forth from the ground. They negotiated the corner with room to spare, and Tob consciously relaxed his grip on the reins. Jordy gave him a pat on the shoulder.

"Next time, plan on outsmarting her before you reach the critical moment."

Stockings settled into her usual swinging walk down the center of the road. Jordy climbed up beside his son as they left the fields behind. On their right, the ridge sloped sharply upward, all rocks and scrub plants. On the left, a narrow strip of pine trees blocked any view of the valley. Only a short way before them the road seemed to end in empty space. Stockings negotiated this sharper, more difficult curve agreeably. Tob supposed even she could see the undesirability of walking off the edge of a cliff.

The road became slightly steeper for a while, and Tob held Stockings to a cautious walk. Finally, they eased around the third curve. Beyond it, Broadford and the river were much closer, although still at a slightly lower elevation than the road.

"I'll take over now, Tob, lad. I've some errands for you. First, run home and let your mother know we're back. But don't stop to spin tales for your sisters."

"No, sir."

"Then get you over to Kessit's place. Tell him we've got his load of stonewood and we'll need his help unloading it at the shop."

"Pross, too," Tob suggested. He liked woodman Kessit's son. Pross, in turn, though several years older than Tob, still seemed to enjoy the occasional afternoons they could steal from their responsibilities. They would wander the riverbank in search of turtles and birds' nests, Pross exchanging his knowledge of current events in Broadford for Tob's news of strange people and distant towns.

Jordy smiled at him. "Aye. Pross will be welcome. Find out when Kessit can get away, then come directly to the inn. It may be that I'll want your help with the rest of the load."

"All right, Dad. Anything else?"

"That'll do. Off with you."

Tob jumped down from the moving wagon and ran across the road, eager for the feel of soft grass beneath his feet. Once in the pasture, his strides quickly degenerated into a series of leaps and bounds, intermingled with rapid sprints and occasional breathless tumbles down some of the shorter slopes.

He reached the bank of the stream at a familiar spot and detoured briefly to check the progress of the blackberry patch. Given enough rain, the patch would provide his sisters with several weeks' work by midsummer. He felt a twinge of nostalgia for summers he'd spent happily roaming this field, but swiftly dismissed it. No more summers at home for him. Blackberry season was also peak trading season. By then he and his father might be anywhere from the northern coast to the edge of the Great Desert, or even high in the Dherrican Mountains, where ponds formed a thin skin of ice every night, even in high summer.

He leapt the stream and cut diagonally across the corner of the pasture. At the bottom of the gentle hill he let himself through the gate. Pepper's pet goat bleated in surprise, bolted a few steps, turned, and lowered her horns at him. Then she flicked her tail and ambled back to her browsing, as if to say, "If I'd known it was only you, I wouldn't have bothered."

Pepper was sprawled in the open door to the stable, petting one of the cats, when Tob climbed over the south gate. The cat looked up, eyes blinking sleepily, but Pepper didn't notice him until he was on top of her, fingers reaching for her ribs. "Tobble!" she squealed, and doubled up into a ball.

He quit tickling her at once and clamped a hand over her mouth. "Shhh," he said. "I want to surprise Mom. Where is she?"

She pushed his hand away. "You're back!"

"Where's Mom?"

"I don't know. The loom, I think. She's been working on

a rug for days." She struggled to sit up. The cat, already disturbed by her giggling, dashed away. "I didn't hear the wagon."

"That's 'cause it's not here yet. Dad's taken a load to the inn."

"I want to see him. Can I come with you?"

"I'm not going there yet, so, no, you can't. Besides, shouldn't you be doing something?"

"I am doing something. I'm staying out of the house while Matti's sleeping."

Tob tickled her again, this time at the juncture of neck and shoulder. She giggled, scrunching her head to one side in defense.

Tob ran for the house while she was still giggling. He crossed the empty living area, putting his feet down with care to avoid making any noise. The trapdoor to the attic was open. He could just hear the sound of Matti's steady breathing. Halfway along the central wall the hearth was unoccupied, trammel hooks hanging empty. The banked embers of the breakfast fire glowed dimly behind a scattering of trivets, but not even the usual pot of cider benefited from the warmth. No reason it should be there, Tob reminded himself. Mom didn't expect them back for two more days.

The steady click of the loom drew him toward the doorway to the right of the hearth. He lifted the curtain soundlessly and peaked through. His mother's hands moved steadily over the loom, the rings on her fingers reflecting a sparkle from the lamp hung over her head.

He grinned in anticipation. "Surprise," he said.

His mother turned sharply sideways on her stool. For an instant her dark eyes registered only alarm, then she recognized him and visibly relaxed. She rose and stepped quickly toward him, hands outstretched. Tob accepted her quick hug, the brush of her cheek against his, and was enveloped briefly in the smells he always associated with her: hearth smoke, cooking spice, and the dust from the loom. Then she stepped back, hands dropping to her sides, and looked him in the eye.

"We were only one day at Fairdock," Tob explained. "And we ended up not stopping at Hillcrest after all. We have to unload at the inn, but we should be home in time for supper."

His mother smiled her acceptance of his words.

Tob continued, "I've got to go help. I just came to tell you we're back. I don't suppose there's anything to eat? I'm starving."

She put her hand on his shoulder and gently turned him toward the outer room. He waited by the table as she rummaged soundlessly in the cupboard. She brought a half loaf of bread, a square of white cheese, and her small, blue jam pot to the table. Before she began to slice the bread, she held up the knife until she had his attention, then pointed toward the ceiling. Tob replied by placing his fingers to his lips. Satisfied, his mother made quick work of fashioning two sandwiches for him, one of sweet grape jam, the other of cheese. He picked them up, one in each hand, and leaned across the table to plant a kiss on her cheek. She tousled his hair and then gestured him out the door.

In the yard Pepper was lying in wait for him at the corner of the house. When she made a grab for his jam sandwich he simply held it in the air over her head, at which point she pretended she was no longer interested.

"Was she surprised?"

"Perfectly. I've got to go."

"Can I come? Please?"

He started down the gentle slope of the lane that connected their yard with the road to Broadford. "No." Tob tore the corner off his sandwich and gave it to her.

She beamed at him. "Thanks, Tobble. Make Dad hurry. I want to see him." She took a big bite of bread and jam.

"Yeah. Bye."

Pepper, her mouth full, could make no reply. Tob waved once and ran for the Broadford road.

CHAPTER 15

Of all the inconveniences of life at Soza, Vray had hated the wind the most. It came up off the plains in great, roaring, neverending gales, full of dust in summer and snow in winter, rain in spring and autumn. There was no escaping the wind at Soza. It pushed its way in through every crack in the windows, under every door frame. It hit her in the face the moment she stepped outdoors, and drove at her back down all the cloistered walkways. Her clothes always seemed too thin to keep the needle-sharp or grit-filled swirls of air away from her skin. There wasn't any corner in the whole House without its own backwash. Vray hid from the wind more than she did from the switches of the Brownmothers.

But at night, locked in and alone on her pallet in the kitchen storeroom, there had been no escaping the soughing, sighing, or howling of the wind outside the thick walls of Soza. It kept her awake, or seeped into her dreams. The noise reminded her of many things. Even worse, it sometimes reminded her of nothing at all. She would lay curled up in the dark, nursing new and old bruises, in terror of falling into chaos, terror that nothing existed but her and the wind. Her past, her identity, threatened to blow away on those long nights, and she feared she was going mad. The only answer was to make a conscious effort to call up memories of her former life.

Her favorite reminder of who she was and why she was in exile at Soza was the exquisitely detailed vision of her brother's smiling face as he bid her a safe journey. In the courtyard of the castle, in the exact spot where poor Emlie had died, he bent to kiss her cheek, helped her into the carriage, told her to be a good student, and wished her a safe journey. All the while, as she'd numbly gone through the motions of accepting that kiss, that helping hand, those kind words, she'd been looking into his eyes. Eyes full of predatory joy, gazing so lovingly on his little sister's defeat.

As the wind and the people of Soza tried to take her mind away, all she had to do was conjure the vision of Damon's eyes, and she found herself again. It was a self she kept well-hidden, deep beneath her genuine fear and confusion, protected from the Brownmothers, the unwanted orphans, the sick who were brought to Soza to die, and the other exiles who'd annoyed Prince Damon enough to be sent to this lonesome place on the edge of nowhere. It was a hard life, without joys or triumphs or kindness.

Another life no longer hers.

Vray brushed a few drops of rain from the tip of her nose. No more days to be spent at Soza. She was almost ready to believe it could be true. Almost. It was so difficult. Soza had drained her of imagination, of hope, of anything beyond itself. It was easier to remember Soza than to believe in the reality of the muddy road beneath her thin boots. A road they'd been on for days. Days and miles lay between her and her last truly coherent moments.

She could remember coming awake to the sounds of a fresh gust of rain hitting against the tiny, cracked window high above the storage shelves. There were rags stuffed in the cracks to keep out the damp, but they didn't do an effective job. In the spring there was always moisture on the thick stone walls. A trail of orange moss grew like a forest through a river valley, edging its way toward the floor. Vray kept her pallet by the door, on the driest bit of floor. In the early days, she'd frequently had to dispute her bit of territory with the storeroom rats who seemed to think they had some sort of precedence, having been there longer.

It hadn't taken her, or them, long to discover who was tougher and more dangerous. That was after she'd stopped screaming in the dark each time she was locked away, after immeasurable days of being laughed at and beaten for daring to ask for a different cell. She'd learned to live in a state of watchful truce with the vermin, and to keep the big kitchen cat beside her. She'd named the ginger tom Dael when she'd first found him—a half-wild stable kitten willing to accept a bit of petting—and he became her ally when she brought him into the kitchen.

She should have taken Dael. She might have, if she'd known she was leaving. If she could have conceived of the possibility of leaving. Instead, she'd last seen him racing across the yard outside the kitchen door, tail high, dashing around the largest puddles as if by his quickness he could defy the downpour and stay dry. Then a senior Brownmother had appeared in the kitchen, her expression sending the two slow-witted drudges scrambling for shelter, her pointing finger stabbing at Vray, choosing her for some unspoken but certain doom.

Vray had followed her away from the kitchen, through corridors, into public areas of the House that had always been off-limits to her, knowing that she would be punished for being presumptuous enough to be there. She hadn't wondered where she was being taken, or why. Curiosity wasn't approved of. She was brought to one of the larger sick halls, and the Brownmother walked away.

Jenil's voice, saying, "I see you've grown, in spite of her," had been enough to send Vray into a dead faint.

That, and the fact that she hadn't had time to steal any breakfast.

Since then she'd had several breakfasts. Midday meals had been less available, not because they were short on supplies, but because the Greenmother seemed in a hurry and resented any interruption to their progress. The first day's travel away from Soza had included several long breaks. Vray could never have walked even those few miles otherwise. Jenil had cooked her a hot dinner, liberally spiced with odd things from her sack of medicines. Whatever was in the food made Vray sleep without dreaming, and walk the next day, and each day since, without feeling tired.

Without feeling anything, she admitted silently. She

161

wished she could feel tired. Or frightened, or grateful, or anxious. Maybe she'd believe in this more if she could feel she was really here.

Wherever here was. Away from Soza. West of Soza, unless the sun had started behaving oddly. As oddly as the people they'd passed walking out the gates of the House. No one had seen them leave. People had looked right at them, but no one had seen. Jenil's only comment had been a reassuring, "Don't worry, dear. They'll never even know you've gone."

At least the wind was familiar. She didn't mind it so much now. Blowing across fields and pastures and stretches of spring-green woodlands was a proper way for wind to behave. She felt no offense, or fear, at its steady tug on her robes and hair.

Jenil was offended about something. Vray hadn't dared ask what and was afraid to guess. It was probably her fault, somehow. They hadn't seen anyone else until yesterday. Then they almost met a troop of guards on horseback, escorting a group of young men and women on foot. Jenil had heard them coming and dragged Vray out of sight to hide in some mulberry bushes. Vray had spent the time cowering, while Jenil grumbled under her breath about too many guards taking too much advantage. But she had done nothing to stop them. Vray had been glad. Guards frightened her. She was grateful that the Greenmother had no more interest in encountering them than she did.

Jenil seemed determined not to encounter anyone. Not to be seen in Vray's presence? *You presume much, girl,* Vray thought silently. *You're not that important. Not to a Greenmother. But if she wasn't valuable to her, what were they doing out here?*

No. Don't ask questions. You won't like the answers. One question kept occurring to her no matter how much she tried to put it out of her mind. Is someone dead? The King? Or Damon? Or Mother? That would change things. Sooner or later they had to arrive somewhere. Perhaps Jenil would tell her then.

★ ★ ★ ★ ★

The village square drowsed in midday solitude as Jordy led Stockings into the inn yard. The horse plodded along at his side, eyes half shut, totally oblivious to her surroundings. Jordy eyed the large front window of the inn, and Stockings's inexorable course toward it. Shaking his head, he stopped and said, "Whoa."

One, two, three, four. After each of her feet had taken another step, Jordy's command filtered through to Stockings's brain, and she halted.

"Someday you're going to misjudge the distance, my friend, and find yourself paying compensation for a trampled fence or broken window."

Jordy turned toward the inn door. "Never, Herri. Undependability isn't one of Stockings's faults."

The innkeeper descended the two steps into the yard to join Jordy in contemplating horse and wagon. "You made good time."

"Aye. The weather helped."

"Any luck finding oranges?"

Jordy stepped up to the wagon and unlashed the tarp, while Herri went to the back to lower the tail board. He leaned one elbow onto the bed of the wagon and reached for a crate as Jordy flipped the tarp aside and said, "See for yourself."

One of the innkeeper's large, meaty hands pried open the crate with a single well-placed jerk. He plucked an orange from the topmost layer and squinted at it. "Very nice."

"There are two more crates just like that one. Yours, if you can use them."

"I can use twice that, and you know it." Herri replaced the orange and straightened. He laced his fingers over his apron and tilted his head slightly to peer under the half-furled tarp. "Don't I see others under there?"

"You do, but they are for Cyril."

Herri made an exasperated noise at the back of his throat. "Must you torment me?"

"Offering three crates of oranges when you ordered only

163

two?" Jordy's face crinkled into a smile. "That's more than generous."

"I don't suppose it occurred to you to get six crates for the inn and two crates for your loving wife?"

"Not if I wanted to leave room for the rest of my goods."

Jordy jumped into the wagon and pulled the other two crates toward the tail board. Getting down on one knee, he slid a few bolts of cloth toward the front of the wagon, then beckoned the innkeeper closer. "These might interest you, Herri."

A pair of squat, dark brown barrels were lashed snugly to the right side of the wagon. Herri's eyes widened with appreciation. "That's not Dherrican ale?"

"Never say I don't give due consideration to your welfare." He began to unfasten the lashings, then paused. "You do want them, I suppose."

Herri growled. "You've a wicked streak in you, carter Jordy. Worse than the children, you are, trying my patience." He stopped, looked up and down the wagon, then turned full circle, scanning his yard and the square beyond. Jordy expected some joke about his having traded his son for the ale. Instead he found himself under his friend's sharpest scrutiny. "Jordy, you haven't lost Tob, have you?"

"No. Of course not. I dropped him at the high meadow to tell Cyril and Kessit we're back."

To his surprise, his explanation only seemed to make the innkeeper more uncomfortable. "Kessit. If only you'd waited."

Jordy dropped over the side of the wagon and faced Herri squarely. "Out with it, man. What's happened?"

"Kessit's son, Pross. They've taken him away."

Pross's family had one of the small farms occupying the fertile lowland between the river and the north ridge. To Tob's eye the decorative carvings on house and outbuildings were far more attractive than some of the ornate metalwork he'd seen used in places like Hillcrest and Edian. Pross was always surprised when Tob insisted that Broad-

164

ford was the best village in the world. But then, Pross never ventured far from home, so his imagination elaborated on the tales he'd heard, making other places seem more marvelous than they actually were. Tob enjoyed the differences in the many places his father traded, but he preferred Broadford. And, for visual variety and sheer three-dimensional exuberance, he preferred his friend's house above any he'd seen.

Tob pushed open the gate—its two posts adorned with six different species of fish cut into the wood—and started across the yard. Several geese took offense and fled, hissing, toward the pond at the back of the house. Their complaint brought Pross's mother out onto the porch. "Tob?"

"Good morning, Jaea," Tob replied cheerfully. "Where's Kessit, please? My father has a delivery for him."

"Oh. You've just returned."

Her voice made Tob suddenly uneasy. She came down from the porch, her hands twisting together until the knuckles bulged white beneath her skin. Tob tried to ignore her tension.

"Yes. Dad hopes we can get the stonewood unloaded before dark. That's why he needs Kessit. And Pross, of course."

Compared to Tob's mother, Jaea was a small woman. When she stood directly in front of him and put her hands on his shoulders she had to look up slightly to catch his eye. "Tob, where's Jordy now?"

"He was going to the inn."

"He'll know then," she said. Tob wondered if she was talking to herself, since the comment made absolutely no sense to him. "Is he expecting you there?"

"Yes, Jaea."

Her hands on his shoulders squeezed him once. He was sure it was meant to be a comforting gesture, but he didn't want to think he might need comfort at the hands of Pross's mother. If he hadn't just been home he would have feared bad news about one of his little sisters, or even Cyril herself.

"Go to your father," Jaea said. "Tell him Kessit will be at the inn this afternoon. Get along with you now."

Jaea was a pretty woman. Her rich brown hair was only lightly streaked with gray, and she had a pleasant face. Tob knew it was absurd to be suddenly, uncontrollably, terrified of her. Yet all he could do was nod, spin around, and bolt through the gate.

Stockings drowsed comfortably in one of Herri's loose boxes and the oranges and ale were safely stowed in the kitchen before Jordy was ready to sit down with his friend near the hearth in the main room. By that time, a small group of people had collected around Herri's two largest tables, some because they made a habit of taking their midday meal at the inn, others drawn by the sight of Jordy's wagon in the yard. Amid a general murmur of greetings, Jordy sat down next to fisherwoman Canis.

She laid one hand briefly on his arm. "What news of the kingdoms, carter?" Her words, pitched at a normal conversational level, still silenced everyone in the room. "Will there be battle?"

"I wish I knew," Jordy said. He searched the faces around him. "There's been no word of trouble from the borders. Did they say anything when they came? Did they show interest in any of the other young people?"

"My sons were on the river, and my grandson is not yet weaned, thank the gods. It's as well you had Tob with you, or they may have taken an interest in him."

Jordy scowled at her. "He's still a boy."

"He's as big as you are, Jordy," said the smith's mild voice. Lannal had the hard-muscled arms and shoulders necessary for his craft. His diffident personality tended to startle people who did not know him well.

"Tob is nearly my height," Jordy conceded, "but he hasn't filled out yet. Strength counts for more than size."

"Tell the guard that," Canis countered. "They seem to go on first impressions."

Herri emerged from the kitchen, a plate in one hand and three mugs of dark beer in the other. He put the plate of cold chicken and bread pudding in front of Jordy, then took a seat next to Canis. He passed one mug to Canis, one to Jordy, and kept the third for himself. "Kessit is going to be lost without him. Pross did all the planting last year, did you know that?"

"Aye, I knew."

Across the table from them, Lannal cleared his throat nervously. "Jaea and Kessit tried to reason with the corporal, Jordy. After they took Pross away, Jaea went to the Greenmother in Garden Vale. She wasn't there, but the Head of the Brownmother House thinks she'll be willing to go to the king and speak in Pross's behalf."

Jordy almost choked. Canis pushed his beer toward him and he took a long swallow. When he could speak, he exclaimed, "Greenmother! Jaea should know better. I'll grant the Mothers due respect as teachers and healers . . ."

"Since when?" Herri interrupted him. "You won't even offer one a civil good morning."

Canis laughed.

A flush warmed Jordy's neck, but he ignored it, and Herri. Lannal dropped his gaze to the table. "The Greenmothers claim more influence than they actually possess," Jordy insisted. "It's not a Greenmother's place to speak to a king on our behalf."

"No," Lannal offered, "it's a wizard's place. But we haven't any."

"We don't need any!" Jordy said, exasperated. "We can speak for ourselves!"

"We can speak," Herri agreed in his most reasonable tone. "But who says the king will listen?"

The great wooden door swung open, spilling gray daylight across the floor. Tob offered a few polite nods to the adults present as he headed for his father's table. Jordy tried to see him as a stranger might. He was a bit large for his age, but then he took after Cyril's people. He had his mother's black hair and midnight-blue eyes as well as her skin, the pale brown of fall grasses, which would deepen toward bronze over the course of the summer spent on the road. Cyril's father and brothers would have towered over Jordy by a head or more. Tob showed every indication of inheriting that trait as well. Still, there was no mistaking him for a mature young man. His face was still a child's face, smooth and slightly rounded. His muscles lacked definition and his voice, when he spoke, was still an unbroken treble.

"Dad, I saw Jaea. She said she'd send Kessit, but I think there's something wrong."

"Pross is gone. He's been taken to be one of the king's guard."

"Taken?" Tob repeated blankly. "Just like that?"

Canis stomped one booted foot on the floor. "Of course, just like that. That's the trouble! In my father's day, we didn't have guards terrorizing honest, hard-working people. In my father's day, we rarely saw the guard at all. All they did was keep the roads free of wandering Abstainers. We had wizards to work weather magic, and a Greenmother in every village."

"We also," Jordy said dryly, "had plague."

"We can blame everything on that," Herri said, and began gathering up mugs for refilling. "Which accomplishes nothing. As Jordy keeps telling us, we can't recapture those days."

Another impatient stomp interrupted him. Canis gave Jordy a sideways glare as she addressed the room at large. "Recapture! He treats half of what we used to have as exaggeration, and the rest as sheer fantasy. Of course he wouldn't want to recapture that."

"What I believe or don't believe makes no difference," Jordy shot back in his own defense. "Whether the gods and their power are real or not, we no longer have wizards to work with them. Whether the kingdoms used to coexist peacefully or not, they lost their stable borders in the years after the plague, and none of the kings wants to re-establish them."

168

"They might go on gathering youngsters for the guard," Lannal said quietly. "But if they do, who'll be left to raise food?"

No one had a ready answer to that.

Chapter 16

Tob drew his hood down over his forehead and watched the water drip past his nose. Contrary to their hopes of the morning, but in keeping with his father's more recent mood, the clouds had darkened as they had struggled to unload Kessit's stonewood at his shop. By midafternoon the rain had begun. Tob hated unloading in the rain. Every time they moved the tarp to get at one item, water leaked in somewhere else. Tob was certain his boots had doubled in weight from the mud they picked up in one farmyard after another. Everything took longer than usual, no one invited them in for a drink or something to eat, and Stockings's always questionable ability to watch where she was going deteriorated completely in the wet. This meant Jordy had to squelch along beside her, one hand on her halter to guard against her stumbling to her knees in some puddle. That left Tob perched on the driver's seat, reins slack in his hands, guilty because he couldn't help with the horse, miserable with the damp. He wondered if it was raining where Pross was. Would he learn to fight on horseback, and go galloping across the country, taking other young people away from their homes? No, that didn't seem likely. Probably, he'd just be a regular guard, destined to march off to a disputed border somewhere.

Tob stared at his hands. He'd never known anyone who had killed another person. Would it feel the same as it felt to slaughter a sheep? He didn't think so, but he couldn't be sure. Pross would learn the answer, if he wasn't slaughtered himself first. If he survived, would he be allowed to come home? If he did come, would he have anything to say to a boyhood friend who knew nothing of man-killing?

Too many questions. From the way the adults had been behaving all afternoon, Tob knew they expected the worst.

Everyone spoke to Kessit as though his son were already dead. *But he's not,* Tob wanted to yell. Guards didn't go to a lot of trouble to carry off some woodworker's son simply to kill him. If they wanted someone dead, they cut him down on the spot. Or so people said. Tob had never seen such an execution. He thought his father had, although Jordy called it murder.

Tob shifted unhappily on the seat. Pross had to be alive. He was just living somewhere else for the summer, that was all. That had to be all.

Ahead of him the horse shook her head irritably. He heard his father's startled protest as she tossed her head, pulling on his arm and splattering him with her mane.

"Easy." Jordy turned sideways, watching her feet as he steadied her. "No mischief now, you foolish beast."

She quieted. Jordy resumed his usual pace, and Tob relaxed. A moment later, the low roof of the goat shed loomed out of the rain on their left, and Jordy turned Stockings into the yard. The stable came into view, one lamp-lit door open, and the chicken coop, and the house. They were home.

Tob jumped down from the wagon and ran to open the double doors on the east side of the stable. Jordy coaxed and threatened the horse until he had the wagon properly lined up in front of the double doors. At the last moment Stockings seemed to remember the procedure, and backed readily on Jordy's command, rolling the wagon into its accustomed place.

"Ho," Jordy said. "Good girl."

Tob ducked gratefully into the dry stable. Splashing footsteps gave them a few seconds' warning of Pepper and Matti's arrival. Tob grinned as his sisters clamored for Jordy's attention.

"Dad, you're home!" Pepper cried.

"Pick me up, pick me up," Matti insisted, knowing exactly what she wanted.

"Just a minute, now," Jordy said. He led Stockings clear of the traces and hitched her to the grooming stand. Then he turned back toward the doorway, arms outstretched. "Come on, then."

Matti ran to meet him, pale braids bouncing against her shoulders, and was swung, squealing, into the air. Jordy pretended to drop her, and hugged her instead, then planted her firmly back on the floor. This made room for Pepper, who received similar treatment amid complaints from her father that she was getting too big and heavy to lift. Tob shook his head. A man who lifted bales and crates and bundles of all shapes and sizes day after day, complaining about a fifty-pound child. Pepper wrapped her arms and legs around him for a moment, clinging fiercely until Jordy's firm tone warned her that enough was enough. Then she slid reluctantly to the ground.

"I made a mash for Stockings," she said.

"I helped," Matti added.

"Mama baked a pie. When are we going to eat?"

"Mama finished that rug last week. The one with the geese in the picture."

"Stockings is very dirty. If you don't wash her legs we won't be able to see her stockings anymore and we'll have to change her name."

Tob turned his back on the controlled chaos around the grooming stand. It wasn't quite so simple to close out his sisters' continuing chatter, but he managed it. As much as he loved them, their nonstop questions and comments would take a bit of getting used to after the long, companionable silences that filled most of his and Jordy's days on the road.

He took off his dripping cloak and spent several minutes hanging wet tarps up to dry, sweeping the wagon, and coiling lines and straps loosely to allow the air to get at them. When he finished, his damp clothes were steaming from his exertion. He walked down the aisle toward the grooming stand. Jordy had stripped off his outer cloak and sweater as his work warmed him. In addition, he'd rolled his tunic sleeves up past his elbows, probably while he was washing the mud out of Stockings's coat. He saw Tob approaching and stepped back, brush in hand.

"What do you think?" he asked.

"She's cleaner than we are," Tob replied. In fact, Stockings looked extremely comfortable, having fallen asleep, one hind leg cocked, during his father's ministrations.

Jordy snorted and put the brush down. "That's not saying much. But she'll do for now. Come along, girl." He patted Stockings's shoulder to wake her, then untied her halter and led her toward her box. Tob clambered up into the loft and forked some hay into her trough. Jordy removed the lead rope as he turned her into the box. She went directly for Pepper's mash and began to eat.

Jordy latched the half door securely as Tob swung down beside him. "You finished with the wagon?"

"Yes, sir." Tob looked around, suddenly aware of the quiet in the stable. "Where are they?"

"I sent them to ask your mother to warm the bath house for us." They returned to the wagon, where Jordy pulled the chest containing their traveling gear from under the driver's seat and balanced it on his shoulder, leaving Tob to collect their damp cloaks and sweaters. Outside, the rain had lightened a bit. Together, they pushed the stable doors closed and hurried across the yard to the house.

Cyril met them at the door. She smiled at Tob and deftly relieved him of his burdens. After she deposited them in her wash tub near the hearth she returned and helped Jordy lower the chest to the floor next to the door. The quality of the smile she bestowed on her husband made Tob uncomfortable, so he turned away. Not that his parents would complain that he was intruding on their privacy. When they were busy looking at one another like that, they didn't notice anyone else.

By the time Tob finished struggling with his mud-caked bootlaces, his mother was back at the hearth, stirring something over the fire, her long, heavy black braids fastened together behind her back to keep them out of her way. Jordy sat on the chest near Tob and drew off his second boot.

Matti trotted in from the other room. "Which shirt do

you want?" she asked Tob. "Blue or green?"

Tob stroked his chin pensively. "Green."

Matti whirled and raced back the way she'd come. "See, I told you!" her shrill voice carried back to them. "He wants green."

"Those two," Jordy said. He waved Tob to the bath house. "You go first, lad. I want to tell your mother about Kessit." Cyril looked around from her cooking. "Just don't be too long."

"No, sir." He left as his mother put down her cooking spoon and gazed expectantly at Jordy.

Sometime during the course of supper the patter of the rain faded and ceased. Through the window, Jordy could see the light in the yard take on a reddish cast as the clouds thinned just in time for sunset.

He pushed back from the table with a sigh. "You can clean those boots out on the porch, Tob. I'll see to the harness."

The boy nodded, his mouth still full of a last piece of lamb. Before any of them could move from the table, however, they were interrupted by a sharp rapping on the front door.

Cyril's expression told Jordy she wasn't expecting visitors. Neither was he. He rose and went to open the door. The women facing him were not neighbors. Both wore the black of the Mothers. One was young, tall and skinny, her damp red hair pulled tightly back, her expression tired. The other's ageless, serene face he recognized immediately.

"Jenil."

"This is semi-official business, carter Jordy," she replied. "You should invite us in."

Jordy stepped aside. "Would it be anything else?" he asked. "Enter, and welcome."

Jenil swept past him in a swirl of heavy cloth. Her young shadow showed less self-assurance. "Come," Jenil said over her shoulder.

The girl jumped as though she'd been stung, and hurried

174

across the threshold. Jordy closed the door. His family were on their feet, watching with varying degrees of curiosity.

"Tob," Jordy said, "outside. Pepper, take Matti and prepare the wash water for your mother." The children scattered and disappeared. Cyril retreated toward the hearth.

Jenil stopped beside his chair and turned toward him. "My business involves your wife as well."

"We'll see," he countered. "Sit you down."

Jenil sank gracefully into his chair, and Jordy pulled out the bench so that he could face her across the table. The girl hovered uncertainly behind Jenil until Cyril stepped forward and placed a hand on her shoulder and guided her to a chair. Then Cyril stepped watchfully back from the table once more, and Jordy eyed his visitor.

"Well?" he said.

"I'll be brief," she said. "This is Iris. She's had a difficult couple of years. I've decided to remove her from an unfortunate situation."

Jordy frowned, puzzled. "You want me to transport her to her family?"

"Just the opposite. I want you to keep her."

"What?"

The Greenmother's professionally benign smile became something more rueful and therefore, if anything, more alarming. "You and I have never liked one another. But there are a few areas in which I trust you. This is one of them. You have a good family. Iris needs that."

Jordy didn't know what to say. He looked at his wife. Cyril's expression was neutral, leaving the decision to him. Then he looked at the girl—Iris—but her gaze was fixed on the table in front of her.

"We don't buy and sell people here in Broadford," he told the Greenmother. "You're treating her as goods to be disposed of."

"I'm acting in her best interest. Somebody has to. You know I wouldn't get myself in debt to you if it weren't important."

"What does the girl herself want? Iris?" When she refused to look up at him, he turned back to Jenil. "Is there something wrong with her? Does she understand when spoken to?"

"She understands. She's just shy." Jenil rose from her chair. "Iris, look at me." The girl raised her eyes immediately. "I'm going now. Remember what I said."

"But I haven't agreed yet," Jordy protested.

The Greenmother faced him, quite serious now. "You are my choice, carter Jordy. There are others who would buy her, you know. To their profit, not to hers. She cannot stay with me. Choose."

Jordy stood and ran one hand through his hair. "All right. She can stay. But only as long as she wants to."

"Good. I won't stay the night myself, thank you," Jenil continued smoothly, knowing as well as Jordy did that he hadn't intended to ask her to. "Good night."

"Safe journey," Jordy responded automatically and moved to open the door for her. He stood on the porch and watched as she strode briskly across his yard and out of sight. Then he went back inside.

Cyril was clearing their empty bowls into the dish water on the hearth. Iris had resumed her original posture, eyes downcast, motionless.

Jordy's head hurt. Dealing with Dreamers always made his head hurt. What he needed was to regain his objectivity, distance himself from the problem. "I've got to oil that harness," he told his wife, and went to the stable to think.

Vray sat stiffly where she was for many minutes after the carter left, waiting for his wife to tell her what to do. The woman, however, said nothing. It was unexpected to find one of the horse people in central Rhenlan. But the woman's cinnamon-brown skin, wide face, and almond-shaped eyes were distinctive of the plains dwellers who roamed the lands east of Soza. She finished straightening up after the family's meal, then refilled a pot with something that smelled like cider and hung it on a spit over the banked fire. After a long while one of the little girls poked her head through the curtained doorway near the hearth.

"Mama?" she asked in a small voice. The woman looked up. "The water's hot." The woman circled the table as though Vray were not there and picked up a low basket filled with muddy clothing. The little girl popped back out of sight, her mother following.

In the next room the two little girls began chattering, their words not quite audible, although Vray could not help but strain to hear them. Asking about the stranger sitting at their table, certainly. She couldn't hear any reply from the woman, and after a few more moments passed began to feel more uneasy than ever. Was she supposed to offer to help with something? How was she going to learn to live among these people?

For a few more minutes she simply sat, uncertain how to behave, unable to summon up the courage to do anything one way or another. In the end, basic practicality forced her to leave the table and walk to the front door. Her bladder needed to be relieved. This was a farm. The appropriate facilities would be outside.

She walked away from the house, then stopped near the middle of the yard and looked around. The sun had just dipped below the horizon, painting the clouds that lingered in the northwest shades of red and purple. To the east, the sky was clear and dark enough to show the first bright stars. In front of her, directly across the yard from the house, was a large building that smelled distinctly of horses. Beyond it and to her right, a chicken coop stood silhouetted against the eastern sky. To her left, the yard sloped gently downhill. Vray thought she could pick out another one or two smaller buildings in that direction, and a low line of hedge or fence. The privy, fortunately, was immediately recognizable at the end of a well-worn path that angled downhill from the house.

When she came out of the privy the sky overhead was black and studded with stars. She started back toward the house, a looming shadow against the lingering light in the western sky. She wasn't ready to go back inside. From a nearby tree came the hoot of an owl. Vray hugged herself under her cloak.

The door to the house closed with a sharp thump, and footsteps descended the path toward her. Vray didn't stop to think. She left the path and moved quickly up the hill, at an angle away from the house. Although it was too dark to see her feet, the ground was smooth and she didn't stumble.

She emerged onto level ground only a few paces away from the stable. Half of a large double door stood open, spilling yellow lamp light a dozen feet across the yard. The effect was too peaceful, too normal. She could almost hear the voice of her nurse, spinning a sweet tale about hard-working Keepers and mellow light bathing the farmyard at the end of the day. Vray made a sour face in the darkness. Tales and songs. How much did they neglect to reveal of what lay beneath the surface of an event, or behind people's actions?

Or, she chided herself, within a picturesquely lighted old barn?

She moved cautiously forward. Only one lantern was lit, hung close to the doorway, so she could make out little of the interior. The musty fragrance of hay hinted at the presence of a loft.

The carter sat on a stool in front of a wagon, vigorously applying a cloth to the set of harness straps in his lap. Vray hadn't dared look at him during his conversation with Jenil, so she was glad of the opportunity to study him from the safe obscurity of the darkness beyond the circle of light. Her first thought was that he was too small to be a carter. Then she immediately revised her estimation. He was actually quite average in size for a Keeper man, but she had been expecting broad shoulders and brawny arms. She guessed his age at something past middle age, perhaps forty. His complexion was pale, the backs of his hands sprinkled with freckles and fine hair that glinted gold in the lamp light. The hair on his head was a sandy yellow, combed straight back from his forehead and showing signs of thinning. He wore no beard. The lines of his face suggested that he smiled more often than frowned, but his eyes as he looked back at her seemed an icy shade of blue.

Vray's thoughts froze. He was looking at her!

He stopped what he was doing and rested the hand holding the cloth on his knee. "Come in, my girl. Don't look away," he added, as she automatically began to lower her eyes.

She jerked her head up and found that it wasn't as difficult as she had feared to meet his steady gaze. She came slowly forward until she was standing only a few feet in front of him.

"Have you known Jenil long?" he asked.

"No." Vray's voice sounded rusty to her own ears, and she hastily cleared her throat. "I don't really know her at all."

The blue eyes narrowed, appraising her. "You have friends though, among the Mothers?"

"No."

His expression softened. "No friends? A child your age? That's not right."

An unwelcome lump formed at the back of her throat. Sympathy from this stranger, to whom she was an uninvited guest dumped on his doorstep, was the last thing she'd expected. It had been a long, wet, exhausting day. She didn't understand why she suddenly had the urge to pour out her life history. Considering how muddled her emotions were, she didn't trust any of them.

"I survive," she answered shortly.

To her relief he changed the subject. "Sit down," he instructed her. The straw covered floor was not uncomfortable. "What do you do, Iris?"

She stared at him blankly. "Do?"

"Aye. Do you cook? Work in the fields? Study a craft?"

"Mostly I clean things." She had no intention of telling him that when she hadn't been slaving in Soza's kitchen, the things she had cleaned had been diseased bodies, to ready them for burial. Honorable enough duty, but not very good to remember.

His response was a considered silence. Vray swallowed nervously, wondering if she should elaborate, at least about the kitchen. Before she could come to a decision he said, "In this family we all do our share of cleaning. You'll have to diversify your talents, my girl." He paused, inviting a response.

Vray only felt more lost. "Oh," she offered.

He put the harness on the ground and leaned forward, resting his elbows on his knees. "All right, child, perhaps I'm asking too much too quickly. We'll take our time, find out where your talents lie. Tomorrow you can help Cyril with her cooking. Have you ever milked a goat, or fed chickens?"

"No, carter Jordy."

"Jordy will do. As for the animals, Cyril will teach you. Have you ever done any needlework?"

Her eyes were drawn automatically to the sleeves of his tunic, dangling less than a foot away from her. She saw that what she had at first taken for a textured weave in the fabric was, in fact, unusually rich embroidery on ordinary cloth. "Not like that," she said.

"I'm not surprised. Take a closer look." He extended one arm toward her. "Go on."

Gingerly, she picked up the edge of the sleeve and straightened it. As a princess she had been taught some intricate needlework, but nothing to match this. It was not, she decided, that the stitches themselves were especially small, for they were not. But they crossed over and under one another in ways her eyes could not unravel.

"You like it," his voice said gruffly above her head.

"It's beautiful," she murmured.

"If you have patience and a good eye, Cyril will teach you, I'm sure."

She dropped the sleeve and sat back abruptly. He looked startled, worried, and offended all at once.

"Now what did I say? What's the matter, my girl? Speak up!"

"I'll do what I'm told, of course, but . . . ."

"But?" he prompted her.

"I don't think your good wife is pleased to have me here."

"I'm sure she's neither pleased nor displeased. We don't know you yet."

All of Vray's misery returned in a rush. Words escaped before she could stop them. "I can't. It's better to be mistreated than to be ignored. She said nothing to me. She won't accept me—"

"By the Rock!" He stood angrily, and Vray cowered, berating herself for a fool for having entrusted any of her thoughts to a stranger. "If Jenil is going to meddle she could at least make a thorough job of it! Did she tell you nothing about us?"

Numbly, Vray shook her head.

He visibly bit back on his anger. "It's not your fault, lass. Jenil should have warned you. Cyril doesn't speak."

He extended his hand down to her. After a moment Vray realized what was expected and accepted his assistance to rise to her feet.

"Doesn't talk?" she asked uncertainly. "To strangers, you mean?"

"She doesn't speak," he repeated. "At all."

Vray tried to absorb the implications. "But then how . . . ?"

For the first time during their conversation, the carter's mouth curved upward in a smile. "I've never known her to fail to make her wishes known. You'll see. The rest of us will help you, until you get to know her. Especially the girls. I don't suppose Jenil told you anything about them, either?"

Vray gave a small shake of her head.

"The seven-year-old is Pepper. Matti is five. Too young for needlework, which is why I suspect Cyril will enjoy having you to teach. And you saw our son, Tob. He and I are gone most of the summer." He paused, obviously entertaining another unpleasant thought. "Did Jenil think to feed you before she brought you here?"

"We had some fruit and cheese on the road." The mention of food caused Vray's stomach to rumble. She hoped the carter wouldn't hear it. "Before the rain."

"I thought as much. Back to the house." He waved her out the door. "No one goes hungry under my roof. Come along."

A thin band of blue was all that remained of the sunset. As they approached the house, someone appeared out of the darkness and said, "Oh, there she is."

"Here she is," Jordy agreed.

Vray stopped uncertainly just within the doorway. A hand on her shoulder urged her further into the room, accompanied by, "Excuse me," spoken in a youthful voice. She stepped aside. The carter's son eyed her dubiously as he passed, but she received a shy smile from one of the little girls who was standing beside the table. The other, smaller one ducked behind a chair to hide. Their mother stood at the entrance to the other room, one hand poised to draw aside the curtain covering the doorway.

"Tob, this is Iris," the carter announced. "She's joining our household."

Jordy walked over to the table. "Matti, come out and say hello. Then get you off to bed. It's time you were asleep. You too, Pepper."

"Daddy!"

"Now."

The five-year-old peeked at Vray over the back of the chair. Pepper walked over and grabbed her sister's hand, as though to drag her out of the house. Cyril took a step toward them. Pepper looked around guiltily, then dropped Matti's hand and crooked a finger at her instead.

"Come on, Matti," she said.

Her words released Matti from her paralyzed fascination with Vray. The little one scampered out the door, with Pepper in close pursuit.

"She hasn't eaten," Jordy told his wife. "I'm going to have a look at the attic."

For the first time Vray noticed a ladder set into the wall in the corner furthest from the hearth. Jordy paused at its foot and looked at her.

182

"You'll have to share with the girls tonight," Jordy continued. "Tomorrow Tob and I will fix you up with something of your own."

"Mom wants you to choose something for your supper," Tob said.

Vray turned quickly. Tob had seated himself on one of the benches next to the table and was watching her with open curiosity. His mother's expression as she stood beside the cupboard was as Jordy had suggested it would be, neither friendly nor unfriendly. Vray's stomach rumbled again. *There's nothing to be afraid of,* she told herself. *These are simple, straightforward Keepers. They don't toy with people.* She walked over to the cupboard and peered inside. Only the heel of a loaf of bread was recognizable. The rest of the contents consisted of various crocks and small jars.

Cyril reached into the cupboard, drew out a small crock and opened it in front of Vray. The sweet aroma of grape preserves set Vray's mouth watering. Cyril pressed the crock into her hands. From a drawer she produced a knife for the bread, and a flat, narrow-bladed spatula. These she also handed to Vray. Then she retreated into the other room, the curtain fluttering closed behind her.

"There's other stuff in there too," Tob offered from the table.

"This is fine." Vray balanced the bread on top of the crock, and carried everything to the table. Her hand quivered slightly as she made the sandwich. The Mothers had never wasted good jam on her. She'd managed to steal a piece of fresh fruit once or twice when it was in season and overflowing the larder in its abundance. She took a wondering look at her sandwich, its thick, lumpy filling nothing like the translucent jellies she had eaten in her father's castle, then took an experimental bite. The bread was slightly stale, but she hardly noticed. The sweetness of the preserves was all she really cared about.

Tob watched her eat without comment. When she finished the sandwich and gazed longingly at the remaining crust of bread, he said, "You can finish it. Mom bakes every

183

morning that Dad and I are home."

It took her two seconds to decide to accept his advice. As she sat there chewing, Jordy climbed down from the attic.

"When you go up," he told Tob, "show Iris where your mother keeps her spare cloth." He turned to Vray. "You might want something more comfortable to wear."

Vray did not tell him that a Mother's robes were remarkably comfortable. "Thank you."

"Have you had enough to eat?"

"Yes, thank you."

"Then you'd best get some sleep. Both of you. It's been a long day for all of us."

Tob obediently got to his feet. Vray started to follow his example, but Jordy pointed at the remains of her supper.

"You can put that away first. The wash water should still be warm."

"Good night, Dad," Tob said from the ladder.

"Sleep well," Jordy replied. He nodded to Vray and went through the curtained doorway into the other room.

Left alone, Vray replaced the crock in the cupboard. She took the knife and the sticky spoon over to the hearth and looked around her. After gingerly uncovering a few empty pots, she finally found one that contained water and a damp cloth. She wiped the knife and spatula clean and put them away. Finally, she swept the crumbs off the table into her hand and tossed them into the back of the fireplace.

She straightened slowly. It really wasn't an unpleasant room. *If you like farmhouses,* another part of her mocked. *I'd rather live in a farmhouse,* she answered herself, *than die in my father's castle, wouldn't I?*

"Might as well get used to it," she murmured under her breath. "Until something better comes along."

Chapter 17

Vray's first day with the carter family passed in a blur of unfamiliar activities and partially understood conversations. The carter himself strode out of the yard directly after breakfast and did not reappear until nightfall. She would have liked to join Tob in his work in and around the stable. She understood horses. But she didn't know how to make the suggestion, so she stayed with Pepper and Matti instead, doing incomprehensible things to a huge patch of ground which they informed her was to be the garden.

After lunch Vray sat on the steps in front of the house for some time, trying not to be ill. She had eaten more over the course of three meals than she had been accustomed to eating in three days at Soza, and her insides protested in no uncertain terms. Once her stomach settled, she spent the afternoon making a spare dress from the material Tob had given her, and in the evening helped Cyril in the kitchen. Matti and Pepper took turns sitting beside her, chattering away. Vray couldn't assimilate a fraction of the information they revealed—names and habits and histories of, it seemed to her aching head, every single person in the village of Broadford. Out of habit she automatically remembered it all, childish jumble or no.

At bed time she discovered that Tob had spent the afternoon re-dividing the attic. The space allotted to her was large in comparison with what she'd had at Soza, but she hardly noticed. Exhausted, she burrowed into the blankets and went immediately to sleep.

The next day she was the last one to wake. Feeling distinctly guilty, she threw on her black robes and hurried down the ladder. The family was already seated at the table, eating breakfast. Matti, her mouth full, waved at Vray with her wooden spoon, which caused her father to look around.

"You slept well, Iris?"

"Yes, sir." Embarrassed, Vray circled the table and took a seat next to Pepper.

The carter's wife slid a bowl and spoon toward her with a silent gesture at the pot of porridge in the center of the table.

"Thank you," Vray added quickly.

Across from her, Matti squirmed on the bench and scratched behind her ear, almost knocking over her milk. Tob reached across the corner of the table and steadied the mug.

At the opposite end of the table, the carter raised his bushy eyebrows at his youngest child. "Sit still now, and eat."

"I can't, it itches."

Pepper, sharing Vray's bench, absently scratched her head, too. "I think something bit us, Dad."

"It's a wee bit early in the year for flies," Jordy replied.

Tob scowled at his sisters. "Stop it, you two. You're making me itch."

"She started it," Pepper complained.

"Momma," Matti whined. She rubbed both hands furiously up and down the back of her neck. "Make it stop."

Cyril twisted sideways on the bench and turned the back of her daughter's head into the light from the window. Under cover of her robes, Vray surreptitiously scratched at one of her own bites. She felt a vague sympathy toward the little one. To itch without being allowed to scratch was unbearable. Perhaps the carter was expecting too much of such a young child.

Tob scratched at his shoulder. Jordy put his spoon down firmly on the table. "Now, that's quite enough—" He stopped in mid-sentence as his wife abruptly rose from the table and drew Matti closer to the window. Jordy got up as well and peered into the child's shock of golden-brown hair. Then he stared at Cyril in evident surprise. "Fleas!"

Pepper looked at her parents. "What?"

"Blechh," Tob said, disgusted.

"It's a little insect that likes to live in hair or fur," Jordy explained in answer to his older daughter's question.

Matti's brown eyes grew round with alarm. Vray listened with growing horror. "You mean I have a bug in my hair?" the child asked.

"Probably dozens," Tob said helpfully.

"Momma!" Matti wailed.

"Tob, that wasn't necessary."

"Well, it's true."

Pepper snatched her hands away from her hair. "Do they crawl on us? I don't like things that crawl on me."

"Fleas hop," Tob informed her. "Hop, hop, hop." He demonstrated, bouncing his hand along the table on two fingers.

Matti, intrigued, paused in her sniveling. Jordy gave his son a look of grudging acknowledgment, and warning not to go any further. "Light the fire in the bath house," he told Tob. "A good cleaning will take care of things." He glanced at his wife. "I'll clear out the attic."

"But if it's too early for bugs," Pepper interrupted, "where did these come from?"

Vray sat very still, hardly breathing, as first the two adults, then each of the three children turned toward her. Jordy said, "Iris, come here please. We'd better have a look at you, too."

Nothing that had happened to her at Soza had felt quite like this. Shame and self-loathing made Vray's skin crawl, far worse than mere flea bites could. Stiffly, she got to her feet and approached the carter—the clean and well-groomed carter. Why hadn't she seen it before? She had been brought to a farm, yes, with a stable and chickens and a dirt yard and a plain, unadorned farmhouse. What she had failed to recognize was the orderliness beneath the rough simplicity. The floor of the house was bare wood—bare and well swept. None of the pots were encrusted with old food. The glass in the windows at either end of the room was rather thick, but it was also clean. Even the rafters were free of cobwebs. The clothing the family wore was

187

unstained by grease or barnyard filth. Their complexions were uniformly free of blemishes or scratches. They were something she was no longer used to: average, healthy Keepers. Obviously they wouldn't have parasites. Matti hadn't been overreacting. She'd been genuinely afraid of an unknown, unimaginable, malady.

Unknown, Vray thought wretchedly, until now.

She bowed her head before the carter. His fingers, hot against skin that had gone cold with the mortification, lightly parted her hair. "Ah, lass, you could have told us you wanted a bath the night you arrived." His voice hardened. "Jenil could have told us."

Behind her Tob said, "You finished that new dress yesterday, didn't you, Iris? So you won't have to put those smelly old black things on again."

Vray shuddered once. Gods, did she smell too? She looked up to find the carter's gaze on her, his mouth downturned with displeasure. "Tob," he said. "I thought I told you to build the bathhouse fire. Perhaps you'd best go first, Iris."

It was too much to bear. Vray whirled away from him, threw her dirty hood over her infested hair, and ran out of the house.

Tob didn't know why both Pepper and Matti began to cry when Iris fled out the door. Maybe because Iris had been crying, her pale face gone dead white. Tob shook his head at the way girls behaved while his father and mother each scooped up a wailing daughter. Iris was an odd girl. Didn't seem to know anything about anything. He sighed and looked around the room. The whole house was going to have to be scrubbed from top to bottom, and they'd probably send him off to Garden Vale for the stinky herbs used for fumigation. Tob wrinkled his nose in protest against aromas to come.

"Should I follow her?" he asked his father.

Jordy spoke above Matti's loud sniffling. "Aye. And no teasing the girl, Tob."

He didn't see Iris out in the yard. He tried the barn, but she wasn't there either, or in the stable. A white kitten followed him from the barn and made an awful racket until he picked it up. Holding it in the crook of his arm, he petted it until it purred louder than anything that small had any right to. Where would he go if he was upset about something? The pasture. He climbed the fence, the kitten contentedly coming along for the ride.

Huddled under the old oak, her black robe was easy to pick out against the browns and early greens of spring. Dead leaves still clung to the tree's branches, although the fresh green buds had started to show. Iris probably didn't hear him over the rustle of the leaves, though the furball's mighty rumbling should have been hard to miss.

Iris sat with her head on her knees, her red hair loose. It hung over her back and arms, as long as his mother's but not as shiny. He looked at it, then deliberately didn't look at it, and tried not to think about bugs.

Tob sat down next to her. Hoping to get her attention, and maybe get rid of the cat at the same time, he asked, "You like kittens?"

Her voice was muffled by tears, hair, and knees. "I'd give it fleas."

"Then we'll give it a bath."

Iris lifted her head. "Stop being so practical," she said accusingly, then sniffed. "I'm sorry."

"Why?"

She snuffled again, and wiped her nose on the black cloth of her skirt. It didn't do her wet, dirty face any good. "I disrupted a Keeper's home. That's the last thing I should do. I'm not supposed to . . ." Her voice trailed off into another sob.

Tob didn't know what to say, so he held out the kitten. "It's got blue eyes," he said. "That's lucky."

Iris's were greeny-gray—where they weren't red. She wiped her hands on her soiled robe and held them out. He gladly passed the kitten to her. She held it close.

"I had a cat at Soza," she said.

"Do you miss it?" he asked.

"No." They lapsed into shy silence for a few minutes while Iris stared toward the woods behind the pasture. "I called him Dael," she finally added.

"The cat?"

The girl nodded. "Everybody spoiled him. That's why I called him Dael." She stared to cry again, very quietly. No snuffling, just big tears rolling down her cheeks.

It made Tob very uncomfortable. His mother never cried like this. He wasn't sure he could remember his mother ever crying at all.

Iris squeezed the white kitten tighter. It meowed in protest. She put it on the ground, but it just climbed back up her robe, hanging on her knees until she took it in her arms again.

"Does it have a name?"

Tob shrugged. "It's just a barn cat."

"I'll call him Nocca then. Cause he's persistent."

"Who's Nocca?"

"Dael's big little brother." Iris shook some of the hair out of her face. She looked at Tob and said sadly, "I miss them. Dael's the only friend I ever had."

Feeling lost, Tob just nodded, and wondered if he should bring up the subject of the bath. He hoped Dad would understand if it took him a while to coax her back to the house. "You talk funny, Iris. How can somebody have a big little brother?"

She almost smiled. "You have to see Nocca. Dael's tall, over six feet. Nocca's the younger of Dael's two brothers, but he's a whole head taller than Dael."

"Who are they?" Tob asked. "Where do they live?"

She bit her lip and looked worried. "They live in Edian," she eventually answered. "Their father's a goldsmith, but they're both in the king's guard."

Tob remembered seeing guards in Edian. He especially remembered seeing them, and being nervous because of them, the day of the Remembering for Princess Emlie. His first summer of traveling with Jordy had been an eventful

190

one. He remembered the guards they'd met on the road, and the smell from the burning bodies of the Abstainers they'd killed. There had been a Dael and a Nocca in that patrol, escorting the goldsmith Loras—surely the same family. He thought about the guards who'd taken Pross away from the village when he didn't want to go. He doubted that he would like this Dael, or his big little brother.

"Why would anyone be a guard?" he asked.

Iris's face, already blotched with crying, reddened further. "Why wouldn't they? Dael's Captain of the Guard, and I—"

She broke off and, as Tob watched with interest, swallowed her anger. When she spoke again, her voice was cool and deliberate. "My—someone I knew once told me that Dael was born to kill people. He didn't want to be a guard. He wanted to make jewelry and beautiful things like the rest of his family."

"Then why didn't he?"

"He killed a man. It wasn't his fault," she added, before Tob could react. "He was young, seventeen or eighteen, I think. A burglar broke into his family's shop. His sister was there, cutting a stone. She was a wonderful gem cutter. The man struck and killed her. Dael heard her scream and ran to help. There was a fight, and Dael killed the burglar. He was arrested for it. He was only trying to protect himself, but there were no witnesses. He would have been sentenced to the work crews for years, or strangled, but Prince Damon witnessed his trial and invoked an old law. Another criminal had been condemned to death the same morning. The prince gave the two prisoners the choice of combat, the winner's sentence to be commuted to life service in the guards. Dael won."

A shadow of sorrow passed over her face, and she seemed to shrink in on herself. "He probably doesn't even remember me. Better if he doesn't," she added in a very low whisper that Tob just barely caught.

Tob thought that it might be better for Iris if she didn't

remember this guard who was good at killing people. He tentatively rested his hand on her thin arm. "I'll be your friend. We all will."

Tears filled her eyes again. "You should hate me." She took a shaky breath. "I don't want to have to face your father again. I just did as the Greenmother told me. I didn't know she was bringing me here. But now that I am here—I don't want your father to send me away."

"He won't," Tob assured her, and patted her arm. "Dad wouldn't turn anyone away. None of us would. Really. Just don't cry. Please."

"I can't help it. I should have more control. I'm sorry." Tears spilled out. She dropped her head and hugged the kitten close again. It happily tried to burrow under the collar of the ugly black robe. Iris absently scratched at her shoulder, then whimpered when she realized what she was doing. "We'd better go back."

Tob nodded and helped her to her feet, wishing that she didn't look and sound so defeated and scared. The closer they got to the house, the more drawn and apprehensive she became. Tob eventually turned his eyes toward the ground and kept them there, not wanting to witness her misery anymore.

Sene remembered the road, though it had been many years since he had been in this part of his kingdom. It had been spring the last time he had made his way to Telina. The little village of pastel-painted stucco, garden plots bright with the first blooms of early flowers, and lemon groves scenting the air for miles around, had been too pleasant a setting for the horrors it had contained. All of the bodies had been indoors. Most had already been dismembered and partially devoured by the hungry village dogs. Gavea had been a substantial black pillar in the center of the road, blocking the passage of the wagon he drove. Her, "Don't bother, they've died, the brave dears. All except this one," was his formal introduction to Filanora. The name was far bigger than she was. Gavea's warning had not prevented him from going to see for himself. That duty fulfilled, he had returned to lift the fragile orphan from Gavea's arms.

"Light as a feather," he'd murmured, surprised when the little girl immediately clung to him and nestled her head against his neck. There had never been a question that he'd take her home.

The lemon groves had deteriorated greatly. None of the houses retained their roofs. The bright colors had long ago faded from the walls. The piebald horse he'd sent to Garden Vale was grazing along the edge of the road near what might once have been a pasture fence.

Corporal Felistinon stood with his back against a lone fence post, his own horse nibbling at the long grass around his feet. He nodded silently as Sene rode up. The corporal, his straight black hair knotted at the back of his neck, was a head taller than Sene, who was by no means a small man. According to popular opinion all horse people were tall. Of course, another commonly held belief was that they never involved themselves with the Children of the Rock except to quarrel over grazing lands, yet Felistinon and his clan had been living in eastern Sitrine for many years in perfect harmony with their neighbors.

"Where is she?" Sene asked.

Felistinon gestured south with a tilt of his head. Beyond the overgrown pasture, in yet another stand of lemon trees, the girl's black robe was visible behind a cascading fall of blossoms.

Sene tethered his horse to the fence and made his way through the tall grass. He had a moment's uncertainty that the child could really be his foster daughter. She was so small. He hadn't seen her since she was ten, but she didn't seem to have grown. As he drew closer he realized he was mistaken. Of course she'd grown. Two inches in six years? His paternal side wondered critically what the Brownmothers fed people in Garden Vale. It wasn't as if she'd been abandoned at Soza. Well, she had been a delicate child. He'd give Jenil the benefit of the doubt.

Bees hummed in the pasture's wild flowers, a soothing

drone beneath the varied noises of rustling branches and bird song. Butterflies floated in the air along with falling petals, spots of blue and yellow amidst the white and green of the grove. Sene came to a halt a few feet behind the girl. She was staring at the remains of the farmhouse at the end of the grove, oblivious to his presence.

"No one lives here anymore," he quietly informed the back of her head.

She jumped, just a little, and answered. "I've noticed that." The girl turned to face him. "I was told there was plague here."

"A few years ago."

"And everyone died. I see it's true. At least, they're gone."

"They're gone," he agreed. "A minstrel named Ivey made a song of it."

"Minstrels do that sort of thing." She seemed more wistful than sad. Sene wanted to pick her up and give her a hug. That had worked when she was four. It had worked for a while afterward. "I suppose Jenil sent you."

"No."

She made a point of looking past him and carefully scanning the road. "Just passing through, are you? I don't see a merchant's wagon."

"I'm on my way to Raisal. For the Festival. People should be with their families during the Festivals."

Feather gestured toward the gray, weathered walls of the collapsing house. "I think my family is there."

"Ancestors don't count," he told her gently. "I was speaking of living family and friends."

"It's a long ride to Garden Vale. I don't think I'll make it back by Festival day." The practical consideration seemed to distract her from her brooding. She cocked her head slightly to one side, regarding him with increased interest. "Actually, I'm not certain I'd be welcome if I did go back."

"Nonsense. A pleasant young woman like yourself? I'm sure you're sorely missed."

The compliment won him the smile he'd hoped for. "You presume a lot on first meeting, don't you?"

He smiled back. "I'm considered an excellent judge of character."

Her cheeks colored slightly. "Thank you." She rubbed her hands uncertainly on the fabric of her brown-embroidered robe. With another glance at the empty house, she said, more to herself than to him, "I can't stay here. I don't want to stay here. I just needed to know it was true."

"Then come with me," Sene suggested. "I've a daughter and son your age. Twins."

His suggestion finally succeeded in capturing her complete attention. "Where did you say you lived?"

"Outside Raisal."

"Jenil keeps telling me I'd like Raisal. It's on the sea. I've never seen the ocean. It's hard to imagine so much water could exist in one place."

"You find it difficult to believe in things you haven't seen for yourself, don't you?"

She shrugged. "I've always believed my Redmother tales, but some things are different. Some things are more personal."

He suddenly understood part of her melancholy. "Not to be able to rely on your memory must be very difficult."

Her frown was extremely suspicious. "Do I know you?"

"We've met, yes."

She glared past him toward the patiently waiting Felistinon. "I suppose he knows you, too."

"He wouldn't have allowed me to come over and talk to you if he didn't."

She considered that, then stated, "Jenil did send you."

"Send? No. She just told me where to find you. You can't get lost from a Dreamer, you know."

She stomped past him in the direction of her horse. "I could lose you."

He followed behind her. "You could try. But I'm very good at tracking. Now, are we going home together or not? You don't want to miss the Festival. Dancing, fresh sea food, a pretty new dress, horse races, sailing competitions—"

"I've been to Festivals," she cut off his enthusiastic recital.

"In Raisal?" he challenged her.

She stopped with her hand on her piebald's saddle. "My legs hurt," she announced.

"It takes practice to ride with a saddle."

She rounded on him. "Do you have an answer for everything?"

He smiled again. "Yes."

"I thought so."

"Come home with me, Feather."

Clumsily and with some effort, she pulled herself the long distance up onto the horse. Out of the corner of his eye, Sene saw that Felistinon had mounted and was keeping a watchful eye on the girl. Except for the brief flicker of annoyance that crossed her face, Feather did an excellent job of pretending the guard wasn't there. Once in the saddle, she looked down at Sene, her angry expression turning to puzzlement. "Didn't you used to have more hair?"

He ran a hand ruefully over the undeniably smooth top of his head. *All right,* he told himself, *you wanted to jog her memory. If that means being reminded of your mortality, it's worth it. I'm not really that old. Just vain. Besides, look around you. No one lives forever.* "Yes, I did. In a few more years I'll probably have none at all."

She made a face. "I wouldn't like that."

"Neither will I." He untied the reins of his horse. "We can at least ride together. That is, if you're going north."

"I might as well. The ocean is supposed to be in the north."

"And the Festival in Raisal? Music? Almond pastries?"

"Are you always hungry?"

"Yes."

"You always have answers, and you're always hungry. What else are you always?"

He mounted his stallion. When he turned the animal's head toward the north, Feather urged her own horse up beside his. As they started along the dirt track, he answered casually, "King of Sitrine."

"Ah. That's what I thought."

CHAPTER 18

Damon leaned back in his heavily padded, carved oaken chair. It was not a throne. Not quite. The room that he used for meetings would never be mistaken for the great hall of the king. There was no dais, no wall-length hearth, none of the generous space required for a royal banquet. He didn't need all that. Damon preferred to give people his personal attention.

He narrowed his eyes, glaring at the stubborn old woman before him. "I won't have it, Vissa."

"I don't see that it's your decision, Highness," the Red-mother countered.

"Everything relevant to the smooth functioning of my father's kingdom is my concern."

"The Spring Festival—"

"The Spring Festival," Damon interrupted her, "is an important ceremony of reunion and rededication after the hardships and loneliness of a long winter. There is no need to mar such a pleasant celebration with religious nonsense."

The woman's careworn face darkened. "You think the gods are nonsense, Highness?"

"I said nothing of the kind. I have no opinion on the subject one way or another. My objection is to the public repetition of childish fables. The Story of Beginnings will not be told this year."

"Your Highness cannot ask such a thing!"

"I do not ask it. I command it."

"The story gives us our identity, as individuals and as Children of the Rock." Vissa's thin hands, folded in front of her, tensed.

"It perpetuates an unnecessary division of the populace. It ties people to hereditary vows, hereditary roles."

"They have to be hereditary. Heredity determines our capabilities."

Damon crossed one leg over the other. "Capabilities are a matter of training. You'd see that, if you hadn't been blinded by your own myths."

"Training? Are the gifts of a Dreamer the results of training?"

"Dreamers are aberrations," he told her. "More dangerous than Abstainers. Don't look so shocked, Redmother. I'm not alone in holding that opinion. They've never been more than a tiny fraction of the population, wielding power over the rest of us on the basis of old legends and a few magic tricks. It's past time we stopped dignifying outdated myths with repetition. Have I made myself clear?"

A log sputtered in the small fireplace as Damon watched Vissa struggle for words. He'd never spoken quite so bluntly to her before. She had an important place in the king's court. Not all of the knowledge she retained in her vast memory was as useless to him as ancient folk beliefs in the Firstmother. However, accepting her value as a tool was one thing. Humoring her superstitions was quite another.

With an obvious effort, she found her voice. "Quite clear, Highness."

"Good. You may go." He lifted one hand to the bell pull suspended beside his chair, signaling the end of the interview to the guard outside, who swung the door open just before Vissa reached it. As soon as she was gone, the dependable figure of his captain filled the doorway.

"You wished to see me, Highness?"

"Have you implemented my plans for the Festival?"

Dael nodded once, his thick gold hair sliding over his shoulders. "The guards are pleased at the chance to display their skills, Highness. There will be maneuvers by patrols and squads in the market pasture, followed by the march round the castle, as you suggested. It will take several hours. I only hope we attract enough of a crowd to give us the attention we deserve."

"Oh, I expect the entire town will be present," Damon

said. Doubt clashed with his captain's usual unquestioning acceptance of orders, providing an interesting display of confusion across the man's features.

"The entire town, Highness?"

"They'll have nothing better to do. I've just arranged it with Vissa. Neither she or any other Redmother will be filling people's ears with old tales at this Festival. I expect my subjects to consider the lessons of the present, not the past."

Dael's perplexed frown gave way to an expression of cautious concern. "That's a significant change in tradition, Highness."

Damon had encouraged his father to choose this particular captain for the king's guards because he was the best—the best swordsman, the best strategist, the best leader, the best thinker—of any Keeper Damon had ever met. In addition, Dael's reactions to Damon's plans provided a reliable indication of how the populace as a whole would respond. Damon found such foreknowledge invaluable. It enabled him to refine his strategies and counter the arguments of those who might disagree with him. At times, by anticipating an area of concern, he could invalidate objections even before they were raised.

"It's an elimination of a complete waste of time," Damon said. "Vows of service should go to the king, not to the mythical founders of a dead society."

"People do cling to their traditions."

"They'll have to be encouraged toward greater flexibility." Damon leaned forward in his enthusiasm. "I suggest you reserve two squads from the maneuvers. Instruct them to pass through Edian after the noon feast and guide any stragglers to the market pastures."

"Yes, Highness."

"You may return to your duties."

Dael inclined his head respectfully before departing. After the captain let himself out, the door guard stepped into view.

"No one else is waiting, sir. Orders?"

"Send to the stables for Second Groom Palim."

"Yes, sir."

Alone, Damon got up, stretched, and sauntered over to the fire. So many plans to put into motion. They'd lost too much during the long plague years to be able to afford to continue as they had for centuries. Admittedly, there had been a few benefits from the loss of population. For one thing, the Dreamers were all but extinct. For another, the plague had eliminated entire Shaper families. The centralization of control in the three largest remaining population centers had occurred out of necessity and over the course of several decades.

What was needed now was even greater centralization, greater efficiency, useful innovations—such as the entire population in the service of one king.

He turned at a muffled rap on the door. "Enter."

"Good day, Your Highness." Second Groom Palim was a barrel-chested, taciturn man a few years older than Damon. His rich brown skin, hair, and eyes indicated an origin along the warm northern coast. The same characteristics that had made him unfit for the plodding life of a fisherman made him one of Damon's most valuable tools.

Damon clasped his hands behind his back. "What shall we discuss today concerning the horses?"

"Frog's healing on that three-year-old filly. Ought to resume training before the end of the nineday."

"Do so. That's the content of today's conversation." Damon resumed his seat and beckoned the other man closer. "Now, on to business. What progress on infiltrating the court at Raisal?"

"No chance. Wizard scares most off. Rest I wouldn't trust near Sene."

"If you don't trust them you shouldn't be using them."

Palim shrugged. "Sitrine court's too small. Folks are too content."

"Well, keep trying. Anything useful from Dherrica?"

"King still chasing prince. Border guard still strong. Guards hate Rhenlan." Palim squinted slightly, as though examining the words he'd just uttered. "Fear us, too."

Damon rested his elbow on the arm of the chair, hand in chin. "Healthy fear is useful, if it's mixed with respect and admiration." Dherrica's strong borders and civil strife provided excellent motivation to constantly recruit more guards to Hion's service.

"Captain Dael's admired."

"I should hope he is. That's one of the primary functions of the captain of the king's guard, to play the hero while the king is busy with real work."

"Hion's been hero and king."

"And wasted both opportunities," Damon snapped.

The other man showed no remorse for making him angry. "Dael's known to honor old traditions."

"He can honor what he pleases so long as he obeys me. Don't look so disapproving. You know I respect your advice. Have you any evidence that my captain's loyalty is in question?"

"No, Highness."

"Do you think that my tampering with established customs will turn Dael against me?"

Palim hesitated. "Not sure, Highness."

"Have your spies watch him come Festival day. I've canceled the Story of Beginnings, and replaced it with a parade of the guards. Weigh your suspicions against his actions, and report back to me."

Palim nodded.

"Dismissed."

Damon shook his head after the departing groom. Palim simply could not imagine anyone in Dael's position not desiring to further his own ambitions. Palim was not a very good judge of character.

Of course, that little personality flaw made Palim a rare and wonderful find in their tradition-blinded world.

"We'll camp here for the night."

Feather guided her tired horse toward the broken stone wall where Felistinon, apparently anticipating the king's de-

201

cision, had already dismounted. Sene remained a moment longer in the middle of the hard dirt road, sitting straight and still in the saddle, one hand shading his eyes against the westering sun as he studied the surrounding landscape.

"Not that there's anything to see," she muttered as she slid shakily to the ground. For a moment she rested her forehead against the saddle's smooth, well-worn leather, too tired to care about getting one more smudge of dirt on her already grime-streaked face. Not once since leaving Telina had they encountered other travelers or the smallest patch of cultivated land. The unrelenting solitude of the Sitrinian wilderness made her feel small and insignificant and far too lonely for comfort.

"I'll take care of that, miss." Feather jumped as Felistinon reached casually over her head to unlace her horse's pack.

She put a possessive hand on the animal's sweaty neck. "I thought I told you not to sneak up on me like that."

His dark-eyed glance was polite but unrepentant. "I don't know how to walk any louder, miss."

"I also told you I can manage my own belongings." It was a futile argument. Her bags were already leaning against the low wall, and as they spoke Felistinon deftly removed saddle and pads as well.

"Oh, never mind. I'll just go stretch my legs before we eat."

"Yes, miss." He took her mount's reins and began to lead it toward a break in the wall.

Feather set off down the line of tumbled stones toward the man who was to blame for all her problems. Sene's horse, stripped and hobbled, grazed beside the guard's rangy bay within the broken circle formed by the old wall. The king himself wandered along the inside of the rough fence, kicking now and then at objects hidden from Feather's view by the tall grass.

Hurrying a little, she caught up to him when they were a third of the way around the wall from Felistinon. "Doesn't this part of Sitrine have anything but ruins?"

"I'm afraid not." The king's broad shoulders moved in a half-shrug. "Trust me. This is a better place to camp than the open plain."

"You've stopped here before?"

"Many times. This used to be an inn, the Blue Bottle. The well was somewhere along here." He kicked aside another fallen stone. "I admit there's not much trade these days between Sitrine and Rhenlan, but Brownmothers at least still travel where they will. We have a Brownmother house at Bren, a day's ride south and east of Raisal."

"I've heard of it."

"We'll pass the turn-off about midday tomorrow." He smiled down at her. "You'll be home in time for a bath before dinner."

Your home, not mine. She thought of Jenil's cluttered rooms and the quiet murmur of the Broad River below the windows of Garden Vale's Brownmother house. She'd yet to encounter a proper river in wide, windswept Sitrine.

Trailing her fingers over the weathered surface of the ragged line of stones she asked, "Is the rest of your kingdom as sad as this place?"

Sene stopped walking. "No, it's not. You'll see, when we reach Raisal."

He swung one leg over the wall and sat there, hands clasped loosely in his lap, at ease in the warm evening air. Feather had the impression he would be at ease anywhere, from the roughest campsite to the finest palace.

"Has Jenil told you nothing about us?"

"She told me I am honored to be betrothed to your son."

"Dreamer or not, I am going to have to have a talk with that woman. Listen carefully, young lady. A betrothal is not a marriage. No one is going to force you and Chasa to marry. No one is going to force you to do anything."

Feather folded her arms. "So why didn't Jenil listen to me when I said I didn't want to leave Garden Vale?"

"Dreamers have the annoying habit of being certain they know what's best for everyone." A smile crinkled the corners of his eyes. "They're usually right."

"Then I'll have to marry your son, won't I?"

Sene grew serious again. "Feather, do you remember any of your childhood?"

"Glimpses, here and there."

"What about the rest of your memory? Since you came to live with Jenil? Did you learn what the Brownmothers teach?"

"I remember everything I was taught in Garden Vale." Faces flashed in front of her mind's eye, beloved teachers, dear friends. Miles and days away, all of them.

"The Story of Beginnings?" he prompted her. "Tales of the kingdoms before the plague, of the war with the horse people, of Hion's hunt for the last fire bear?"

"Yes, yes. I've heard them all."

"But you don't believe them." Feather dropped her gaze, hoping that the growing darkness hid the flush that spread up her neck and warmed her ears. The too-astute king continued, "It's not easy, I know. For years Keepers marry Keepers, and Shapers marry Shapers, and we raise our children and go about our own business without bothering anyone else."

His rumbling voice deepened. "Until the rules change and we're suddenly expected to marry outside our own kind, to produce children who'll never get married themselves, but who will live for hundreds of years, bending the power of the gods to benefit all of the Children of the Rock."

In spite of herself, Feather shivered. "Maybe that part is true. I know Jenil is real. Her power is real. And I can believe that Dreamers are infertile, just as Shapers and Keepers are usually infertile with each other."

"Dreamers have to come from somewhere."

"From your generation, Your Majesty. Not mine! New Dreamers were supposed to have been born ten or fifteen or twenty years ago."

"Two were. My cousins followed tradition."

"What of Hion's cousins, and Dea's cousins, and all the other Shaper families? Where were they when the Dreamers were killing themselves, searching for the cause of the plague?"

"Some of them were dying, too," Sene said. "Others were too frightened to realize what was happening, or too bitter to care. None of which matters now. We missed our chance."

"So you pass the burden to your children."

"Not a burden. A gift. Do you believe in the gods, Feather?"

"I don't know. Jenil does."

"So does Aage. He doesn't just believe, he knows. They talk to him. They're giving us another chance. Maybe our last chance."

"And that's supposed to make me feel better?" Feather demanded.

"I beg your pardon?"

"It's all very well your being kind and charming and promising that no one's going to force me into anything, except how can I say no when everyone says my saying no will mean the end of the world!"

The king's big, callused hand cupped the side of her face. "Gods, I'm getting as bad as Jenil."

His thumb gently wiped away the single tear of angry despair that escaped her rigid control. "None of us is that important, little one. I believe more Dreamer children will be born. If not to you, then to someone else. You're not alone. You've been given an opportunity, yes. But what you do with that opportunity is up to you. All I ask is that you give the matter some thought before you make your decision. Talk to Chasa. Get to know the people of Sitrine. You were happy, once, in Raisal."

"I was happy in Garden Vale."

"Your Majesty!"

Sene jerked around at Felistinon's warning shout. The guard was running for his pile of gear, pointing urgently into the darkness beyond the tumbled remains of the inn. Sene slid off the wall, grabbed Feather under the arms as if she were a child, and swung her up and over the low barrier. Before she could draw breath to protest he grabbed her by the hand and started to run, leaving her no choice but to run with him.

His wordless urgency lit the first spark of fear in her. The grass hissed past their legs, the thick growth hiding broken stones and half-rotted beams of wood that moved treacherously under her feet. Twice she tripped and almost fell, the king's iron grip tugging her upright and onward.

"What is it?" she gasped as he finally dropped her hand and slid to a halt next to his saddle. The last light had faded from the horizon, where a faint band of orange lingered at the edge of the arching blue-black of the night sky. Moonslight cast conflicting shadows over the wide plain, altering the shapes of familiar objects and making it difficult for Feather to judge distances. But Sene was right in front of her, and there was no mistaking the size of the sword he pulled from his saddle scabbard, or the deadly intent with which he spun to search the darkness.

She saw them at the same moment he did, crouching figures that clambered over the wall near the point where Felistinon had left Feather's horse. The animal threw its head up and shied nervously as one of the figures broke away from the group and ran toward it. The corporal was nowhere to be seen.

"Don't move," the king told her. Lifting his head he roared, "Stay away from that horse! Guards, attack!"

The dark shape paused, then resumed its scurrying rush forward, one hand raised. Pale Keyn-light glittered off a knife blade. The horse swerved awkwardly, its hindquarters bumping up against a section of wall. Feather's throat went dry with helpless terror.

She didn't hear the twang of a bowstring or the whirring flight of the arrow. Its feathered shaft seemed to materialize in the center of the man's chest with the suddenness of Dreamer magic, stopping him in midstride. The horse neighed frantically at the sharp scent of blood and skittered away along the wall as the shadowy figure toppled over and vanished from view in the tall grass.

Then the rest of the dark shapes were running toward Sene, and Feather didn't have time to think of anything except staying out of the way. The low wall at her back provided a little comfort. The steady support of Felistinon's marksmanship provided more. From the corporal's vantage point somewhere in the darkness he picked off three more of their enemies with well-placed shafts, leaving only five knifewielding adversaries for the king.

They had the advantage of numbers. Sene had the sword. If they had coordinated their attack they might have brought him down. Feather crouched low in the grass, hands searching desperately for something of manageable size she might use for a weapon. The first attacker died soundlessly, head flying one way, body falling the other as he ran straight into Sene's sweeping sword stroke. Momentum carried Sene around to block two more jabbing knives. Another swift beheading. The third screamed high and bubbly as she fell, Sene's back swing slicing her nearly in two.

The last two came at the king from opposite sides. Without seeming to hurry Sene turned and twisted, facing first one, then the other, sword whispering in the moonslight, its blade dark with blood. Feather heard a sound on the wall behind her. In a flurry of long legs and long hair Felistinon launched himself over her head, sword in hand. As he thrust his blade through the nearer man's back, Sene dispatched the other one with a final neat, two-handed swing.

Without a word, king and guardsman turned their backs on one another. They circled slowly through the trampled grass, their eyes searching the ruins, the line of the broken wall, the empty plain beyond. The only sound in the night was Sene's heavy, gradually slowing breathing.

Feather was ready to burst with tension by the time Sene lowered his sword and glanced over his shoulder at the corporal. "Well done."

Felistinon took one last look along the wall, then knelt to wipe his sword on the grass. "Do we leave them and move on?"

Sene walked toward Feather. The coppery smell of blood hung around him like a cloud. "Are you hurt?"

"No, Sire." She pushed herself upright, determined not to let him see how badly her knees were shaking.

He guessed anyway. "It's never easy," he said gently. "Still, I think we should stay here tonight. The bodies must be burned." He glanced at Felistinon. "The wind's in the north, I think."

"Outside the wall?" the corporal replied. At Sene's nod he said, "We'd better stake the horses."

"I'll be with you shortly."

Felistinon walked off to retrieve his bow. Feather stared at the crumpled, broken bodies scattered across the grass. Sene said, "They were Abstainers."

"They're the first I've ever seen."

"They would have killed us."

"I know. I just wish—"

"What?"

"I want to understand why."

"Why Abstainers kill?"

The bitter taste in the back of her mouth had little to do with the deaths she'd just witnessed. "Why Abstainers exist."

"I wonder if any of us can understand. We are the Children of the Rock," he said, and the low rumble of his voice came close to the somber rhythm of ritual. "We make our vows before the gods, to live for one another, to shape or keep or dream according to our natures, to fulfill our duties to the rest of the Children. To forsake our vows is to forsake our deepest, truest selves. Abstainers have chosen to forsake the foundations of life. Once that happens, perhaps they simply can't stand to see anyone else in possession of what they've abandoned."

"You don't hate them, do you?"

"No. I pity them with all my heart."

"But you kill them."

He looked around at the corpses, his expression calm. "Yes. I do. And have before, and will again."

"Doesn't it bother you? Even a little bit?"

He placed his warm, callused hand on her shoulder. "I don't question the will of the gods. It only wastes my time, and theirs, and doesn't change a thing."

Feather held her peace as Sene walked away. He didn't question tradition and law. Fine. Perhaps that worked, for a king. Perhaps it had once worked for her. No longer. She had thought she understood her life, a single thread in the open weave of a simple fabric. Jenil had shattered that illusion. The pattern of Feather's life was more complex than she could ever have guessed, interwoven with people she did not remember and a purpose she had never anticipated. Or so they told her, Sene and Jenil and who knew how many others who would claim to know her better than she knew herself.

They could claim whatever they wished. She would believe them, or not, as she saw fit. From now on, she was going to question everything.

CHAPTER 19

Vray sat on the edge of the porch and tried to massage the kinks out of her aching right hand. The touch of the clean skirt against her legs distracted her briefly. A few days of clean clothes and clean surroundings hadn't been long enough to make cleanliness seem normal. Her healing flea bites no longer itched, and she entertained the thought that eventually even the marks would fade. Eventually. She'd have to start thinking in terms of long periods of time again. Forgetting habits she'd worked three years to acquire was going to be hard.

The afternoon had turned pleasant. The only reminder of the morning's thunderstorm was a puddle in front of the chicken coop. The carter emerged from the stable, wiping his hands on a cloth, then saw her and began walking toward the porch. *I'm too tired,* Vray thought. *He's either got some work for me to do, or he's going to make friendly conversation.* She hoped it was work. She didn't want friends.

"Done something to your hand?" he asked.

Vray became aware that her left hand was still massaging her right. "Sewing. I'm out of practice."

"You've been at it all afternoon?"

"There's a lot to learn."

"Your fingers will be stiff in the morning if you don't get rid of that tension. I've an exercise you might try. Very relaxing." Before Vray could think of a way to politely decline, he reached into his trousers' pocket and pulled out a smooth gray rock. "Here, catch," he said. "Now, just toss it gently from one hand to the other. You'd better stand up."

Vray stood. The rock was a nice size and weight for throwing. She tossed it from her right hand to her left.

"Good. Now back again. That's right. Now, make it a slow, high arch. That's better. Your arms and shoulders should feel relaxed. Don't watch your hands, just let the rock travel. If the upward toss is accurate, the catching is automatic."

He was right. As she fell into the rhythm of tossing the rock back and forth, her right hand began to loosen up. "It works."

"Good. Don't stop, I'll be right back."

Jordy went into the house. Vray made a few more tosses. Relaxing it might be, but it was also boring. Behind her the door opened once more and the carter returned, Matti at his heels. His hands were full of what Vray at first took to be multicolored stones.

"You've mastered that," he said. "Now try it with two."

"I want to play, Daddy," Matti said.

"You can catch for Iris." He held out his hand and Vray returned the rock in exchange for two of the brightly colored objects, which were not stones after all but soft, heavy bags about the size of a child's fist.

"And one for you," he said to his eager daughter.

Vray looked uncertainly at the sacks in her hand.

Jordy said, "One in your right hand, one in your left. As the first one passes in front of your eyes, toss the second. Like this."

She looked up. He took two of the balls and tossed them in the air one after the other. Each arched gracefully over and down into the hand opposite from the one it had left.

Vray tried it. One bag shot out in front of her while the second fell wide of her belatedly groping hand. Matti ran to retrieve them while Jordy offered her two more.

"Try again."

She tried several times. Pepper came around the corner of the house, and her face lit with excitement when she saw what they were doing.

"Daddy, let me try!"

"Not too close." Jordy handed two balls to her. "Give Iris plenty of room."

Pepper tossed one of the balls back and forth a few times, then started on two. Jordy demonstrated for Vray yet

211

again, each of his tosses a perfect arc from one hand to the other. "Slow and easy," he told her.

Vray, watching his hands, blinked. "This is juggling!"

A smile crinkled the corners of his eyes. "Not yet. Three objects, now that's juggling." With that, he picked up a third little sack, and toss toss toss, all three were moving, arcing before his eyes, falling into his hands, only to be gently tossed upward again. It looked so simple, so easy. So relaxing. Vray looked from him to Pepper, who was making symmetrical tosses with her two sacks, then back to her own hands.

After a few more false tries she did it. Toss toss, catch catch. After that the yard was filled with flying colored sacks and the excited squeals of Matti as she chased those that escaped from Vray and Pepper. Vray stepped away from the porch to give herself more room, and so that she could face away from the westering sun. Jordy, juggling all the while, took her place and sat comfortably on the edge of the porch. Vray noticed that the pattern of his juggling varied every few moments, the sacks arcing now higher, now lower, now moving in circles instead of arches.

Pepper picked up a third sack. She could get all three in the air but couldn't keep going for more than a few seconds. However, Matti was more than willing to chase the ones she dropped, and Pepper kept practicing.

Just as she was considering trying a third sack herself, Vray saw Tob climbing the hill from the road. A very odd expression crossed his face as he saw what they were doing.

"Not you, too!" he said to Vray.

"Now, Tob," his father cautioned from the porch.

She stopped uncertainly, and glanced from Jordy to Tob. "You don't like juggling?"

"Oh, I like it. It's just beginning to seem I'm the only person in the kingdom who can't do it." He made a sudden, playful grab at Pepper, who retreated, giggling. "And no gloating from you, either."

"It's a matter of coordination," Jordy explained calmly. "Tob simply hasn't the eye for it."

"Tobble can climb trees," Matti announced.

The door of the house opened soundlessly and Cyril came onto the porch.

Tob smiled at Vray. "Anyway, don't let me interrupt. Just watch where you're throwing those things."

"Actually," Jordy began in a distinctly lecturing tone. "The knack is in not watching them."

Behind him Cyril had picked up her broom. As one of the sacks Jordy was juggling rose to the peak of its arch his wife, a hint of a smile on her face, knocked it aside with one well-aimed swipe of the broom.

"Wha—?" His rhythm hopelessly broken, Jordy's hands faltered and the other two bags fell around him.

Tob grinned. "Weren't watching that one, were you, Dad?" The girls giggled as their father twisted around and reached for Cyril, who stepped nimbly away.

Vray, completely caught up in the relaxed, unthreatening mood of the family, laughed too.

"Where's Rose?"

Ruudy glanced around the kitchen as though noticing for the first time that his wife was not there. Dael smiled behind his hand. Rose was usually in the same place, but Ruudy never seemed able to remember where that was.

"In the workroom," Dael suggested to his mother.

"Well, of course she's in the workroom." Deenit finished removing a large pan of nutbread from the oven as she spoke. The honeyed aroma had been filling the kitchen for the past hour, attracting every male in the family to the large, high-ceilinged room at the back of the house. Dael sat with his father and two brothers, each with a mug of herb tea on the table in front of him.

Deenit continued, "She said she only had to finish one gem and then she would help me pack the food."

Loras gestured casually toward his middle son. "Ruudy, go get your wife."

"She'll yell at him," Nocca offered helpfully.

"I know that. That's why I'm sending him instead of

going myself. She's the best gemcutter I've ever worked with, but she doesn't appreciate having her concentration broken."

"That's probably part of what makes her such a talented gemcutter." Deenit swung her single long, graying yellow braid behind her back with a twist of her head. "Loras, what did you do with the basket?"

Dael watched his father jump obediently to his feet. "It was in the shop. I'll get it."

"You could get Rose while you're out there," Ruudy called to no effect. Loras was already gone. Sighing, Ruudy pushed his chair away from the table and announced to the room in general, "I love my wife. She loves me. Dael, can I borrow a shield from the guardroom?"

"The guardroom is fifteen minutes' walk from here," Nocca said.

Ruudy nodded. "I know."

"Go," his mother commanded.

Ruudy went. Dael finished his tea, then wandered to the fireplace to pour himself another mug. Festival day. It was good to be with family. He would have liked to spend the whole day listening to his parents tease each other and all of their children, watching Ruudy and Rose's quiet romance, eating his mother's and every other neighborhood household's best cooking. He would at least get a slice or two of that nutbread before he left for the castle. No Spring Festival was complete for anyone living in this section of the city without Deenit's nutbread. People remembered it from year to year as much as they did the Story of Beginnings.

This year they'd have only the nutbread.

Being captain of the guard and a disciplined man, he turned his mind back to nutbread. When he was very young he had gone through a year or two of resenting the fact that his mother shared such a wonderful food with all their neighbors. He had been sure that if their family kept all that she baked it would last several ninedays and he could have most of it for himself. But Deenit had always insisted that it was the one dish she wished to share at Festival time. "Festivals are for celebrating," she would lecture him. "I celebrate my heritage with foods I ate as a child in Sitrine." Dael had never wanted to hear the explanation. Later, he'd come to be proud of her accomplishments, of her popularity and generosity, of the contributions to their lives that were uniquely Sitrinian.

The very Sitrinian smells of lemon, almond, and saffron had by this time permeated every corner and crevice of the big kitchen. When they returned at nightfall, the aroma would be lingering in their bedrooms. One more good reason to come home to his family's house on Festival night. Dael returned to the table, to stand behind his mother's shoulder. "Don't hover," she said, "and before you ask, no."

"But Mom . . ."

"At the Festival."

"I may not make it for the meal," he said, then regretted the admission as she whirled around, hands going to her hips.

"What is that supposed to mean?"

"It means I have to be at the castle. Orders."

"It's Festival day! Those at the castle won't need guards today."

"Mom, I won't be there either," Nocca admitted. Dael flashed him a quick smile of gratitude. Their mother's anger was usually easier to take when it was divided among several of them. "We're having a parade."

Loras came back in time to hear that. "A parade? A parade of what? Why?"

"You'll see," Dael said. He had no intention of trying to explain. Loras and Deenit would be upset enough when the decision to cancel the Redmother tales was made known, unlike others in the town, who either wouldn't care or would be glad to be relieved of the boredom. He wasn't going to ruin his parents' morning with news they'd hear soon enough.

"That's not an answer," Deenit began.

Before she could get truly started, the door from the

215

front of the house swung open to admit Nocca's girlfriend and partner in the guards, Peanal. Peanal was a small young woman, freckled and cute, a short sword swinging from her belt. She had a pleasant disposition and a wicked technique to her sword work, fast and agile. All were traits that Dael liked in one of his guards. He wasn't as sure how he'd like her as a sister-in-law, but then she and Nocca had only been together since late winter, and hadn't yet made up their minds about anything.

She was on duty, so she ignored Nocca except for a passing grin, and came directly toward Dael. "Captain, you asked to be informed of the inspection. It's time."

"I'll be right there." He turned his best wheedling look on his mother. "Can I take just one piece? Please?"

She sliced the bread, sending wisps of fragrant steam upward. When she removed the first piece she placed it on a cloth and handed it to the girl. "Here, dear. You must be hungry."

"Mother!"

Nocca slipped past Dael and stood next to Peanal. "I better go, too. I'll share yours, all right?"

"You'll do no such thing." Deenit handed out a second portion of the bread. When Loras moved toward the table, Dael planted himself squarely in the way.

"My turn," he announced firmly.

His mother kissed him on the cheek and handed over the rest of the loaf. "Don't eat it all at once," she warned. "You know what a stomachache it used to give you."

"Mother!"

"Yes?"

"Don't embarrass me in front of my guards," he muttered.

"It's just your brother and Peanal."

"I'm leaving now." He knew when to retreat. "Enjoy yourselves. We'll be back as soon as we can. Tonight at the latest."

"Where is Rose?" His mother waved them out the door as she turned her attention back to the work to be done. "If she's injured Ruudy it will ruin the entire day."

Chuckling under his breath, Dael shepherded the two younger guards out of the house.

The largest barn in Juniper Ridge was just large enough to accommodate all of the tables and benches required by the village population for the Spring Festival. Doron placed her crock of vegetable stew at the edge of the makeshift hearth in the center of the floor, then squeezed through the crowd in the direction of the wine barrels. Outside, a late season storm was coating every fence post and tree trunk with damp snow. Inside, the well-tended fire, combined with the warm breath and bodies of many people, made the barn completely comfortable.

Doron smelled wet wool as a strong, slender hand came to rest on her forearm. "The joys of the season to you, dyer," said the familiar voice.

"So it's you, is it?"

Pirse, with typical Shaper arrogance, ignored the challenge in her tone. "I've told you before, I just can't seem to stay away."

She allowed him to draw her away from the dense knot of people near the wine table. He had obviously just arrived. The shoulders of his cloak were dark with damp, and melting snowflakes glistened in his black hair and eyelashes.

"The whole winter we heard nothing of you," Doron complained.

"I went so far north that I saw no people for ninedays at a time. Which reminds me, I have a favor to ask."

"Naturally."

Others were becoming aware of the prince in their midst. Pirse acknowledged some greetings and allowed a youngster to carry his cloak up to the loft to dry. *He looks well, at least,* Doron thought. The prince may have been in exile as far as Bronle was concerned, but he hadn't been abandoned by Dherrica itself. As long as he stayed true to his vows, Keepers wouldn't be able to help themselves responding to him and sheltering him. And Doron was no exception.

A shift in the throng left them alone again. "It does seem that all I ever do is ask for things," Pirse said in answer to her comment. Or perhaps, her thoughts. "But this is important. Dragon's ears. Three sets. I would have left them with Morb at Dundas, but I had to bypass a patrol. Then the weather worsened and I didn't want to double back."

Doron pursed her lips. "There's Damic in Dundas. He usually comes south for a bit of trading around midsummer. Will he know how to find your wizard?"

"Aye. But it needn't be someone from Dundas. If Jordy comes through first and is willing to take them to Garden Vale and the Greenmother there, that would be fine."

"Fine indeed. You won't be here to listen to him complain."

Pirse slid an arm around her waist and bestowed one of his more charming smiles upon her. "So, you do miss me when I'm gone."

The impulse to slap the knowing smirk off his pretty face wrestled with an equal impulse to entwine her body around his then and there. She compromised by leaning into his embrace long enough to bite him, not gently, on the nose.

His hand moved from her waist to cup her breast from beneath, half warning, half promise. She didn't know her mouth was still open as she gazed into the sparkling eyes level with her own until he tilted his head slightly and caught her in a kiss. She stopped hearing the conversations going on around them, stopped thinking, stopped breathing. Nothing was real but the taste and smell and touch of this one aggravating obsession.

They separated reluctantly. Doron's mind resumed working, and thoughts assumed astonishing clarity. What was the matter with her? With him? With them? She knew the prince was as unnerved by their mutual attraction as she was. Each time they met, they were drawn together more strongly, more insistently, than the last. Unnerving, because on all other levels they tended to bicker and disagree. He was a Shaper, by the gods! She didn't like Shapers. There was certainly no rational excuse for his behavior. Anyone would have thought that dragons, roving Abstainers, and the enmity of his uncle would have required Pirse's full concentration. Yet ever since the few ninedays he'd spent recuperating in her care, he had returned to Juniper Ridge for each Festival, as well as scattered days between when time allowed. One or two casual stops she might have considered gratitude. But gratitude had long since ceased to be an adequate explanation.

"Are you busy after lunch?" he asked.

It made no sense. Even as she thought it she found herself saying, "Only with you."

CHAPTER 20

"This village needs another Redmother," Canis said as she took a seat next to Jordy on the inn steps.

Jordy turned his head to look at the fisherwoman. The steps were still in shadow, not yet warmed by the early spring sunlight. A mug of warm cider steamed between Canis's bony hands. He drained his own mug and glanced from Canis to the girl folded up in the shadows and one of Cyril's old shawls. He tipped his head toward the group of children he hoped she would soon decide to join, but Iris ignored the prompting. Most of the young people of Broadford were in the square, preparing it for the Festival. Some draped garlands of mixed dried and early-blooming flowers on every building eave, rail, and fence post, while others were setting up trestle tables for the feast. A double dozen youngsters laughed and enjoyed each others' company in the dawn-lit square, while Iris clung silently by his side. Even Ivey, who'd arrived late the night before, was up on a ladder, taking directions meekly from the prettiest girl in the village.

Jordy'd brought Iris, along with Matti and Pepper, to help with the decorating. The little ones were doing what they could and not getting too much in the older children's way, but his new charge didn't seem to know how to join in the fun. Jordy scowled and turned his attention back to Canis.

"We have a Redmother, haven't we?"

Canis gave a gusty sigh. "You've been gone, carter, but I'd think Herri would have caught you up on all the news by now."

"Redmother Driss was pregnant when I left. Has she had the baby?"

"Twins. Four ninedays early. She's very ill. A wet nurse has been found, but the babes may not live. Brownmother

220

Mellany from Garden Vale has done all she can. She's hoping Greenmother Jenil will return from Sitrine soon. Her magic's about the only hope Driss has."

"Greenmothers," Jordy growled.

Canis rapped him sharply on the head with her knuckles. "Not a word against any of the Mothers from you today, carter. Jenil can't always be where she's needed, and we Brownmothers serve when we can. Driss is so young. We didn't think she'd need to start training another Redmother for years yet. If she dies, our memories die with her." Canis sighed. "Without Driss, we've no one to tell the Story of Beginnings today. And don't tell me we can do without the story, carter."

"We'll have to," Jordy said. The old tale was entertaining, but hardly necessary to the festivities. There were more important rituals to fill the day, plenty of games and food and talk to fill the time. Not wanting another rap on the head, he didn't say so.

The girl had drawn closer while Canis spoke. Ivey jumped lightly down from the ladder and came up to them. "Will you have some cider?" Jordy asked the minstrel, but Ivey ignored Jordy's question.

"We'd enjoy your company, pretty one," Ivey said. Iris's head lifted sharply at the compliment. She pulled the shawl closer around her narrow frame, her fingers playing nervously with the long red fringe. Despite her silence, Ivey persisted. "We haven't been properly introduced."

"Iris," Jordy answered for the girl. "Why don't you run along and help?" he added, keeping his tone gentle. He had to be careful. She tended to take every word he said as a command.

Paying no attention to either Ivey or himself, she addressed Canis, her voice soft. "Brownmother Canis?"

"Just Canis will do, child," the fisherwoman told her. "I don't do much these days."

"Nothing much," Jordy agreed, "but supervise the Festivals, and see the poor and sick are tended through the winter, and—"

221

"No more than a little organization," Canis grumbled. "Now, child, what is it?"

Iris hesitated, then straightened her shoulders. "I've had some training as a Redmother. I could tell the story for your village." She made a half-furtive gesture toward Jordy. "If it's permitted."

A sudden smile lit Ivey's face. "I thought you looked familiar. You wouldn't know me, lass, but I know of your family. It's more than some training she's had," he explained to Jordy and Canis. "It was to be her profession."

The girl's skin had gone as red as her hair. Jordy flushed. He'd just learned more about his fosterling from the minstrel than Greenmother Jenil or the girl herself had seen fit to tell him. Before he could say anything, Canis handed her empty mug to him and got to her feet.

She wrapped an arm around Iris's thin shoulders. "We'll go to Driss's house now. If she has the strength, perhaps she can help you practice. How long has it been since you told the story?"

Iris mumbled something in answer as Canis led her across the square. Jordy turned his attention to Ivey. Or would have, if the minstrel had not already slipped away to join the crowd of young people setting up targets for the archery competition. Jordy intended to have a talk with the lad—but it could wait. They had the whole day ahead of them.

"I said I was never going to leave Garden Vale. So where am I? Not in Garden Vale." From her seat on her cushioned stool, Feather glowered at a passing servant, who cringed and quickened his pace. That was one of the things—one of the many, many things—that annoyed her about the king's household. No one was willing to fight with her. If she glowered at someone they had every right to glower back. The king's daughter was nice to her, the servants were polite, the townspeople smiled constantly. Everyone was being entirely too tolerant of her bad moods.

I know I'm being a brat. Anyone from Garden Vale would

know I'm a brat. Why can't these people accept me as I am and snarl back?

There were lots of things Feather didn't like about Raisal. For one thing, oceans were boring—even if she had wanted to see one. The shore smelled of fish. Dead fish. And salt. And gull droppings. From a distance she supposed it wasn't too bad. Just a fresh salt tang to the breeze. You needed a breeze on a day like this. Spring Festivals weren't supposed to be this warm. In Garden Vale, they'd been happy if they didn't have snow. They would never risk putting the entire feast outdoors.

She looked disdainfully at the field full of open-sided pavilions. The amber- and scarlet-patterned cloth moved with the breeze, brilliant in the morning sunshine. Her cushioned stool was still in the shade, just beneath the awning of the large tent nearest the main building. No doubt a servant would be by to move it, and her, before the sun progressed much further. Since her feet did not quite reach the ground, she was tempted to command the man to move the stool with her on it. He wouldn't want her to risk getting her lovely white dress and soft shoes grass-stained, would he? Of course not.

How can anyone have fun at a Festival if they're not allowed to get dirty?

She wanted to be in Garden Vale. She wanted to eat dried berry soup and let it dribble down her chin. She wanted to win the foot races. She wanted to go wading in the Broad and complain to her friends about how cold it is.

I am pouting. Pout pout pout.

No one knew her here. How could she play games she had never even seen before? What was she going to eat? They put almonds in everything. And lemon juice. That wasn't so bad, maybe. The lemon drink sweetened with honey was good. Feather squirmed restlessly on her stool, picking at the golden tassels on the cream-colored cushion. People were arriving in huge numbers now, streaming up the road out of the town of Raisal to enjoy the feast on the grounds of the King's estate. According to Princess Jeyn, the court and the town had been sharing Festivals for generations. The ruler provided the physical setting and large quantities of various meats, and the townspeople brought the rest.

"Keep frowning and your face will freeze that way."

She looked up at the familiar rumbling voice, tilting her head to see behind herself. King Sene returned her frown with raised eyebrows. "It hasn't so far," she informed him.

"You've been lucky." He continued to stand behind her. She stubbornly continued to stare up at him, cricking her neck but ignoring the discomfort. "Where's Jeyn? I told her to keep an eye on you."

"She was called away."

"You've been sitting here since breakfast. Why didn't you go with her? You won't enjoy the Festival rooted to one spot all day."

"I don't want to enjoy the Festival. I want to pout."

"Ah. Of course. You're homesick."

"Children get homesick," she announced. "I simply prefer Rhenlan customs to yours."

"You don't know our customs. You're homesick."

"I can't be homesick. I don't have a home."

"Nonsense. Now you're being pitiful. It's not very becoming." His hands gripped her shoulders, and she found herself suspended briefly over the stool before he took a step to one side and placed her on her feet.

"I'll get my shoes dirty." She turned to face him.

"That's what shoes are for."

"These?" she demanded, lifting one foot gracefully. "Soft linen like this is too delicate for the outdoors."

"Then why are you wearing them?"

"Jeyn picked them out and told me to wear them!" she snapped.

He took a step back and looked her over. "You do look nice. Pretty dress. Jeyn was just trying to be helpful. She wants you to make a good impression on Chasa."

Chasa. She kept hearing about Chasa. This person she supposedly had adored as a child. This person she was betrothed to. This person who hadn't put in an appearance since she got here. She only got here yesterday, but that was no excuse, considering this was his home. "When is he going to make an impression on me?"

"He should be out any minute. Would you like to come with me to the craft display? I'm told that you're an embroidery expert. Perhaps you can help with the judging."

Placing one hand on her shoulder, the king steered her out of the shade. She squinted in the bright light, smoothing her skirt as they walked. Away from the relative quiet of the house, the bustle and excitement of the crowd was even more noticeable. Raisal was a big town, to be home to so many people.

Garden Vale was much cozier.

The pavilions had been arranged in a rough horseshoe, with the open end partially closed by the north wall of the house. Singing had already begun on a stage set up near the orchard. A huge oval had been staked out just beyond the west side of the horseshoe, near the stables. That was something she'd like to see later. Garden Vale never raced its horses. Farm horses weren't exactly built for speed.

As they approached the craft tent, she noticed someone cutting across the field to intercept them. At first she thought it was the wizard she'd met last night. The hair color and length was the same, silver blond brushing his shoulders. But the long bangs drifted in front of his eyes. Aage wore his hair swept back from his high forehead. This man wasn't wearing black robes, either, which she should have noticed first. In fact, he was wearing amber and scarlet. Like Jeyn. And the king. The family colors of the ruling house of Sitrine.

"Uh oh," she muttered.

Sene smiled down at her, then raised a hand in greeting. "Chasa!"

The prince quickened his pace. He was built like the king, if a bit more slender. The relation between father and son was apparent in several subtle details—the eyes, the dimpled smile, the way each man moved. But there were differences, too. Sene's warm eyes were surrounded by tiny laugh lines which were emphasized whenever he smiled, and he smiled often. He carried himself with complete self-assurance, a jovial bounce to his stride that was not quite a swagger. Reluctantly, Feather turned her attention to Chasa. The boy stopped in front of her, looking oddly surprised.

"It's Filanora," the king said in introduction.

As usual, she winced at the sound of her name. Chasa broke into a huge grin. "Feather!"

That was better. But spoken in his voice, the word produced a shudder. She pulled back slightly, scowling. "Your Highness," she responded coolly.

His smile faded. The king stepped into the conversation with a cheerful, "Hasn't grown much, has she?"

"Only more beautiful," the prince offered.

She had no intention of listening to any more of that. Not in that uncomfortably familiar, unfamiliar voice. "Your father wants me to look at some embroidery. Excuse me, please."

She escaped into the tent.

As midday approached, the entire village began to gather in the square. Tob looked for his parents. Jordy was easy to find, walking here and there around the square and collecting small children who had grown tired and restless with the long morning's wait. When he had gathered a sizable group, he led them to an unoccupied patch of ground in front of the inn. They surrounded him, smiles replacing their expressions of tedium as he began to juggle a variety of odds and ends he pulled out of his pockets. Pepper and Matti were right there in front, as though they couldn't enjoy their father's skill every day. Tob almost regretted being too old for that circle of children. Jordy said something and the group squealed with laughter. Nearby adults turned their heads and smiled.

The last few fisher folk hurried up the road from the river, and Herri came out of the inn. As the sun reached its highest point in the pale blue sky, Canis shooed the innkeeper onto the platform in the center of the square. Jordy dispersed his flushed and cheerful audience to find their parents. The villagers settled down on cloaks and blankets spread on the damp earth, rustling and murmuring like a great flock of birds.

When all was quiet, Herri spoke. "We are the Children of the Rock of the village of Broadford. Today is a day when all things are in balance with one another. We stand poised between the cold of winter and the warmth of summer. This reminds us to seek balance everywhere in our lives, misfortune balanced by happiness, death balanced by life." He turned slowly in place, projecting his voice equally to each side of the square. "The year has turned behind us. Things change. Let anyone who has experienced change since the Fall Festival stand and speak."

First on his feet was Shar, who had a farm on the river at the eastern edge of the village. Shar's grin gave away his news before he even opened his mouth. "We have a daughter!" he called happily. Approving smiles answered him from all sides. His wife tugged once on his tunic, then handed up a tiny bundle. Gingerly, he folded the blanket back from a tiny face then held the baby high for all to see. "This is Baisch," he announced. "Born a nineday ago, with Keyn at the full, Sheyn at first quarter, and Dreyn waning."

Tob folded his legs and laced his fingers around his knees. As soon as Baisch had been inspected to everyone's satisfaction, one of the fisherwomen bounced to her feet. Tob listened politely as several more births were announced. The Redmother's husband said a few words regarding his twins and his wife's illness. Their friends and neighbors were respectfully silent. Tob didn't know the family very well, but he felt sorry for the babies.

One by one, speakers continued to stand forth in front of their friends and neighbors with good news and bad. Then, to Tob's surprise he saw his father get up and beckon to someone seated on the ground near him. Iris's red hair appeared out of the crowd. Most of the villagers stared at the girl curiously. She stood pale and motionless at Jordy's side.

"This is Iris," his father announced simply. "She has been fostered into our family at the request of Greenmother Jenil. She will live with us as our eldest child from now until the day she chooses to leave and make her own home." He sat down. Iris stood a moment longer, turned so that she could be seen by the people behind them, and resumed her place on the ground. Tob caught a glimpse of Matti's smooth brown hair as his youngest sister climbed into Iris's lap.

The last person to stand before the village was Kessit. He announced the day and manner of Pross's departure. Hearing it announced openly in Festival ceremony brought frowns to many faces. Herri called for any final announcements, then invited the village to the yard of the inn for lunch.

Matti's firm grip on her hand was the only thing that stopped Vray from running off in a blind panic. As it was, she was forced to stay close to the child, who in turn was clutching Cyril's skirt in her other hand. Eldest child. By the Firstmother, Jordy had adopted her! *He doesn't know anything about me,* she thought in panicky wonder. Yet he had assumed parental responsibility for her in front of the entire village. Whatever she did was going to reflect back on them.

Gods, I'm not ready for this.

The inn yard was filled to overflowing with long trestle tables and hungry villagers. Tob appeared through the press of people, eyes shining, and grabbed his mother by the arm. "Come on, I know a shortcut."

Vray felt her free hand grabbed by Pepper. They snaked their way, Tob leading, between clumps of people, and eventually reached a narrow gap between a table and the inn wall. They squeezed through, the carter last, to find themselves virtually alone on that side of the table. Tob unashamedly helped himself to a choice bread roll and bit into it with enthusiasm. Vray found herself next to Tob as they moved along the amply laden table.

The boy finished his roll and grabbed another before moving on to a huge kettle of some sort of stew. Vray identified mushrooms floating on the steaming surface. It smelled delicious. Tob served himself, then passed her the ladle. "Which is your favorite?" he asked.

"Favorite?"

"Festival. Spring or Fall?"

With difficulty, Vray pictured the banquet hall in Edian: servants everywhere, and Damon laughing with his friends through Redmother Vissa's recitation. "I don't really have a preference."

Tob gave her a skeptical look. "Most people prefer the Fall. There's all the fresh food from the harvest. Dad and I usually try to get back with something interesting from southern Dherrica or the lake country." He sniffed at a pie, then took his knife from his belt and cut a large wedge which he somehow balanced on the edge of his bowl. "This is only half what we have in the Fall." He eyed her again. "If you like stews and soups and things, Spring's the better Festival."

"I enjoy all kinds of food." She would never take food for granted again. Not after Soza. Each family in Broadford had produced their best to share with their friends and neighbors. The precise sequence of events at a Festival varied from village to village, from kingdom to kingdom, but one element was never overlooked, the day-long feast. As Vray scanned the tables again she saw none of the delicacies that she would have seen at court, but she doubted she would miss them. At one end of the yard, Herri was overseeing a whole pile of barrels of cider and wine, his contribution to the festivities. On the table at his elbow was what looked suspiciously like an entire basket of fresh oranges.

"Well, besides food," Tob pressed on, "maybe you like the Fall Festival for the weather. It's usually perfect then. Warm during the day, cool at night. At Spring Festival it's cold and rainy, often as not."

"Which do you prefer?"

"Spring."

"After all those arguments you made for Fall?"

"Spring is about beginnings. It's exciting." They waited at the end of the table for Jordy and Cyril to finish helping the girls. "Now you choose," Tob insisted.

Vray matched his challenging tone. "Then I choose Fall, of course."

She didn't have time to defend her decision. A commotion rose among the people who'd already collected their food and moved out into the square. Voices shouted "Kessit!" and "Jaea!" A tall boy with wavy brown hair and a filthy tunic burst through the throng of people and paused at the edge of the yard.

"Pross!" Tob exclaimed. "It's Pross!"

Other voices repeated the cry. Jordy left Pepper in his wife's care and pushed his way toward the boy. Kessit appeared from the other side of the yard, calling his son's name. People stepped aside to let him pass. He reached Pross and enveloped him in a hug. The boy's mother and Jordy arrived simultaneously. At Jordy's urgings, the reunited family moved across the yard and through the door to the inn. Jordy, with Herri at his heels, followed them inside.

Excited chatter broke out around Vray. Her trained memory connected the names with the announcement made during the ceremony. "What has he done?" she demanded.

"Left the guards, that's what." Tob's proud smile chilled Vray. "Good old Pross. I knew he'd be back." His mother patted his arm, attracting his attention. He looked around, saw that Cyril needed help with the girls' food, and took one of the bowls.

They spread a cloth on one of the mounds of straw scattered around the square, and sat down to eat. Jordy rejoined them after only a few moments.

"Can I go see Pross?" Tob asked immediately.

"Wait yet a while. There'll be time enough after we've all eaten."

The carter said nothing more. Because there was nothing

to say. A boy was chosen for the guards and declined the honor. There was nothing disturbing in that. It would be different if he lived in Edian. It wasn't wise to defy guards there. But these were good people, and Damon's influence hadn't extended this far.

Thank the gods.

CHAPTER 21

Vray was oddly unsurprised when the minstrel appeared beside her during a break in the music. She looked up from her seat on the straw and was caught by a dimpled smile so infectious that she had to smile faintly back.

He offered her the blue-glazed cup in his hand. "Wine. Cool to the taste, warming as the gold sunlight of Sitrine. Brought by our carter friend for the occasion."

His glance flicked toward Cyril. "May I borrow your companion?"

Jordy's wife took no notice of him, and he turned his attention back to Vray.

No doubt it was Cyril's unresponsiveness that Ivey found disturbing. Vray knew it would bother her, if she made her living by her charm. The minstrel still held the cup before her face, so she took it and sipped cautiously. She'd been drunk twice, and hadn't liked it. Words had spilled out of her as if there wasn't room for them in her head anymore. She remembered reeling in circles, and the sound of mocking laughter, while whole family histories, mixed in with Mother tales and a year's worth of law reader judgments, tangled themselves together and got told to people who didn't care. Did Cyril have words trying to burst out of her? Did she long to communicate, but know of no way to free the words, even if she drank a barrel of wine? It didn't seem so. She didn't have to talk in order for her husband and children to understand her.

"Iris?" Ivey studied her, his expression thoughtful, as he spoke. "Canis will come looking for you any minute now. Will you walk with me first?"

"And talk with you?" She stood and let him lead her away from Cyril. "Since you know of my family."

"Since I know of your family," he agreed, then said

232

nothing else until they entered the shadows of the inn stable.

A horse nickered faintly, but they didn't seem to have any other company. Ivey scooped a handful of grain from a feedbag and offered it to the horse in the nearest stall. The animal's velvety lips covered his palm.

"It's Feast day, children. Plenty for everyone." He scooped up another handful and went to the next stall. Vray followed him. "I'm having trouble remembering 'Iris,' though I doubt I'll foolishly slip and call you Your Highness."

If he could come so directly to the point, so could she. "What are you asking for your silence, minstrel?" She raised her eyes to the stable loft. "I expect the straw is comfortable. To be honest, I've nothing but myself to offer." She also had no way to keep him from going to her brother, if that's what he decided to do.

Ivey turned to face her. The horse butted him with its head, and the minstrel steadied himself by grasping Vray's shoulders. She flinched, but he just pulled her closer, kissed her on the forehead, then let her go. "You flatter me, lass. But I don't think Jenil had me in mind as a lover for you."

This was not the conversation she had expected. "Jenil?"

"She brought you to this village so you'd find some sturdy farmer lad to make Dreamers with."

Vray sat down, rather abruptly, on a feed bin. "What?"

He flicked his curls behind his shoulder. "You know of Aage's prophecy, Redmother?"

Numbly, she nodded.

"I'm good at keeping secrets," he went on. "People seem to trust me, so I hear and see a great deal on my travels. King Sene told me the Greenmother wanted to find you, and I remembered a tale I'd heard of a red-haired Soza girl."

"I'm hardly the only red-haired girl in Rhenlan."

"Your pardon, Princess, but to be specific, a guard told me of a drunken girl he'd bedded, and how she told him his family history the whole time he was with her. He wanted to know if I sang the whole time I was with a woman. I told him, yes, but only with very ugly bed partners." His dry recitation did not force her to relive her humiliation. In fact, Vray found herself smiling, and wondered how he managed to make the incident seem amusing. "I could think of only one missing red-haired Redmother. I made my way to Soza to sing for the Brownmothers and guards and the dying and the orphans. Don't you remember? I was very entertaining, Highness."

"I heard talk of a minstrel. I didn't see you, though."

"A pity. I saw you. At least, I saw an underfed kitchen maid who bore a strong resemblance to Soza's senior Brownmother, and to the man in charge of the local border guard. Cousins or some other kin of yours, yes?"

Vray could only nod again.

"I didn't think it would be wise to actually try to speak to you, so I sent word to Jenil of your whereabouts—and she brought you here."

"To marry a Keeper?" Vray frowned.

"She didn't actually say that. It's just my guess. Maybe she just didn't want to see you wasting away at Soza. Broadford's a much nicer place to be. I hear they've already found a use for you."

Vray considered the cup in her hand, and the villagers she was about to face. She poured the wine on the stable floor. "Canis will be looking for me."

He offered her his hand and she took it. If he noticed that she was shaking, he gave no sign. But then, it was only natural that a seasoned performer like Ivey would recognize an attack of nerves.

Grateful for the minstrel's silent support, Vray allowed him to lead her out of the stable, toward her first public appearance as a Redmother in three years.

Vray stood before the villagers and tried not to see them. It helped to have Ivey, with his confident smile, in the front of the crowd. Canis sat in the front rank as well, arms crossed, pleased with herself for having saved the day. Vray looked past the fisherwoman to find Jordy's sandy head. His eyes were on her, as well. Everyone's eyes were on her. The whole village had gathered in the square. A patient, expectant silence grew as people found seats on the grass, silence soon to be broken by a crying child or teenage giggles, but complete silence for now. Vray concentrated her attention one moment longer on Jordy. His pale eyes seemed to bore into her, not in anger or disapproval, but with reassurance. She swallowed, close to tears, but her hands no longer shook.

She took a deep breath, then stooped over the three objects that waited on the inn steps: a bowl, a smooth stone, and a pitcher of water. She placed the stone in the center of the bowl, then poured water over it, enough to form a pool. As she straightened, she carefully chose her words. A Festival, of all days, was not a time for lies. "I am called Iris, of the town of Edian, Redmother student to Danta. I speak in place of Driss the Story of Beginnings.

"The world was formed as worlds are formed, in company with the sun and moons and planets and gods in the empty chaos between the stars. For centuries of centuries, the world remained young and barren, and the gods were lonely. So they Bent their power upon the fabric of the world, and the water, which has substance yet is malleable, brought forth life, plants and creatures of the sea which grew and multiplied and became many.

"Centuries of centuries passed, and the gods were lonely. So they Bent their power upon the fabric of the world, and the air, ever changing and limitless, acted upon the life of the water, encouraging greater growth and variety until the plants and the animals burst forth upon solid ground and spread across the world.

"Centuries of centuries passed. The world was fair and the gods were pleased, but still they were alone. As they journeyed across the world they saw that it was ignorant of its own marvels. This ignorance saddened the gods.

"At last they came to the mountains. In the mountains was a cavern. In the cavern was a pool. In the pool was a rock. For the third time, the gods Bent their power upon the fabric of the world, and the Rock, which is the foundation and the source upon which all else rests, and from which all else comes, brought forth a woman in the fullness of her maturity, heavy with child. The woman opened her eyes and looked upon the world, and the gods spoke to her, saying, 'Know the world and marvel in it.' She saw and understood and marveled.

"The woman gave birth upon the Rock in the midst of the pool within the cavern. She bore three children, and felt great joy, for they were beautiful, and she was eager for others with whom she could share her knowledge of the world.

"These are the children of the Firstmother, who are the Children of the Rock. The girl child grew to be the Keeper. Her delight was to maintain the land and the waters and the living creatures as they had always been, guarding against any mischance, keeping them in balance with one another. The boy child grew to be the Shaper. His delight was to examine the land and the water and the living creatures, discovering where unbalance disturbed the Keeper, and shaping any necessary change.

"The third child of the Firstmother, neither boy nor girl, grew to become the Dreamer. The Dreamer's greatest delight was to remember the land and the water and the living creatures as they had been through the centuries of centuries past, and to anticipate what they might be in the centuries of centuries yet to come. The Dreamer alone of the Children of the Rock could bend the power of the gods, using it for purposes suggested by the Keeper or the Shaper.

"The Firstmother was pleased with her children. Each was different from the others. None shirked responsibility. They came to their Mother and vowed before the Rock to be true to themselves, to keep or shape or dream as their gifts allowed. And the gods heard their vows and were satisfied.

"Now, the Children of the Rock loved one another. The

Firstmother and the Dreamer spent much time in conversation, as was fitting. She had been born to hunger after knowledge and wonder at it, and the Dreamer was capable of seeing and teaching much. The Keeper and the Shaper copulated together, as was fitting. They were female and male, after the manner of most living creatures, even though their differences prevented them from producing offspring. And the gods were pleased with their happiness.

"But time passed, and the Children of the Rock grew less content. They saw that the world was large and they were few in number. They feared greatly that they would be forced to break the vows they had made to keep and shape and dream.

"So the Firstmother went back to the pool and the Rock that had borne her, and contemplated within herself what was to be done. The years had taken her well beyond the time of child bearing, and her children were infertile. Understanding all this, she saw that there was no solution, and wept.

"The gods saw her sorrow and spoke to her, saying, 'Go back to your children. Tell them that if they have been true to their vows, their vows will not be broken.'

"The Firstmother did as the gods commanded. The next time the Shaper and the Keeper had intercourse with one another, the Keeper became pregnant. At the proper season she bore two children, a boy and a girl, who grew and matured after the fashion of their mother and became Keepers.

"Then the Keeper and the Shaper had intercourse once more. Once more the Keeper became pregnant. In the proper season she bore two more children, a boy and a girl, who grew and matured in the fashion of their father and became Shapers.

"The Keeper and the Shaper felt great joy in their children. The Keeper taught her son and daughter to maintain and guard the world. The Shaper taught his son and daughter to examine and change the world. The Keeper's children produced children who were Keepers after the fashion of their parents. The Shaper's children produced children who were Shapers after the fashion of their parents. And the gods were well pleased, for they saw that they would never be alone again.

"But the sorrow of the Firstmother continued, for her most beloved child was the Dreamer, and the Dreamer remained alone. She called her other two children to her, to see if one of them might give the Dreamer a child. But the Shaper could not impregnate the Dreamer, for the Dreamer was not female. The Keeper could not bear a child for the Dreamer, for the Dreamer was not male. So the Firstmother returned to the pool and the Rock that had borne her and contemplated within herself what was to be done.

"The gods saw the sorrow of the Children of the Rock. They spoke to the Firstmother, saying, 'We value the vows of the Dreamer and would not see them broken. Therefore we shall bend our power upon the Shaper and the Keeper a third time, and they shall bring forth a child for the Dreamer.'

" 'One child?' the First Mother asked.

" 'One child,' the gods affirmed. 'Dreamers need not be many, for they bend the power and live long lives.'

"The Firstmother returned to her children. The Keeper and the Shaper had intercourse with one another, and the Keeper became pregnant. In the proper season the Keeper bore a child, neither Shaper or Keeper, a girl but not female, who grew and matured with the gifts of the Dreamer.

"The Children of the Rock increased in number and spread over the world. Keepers guarded it and Shapers guided it and Dreamers envisioned it, according to their vows. The Keepers were fertile among themselves and produced many children and became numerous. The Shapers were fertile among themselves and produced sufficient children for their needs, and lived among the more numerous Keepers as their helpers and guides.

"A Shaper child and a Keeper child may love one another, but they are not fertile together. Only in every third generation do the gods Bend their power over certain unions, to produce children for the Dreamers. Only then will a child be born, boy or girl according to the will of the gods, who will grow and mature to become a bender of the power among the Dreamers."

Vray fell silent. No one stirred. The stillness was complete. She could believe that even the gods were listening, remembering how it had been. Vray's heart pounded in her ears, but with relief, not fear. She had not forgotten her training. She had not embarrassed herself before the people of Broadford.

"This is as it has always been for the Firstmother's Children. This is as it always will be. The Story of Beginnings is our story. We are the Children of the Rock."

CHAPTER 22

The afternoon was devoted to games, gossip, and return visits to the food-laden tables in the inn yard. There were races and contests of every variety. The young women, and not a few of the matrons, exchanged their pretty skirts for loose trousers, the better to compete.

Ivey remained on the sidelines, the better to observe the carter's daughter. The exiled princess was among a limited number of nonparticipants. Jordy's wife sat on the side of the square, embroidering a fine, russet-colored tunic and keeping a watchful eye on the family's youngest daughter, Matti. Vray—Iris—stayed beside her. As far as Ivey could tell, she seemed content. She watched Pepper and another girl win a relay race from the platform in the square to Kessit's woodshop and back again. Tob and the other boys and girls his age played a game that had the two teams scattered around the village for much of the afternoon.

Some of the adult games of skill were very well played. Ivey knew of good darts throwers in Bronle and Edian who would have had difficulty scoring higher than Jordy, who only lost in the final round, to Herri. The carter tried his hand at several games, doing well without winning until the end of the day, when archery targets were set at the far end of the square. The archers, Jordy among them, lined up close to Cyril and a crowd gathered to watch. The carter's performance was flawless. The reaction of the rest of the villagers indicated that this was considered normal. The real competition had been between the others, for second place.

The contests ended at dusk. Tob and his friends returned from their game, hungrier than ever. Torches were set out, and the corner of the square nearest the inn was cleared for dancing. Pepper came over to where her mother was sitting. Cyril folded her embroidery and put it away, then led Iris and the child back to the inn.

Ivey joined the crowd of people in the inn yard. He inched past burly farmers and chattering youngsters until he was standing beside Iris.

"I hope some of that's for you," Ivey said.

The princess jumped at his voice, and nearly dropped the bowl she had been filling. The little girl with her didn't notice, just continued to chatter as she tugged Iris along the serving table. Ivey slowed, hating the fear he saw. She'd done well with the Story of Beginnings, and he'd seen her laughing at least once with the carter's stocky son. She seemed comfortable in the presence of Jordy and Cyril, if not relaxed, but now he'd caught her away from that security, and the fear was there again.

"This is Pepper's bowl," she said.

Around them, other people moved leisurely past the tables, some in search of food, others more interested in Herri's kegs of ale and wine.

"Iris!" Pepper tugged on her skirt. "I don't like cabbage!"

"Well, maybe Iris likes cabbage." Ivey moved up beside them, took the serving spoon from the princess's hand, and held some of the pale vegetable over the bowl. "Do you like cabbage?"

"Yes, but . . ."

"Then have some cabbage."

"That's my bowl," Pepper complained.

"Share with your sister," Ivey shot back. The child scowled, then reluctantly acquiesced.

"Just don't get any on my bread." She pulled Iris's hand down so that she could reach into the bowl and rescue a square of raisin loaf.

"There. What else would you like?" Deftly taking the bowl, Ivey ushered the princess ahead of him along the table. "You need some meat. Is this goose? Goose is good, especially if Herri provided the stuffing. He does a wonderful sage stuffing."

Pepper, with a disgusted look at Ivey, took her bread and

wandered off. Iris almost followed her; would have, if Ivey had not taken a firm grip on her elbow.

"Pretty girls need to eat," he told her.

"I've eaten already today."

"People eat more than once a day." He kept his tone gentle, despite an urge to stride off at once and strangle the entire population of the Brownmother House at Soza. "Are you hungry?"

She had to think about it. "Yes."

"Then eat." He piled some goose in the bowl, reached for a slice of honey-cake, then chose one of the last of the northern oranges for himself. "This is a Festival. We're supposed to feast."

"True." She accepted the bowl from him and bit into the honey-cake. "I'd forgotten. I never went to the Festivals at Soza."

"Soza?"

The voice behind them did not sound pleased. Ivey turned to find Jordy watching them, the ever-present mug of cider in his hand. "Soza? Did you say you were at Soza, m'girl? Living at Soza?"

Ivey caught the bowl as it dropped from her hand, and set it on the table beside them. What good humor the princess had been enjoying vanished in an instant. The way she lowered her head, body tense, he expected her to make a run for it. She'd been taught too well how to react to displeasure.

"Yes," she whispered.

"Your family sent you to Soza?" Jordy insisted. "Why? What did you do?"

She shrank further. "I was sent, yes, because . . . I was . . . I had . . ."

"Trouble at home," Ivey finished for her.

As he'd hoped, Jordy turned his indignation away from the princess. "You know all about this, I suppose? You seem to know everything else about her. Certainly more than that Greenmother saw fit to tell me, and I can guess why. I've got young children, too young to be threatened by the sort of violent troublemakers who have to be sent to Soza. Rock and Pool, how dare she put innocent children at risk for the sake of someone else's failure!"

"Someone else's!" Ivey yelled back. People around them backed away, staring. "Not half a day has passed since you made a vow to take this child as your—"

"I know what I vowed! I don't regret the vow. I resent the lies!"

"Jenil hasn't lied to you!"

"She obviously didn't tell me the truth!"

"You want the truth?"

With a strangled whimper, Iris grabbed Ivey's arm, pulling him frantically away from Jordy. Tears leaked out of the corners of her eyes. "Please! No!"

"You have nothing to be ashamed of!" He did not allow her to drag him a single inch. The entire village was listening now, just as they'd listened to the songs and tales of the afternoon. Having an audience calmed Ivey. He had to say something, and fast, to put Jordy's suspicions to rest. "And you, carter, know less of Soza than you seem to think you know!"

"Do I indeed?"

"You do. People nobody wants are sent there, true. That says less than you think about why they are unwanted. Yes, some of them are uncontrollable, perhaps on the brink of becoming Abstainers. But some are just unloved. Unwanted not for any lack in them, but for lack of proper feeling in their parents, their families. Iris's family did not know love. Husband and wife didn't love each other. They don't even live together. Her brother thinks nothing of Iris, except as a rival for their parents' inheritance. She was sent away because she was an inconvenience. The father didn't care. The mother wasn't there at all.

"So the girl lived in Soza for years, her Redmother talent going to waste. Somehow Jenil found out about her, and brought her here. Here, where Jenil thought she might be wanted at last. To a family where Jenil thought there was understanding, and caring, and love. Of course, knowing how you feel about Greenmothers, I suppose you consider that wrong."

Iris had stopped crying in blank amazement at Ivey's impassioned—and brilliantly misleading—speech. He only watched her peripherally, however. Jordy was the one he needed to convince. A buzz of comment rose from some of the nearby villagers. Ivey ignored that, as well.

The carter's expression became thoughtful, and he took a step toward Iris. "I shouldn't have lost my temper, lass. He's right. I don't know enough about Soza to judge it, or you. I'm sorry." He put a hand on her shoulder. Ivey half-expected Iris to cringe away, even scream in terror, but to his surprise and the carter's evident satisfaction she moved closer to him. Jordy's arm went around her shoulders. He kept her at his side as he turned back to Ivey.

"Even Jenil is entitled to the occasional correct guess. Iris will have all our love. All our understanding, if we're told what there is to understand. There's no fear of her being unwanted. Not anymore." He gave her shoulder a squeeze. "But what about those parents? That brother?" His voice grew angry once more. "Did the Greenmother give any thought to them? Edian isn't so far away. Does their law reader know that they sent away a perfectly blameless child for their own convenience?"

"Edian knows." Ivey tried not to let panic change the timbre of his voice. It would be just like this man to go storming right up to the king's gates, demanding justice for his new daughter.

"I don't want to see them again." Iris's voice was soft but very sure. "I don't want to see them at all. They aren't my family. My life is mine, not any concern of theirs."

"Are you sure, lass?" Jordy looked down at her. "I'm often in Edian."

"It's been three years. They won't even remember me." Her voice fell further. "And I don't want to remember them."

Seeing that the shouting was over, most of the people grouped around them began to drift away. With a certain

244

amount of resignation, Jordy said, "We'll leave it, then. If that's what you want."

"Thank you."

Ivey clapped his hands together once and announced, "Time for dancing!" Several young people took up the shout, and ran to fetch instruments or partners. Jordy reached behind Iris for the bowl of food and pressed it into her hands, then walked with her toward the square. Left alone, Ivey gazed gratefully at the earth. *Thank you, gods, for letting me distract a very stubborn man.*

He went to find his guitar.

"Well, carter."

Jordy glanced up at the greeting. "Well, innkeeper," he countered. Herri stepped over the bench and sat down, a large cup of wine in each hand. He passed one to Jordy.

"It's been a fine day for it."

"Aye." Jordy took a swallow of wine. In front of them a new dance began. Young Pross had recovered enough from his adventure with the guards to take a turn on the drum. Farther along the square, Ivey stood in the flickering light of three or four torches, gesturing broadly as he told some tale or another to a circle of fascinated children. Villagers stood or sat in small groups around the square. When there was a pause in the dancing, snatches of talk and laughter could be heard from every direction. Keyn, just passing full, added her gentle illumination to the scene.

"Your Iris is a quiet one." Herri nodded toward the girl, hiding as she had been most of the day in the shadow of Cyril's silence. "You can't tell what she thinks of our Festival. Is she still frightened of you?"

"Can you blame her? Soza's the last place a child would learn to trust an adult. At least she gets on well with Tob and the girls."

"Give her a few ninedays, Jordy. She'll settle in."

"I haven't that much time." Jordy finished the wine and set the cup between his feet for safekeeping. "Tob and I have to get back on the road."

The dance ended with a trill from the flutes, a crash from the drum, and an exuberant shout from the dancers. In the lull that followed, other, fainter sounds carried clearly through the night air. Jordy stiffened.

"What is it?" Herri asked.

"Horses."

Around the square, conversations died and heads turned in the direction of the road. Herri's black brows knotted in puzzlement. "Who would be abroad on a Festival night?"

The blacksmith, still panting from the exertion of the dance, looked toward Herri in alarm. "Not Abstainers!"

The riders cantered into the square from the north road. Pale Keyn-light reflected off the metal they wore, helmets, ring-sewn leather vests, and forearm guards. The leader wore not leather, but chain mail. Their equipment and the cut of their tunics made them immediately identifiable. King's guards.

They did not slow. The surprised silence at such an unexpected interruption gave way to shouts and curses. Nearby adults snatched up children, their own or anyone's, and hurried with them toward the wall of the inn. Others tried to wave the onrushing horses away as they would a herd of panicked sheep. The horses, trained to fight, came on without pause, and farmers and fishers scattered to avoid being trampled.

Jordy counted eight guards in the square. Four others waited with the pack animals and spare mounts at the entrance to the north road. Herri leapt to his feet as one of the riders bore down on the dance square. Ignoring angry shouts to keep clear, the guard jumped his horse into the ring of benches, its hooves narrowly missing heads as people ducked out of the way. He pulled his horse to a stop in front of the musicians, and turned back toward the rest of the guards.

"Here, sir!" the guard called.

Three other riders began to close on the dance area. Jordy pushed past the innkeeper and under the nose of the horse to grab Pross by the elbow. In a low voice, he said,

"Run, boy," and pushed him in the direction of the river.

A boot planted between Jordy's shoulder blades sent him sprawling. He rolled away from the thudding hooves, heard people scatter all around him. He bumped into an overturned bench and scrambled to his feet. Herri had grabbed the first horse by the bridle. Two mounted guards bore down on the running Pross. Kessit's outraged cry carried above the confused shouting. "Stop them!"

The rider in the middle of the dance area drew his sword. "Let go, or I'll remove your hand from your arm."

"You have no right here," Herri told him. "You should be at home with your families."

The young guard laughed. Pross's pursuers caught his arms and lifted him from the ground. They slowed their horses to a walk and turned back toward the square, the boy struggling in mid-air between them.

Another guard urged his mount toward Herri. Onlookers fell back at the sight of the naked sword ready in his hand. "Don't be a fool," he said. "We have any right we choose to take."

Ivey took one look at the reckless approach of the leading guard and turned away to quickly scan the crowded square for that distinctive red hair. Where was she? Jenil would skin him if Vray was caught, and leave what was left for Sene. He had seen the girl just a few minutes ago!

People were scuffling in the dancing ring. Herri's voice carried, although the words were indecipherable in the general noise. Too many horses jostled each other and threatened the people around them. Ivey remembered where he'd seen the girl, sitting near Jordy's silent wife on a bench against the smithy wall, a quarter of the way around the square from the dancing ring. Keeping close to the wall of the inn yard, he started in that direction, and broke into a run as soon as he could.

He was the only one moving away from the disturbance. A few parents had scooped up children, but curiosity and concern drew everyone closer to the group of riders. He almost missed seeing the tall princess. The diffident girl of the tale-telling had disappeared. She was pale, but the tension in her was not fear. She was furious, and she intended to do something.

He snagged one arm around the girl's waist and dragged her back against the inn yard wall. "Hold it!" he growled in her ear.

She snapped her head to the right, meeting his eyes. The expression in hers was nearly enough to wither him. "Let go of me!" she shouted.

"Don't do it, girl."

Her body went stiff against him. "They have no right to do this. I'm going to stop it!"

"You can't."

"Let me go and I will!"

"How? Who do you think you are? Who would they think you are?"

She blinked. "What?"

Confusion caused her to stop resisting him, long enough for him to pull her the rest of the way into the yard. Once behind the wall, they were out of sight of the square, out of the view of any guard who might glance their way. A guard who might notice a red-haired woman, or remember her later.

"Are you really going to command that troop to cease what they're doing?"

"I have to." Now she sounded more confused than determined. Her anguished gaze turned toward the sound of raised voices, the harsh laughter. "The boy belongs here. He's their only son. Dael would never . . ."

"Send the guard out to steal children? Perhaps not, but that's not your concern. Do you want to repeat the last three years?" She shuddered and, abruptly, leaned against him. He spoke rapidly. "Jenil could have brought you to Edian, you know. She would have, if she thought you could help by being there. She chose to bring you here. Whatever her reasons, she means you no harm. Stay safe, Vray. Trust us. Stay here with me until the guards are gone."

Her protest was weak, barely a whisper. "But they need me."

He patted her shoulder. "These are good people. Strong. They can take care of themselves."

Jaea tried to throw herself at one of the horsemen who held her son. Kessit stopped her. "The boy doesn't want to serve in the guards. Leave him alone!"

"No one asked what he wants. No one's going to ask what any of you want," the rider shot back.

Jordy tried to catch the eye of some of the villagers nearest him. Any moment now, someone would notice that they outnumbered the guards four to one. Jordy could just imagine the unplanned rush against the intruders, and the bloody results. He finally got Herri's attention, and signaled frantically for him to step back.

The leader of the guards was also aware of his position. He raised his voice. "We serve the king. So does this boy. So does anyone we choose. Interfere at your peril." He turned his head toward the edge of the square. "Torch!" he yelled.

Grinning, two of his men snatched up the nearest torches. One rode for the smithy, the other for the inn. Other guards grabbed yet more torches and swept toward their chosen targets.

The diversion worked perfectly. Children screamed as flaming brands flew over their heads to bounce off the walls of the inn and roll under wooden tables. Herri released his captive with a curse. Five riders piled their torches, and branches torn from nearby trees, against the wide wooden doors of the smithy, which began to smolder. At the inn, dried flowers and gaily colored decorations burst into flame.

For most, the choice was automatic. Everyone knew how to deal with fire. The villagers scattered, not out of fear of the guards, but to fetch water. Pross was swung up in front of one of his captors. Another rider thundered close behind Kessit and Jaea and tumbled them to the ground. The rest

threw torches high into the branches of the trees surrounding the square, where they caught and flickered omi-
nously.

Herri bellowed instructions. Canis knelt beside Jaea and
Kessit. At the smithy, Lannal formed a chain of villagers
and buckets between his well and the burning door. Jordy
found Tob beside him. "Rope from Herri's stable. Be
quick. We have to get into those trees before the fire
spreads."

Tob ran off. Jordy hurried to find some agile assistants
and a few hatchets. He spared no further thought for the
king's guards, who cantered off into the night.

By the time the fires were extinguished, the doors to the
smithy were gone, along with their frame and part of an adjacent wall. At the inn, the yard was a shambles of charred
wood and trampled food. One outer wall was scorched, but
the rest of the building was undamaged. The trees around
the square still stood. Rocks, well thrown by Jordy, had dislodged most of the torches before they could catch among
the green new leaves. A trio of oaks on the east side of the
square lost the entire upper portions of their crowns, thick
with last summer's tinder-dry dead leaves. Villagers had
climbed as high as they could to chop away the burning
branches and stop the fire spreading to neighboring trees,
while people below extinguished the fallen brands.

People left for their homes and farms, neighbors walking
with neighbors. Jordy found his wife and children near the
inn. Iris and Cyril were seated on a blackened bench, Matti
stretched out beside them with her head in her mother's
lap. Tob and Pepper were on the ground, Jordy's cloak
thrown over them. Keyn, now high overhead, lit Cyril's expression clearly.

"A few more minutes," Jordy told his wife. "I'll just look
in on Herri."

He passed through the ruined yard, stepping over or
around puddles and debris. In the main room, Herri sat
slumped at a table. The minstrel stood nearby, bare-

chested, wiping soot from his face with the lower edge of his damp tunic.

"It could have been worse," Jordy told them. "At least no one was hurt."

"Not hurt?" Ivey complained. He lifted an imaginary bucket of water and groaned. "My arms may never recover."

Herri snorted wearily. "Don't expect sympathy from him. A few hundred buckets of water would mean nothing to you, would they, carter?"

Jordy lowered himself into a chair. "They may have meant the difference between saving or losing this inn, or the entire village. We owe you our thanks, minstrel."

"You shouldn't have needed such help. This should never have happened."

"The worst of it was letting them ride out of here with the boy." Herri's great fists clenched on the table. "When do you leave for Edian, Jordy? You'll have to carry our grievance to the law reader. Not just for Kessit and Jaea, but for all of us."

"Don't expect too much," Ivey said. "The men who were here tonight may be conveniently unknown in Edian."

"D'ye see, Herri? It's as I've said before. We can't look to Shapers to solve our problems."

"It's one thing to fight a fire. It's another to expect villagers to stand against the king's guard. You saw what happened tonight."

A gloomy silence settled over the room. Ivey said, quite casually, "I would think it's a matter of planning. Organization. Your people aren't helpless. They defend their families and property from bears in the fall, and wolves in the winter."

"Our fellow Keepers aren't marauding animals to be hunted down, no matter how they might behave," Herri said.

Jordy pursed his lips thoughtfully. "It's not a question of killing, necessarily." He had not liked feeling helpless, and his fingers had itched for his bow. "If a few of our best ar-

251

chers had slipped away in the first confusion, gone onto the roof here, or into the shadows of the trees, we would have controlled the square."

"As if anyone could have imagined such a thing," Herri said.

"Proper leadership," Ivey said. "That's what's needed."

Jordy eyed the two men. "What about discipline? Instant obedience. There's no time for questions when a crisis comes."

"You're respected, Jordy," Ivey said. "You'll find that people listen to you. Besides, I've no fears for Broadford." His pointed emphasis on the name was unmistakable, his implication clear.

"I agree. We can't ignore the rest of Rhenlan. The other Shapers won't object to Hion's abuse of power. They've found too many ways to profit from it, their responsibilities forgotten or ignored. Until every town, every village in Rhenlan takes control of its own affairs, defies the abuses of the king, things will only get worse."

Herri lowered his gaze to the table. Ivey's quiet voice said, "You're suggesting revolution."

"Aye. Do you not agree with me, Herri?"

Herri sighed as he met his gaze. "I agree with you. And may the gods protect us all."

CHAPTER 23

The minstrel looped his pony's lead rope around his hand as they approached the ford. "The law reader in Edian is a good man," Ivey said.

"He's a Shaper."

"Those two qualities aren't mutually exclusive, you know."

Jordy grunted. It was the morning after the Festival, time for the minstrel to be on his way. He'd asked Jordy to accompany him out of the village. "In your opinion," Jordy answered the younger Dherrican. He forestalled a lecture on the perils of generalization by adding, "Which I respect. You don't have to tell me my business, laddie. I'm not prejudging the man. He may be honest, aye, and conscientious. What I'm doubting is his influence."

"King Hion wouldn't keep a law reader if he wasn't making some use of him."

They reached the bank of the river. The first snow melt in the mountains far to the west was just beginning to be noticeable in the behavior of the Broad. The waters were still placid, but they had risen several inches in as many days. Ripples marked the location of most of the flat stones of the ford; the chatter of the water was loud enough to force them to raise their voices.

"Using him to placate the ignorant," Jordy said. "Well, I won't have it."

Ivey stopped and turned toward him. "This wasn't an isolated incident. He'll have heard other stories like yours."

"And done nothing. I told you what they're saying in Cross Cove."

"Dissatisfaction is growing everywhere, Jordy. Even in Edian itself."

Jordy studied the minstrel's serious face, then gave a reluctant nod. "Even in the court itself?"

"Aye." Ivey urged the pony into the water. "Should I wait for you in Atade?"

"Not this year. You might wait a long time. I'm going to be in and out of Broadford to keep an eye on the girl." The minstrel looked surprised. Jordy shrugged. "There's no help for it. If my usual customers can't wait for me, they'll just have to find someone else."

"I'll pass the word. As for the king's guard, if I learn anything that I think might interest you I'll leave messages where I can."

"Good. I'll be listening."

Ivey waded across the river beside his pony. "Travel safely, carter," he called in farewell.

"And you." The younger man raised a hand in acknowledgment without looking back.

Jordy stayed on the river bank until Ivey and the pony were safely across and had disappeared into the thick woods on the other side. Then he started back for the village square. He had several people to visit this afternoon if he and Tob were to get off to an early start in the morning.

Frost silvered the roof of stable and goat shed, glistened treacherously on each blade of grass, but his exertions warmed Tob as he helped his father load the wagon in the pale, clear dawn. Stockings's breath drifted gently upward as she waited patiently, undisturbed by the thuds, rattles, and creaking going on a few feet behind her. Jordy paused occasionally in his arrangement of the crates, rolls, and parcels to visually measure the space remaining and compare it to the piles of goods still to be loaded. Sometimes he asked Tob's opinion, not because he needed advice, but to test his apprentice's eye and memory. When he could, Tob waved to Matti, who watched wide-eyed from the window. Pepper was still asleep. She didn't like to get up early, and she didn't like to say good-bye.

Iris came out of the house, her arms barely long enough to manage Cyril's largest wicker hamper. Tob lifted the last sack of feed onto the tailboard of the wagon, then helped the girl place the hamper next to it. Jordy lashed the final barrel into place before coming to examine the hamper.

"Cyril wants you to take it," Iris offered diffidently.

Jordy lifted the lid. "Extra honey, good. And grape jam. Surprised your mother parted with that. I suppose we can trade it."

"Dad!" Tob protested.

"Just teasing, lad. Thank you, Iris. I see you're learning to understand Cyril."

"I suppose so." She fidgeted with the handle on one side of the hamper. "Jordy?"

"Yes, lass?" He closed the hamper and fastened it. When Iris didn't continue, Jordy sat down on a crate. "Now, you're not still worried, are you? I know Matti's hardly more than a baby, but Pepper's a good girl. She'll be company for you. And when you need someone older to talk to, Canis would welcome a visit anytime. You remember where their house is."

"Jordy?" Iris repeated, as though she hadn't been listening to a word he said. "May I ask a favor?"

Tob shifted his feet. At this rate, Iris was going to dither half the morning away. A band of pink stretched along the horizon now, brightest in the east. The last stars had faded to invisibility behind the growing lightness of the sky. At the bottom of the hill the birdsong from the hedgerow had risen to clamorous levels. If they didn't leave soon, they'd never reach their usual first campsite by nightfall.

Jordy gave no sign that he was aware of the impending sunrise, the miles to be traveled, Tob's existence, or anything other than the girl who struggled to look him in the face. "If I can," he told her. "What is it?"

"Broadford needs . . . that is . . . Canis says . . . since my aunt, actually my cousin—" She bit her lip and started again, the words finally tumbling out in a coherent order. "If Driss dies, Broadford will have no Redmother and that's not right. I have the training. Let me spend some time with her. Let me become the new Redmother. Canis says there's no one else. I won't let it interfere with what needs to be done here. I can get up early, or work after the rest of the family's in bed if that's what it takes, but I really should spend as much time as I can with Driss, as long as she's strong enough to talk, to learn the village history—"

As soon as she paused for breath, Jordy said, "Iris." She flinched, although Tob saw no reason for it. His father wasn't angry, just anxious to get a word in while he could. "I approve."

She looked at him as though he'd said something complicated. "You do?"

"Aye. It's a fine idea. Herri asked me if you would consider it, but I told him you might need time to become comfortable with us before committing yourself. Being Redmother can be a big responsibility."

The girl slowly—very slowly as far as Tob was concerned—absorbed a few fragments of meaning from Jordy's words. "The innkeeper thought of me? He doesn't know me."

"He heard your Story of Beginnings at the Festival. We all did." Jordy's exasperation finally broke through. "Stones, girl, this isn't Soza. No one's going to stop you doing what you do best. I'm not going to insist that you muck out the chicken coop or reshingle the stable roof if you're ready and able to use your Redmother skills instead. Neither is Cyril. Don't imagine you have to work all day and half the night to please her. Ask Tob here."

"Mom's very independent," Tob assured her. Then he glanced involuntarily to his right. The first sliver of sun peaked over the horizon and began to expand.

Iris caught the direction of his gaze and looked guilty. "I'm sorry. I'm keeping you. I should have mentioned this earlier."

"You're not keeping us." Jordy pushed to his feet. "Anything left?" he asked Tob.

"The bedrolls, and Stockings's grooming kit."

Jordy jumped down from the wagon. "Iris will help you. I'm going to talk to your mother."

Tob didn't really need any help, but he led Iris into the

stable and allowed her to carry the sturdy sack of grooming supplies back to the wagon. Tob stowed the sack and bedrolls near the hamper, raised the tailboard, and hooked it in place. "Well," he said to the silently watching Iris. "That's that."

The door of the house swung open, and Matti tore across the yard. Jordy followed, Pepper clinging to his back with her arms around his neck and her bare legs jutting out past his waist.

"I want to go with you as far as the square," Pepper said as Jordy reached the wagon, turned around, and deposited her on the footrest below the driver's seat.

"No."

"You've got chores," Tob reminded her.

"It's too cold for bare feet," was Matti's helpful comment.

"You could run and get my shoes," Pepper suggested to her little sister.

Tob hugged the two little girls, one after the other, without interrupting their conversation.

Matti smiled up at Jordy and held out her arms. "I love you, Daddy."

"My wee mischief maker," Jordy told her as he swung her into his arms. "You've two sisters to listen to now. That's twice the work, you know."

"I can do it," Matti answered with unshakable confidence.

Jordy put her down, received a fierce hug from Pepper, and firmly disentangled himself from her. "Off you go, now."

Pepper looked down from the wagon, appalled. "My feet will freeze!"

"Now, Pepper."

Iris stepped closer. "I could carry you," she suggested.

Pepper considered the distance back to the house, considered the set to Jordy's jaw, smiled brightly, and said, "Thank you," as she clambered onto Iris's back. They moved away from the wagon, Matti trotting after them.

Jordy took Stockings's lead rope in his hand.

"G'dup," he told the horse. Over his shoulder he said, "We'll see you in a few ninedays."

"Bye, Daddy!"

"Bye, Tobble!"

Stockings leaned into the harness and the wagon began to roll. Tob followed it, walking backwards a few paces to wave to his sisters. He caught a glimpse of his mother watching in the doorway and waved at her, too. One of the cats emerged from the stable, blinked in the sunlight, and stretched. Matti went toward it. Iris started to carry Pepper back to the porch.

Tob turned around and ran to catch up with the wagon.

The attic was very quiet. Vray knew she was only imagining it, but the house seemed to echo with emptiness in the absence of the carter and his son.

A small voice spoke in the darkness. "Iris, are you asleep?"

"No, not yet."

"We're glad you're here. Me and Matti. It used to always be lonely when Tob was away."

"Thank you. I miss him, too."

"Iris, do you know any stories?"

"A few," she admitted. Her training as a Redmother had begun when she was younger than Pepper. As far as she knew, Vissa had told her every story that there was. Much of the oral and written tradition and history of a dozen kingdoms was stored in her memory.

"Will you tell us one?"

"You're supposed to be going to sleep."

Rustling noises came from the direction of the little girls on their bed. "Just one or two. Please?"

Vray relented. "About what?" She sat up and clasped her arms around her updrawn knees. A scuffle in the darkness warned her just before two small bodies joined her on her bed.

"Monsters," Matti announced immediately. "One we've never heard of before."

"You've heard of dragons?" Vray asked.

"Lots of times."

"Wind demons?"

"They're boring," Pepper complained.

"How about fire bears?"

The suggestion earned her an enthusiastic "Oooh," from her audience.

Pepper said, "I've never even heard of a fire bear. Where do they live?"

"There aren't any anymore. Originally they lived only to the north of here. But for a while there were some as far south as White Water, and all through the Dherrican Mountains."

"What did they do?" Pepper asked.

"Why aren't there any anymore?" Matti added.

"Tell us about one."

Vray rocked thoughtfully on the base of her spine. "I can tell you a couple of short stories about long-ago heroes who killed fire bears, or I could tell you one kind of long story about the last fire bear. Which will it be?"

"The long story," Matti replied instantly.

"All right," Pepper conceded.

"Fire bears lived along the seacoast of Rhenlan for centuries of centuries," Vray began. "They were taller than any other bear that ever was. Taller even than the gray bears of the cold south in Dherrica. They had no fear of the Children of the Rock. Usually they hunted alone, but sometimes a whole pack would attack a village and the people would have to find ways to fight them off until the nearest king could send a brave Shaper hero to kill them."

"Why were they called fire bears?" Matti interrupted.

"Because the tiniest bite or scratch from one of them would burn like fire. Even a small injury could kill a person."

"What did they eat?" Pepper asked.

"What does any monster like to eat?" Vray answered question for question.

"Us?" Matti asked.

"That's right. Now, let me go on. A time came when people noticed that fire bears were beginning to change. From one summer to the next, Keepers and Shapers all through the kingdoms found hundreds and hundreds of dead bodies of old fire bears, and tracks of a new, smaller sort of fire bear. At first, the Shapers and Keepers who usually had to fight them thought this was a good idea. But the Dreamers warned that it wasn't right. Some evil magic was working, and the gods were displeased."

"Who was working the evil magic?" Pepper asked.

"The Dreamers say we have enemies outside the world who are always trying to find a way in."

"Everybody knows that," Matti complained.

Pepper was not satisfied. "How can there be anything outside the world? The world is the world."

"I don't understand it either," Vray said. "But monsters aren't like other animals, are they? The wind demons don't even have bodies."

"Maybe they're just bad weather," Pepper suggested.

"You wouldn't think so if you felt one," Vray told her.

"I want to hear the story," Matti said.

Pepper remained silent, so Vray continued, "Soon Shapers and Keepers, children and adults, began to die. The medicines that Brownmothers could use had no effect. All of the Greenmothers spent days and days trying to heal people. Then the Dreamers began to die, too. Finally the wizard Herfin realized that a new sickness had come into the world."

"I've heard this," Pepper interrupted excitedly. "Wizard Herfin is the one who discovered the plague, and Greenmother Gavea is the one who cured it."

"That's basically right," Vray said. "But I'm telling you a more complicated version. Should I keep going? Or isn't it interesting?"

"Keep going," Matti said. "I want to know what happened to the fire bears."

"The new sickness came from the fire bears. Many, many of the Children died before Herfin discovered that the

260

droppings of the fire bear could put the illness into the soil or the water, and from there into us. Not everyone who had the illness, the plague, died. Some became very sick. Some didn't become sick at all. But very often, when it was time for them to have children, the children died."

"Not all the children," Pepper said. "Otherwise we wouldn't be here."

"That's right. But in many cases, a husband and wife watched four or five or six children die before they finally had one who survived. Most of the Greenmothers were concentrating on helping those who fell sick to recover. It was Gavea who saw that the only way to remove the threat from the Children was to completely eliminate the fire bears."

"Is that why people like Herri don't have any brothers or sisters?" Pepper asked.

"Probably."

"Did the wizards kill the fire bears?" Matti wanted to know.

"The wizards helped, but there weren't very many of them left. It was time for a new generation of Dreamers, but few children of any kind were being born. With so many Keepers dying, many places in Rhenlan and central Dherrica could no longer produce enough food to feed their own people. Some Keeper families moved south, away from the fire bears' influence, only to die of the cold. Whole Shaper families disappeared. Those that remained began to fight over who would rule certain areas. But Gavea went to Sitrine and told the newest of the Dreamers, Aage, what needed to be done. Aage took the best of the kings' guards and they went from village to village all along the great sea, across the plains north of Edian, through the forests surrounding Long Pine, in and out of the foothills of every range of the Dherrican Mountains, finding and killing fire bears."

"How long did it take?" Pepper asked solemnly.

"Sixty years," Vray replied just as solemnly.

"Not with the same guards!" Matti protested.

"No. Of course not. It took many, many people, and all

261

of Aage's magic, to do such a thing. But finally, Gavea and Aage knew that only one fire bear remained. It lived in the ruins of an empty village on the edge of a great marsh. Aage took two archers and a swordsman named Hion, and they sailed west along the coast, because it was the height of summer and the northern swamps were impassable. Twice they were almost swallowed by sea monsters. Once they had to go ashore so that Hion could slay a dragon, which had been flying after them. When they finally reached the fire bear's lair, Hion coaxed it out, using himself as bait. Its claws scratched him and he was sick for a very long time. But while he was fighting it, the archers were able to shoot it with arrow after arrow until finally one of the arrows pierced its eye and brain and killed it. That was in the year that Prince Damon was born. It marked the beginning of the end of the plague."

"What does that mean?" Pepper asked. "Beginning of the end?"

"Anything that doesn't end all at once has to start ending somewhere. The plague was spread by the bears; spread very far. Sickness appeared in some villages years after a bear had been nearby. But once Hion had killed that last bear, the Dreamers knew the plague would die out, too. Does that tell you enough about fire bears, Matti?"

Her bed shifted slightly. Pepper whispered, "She's asleep."

"I guess that tells me what kind of storyteller I am."

"Oh, no, you were wonderful. Matti's just too little to be up so late."

"We'd better put her back on your bed." After a brief fumble, Vray lifted the small child and cradled her against her shoulder. She found herself wondering if the prince who'd been born in the year of the last fire bear had ever been this little and curious, and fallen asleep when told of his father's exploits. Pepper led her to the other bed, and together they tucked Matti under the blanket.

"Go to sleep, now, Pepper."

"I will. Do you know more stories?"

Vray smiled into the dark. "A few." She climbed back into her own bed and closed her eyes.

"Good," was Pepper's final comment for the night.

Chapter 24

Jordy followed the porter up the stairs to the law reader's room. The white-haired Shaper behind the table identified himself as Reader Oskin. Beside him stood an old woman in Redmother's robes—the witness. The captain of the king's guard, the man Jordy had come to challenge, stood just in front of the dark wooden table, arms folded over his chest, aquiline features impassive. He gave no sign that he recognized Jordy. So much, Jordy thought bitterly, for fine words spoken around a summer campfire.

At the law reader's command he made his statement. The witness listened attentively, her mouth a small 'o' of sympathy as he described torches falling among the children in the inn yard. Reader Oskin scratched lines in a book with a feather. Captain Dael saved his response until Jordy had finished.

"It seems the guards let their enthusiasm get the better of them," he said.

Oskin raised his white eyebrows. "Enthusiasm for an action that was in itself of dubious legality."

Dael flipped his long blond hair back over his shoulder with an impatient movement of his head. "They'd found a suitable candidate for the guard. They didn't want to lose him."

"They took him forcibly from his family and village. Twice," Jordy stated.

"It is an honor to serve the king."

"A voluntary honor."

"One to be encouraged. The guards were simply doing their duty."

Oskin interrupted the rapid exchange of words. "What action am I expected to take in this matter?" he demanded.

Jordy had his reply ready. "Return Pross to his family.

Discipline the guards. Reimburse the innkeeper and the smith for their lost property."

"Guard discipline is my concern," Dael replied. "Even if I could identify that troop from your description, which is doubtful, you can't expect me to tell them not to protect themselves from an angry mob."

"Mob? A village at its Spring Festival is not a mob!"

The captain spoke over his objection. "The boy is probably enjoying himself by now. He could be anywhere in Rhenlan. If I encounter news of him, I'll see that he knows he's been missed at home. As to the property damage you mentioned, what was it? A door? A few tables? That's a matter for the treasury, not for me."

With an effort, Jordy held his temper. The law reader said, "Prince Damon administers the treasury. You can tell your village that its claim will be considered. But I warn you, the prince it not likely to trouble himself with such an insignificant amount."

"His attention is on larger affairs," Dael added.

"That's all, then." Oskin raised his voice. "Next." The porter opened the door.

Jordy left the law reader's house and returned to the marketplace in a haze of bitter fury. At the wagon, he answered Tob in monosyllables until the boy wisely vanished. He worked off his anger by giving the already clean Stockings a vigorous grooming. He hadn't really expected anything better of the law reader. It had been foolishness to think that his single, chance encounter with Hion's guard captain three years earlier would influence the man's present behavior. Jordy knew his anger was the result of disillusionment. More foolishness. He should know better than to harbor illusions about anyone as close to Rhenlan's prince as Captain Dael must be.

Jordy allowed the horse to go back to her grazing. He circled the marketplace, arranging for his next load of goods, taking requests for the return trip. Tob caught up with him late in the afternoon, in time to share flaky fish pastries from a market stall.

As they finished, a boy perhaps a year younger than Tob, brown hair a shade lighter than his skin, ran up to Jordy and touched his sleeve. "You're the carter, Jordy?" he asked.

"Aye."

"My father is a glass maker, Bellon. He'd like to speak to you about carrying some merchandise for us."

Jordy brushed the last crumbs off his fingers. "I'll have to see it."

"I can take you to our shop now, if you like."

They threaded their way out of the square into a street lined with equal numbers of shops and residences. Tob and the boy soon fell into conversation. Jordy allowed them to walk a little ahead while he calculated how much room he could spare for this man Bellon's cargo. At the shop, the boy held the door open and Tob stepped aside to allow him to enter first.

The interior of the shop was tall and spacious. Thin spring sunshine entered through dozens of clear windows set in the upper portions of all four walls. Lower windows stood open to admit the cool afternoon breeze. Light sparkled and reflected between glass objects of every shape, size, color, and purpose. A large workbench occupied the center of the room, midway between the door and the fiery mouth of the furnace. Jordy halted in mid-stride.

Seated at the worktable was Dael.

"Carter, don't leave. We should talk."

Three others sat near the captain. A man with the boy's brown skin rose. "I'm Bellon. I do need someone to bring me a mineral from Atade which I use to color my glass. This is my wife, Thena, Senior Brownmother for Edian."

The woman beside him nodded, her dark eyes and long face worried.

The glassmaker gestured to the remaining man, seated between him and the guard captain. "I understand you know my friend the goldsmith?"

"Loras. It's been a long time since the lake country." Then he glared at the young guard captain. "It seems things have changed."

"Come in, boys. Close the door," Bellon said. "Sit down and be quiet. That is, if that's all right with you, carter?"

"I won't say anything my son shouldn't hear."

The glassmaker's son led Tob to a pair of stools under the south windows, where they perched, wide-eyed and solemn. Jordy took the single vacant stool, across the workbench from Loras and Dael.

"The situation has changed, for the worse," Loras answered his accusation, an unhappy frown on his weathered face. "Dael told me what happened in Broadford. It's appalling."

Jordy's eyes narrowed. "Your son didn't seem to find it appalling."

"Not in front of Law Reader Oskin. In public, I'm completely loyal to my prince and my king. Stop feeling offended for a moment, and think about my position. I'm the captain of the king's guard!"

In the pause that followed, the fire in the furnace crackled and hissed. The tight knot of outrage in the pit of Jordy's stomach didn't ease. "So, you don't agree with present Shaper policy?"

"What do you know of Shaper policy?" Dael countered with no little fury of his own. "Policy is something that concerns whole kingdoms. You're worried about one village!"

"This isn't just about Broadford! I'm looking beyond Rhenlan. So should you be!"

"What can he do?" Loras spread his large hands, palm upward, on the table. "In his position, he answers directly to the king."

"To Damon, more often," the captain said. "Hion rarely concerns himself with the guard these days."

"Hion or Damon, it makes no difference," Loras said. "If Dael were to defy them, they would simply dismiss him. At least this way he can try to do some good."

"I am sorry about Broadford," Dael said. "Forget what I said to the law reader. I will try to find Pross and get him back to your village. I think I know the identity of the troop involved. Knowing what you've told me confirms that I can't trust them. They've become more Damon's men than mine."

Jordy leaned forward, interested in spite of himself. "There's that much division in the guards?"

"On the surface, no. Discipline is good. I'm respected and obeyed. I also make a point of keeping well informed. I know which of my people enjoy the attentions and special favors of the prince, and which of them remember their proper duties as guardians and protectors of the common good." He made a helpless gesture. The dissatisfaction evident in his expression paralleled Jordy's own feelings. "The first group I watch diligently. The second group I trust. If it weren't for the responsible ones, the ones who really care, maybe I wouldn't stay. Maybe that makes me a fool."

"Dael—" his father began.

"You say I should think beyond Rhenlan? I do. If I had some freedom of movement, instead of being trapped here, there's no end to what I could do." Dael straightened on his stool. "We've heard of your dissatisfaction, carter. We think we should help each other."

"Heard?" Jordy asked skeptically. "Where?"

"A friend of yours," Loras added. "The minstrel Ivey."

"He told us you're always interested in news of our rulers," Dael said. "I can give you that."

Jordy looked around the table. "You should know that I believe the very concept of the ruling and the ruled needs to be questioned."

Loras gave a long, low whistle. "And we thought we were dissatisfied."

"We?"

"Some of us here in Edian, who don't like the direction Damon's been taking. He's supposed to be responsible—actually, his father's supposed to be responsible, but Damon does everything these days in his father's name—for our welfare. Instead he's busy trying to extend his influence farther and farther from home. Where's the sense in his claiming taxes and services from more and more Keepers, when he has yet to fulfill his vows to those of us who are already his responsibility?"

"Where is the sense," Jordy countered, "in continuing to acknowledge his authority?"

"It's the same common sense that causes a small child to run from a bully," Brownmother Thena snapped. "Self-preservation, carter."

"The strongest bully is helpless against several children capable of cooperating against him." Jordy saw the others' doubtful expressions, but continued resolutely. "You said it yourself, Dael. Many of the guards are good people who'd never put a village to the torch, no matter what Damon ordered. Just imagine what we could accomplish if Keepers all across the kingdom joined together to deny all Shaper injustice."

Dael tilted his head to one side. "I can imagine certain Shapers feeling threatened by an idea like that."

"That's one of its dangers," Jordy agreed.

"That sort of cooperation won't develop spontaneously." Loras gave them a few seconds to consider his opinion before adding, "It will take a tremendous amount of work to organize."

"Organization would be the least of our worries—" Dael began.

"It's ignorance of the danger that—" Jordy said at the same moment.

Conversation around the table fragmented. Dael and his father fell into one loud discussion, while Jordy found himself arguing equally vehemently with Thena. Then something Loras said drew her attention, and Dael asked a question which Jordy had to answer with a long description of the hard realities of life in the villages. He spared a reassuring nod for Tob, who was watching the group of adults with a worried frown.

Bellon, who had remained silent, suddenly leaned across the work bench and heartily clapped Jordy on the shoulder. "By the Firstmother, we can do it! And if you can convince me, carter, you can convince anyone."

"We'll have to proceed very carefully," Dael warned.

"Of us all, you have the most freedom of movement, Jordy. All of the initial coordination, at least, will fall on you."

"There are others we can count on," Jordy replied. "Ivey, for instance."

Loras nodded. "Yes. He'd be helpful, if he's willing."

"He's willing," Jordy said.

While they'd been speaking evening had fallen. Thena got up from the workbench and went to light the lamps.

Dael also rose. "I've got to get back. Thank you, carter." He paused, obviously searching for words, but finally said simply, "Good night," and left.

Bellon got down from his stool, stretched, and sighed. "We've all had enough food for thought for the time being. Join us for supper, carter. You and your son. There's still that Atade shipment to consider."

"Thank you. We'll do that."

Jordy beckoned to Tob. Thena and her son went out the door first, followed by Loras.

The goldsmith paused in the doorway. "I'll be going home," he said. "How long will you be in Edian?"

"Another day. Two at most."

"See me before you leave. I might know a few useful people in the villages and towns you'll be visiting."

Bellon closed the shop behind them. He motioned Jordy and Tob toward a handsome house next door. Loras said his farewells and went off down the street in the opposite direction.

Jordy exhaled a long, tired sigh in the darkness. He hadn't accomplished what he'd set out to accomplish on this visit. He wasn't completely sure how circumstances had come to shift the way they had. Aye, well, he wouldn't take back a word. If they'd begun something, so be it. For better or worse, they'd just have to see it through to the end.

"Any land, any group of people, needs one ruler, one ultimate authority who takes final responsibility for all decisions made." Sene clasped his hands behind his back and refused to flinch under the pressure of Feather's skeptical gaze. Jenil had taken care of the girl's physical and emotional well-being during her years in Garden Vale, but Feather had a great deal to learn about how to be a member of the ruling family of an entire kingdom. Since the Spring Festival, Sene had made an effort to spend time with her every day. Sometimes they walked to Raisal, or rode to a nearby village, and Sene introduced her to Redmothers and community leaders. Other times they stayed home, where Feather could learn the day-to-day details of the life she would one day share with his children.

"In Sitrine," Sene continued, "the responsibilities of the throne will go to Jeyn rather than Chasa. However, there is a great deal of hard work that comes before any decision—work which should be shared. That's been part of the problem in Dherrica for years."

Feather cocked her head. "What has?"

"One person holding too much power. Farren started it, when he diminished the size of his court and eliminated his council entirely. Dea only made matters worse by banishing Bronle's wizard. Hion has his faults, but at least he's training Damon to rule, and he keeps up his council meetings."

"Greenmother Jenil doesn't have a very high opinion of that council."

"Compare conditions in Rhenlan with those in Dherrica. A weak council is better than none at all."

A breeze played idly with the flowers set on a stand near the window. Other than that spot of color, Sene's audience room had very little in the way of decoration. One entire wall and the adjacent corner were filled with a map table. The other walls, except for the space needed for windows and doors, were covered with book shelves. Once every few ninedays, Sene used the room to hear disputes referred to him by law readers. He liked the convenience of having his references near to hand, but he suspected that his reputation for wisdom occasionally suffered in the eyes of his Keeper subjects, who didn't need books and weren't always generous about allowing that other people did.

Through the house door, propped open to catch the cross breeze, Sene heard the rap of boot heels on the corridor's tiled floor. Feather exclaimed, "Not another one! And don't tell me that listening to your arbitrations is an opportunity to broaden my education, because I am never going to be a ruler of Sitrine. And that's that."

"Define 'ruler.' No, never mind. We'll discuss it later." Boot heels—not the softer, formal footwear of a law reader—implied one of his guards or a traveling messenger. Sene hid a smile. He would point out that detail to her later—educationally, of course.

The man who entered was not a member of Sene's guard.

"Ivey!" Feather exclaimed.

"Your Majesty," the minstrel said to Sene. "Dektrieb told me I'd find you here. Hello, Feather."

"Welcome, my friend." Sene gestured Ivey into the room. "You bring me news of the wide world?"

"Quite a lot, actually."

Sene took a seat at the table as Ivey began his report. Feather made no move to leave, which pleased Sene. The sooner she understood the complicated issues involved in ruling Sitrine, the sooner she would be ready to marry Chasa. Afternoon faded to twilight, then to full dark. The minstrel had not been exaggerating. He had a great deal of news indeed. Sene had drawn paper, pen, and ink from a drawer and made notes as Ivey spoke. He looked them over now. Unrest in Edian, the sorry state of the Brownmother house at Soza, the guard attack on Broadford, and Jenil's choice of a Keeper family to shelter Vray.

"This carter," Sene said. "Do you trust him?"

Ivey looked surprised. "Jordy? Yes, of course."

"From what you say, he has little use for Shapers. What would he say if he knew that you served me?"

"He would call me a fool." Ivey leaned back in his chair with a smile. "He says what he thinks. He's an honest man, Your Majesty."

"Honest men don't like being deceived."

"True. He'll be furious. But there's no sense worrying about that until it happens. Right now, I need your advice about another Dherrican entirely."

"Very well. Palle, or Pirse?"

"Both, actually."

"I was under the impression that the prince spends his winters hunting Abstainer bands and his summers killing dragons."

"Aye. Quite successful he is, too. The villagers honor him for it. Palle, on the other hand, never stirs from Bronle. His troops guard the important trade routes between Dherrica and Rhenlan, make a show of patrolling the border, and are quick and efficient when it comes to the collection of taxes and tribute."

"Nothing wrong with any of that."

"Except for the way certain merchants are given all the best trade, and certain goods are available in some villages but not others, and certain Shaper families receive favors from the king while others do not."

"Choices must be made." Sene glanced at Feather. "The art of arbitration."

"Palle renders judgment based on who is the highest bidder. Those who can buy his favor are pleased with the system. Those who cannot have no voice with which to complain. Rather neat, don't you agree?"

Sene studied the young man's bitter expression. "None of this changes the fact that, with Dea and Emlie dead, and Pirse declared Abstainer, Palle is the lawful king."

"Pirse is no more an Abstainer than I am. He did not kill the queen. Half of Dherrica knows it, and the rest have their suspicions."

"Can he prove that? Can you?"

"Stones, no."

"He can't challenge his uncle's accusation in front of the law readers without some evidence to support his version of what happened."

Ivey snorted. "He doesn't know what really happened. He also can't enter Bronle. Some of the guards might deliver him to the law reader for judgment—but most would rather please Palle than serve the law."

"Then the impasse continues."

"Not necessarily." Ivey sat forward. "It occurred to me that Pirse could challenge his uncle's right to the throne without ever placing himself in his uncle's power."

"How?"

"By fathering a child—a direct descendent to take Dea's place."

Sene twirled his pen between his fingers. Feather, who had not spoken since the minstrel began his tale, identified the most practical flaw in Ivey's plan. "Has Palle claimed blood debt against the prince?"

"Formally, no," Ivey admitted. "But isn't it implied? Pirse is accused of murder, of stealing the life of Palle's sister. By law, Palle has every right to claim new life for old."

"By declaring Pirse Abstainer, his life forfeit, he made his claim clear," Sene said. "He wants Pirse to pay the debt with his own life."

"Ah, but that's my point. Palle can lay the claim, but it is up to whoever judges the case to decide the method of payment."

"But, you said Palle has not claimed blood debt," Feather argued.

"With good reason, if Ivey is correct," Sene said. "The last thing he needs is for Pirse to father and raise a child to succeed Dea as ruler of Dherrica. Not only would such a response to the blood debt claim save Pirse's life, it would also relegate Palle to the role of regent, at best. Not even that, if the mother's family claims the regency for her."

"Can Pirse answer a challenge before it's presented?"

Sene nodded slowly. "In the case of a member of a ruling house, like Pirse, claims are settled by a council of the Children, rather than a single law reader."

"I don't know if it would work," Ivey said. "That's why I'm asking." He pointed to the book-lined shelves. "If there's a precedent anywhere in there, Sire, to get Palle off the throne, all of Dherrica would be grateful."

"I can't guarantee anything. But I also can't see Pirse remaining a fugitive for the rest of his life. Have you discussed this with the prince?"

"Aye. We spent a nineday together last winter, near Dundas."

"Do you have a mother in mind for this child?"

"We do."

"And you have reason to believe she'll accept this proposition? Her and her family? For the sake of the child, this will need to be more than a passing relationship between Pirse and the girl."

"The family has no great love for Palle." A blush colored Ivey's fair Dherrican skin. "As for Kamara, Pirse won't know for certain until he asks her, but he told me the two of them were childhood friends."

Sene heard tapping. Distracted, he glanced toward Feather. She had her arms folded and a frown on her face. The toes of one foot beat impatiently against the floor.

"I see you've got it all figured out," she said. "But what if it's all a waste of effort? What if Palle refuses to acknowledge the child?"

"I know the solution to that problem," Sene said. He smiled at Feather. "And you, my dear, can help."

Her foot stopped its tapping. "Me?"

"In fact, the task is perfect for you. An opportunity to broaden your base of authority here in Sitrine."

"But—"

"You will summon a Council of Judgment," Sene continued over her protest. "Aage is the only Dreamer available, but you've got hundreds of people to chose from for the Shaper and Keeper positions. We'll make a formal presentation of the case and let the Council respond. That should answer your questions, Ivey."

"We?" Feather repeated.

Sene pretended not to notice the icy skepticism in her tone. "Feather, you will speak for Pirse in his absence. The judgment of the Council will resolve nothing between Pirse and his uncle, of course, because Palle hasn't presented the challenge to us. But we can judge whether or not this child would be fair compensation if Palle ever does claim his blood debt."

Ivey nodded. "That's all Pirse asks. Thank you, Your Majesty."

"Yes," Feather grumbled. "Thanks."

CHAPTER 25

Sene knew better than to be out from under a cool roof at midday in summer-baked Raisal. Even worse, he walked the main street bare-headed. The bald spot on the top of his head would crisp in the strong sunlight. He'd go home burned, and Jeyn would nag at him. He wiped a trickle of sweat from his cheek.

"Should have brought a hat."

The market was over for the day, and the street nearly empty. As he passed a tavern, a few people lounging at the awning-shaded tables called to him, but he declined their offer of a refreshing drink and hurried on. He needed to be alone, to bring his anger and frustration with Jeyn under control. He had shouted at his daughter, she'd shouted back, and they'd stomped off in opposite directions—which didn't solve a thing.

When his grandmother was ruler, Raisal had been the largest town on the continent, its market and workshops and wharves bustling with activity. Sene barely remembered those days, when he rode his father's shoulders through the noisy, crowded streets and watched ships sail in and out of the harbor. He remembered the plague better—mass graves, Redmothers reciting by the hundreds the names of the dead, and whole streets of houses emptied and left to fall to ruin. Ruin that still hadn't been completely cleared away, despite years of effort. Now he walked the streets of a much smaller town, toward wharves where only a few fishing and trading boats waited for the tide.

Both his parents had died from the plague. His grandmother lived until he was fourteen. From her, he inherited a town and countryside ravished by loss and reeling with despair. In the waning years of the plague, representatives of more and more villages came to him with the news that the

277

Shapers who had led and protected them were dead. In the end, only three other Shaper families survived in Sitrine, all close relatives of the ruler of Raisal. The consensus among Keepers, Shapers, and Aage was for Sene to organize and care for the populace of the northeastern lands. Instead of concentrating on his city and its surrounding villages, Sene began the task of rebuilding an entire region. More responsibility than any one person should have to bear, but there hadn't been any choice. The rulers of Rhenlan and Dherrica, whose territories had grown in much the same way, seemed to take pleasure in their expanded kingdoms. He did not.

Sene approached the dock. A breeze tempered the heat and disguised the fierceness of the sun. Perhaps the comparatively cool air would help clear his head. He had to think this situation through before he went home and tried, again, to have a reasonable conversation with Jeyn.

He wouldn't be quite so annoyed if both Aage and Jenil weren't nagging at him. They were impatient to get on with their plans for a new generation of Dreamers. Hion's daughter had been established in her new home, and Feather was settling in to life in Raisal. The only one unwilling to cooperate was Jeyn. Over lunch, Sene had tried to have a fatherly talk with his gods-favored daughter. It wasn't that he wanted to push her into marriage, exactly. He had merely hoped to advise her on her relationship with her betrothed. Jeyn had not been interested in his advice. As the conversation grew more heated, Sene discovered she wasn't interested in Daav, either.

Sene took a seat on the weather-worn planking of the dock and leaned his back against a piling. Through the purposeful bustle of traders, sailors, and hungry gulls, he spotted Chasa's boat at the end of the jetty. His son had been called away on a sea-dragon hunt just after the Spring Festival, and had only returned last night. Sene didn't remember so many monsters slipping through the cracks between worlds when he was young. Maybe because the cracks weren't so numerous then, or because there had been more wizards to defend against the magic.

They needed more Dreamers, and soon. The gods had provided a way, and Sene had vowed to obey the gods' will. Jeyn was old enough to be wed. It was time she and Daav made peace with each other and got on with giving him grandchildren. Sene sighed, and knocked the back of his head lightly against the wooden post. It didn't help his frustration any. What was he going to do with that girl? She had too much mind of her own. Always thought she was right. A chuckle rumbled up from his chest.

"Takes after her father that way," he admitted. With renewed determination, Sene got to his feet. Time to go home and try a little more fatherly persuasion.

Chasa pulled off his vest as he came into the hall as the head of the household staff entered through another door. "Have you seen Feather this morning, Dektrieb?"

"Gone into town, I believe. She's been complaining about being cooped up in the house." Dektrieb muttered something else under his breath, about Feather, but Chasa couldn't catch the words.

Chasa hid a smile with his hand. "You don't remember when we were children, do you?"

Dektrieb shook his head. "I was with the guard then, Highness."

A wound and the permanent limp that resulted had forced Dektrieb to retire from the guard and come to work on the king's estate.

"Well," Chasa went on. "Feather's always been adventurous. And kind of stubborn and touchy. We used to get into a lot of trouble together."

He remembered the time they'd stolen a basket of freshly caught fish from the kitchen—so fresh they were still wriggling. Feather wanted to get them back in the water before they died, and they got to the shore and tossed the basket in before they'd been caught. They had gone to bed hungry, and had to listen to a long, dull lecture from Aage on the differences between fresh and salt water fish, but they'd still felt they had managed a victorious deed. They used to make plans about all the victorious deeds they'd accomplish when they were grown up and no one could stop them from saving the world. Then Feather had gotten sick and been sent away and a great deal of mischief had left Chasa's life. Jeyn liked to tease, but Feather had been a true instigator of rebellion.

Bright sunlight hit Chasa in the face as he left the house. She could have waited a couple of hours, he thought, and sighed as he set off toward town.

Raisal slumbered in the midday heat. The few people Chasa encountered were happy to report that the new princess and the king had wandered by at different places and times. Chasa followed on Feather's trail. It led down a wide street of small shops interspersed with vegetable and flower gardens. Vine trellises climbed the stucco walls, waxy green leaves and explosions of purple flowers dark in contrast to the sun-catching whitewash beneath them. Chasa lingered in the shade of a building for a few minutes. In the garden behind him, a songbird trilled. He didn't have to wait long before Feather emerged from a doorway. She carried a cloth bag and wore a green dress belted with a red sash. A silver chain glinted around her delicate throat. She plopped a wide-brimmed straw hat over her fine, straying hair as she stepped, barefoot, into the street.

Chasa took a steadying breath and hurried to catch up with her. He touched her lightly on the shoulder. "Lost?"

She turned her head, looking up sourly from beneath the hat brim. "Of course not."

"Can I carry your bag?" He fell into step beside her. "No."

"What have you got?" *I sound like a five-year-old*, he told himself. *Next I'll be asking if I can see. Then I'll go on to the banality of commenting on the weather.* He decided to start over. "Hello, Feather."

"Hello. Embroidery thread."

They continued walking toward the main square. "Do

you like lemonade?" he asked.

"Yes."

"There's an inn nearby where we could get out of the sun."

"I like the sun."

"So do I. But aren't you thirsty?" He couldn't see her face under the hat. He noticed the tension in her and wondered what was wrong. "You don't remember me, do you?"

"No."

"Then maybe we could sit and talk and get to know each other." They entered the square in silence, and he steered her toward the inn. "For example, you could tell me what you like to embroider. Do you still hate to eat fish?"

Feather stopped walking and glared up at him. "That's not fair."

"I know," he said. "I remember lots of things about you and you don't know a thing about any of us."

He didn't want to tell her how angry that made him. The thought that Dreamers could make mistakes made him extremely uncomfortable.

He motioned toward the inn. "Why don't we have some lemonade? Then we could go home and I'll hunt up a book of embroidery patterns in the library. There's a text all about the history of embroidery. I could read that to you, if you like."

"I don't need to hear a history of embroidery."

"You'll like the pictures."

Her frown eased. Grudgingly, she nodded. "That might be interesting."

"Chasa, Feather!"

They turned to see the king approaching them. "Sir?" Chasa said.

"Your Majesty." Feather's expression brightened as the king came up and put a hand on her shoulder.

"A warm day," Sene said. "Lemonade at the usual inn?"

She looked up at him with a friendly smile. "Yes, Sire."

Chasa gaped at the obvious fondness between his father and his betrothed. The king did not seem to notice. "Son, do me a favor. Ivey's back at the house, and your sister and Daav have been fighting again. I've got a suspicion she might try to make Daav jealous, and I don't want her embarrassing herself or Ivey. Might be a good idea if you spent some time with her until I get a chance to talk to her." Without waiting for Chasa's reply, he steered Feather toward the inn.

Chasa tried not to frown as he started back toward the estate. He heard his father call after him, "We'll see you for supper."

Feather's voice, lively with affectionate teasing, carried clearly down the quiet street. "Shouldn't you be wearing a hat?"

His father laughed ruefully. "Not you, too!"

"Here."

Chasa glanced behind him. Feather stood on tiptoe to settle her new hat on the king's head. It looked ridiculous.

"I look ridiculous," his father complained. But he did not reach up to take it off again.

Chasa turned his back on the conversation. Uncomfortable and unhappy, he continued slowly back to the house.

"Hi."

Ivey looked up sharply. "Your Highness?"

The very attractive princess of Sitrine stood near the arched trellis that served as entrance to the garden grape arbor. Ivey, sitting on the railing of the terrace outside the garden with his eight-string guitar on his thigh, smiled his pleasure at seeing her. Jeyn's pale hair hung loose around her shoulders. Her blue silk dress, high-waisted and low-necked, displayed her advantages—to advantage, Ivey concluded with an appreciative smirk. When he'd passed through Raisal last fall she had been off somewhere checking on the kingdom's law readers, and the spring before that he'd been on and off of the royal estate so fast he'd only had time for one audience with the king. With one thing and another, it had been nearly two years since they'd had a real conversation. The last time she'd bent his ear with news of Aage—that is, when she wasn't complaining about her betrothed, the builder. She had asked him a lot about his travels, too, and about his family, his friends, and whether he had any current girlfriends.

"I didn't know you were here." She came through the archway, a book in one hand. "Are you busy?"

"No. Not at all." He hastily put his guitar aside. "Just practicing."

She came up to the terrace and rested her elbows on the railing beside him. "That sounds like work. I shouldn't disturb you."

"Don't think of it as a disturbance. Think of it as inspiration. Artists need inspiration."

"Overt flattery." She nodded emphatically. "I like that. Do some more."

"It is my profession."

"Part of your profession. What have you and Dad been up to lately?"

"I thought you wanted to be flattered."

"I can be flattered anytime." She turned and set the book on the railing, then gracefully vaulted up to sit beside him. "I was busy when you met with Dad this morning."

He folded his arms. "That's right. The king was annoyed that you weren't there."

She looked a little sheepish. "I was busy."

"Oh?"

"Having a fight."

"You're still not married to Daav. The king mentioned that, too. You're lucky your father is so fond of you. He wouldn't put up with that much dereliction of duty from any other member of the court."

"We've talked about that," she admitted, then changed the subject. "About the meeting?"

Should I humor a pretty girl? Ivey thought with amusement. All blonde and tan, brown-eyed like her twin and outwardly much more clever. Would a clever girl allow herself to be humored? Only if she wanted to be. She did say

283

she liked being flattered. "It was a nice meeting. You should've been there."

"Ivey!"

"Not that we really missed you. There was another pretty girl there."

"You've met Feather."

"Cute name. Cute kid. She and Chasa will make a nice couple."

"If they ever get the chance. He's hardly been home since she got here." She drummed her fingers on the stone surface of the railing. "And you're not telling me about the meeting."

"Do you really want to talk about the meeting?"

"For the moment, yes."

"Yes, tell us about the meeting," Chasa agreed, coming onto the terrace from the house. He sat down beside his sister, who absently put a hand on his shoulder and brushed aside his windblown hair. Chasa turned his gaze on Ivey. "We just love hearing about meetings."

The prince sounded annoyed. He and Jeyn shared the same expression of dissatisfaction, which made their resemblance even more striking.

"Among other things, your father asked me to determine if there's been as much increase in Abstainer activity on Rhenlan's side of the border as there has been here."

"He doesn't ask much, does he?"

Jeyn elbowed her brother to silence. "Did you bring him an answer?"

"Do I ever fail an assignment?" She eyed him skeptically, so he temporized, "Do I often fail assignments? Never mind. Yes, I was able to answer a few of his questions. My friends in Rhenlan haven't noticed any increase in Abstainer activity. If anything, there've been fewer incidents this year than last."

"The weather's been mild. That could account for it, I suppose," Jeyn mused.

He nodded. "That's a nice, common sense interpretation."

"But not Dad's interpretation, I bet." Chasa shook his head. "I wish he didn't always have to look for the larger pattern behind every single thing that happens."

Jeyn cut across Chasa's complaint. "What did Aage say?"

"That our problems with Abstainer attacks may be part of a larger pattern."

Chasa groaned.

Ivey ignored him, and continued, "Several things could be happening here to explain the rising number of incidents. One: more Sitrinians than usual may be forsaking their homes and families and becoming Abstainers."

"They're not," Jeyn protested. "I know. I keep in touch with the Redmothers of all the villages. Our people are prospering. I can't even remember the last time anyone reported losing a loved one to the Abstainers."

"Two: the Abstainers are migrating here from somewhere else. Specifically, from Rhenlan. Which, according to some people at least, has not been prospering these past few years."

It was Chasa's turn to drum his fingers on the railing. "Abstainers don't just migrate. That suggests forethought, planning—and Abstainers don't plan. They just act."

"And react," Jeyn said. "They couldn't plan, as in thinking things through and coming to a decision that Sitrine would be a good place to live, but they might leave Rhenlan in reaction to a direct threat. We know King Hion has been adding more and more people to his guard."

"More guard patrols should mean more Abstainers killed," Chasa replied. "Then we'd have fewer of them on our border, not more."

"Three," Ivey said. "They're not simply Abstainers. According to Aage, they might be sent by the Others."

Jeyn's eyes widened. "They're monsters? Like phantom cats, but not in animal form?"

"Impossible," Chasa snapped.

"Aage knows about monsters," Jeyn insisted.

"He knows about bending power," her brother corrected

her, "in places none of us can go. I know about monsters, the physical kind that Shapers kill with magic swords and spears. That we can only kill with magic-enhanced weapons. Abstainers don't have anything to do with the Others. If they did, Felistinon's arrows wouldn't have helped against the band that attacked him and Dad and Feather."

"That's more or less what your father told Aage," Ivey said.

Jeyn set her jaw stubbornly. "Aage wouldn't suggest it if it wasn't possible."

"There's possible, and there's practical," Chasa said. "Dreamers are not practical. They don't have the same concerns as the rest of us. They don't even see facts that are obvious to the rest of us."

Ivey looked from one tense twin to the other. He hated to see them fighting. "Of course Dreamers share our concerns."

The two blond heads turned toward him.

"We're all Children of the Rock," Ivey continued. "We need each other. We need Aage's vision, his wisdom. And he needs us—specifically, you two." When they didn't respond at once, Ivey waggled his eyebrows suggestively. "To do certain things with two certain Keepers."

It was the right thing to say. Jeyn made a very sour face and Chasa mirrored it.

"Breeding stock," Jeyn complained.

"That's us," Chasa agreed. "I don't mind, not really."

"I do."

"Feather doesn't like me."

"I wish that was my problem."

"Ah. The fight was with Daav."

She blushed, as much with anger as with embarrassment. "The fight is always with Daav." She swung her legs over the rail and got up to pace across the terrace. "I do not see what Father likes about that man!"

When Chasa didn't continue the conversation with his twin, Ivey said, "I thought he was chosen by Savyea."

"Father approved it. Father can spend hours with him, walking around buildings and discussing stonework. I have no interest in stonework! I'm the one who would have to live with him, not Father!" She strode back toward Ivey and Chasa, hands gesturing widely. "He's got bricks for brains, I'm sure of it. He's not interested in a single thing I'm interested in. He doesn't like horses, he doesn't like music, he's nervous around Aage, he falls asleep during Redmother stories. When I try to talk about running the country, he just stares at me!"

"So do I," Chasa said.

"Maybe he's overwhelmed," Ivey suggested.

"Nonsense. He's just an idiot," she snapped. "What sort of Dreamers would a man like that father? Magic builders. Just what we need. A child who can make palaces appear out of thin air? Then where would all the carpenters and stonemasons and thatchers be, hmm?"

Ivey caught one waving hand. "Jeyn. Calm down."

"Easy for you to say. Nobody's asking you to marry someone you don't like." She looked up into his face with a sudden, conspiratorial gleam in her eyes. "You know what? No one's going to make me do that, either."

"Make you ask me to marry someone I don't like?" he asked, stalling for time.

"I don't think I want to hear this." Chasa gave a decisive nod. "In fact, I am not going to hear this." Before Ivey could protest, the prince disappeared into the house.

Jeyn reclaimed his attention. "You know exactly what I meant!"

"You're not marrying Daav."

"Got it in one."

"Does the king know this?"

"Not yet. But Daav does. I think that he's the most important person to know it, don't you? It is between us, after all. It's not as if I won't marry a Keeper. It's just got to be the right Keeper."

"Got anyone in mind?" He said it without thinking, then felt a hot flush spread up his neck. He dropped her hand

and stepped quickly back. "No. That's not a fair question. I apologize."

She smiled at him. The smile was pleasant, the tilt of her head decidedly speculative. "I was hoping for a bit of that overt flattery you mentioned earlier."

"Maybe later." He looked over his shoulder, craning his neck to glance at the westering sun. "Actually, I really have to practice. I'm supposed to play for dinner tonight."

"Fine. I'll see you then." Still smiling, she picked up her book and moved toward the door into the house. "Thank you for listening to my problems."

"You're welcome, Your Highness." She went into the house, and Ivey sat down heavily on the stone railing.

She likes me. I think I'm in trouble. He picked up his guitar once more, and absently fingered a few chords. A little flirting was nothing to worry about. Neither he nor Jeyn had been serious. She was just bored with Daav. The builder was a good man, but deathly dull. Ivey wondered when Jeyn would gather the courage to tell her father that she could not accept Daav as her husband—and who she would find to replace him. Daav couldn't be the only Sitrinian Keeper worthy of marrying the princess. To win Jeyn, however, he would also have to be a man with wide interests and good taste.

Whoever he is, I wish him luck with the king.

CHAPTER 26

Vray sat back on her heels and twisted her stiff back. Around her, hundreds of tiny plants poked through the brown soil of the garden in orderly rows. Vray removed her woven hat and fanned herself with it. With midsummer only two ninedays away, the morning sun was already hot.

Pepper, working at the other end of the row, stood up. "What's the matter?"

"Nothing's the matter," Vray returned. "I'm just resting."

"Then you'll never finish."

"Look at this," Vray said, pointing down. The summons was enough to distract Pepper, at least for the moment. She hopped nimbly through the garden to Vray's side. "What do you suppose that's doing here?"

Pepper peered obligingly at the little plant. "That's a radish," she announced with great authority.

"I know it's a radish." Vray supposed she would never live down her initial inability to tell one tiny, two-leaved seedling from another. "These are supposed to be carrots."

"Sometimes a few seeds get mixed up. Let's move it where it belongs." The girl dug around the seedling with her fingers and carefully uprooted it, then confided, "Mama would probably just throw it away, but I love radishes."

She straightened and looked beyond Vray, eyes widening. "Daddy!"

Vray turned as Pepper dashed past her, abandoning the now unimportant seedling. The big bay mare was hauling the wagon up the hill, Jordy at her head. The carter looked up at Pepper's squeal, smiled, and said something to her as she drew near. He waved to Vray.

Vray did not leave the safe, familiar haven of the garden. From there she watched Jordy maneuver the horse and wagon into the stable, listened to Pepper's excited commentary, and saw Matti come careening out of the house, dragging her mother along by the hand. Vray resumed her weeding.

"Where are you? Iris!"

Pepper beckoned to her from the stable doorway. Vray got up and crossed the yard, self-consciously rubbing the dirt off her hands.

"Hello, lassie," Jordy said as soon as she entered the stable. "I brought something for the three of you. Pepper will show you which crate."

Vray obediently went to the back of the wagon, where Pepper and Matti crouched over one of the boxes. They watched eagerly as Vray pried up the lid. "Just the top package, mind," the carter added.

"What is it?" Matti demanded.

Pepper, more experienced, was already unwrapping the outer layer of brown paper. Inside nestled dozens of small, squarish objects, each within its own twist of the sort of smooth white paper Vray hadn't seen since her last visit to the markets of Edian.

"Taffy!" Pepper shouted. "Daddy, thank you!"

"Pecan taffy." Jordy, who had begun to rub down the horse, put aside his cloth and came over to the wagon. "I expect you to make it last."

"Can we have some now?" Matti asked.

"One piece."

Pepper and Matti didn't waste any time. Their small hands dove at once into the rustling pile. Vray picked up a piece of the candy and slowly unwrapped it. Chunks of pecan jutted from the surface of the otherwise smooth brown candy.

"I wasn't sure if you had a sweet tooth."

She glanced quickly at the carter. Was the man apologizing? Her unreliable emotions threatened tears, but she mastered the feeling at once.

"It's a lovely treat," she assured him.

Matti jumped down to the ground. Pepper asked, "Where's Tob?"

"We had a small delivery for Herri. He'll be home for supper."

Jordy waited while Cyril escorted the happily chattering Pepper and Matti from the stable to take their treasure to the house. Then he pulled out a small chest, lifted the lid, and dug past the layers of protective wrapping until he uncovered folds of rust brown wool. He straightened and handed the bundle to Vray.

It was heavy, and far too hot draped across her arm. She held it away from her. "A cloak."

"Aye. The weave is plain, but it wears well. I thought you might decorate it to suit yourself, seeing as you have quite a few ninedays yet before the weather cools."

"To suit myself," she repeated.

"It's for you. A winter cloak." Her continued puzzlement seemed to make him uneasy. "Unless you don't like the color."

"I do! It's beautiful!" she said hastily. She thought that in a moment she was going to cry. "It's just that . . . Do you return from all your trips with so many gifts for—for your children?"

"I'm only bringing things you need, my girl."

She clutched the cloak in both hands. The wool smelled faintly of sweet herbs. The man's generosity overwhelmed her—how could she possibly express her gratitude?

"I have to finish the weeding," she said, and fled to the solitude of the garden.

"I don't want to be here, you know. What's this one? I'll have more, please."

Chasa overheard the girl's precisely enunciated words as he walked past the dining room several hours after the end of dinner. Feather was seated by herself at the big table. Dektrieb placed a glass of wine beside her hand, and started to move away.

"Just leave the bottle," Feather ordered after taking a long drink. "Save you having to run back in here every few minutes."

She held up the glass to the light. "I like this one."

Chasa watched silently from the doorway, not sure whether he was amused or annoyed. Dektrieb did not look happy, but did as he was told. The servant saw him as he turned away from Feather, and shook his head as he went out. It was up to Chasa to see what he could do. He took a deep breath and entered. Several glasses of different shapes and sizes cluttered the table in front of the girl. Two were empty, and four more held various amounts of wine in shades of red, purple, gold, and sparkling clear. Each vintage looked to have been tasted. Probably more than once, if the unfocused look on Feather's face meant anything.

Chasa sat down beside her. "Hello."

She took her attention away from the glass only momentarily. Just long enough to rake a contemptuous look over him. "Oh, it's you."

"So it is."

"I want to be alone."

She took another long drink. Chasa remained where he was. After a while she spoke again.

"This is very good."

"Is it?"

She favored him with another cold look. "I just said so. Gods, but you're stupid. Stupid and dull. Not ugly. I'll give you that. Very pretty. Too pretty. Too young and muscled. Muscles and no brains."

Chasa winced at her words, but spoke patiently. "You're drunk, you know."

"How would I know?" She banged a small fist on the table. One of the empty glasses turned over and rolled toward Chasa. "I've never been drunk before. I'm just . . . learning new things. Sene wants me to learn new things. So I'm learning about wine. It makes me numb, so I think I'm going to try it a lot. Do you ever learn new things?"

"I try. About wine, for instance. In the morning you won't feel so numb. I learned that several years ago."

"You learned something? It stayed in your pretty yellow head?"

Chasa set the empty glass upright. "Yes."

She banged her fist again. "That's not fair!" She began to snivel. "Nothing's ever fair!"

"What isn't fair?"

"You know things," she told him. "You remember things. And you're only a Shaper. Why do you have memories when I don't?"

Because Jenil's an idiot, he said to himself. "I don't know."

Feather's lips drew back in an angry snarl, and she threw a glass at him. "Of course you don't know! I don't want to be here! I don't want to be with you! I don't want to hear your voice! It scares me to hear your voice."

Tears rolled down her cheeks. More glasses were overturned, wine splashing everywhere as Feather lay her head on her folded arms and began to sob.

Chasa hurried around the table to her, then hesitated to touch her. "Why does it scare you, Feather? How can I help?"

"Go away." She lifted her head. Her face was stained with tears and wine and she looked thoroughly miserable. "I don't want to be here. I want to go back to Garden Vale."

"You can't."

She found another glass to throw at him. "Why not?"

"Because it wouldn't help. You know about us now, and about your family. You can't hide from things you know."

"But I don't remember!"

He hesitantly touched her shoulder. She shook him off. Chasa took a step back, hands behind his back. He waited for her to throw something else. When she just sat there, looking down as wine dripped from the table onto her skirt, he said, "Feather?"

"What?" she shouted. She got unsteadily to her feet, then slipped in the puddle that had formed beneath the chair. He didn't try to catch her, just let her grab the table instead.

"Why do I frighten you?"

"I'm going to be sick."

293

"It's probably for the best," Chasa assured her. "You shouldn't mix so many different types of drinks. Why do I frighten you?"

She gulped. Her pale complexion began to look decidedly green. "Because sometimes I almost remember you—but only almost. Like hearing things on the other side of a wall that's too high to climb."

She gulped again, and cupped her hand over her mouth. Behind it she said, "Go away."

Chasa moved toward the door to call for Dektrieb and Feather's maid. As he reached it, he heard her gag and begin to vomit. He wanted to turn back and help her himself, but his bad-tempered, drunken betrothed wouldn't appreciate it. Wouldn't want to hear his voice.

By the Firstmother, Jenil, he swore under his breath, *this is all your fault! You had no business taking her away.* So far away from herself that maybe no one could bring her back again. She had no memory, and there was nothing Chasa could do about it. Nothing he could do but go away.

Dreamers were no use at shaping things. Look what Jenil had done to Feather.

"For her own good," he grumbled as he marched into his own room and slammed the door behind him. In the soft glow of the bedside lantern he saw that the linens were turned back, the pillows fluffed. It had been a long day, but sleep didn't tempt him. He needed activity. There had to be something he could do, some help he could offer someone. The Dreamers weren't enemies to the rest of the Children of the Rock. They just had no talent for making decisions. They forgot that the people they "helped" should have a say in their own fate.

His thoughts shifted from Feather to the afternoon's conversation with Jeyn and Ivey. Abstainers who were really phantom cats or dragons in disguise? A terrifying thought, if it were true. Which it couldn't be. Still, there was something odd going on. Abstainers tended to stay away from settled areas. They preferred to hunt and glean in the wilderness, surviving with as little regulation or pattern in their lives as was physically possible. In winter, they sometimes had no choice. If they didn't raid the occasional isolated farm, they starved. But it was summer. Recent attacks couldn't have been motivated by need.

By what, then?

Chasa went to the chest at the foot of the bed and took out the sword he'd put away only last night. Aage was a great one for presenting ideas, not so great at proposing a course of action. Ivey collected information, but choice tidbits of village gossip and snatches of conversation overheard in a bar weren't much use unless you knew what was behind them. Dad could speculate for the next three ninedays and be no closer to coming up with a solution than they were now. There was only one way to find out what was driving the Abstainers into Sitrine.

Someone would have to ask them.

"Iris?"

She hadn't responded when Matti had tugged on the light blanket she had wrapped around her, or when she'd yanked on a strand of hair sticking out from under the cover. At the sound of the name, however, Vray moved, rolling over before Matti could go on to the next phase of what was becoming a ritual. Vray hated to be tickled. The children had been excited to have their father and brother home. They'd concentrated their attention on Jordy and Tob up until bedtime. Now they were alone in the loft and had no intention of falling immediately to sleep.

"Hmmm?" she asked, even though she knew full well what was coming.

Pepper answered, "We'd like a story."

"It's storming," Matti explained. The loud rumble of thunder that rolled across the house briefly distracted Vray's attention from the wind. "We can't sleep."

Vray didn't like storms, either. She'd been trying her best to get to sleep so she could avoid listening to wind and rainfall and thunder. With a sigh, she sat up and moved over to let the girls clamber into the bed. She draped an arm over their shoulders, pulling them closer.

"A story?"

"Yes, please," Pepper said.

"Do you know any about horses?" Matti asked.

"Horses? Yes. A few. Your mother's from the horse people, isn't she? I saw some riders once, near where I used to live. Near the southern border." That was why guards were sent to stay at Soza, she added silently. Sent to "protect" Soza and the border villages.

"I think so." Matti's answer distracted her from her memories.

It's the storm. She shouldn't let it remind her. This was nothing compared to storm season in the south.

"The horse people didn't used to be our enemies." She wondered if the girls were old enough to have any interest in part of their history. "The horse people are divided into tribes, not kingdoms. They move from place to place in search of the best pasturage for their horses."

Matti said, "I want to hear about horses, not horse people."

"Horses. Hmm. Have you ever heard of Captain Dael of the king's guard?"

"No," they echoed each other.

"No? Well, he's very famous in Edian."

"We've never been to Edian," Matti told her.

"Daddy has. And Tob. All the time in the summer," Pepper added.

"With Stockings."

Vray smiled. "Stockings is a very nice horse."

"Daddy says she's stupid."

"Well, she's a pretty horse. Not as pretty as one of the queen's, but pretty for a cart horse. Would you like to hear a story about a very silly princess and a horse?"

"In Edian?"

"That's where this princess lived. Once a year, they hold a horse fair. It's very exciting. When the princess was eight, her mother the queen brought her best horses in for the fair and put them in the royal stable. The princess was just learning how to ride. She was a little bit afraid of horses, but since her mother loved horses so much she thought she had better learn to ride if she didn't want the queen to think she was totally useless.

"Among the queen's new horses was a stallion. It was black as night, with a neck arched like a crescent moon and a mane that fell to the ground. This was the most beautiful horse the princess had ever seen. She wanted that horse more than anything she had ever wanted in her whole life. Day after day she watched the grooms working him, she watched him in the pasture, she watched him with a mare, she went to his stall and fed him oats. She avoided her lessons so she could be near that one horse. She'd been given a pony, but he meant nothing to her. She begged the queen for the stallion. She was told not to be ridiculous. She begged the king, and was told she was too young. She asked the prince to talk to their parents and was told it wasn't any of his business. She asked her uncles and her aunt. She offered to buy the stallion from her household money. Except that eight-year-old princesses don't have very much household money. She knew that some day she would be given an estate of her own outside Edian, so she offered to sell that. Nobody paid her any attention. So she decided to steal the horse."

The girls made shocked noises, and a fresh clap of thunder punctuated the enormity of the crime. Vray blushed hotly with the memory, thankful for the concealing darkness.

"She didn't think of it as stealing. I don't think she'd ever been taught any better. She was only eight, there was something she wanted, and she decided to take it. So, just before the fair, when all the royal horses were gathered in the courtyard of the castle and the grooms were getting ready to herd them down to the stalls in the market square, the princess snuck up to her stallion. When his groom turned away, just for a moment, she managed to get on the horse's back. She grabbed hold of his silky mane and hung on for dear life, shrieking in the poor thing's ears.

"I think the stallion was about as stupid as Stockings. At least, he hadn't been trained for the possibility of having an excited, frightened child land on his back. He was skittish enough to begin with. The girl panicked him, and he bolted. And that panicked all the other horses. The court-yard was chaos, with horses stampeding and grooms and guards shouting, trying to prevent a disaster. The stallion, in the middle of it all, tried to throw the princess off. The princess, meantime, just screamed louder and louder. The only thing she could see were all these heavy bodies and flashing hooves. She knew that when she fell off she was going to be trampled—and it was certain she was going to fall off. There was no way she could hold on for very long.

"In all this noise, with all the people and horses rushing around, there was only one calm person. Only one person saw that there was a little girl in danger. He was a young guard named Dael. While everybody else was trying to get the horses under control without getting trampled them-selves, Dael pushed his way through the frightened animals. He didn't think about getting hurt. He made his way to the stallion and grabbed the princess just as she started to fall under the horses' feet. He saved her life."

"I hope he was very angry with her," Matti said.

Vray laughed. "He was. But he didn't say anything just then. She held onto him as hard as she had the horse and he carried her from the courtyard to the guard room. There weren't any guards there. They were all outside with the horses. He had to pry her fingers out of his tunic before he could set her down. First he made sure she hadn't been hurt. Then he asked her what she'd done, and why she'd done it. He listened very solemnly. At the time she thought he was very ancient and wise. She didn't know he was just nineteen. But when you're eight, nineteen is very old.

"After she finished, he explained that she had no right to take something that wasn't hers. He explained that someone might have gotten hurt or killed and that a person had to be very careful to never do anything to hurt anyone else. She realized that he might have gotten hurt, and that frightened her more than knowing she might have gotten hurt. She promised him she'd be good. Then she had to go and face her mother, who was very, very angry."

"Was she good for ever and ever after?" Pepper asked.

"She tried, most of the time. And even if she didn't get her beautiful horse, at least she'd made a friend." Vray sighed. "That's not a very good horse story, is it?"

"It was all right," Matti judged. "I wish it wouldn't rain so loud."

"Me too," Pepper said.

"Me too," Vray agreed. "Would you like to sleep with me?"

They crawled under the cover without asking for any more stories. Vray was glad of their company, though there wasn't enough room for three bodies in the bed, even though two of them were small. She settled down between them, as appreciative of the warmth and contact as her eight-year-old self would have been, and tried not to think about the wind and thunder as she drifted off to sleep.

Chapter 27

Vray was up off her pallet in the Brownmother house store-room with the first flash of lightning. As the storm gathered force, rolling up from the plains and battering at the mountain, she paced, arms clasped tightly at her waist, back and forth across the width of the room, driven by the howling of the wind. That the old stone building was perched on the edge of a clifftop did not help her sense of vulnerability to the elements. She'd always been afraid of the wind, terrified at the thought of wind demons.

Another boom of thunder made Vray jump, but she was immediately distracted by the creak of the door. Although the sound of the storm had covered the sound of the lock being turned, nothing could disguise the jarring noise made by those rusty hinges. Vray turned toward the door. Brownmother Muraje's scowling visage was lit by a lighting flash and the candle in her right hand. "Vrain's hungry. Get to the kitchen." She boxed Vray on the ear for emphasis. "Don't keep the guard leader waiting, or he'll take it out of your hide himself."

Cousin Vrain was always hungry. Vray piled potatoes into a bowl, searching through the bag in the dark store-room by touch. She found a certain pleasure in the dusty feel and pebbly surfaces as she pulled the vegetables out of the burlap storage bag. When she'd counted out two dozen, she picked up her bowl and headed for the kitchen where Theka, one of the other kitchen girls, had built up the fire and set water to boil.

She'd left Theka slicing a loaf of bread. As she reached the kitchen door, she heard a high-pitched squeak from Theka, answered by a laugh and words, masculine and slurred. Guards. Come to see their commander's orders were being carried out? She peered toward the work table,

300

then at the hearth, but didn't see the girl. She did hear her crying. Then she caught sight of her, a little thing pressed against the wall beneath the kitchen's one window. A pair of men flanked her, making the twelve-year-old orphan seem even smaller. Both of them had their hands on the girl. One of them forced a kiss on her.

Vray drew back, safely unnoticed in the shadows. Theka had said she was afraid of the guards. Perhaps this sort of thing had happened to her before. But she was only a child!

What should I do? What can I do?

Would it do any good to run to cousin Vrain, beg him to stop his men from molesting a servant? At Soza?

Can I hide here and let her be raped? Can I let anyone else get hurt?

The knife still sat on the table beside the abandoned loaf of bread. She almost laughed. She was a skinny girl, and they were two guards. Drunken, probably, but they were still trained killers. No. Heroics weren't in order. She put her bowl of potatoes on the floor. Knees shaking, she stepped out of the shadows and went to the trio by the window. She touched one of the guards on the shoulder.

"Leave the girl be." When a bloodshot eye was turned on her, she smiled, hoping it was suggestive. "She's got a meal to cook for Vrain. You don't want him angry, do you?"

The second guard made a grab for her. Vray danced back. Drunk, all right. She almost gagged from the stench of his breath. The first guard released Theka. The girl scrambled away as he planted his hands on his hips. His eyes raked Vray with interest while she kept smiling at him.

"You're a pretty one."

She gestured toward the dark storeroom. "Why don't we go in there? You, me, and your friend."

The second guard pushed her forward while his hands tugged at the fastening of her robe. "Good idea," he slurred in her ear. "Pretty girl."

The first man laughed. Retrieving a wine bottle from the table, he hustled them into the storeroom and slammed the door. Vray was glad of the darkness as she was pushed to the floor between the two guards.

Tob hit the floor, not sure if he was awake or asleep, not sure if the scream was real or something he'd dreamed. He did know, groggily, that he'd rolled out of bed and was sprawled on the rag rug spread on the attic floor. He climbed to hands and knees, shaking his head just as thunder cracked overhead and Matti and Pepper began shrieking.

"Uhh," he groaned muzzily. "What?"

"Iris! Wake up!" Matti called. "Tobble!"

Tob blinked, rubbed the sleep from his eyes, and stumbled as quickly as he could to the girls' side of the attic.

"What?" he asked again. Matti, Pepper, and Iris were all huddled on the same bed. The girls were pummeling Iris, trying to shake her awake, and both of them were crying. He said, "Stop that," and moved forward just as Jordy's head appeared at the top of the attic ladder.

"What's going on?" his father demanded irritably. "Do you know what time it is?"

Tob started to say something, but it was Iris's voice that answered from the pile of girls. "I'm sorry. I had a nightmare."

Jordy grunted. "You all right now, lass?"

"Yes."

She didn't sound all right. Pepper and Matti were still snuffling. "I'll take care of it, Dad," Tob promised. "Go back to bed."

Jordy grunted again. "Good lad. Good night." His head disappeared once more.

Tob came forward, plucking first one sister, then the other out of Iris's bed. He hugged them and got them settled under their own covers without too much trouble. Both of them were sleepy, and it was easy enough to soothe them.

When he finished he turned back and found Iris sitting in the center of her bed, arms wrapped around her drawn-up knees. He came and sat down beside her.

"You all right?" he whispered.

She scrubbed at her face. Tob wondered if she'd been crying, too. "I'm sorry," she repeated.

He would rather she answered his question. "You afraid of storms?" He hoped not. He didn't want to have to share the loft with a girl who screamed every time it rained. He wouldn't get much sleep that way.

"No. Yes."

"Which is it?"

"Yes." She was silent for a while, then said, "My memory's too good."

"You're a Redmother," he reminded her. "Do you remember your nightmares?"

"No. I make nightmares out of memories."

"You should try to dream good memories, then."

"Do you believe in wind demons?"

"Of course. Don't you?"

"I used to be afraid of wind demons. Silly. All a wind demon can do is kill you."

"That's scary."

"No."

He shook his head. "You're a strange girl, Iris."

"I'm sorry."

"Stop being sorry," he said irritably. Getting up, he did his best to sound like his father. "You go to sleep, now."

She nodded and stretched out on her side. He started to smile, elated at the sudden sense of authority, but a yawn interrupted his new feeling of power.

"Good night, Iris."

She turned over. "Good night, Tobble."

She called him Tobble. He went back to his bed.

As if she really is my sister. I think I like that.

Feather stumbled into the dining room just as Dektrieb collected the last of the dirty dishes. Her head hurt. She didn't quite remember why, but knew it had something to do with the dining room.

"Why aren't I in bed?" Feather asked.

The man looked up from the dishes. "Good morning, ma'am. No, you're not late."

Which wasn't what she'd asked. He was being circumspect. She hated it when people were circumspect. Feather approached the mostly empty breakfast table with careful steps, mouth pursed with the effort of swallowing a tart rejoinder.

"I was drinking." She blinked her nearly swollen-shut eyes. "Don't ever let me do that again."

"I'll bring your orange juice with a restorative right away," he said. "What else would you like? Cook saved some eggs for you."

Her stomach lurched. "No."

Feather sat down in front of the sole remaining place setting as Dektrieb nodded agreeably and hurried off to the kitchen. When he was gone, she leaned her head on her hand.

"I don't like breakfast anyway," she told the empty verandah. A stray breeze fluttered the corner of the pale green tablecloth. "I came for the first council meeting of the day. Not for the food. Me and a plate of eggs. I should forget the whole thing and go back to bed."

Her stomach rumbled.

"How dare you," she muttered. Her stomach thought it belonged to a princess getting an early start on her day. Her body got out of bed despite how it felt. She was getting used to the routine of this place. The king was very well organized, and his good habits seemed to rub off on everyone else.

Thoughts of Sene focused her attention, and she took another look around the empty dining room. Empty? Sene changed other people's habits, but he didn't change his own. He lingered over meals, waited for everyone in the household to put in an appearance at the table so he could give them their orders for the day. So, something had happened. Otherwise he would still be at the table. Feather thought she would be worried if her head felt better. Or be furious at being left out. Not that being worried should necessarily stop her from being furious. Except Sene would say that being furious all the time clouds one's judgment.

A clatter of hoof beats distracted her. She groaned but turned in her chair. The king rode up from the direction of the road, his white stallion's flanks glistening with sweat. A stable boy came running around the side of the house. Sene gave him the reins, then climbed directly from the saddle over the railing of the terrace. He was bare-headed, and his clothing was dusty. He stamped dirt off his boots before coming to the table.

"Feather. Good," he greeted her. "Have you been waiting long?"

She hid her misery and answered, "Only a few minutes."

"I asked Jeyn to wait for you, but now I'm told she was called away as well. Quite a morning, eh?"

"Apparently so."

Sene took a seat just as Dektrieb appeared with a glass for Feather. The servant accepted his master's appearance without surprise. "May I bring you something, Sire?"

"Another melon, Dektrieb. And a wash basin."

"Yes, Sire."

Dektrieb left. Feather watched Sene expectantly over the rim of her glass as she gulped down the restorative. He said, "A sea monster. We received the report just before dawn. And Chasa's nowhere to be found."

Feather stopped feeling sorry for herself. The only thing she knew about hunting sea monsters was that an expedition needed to be launched as rapidly as possible.

Sene glanced in the direction of the harbor, out of sight beyond the headland to the west. "The boy needs to be at sea." He frowned at the door leading inside. "I wonder where Jeyn went?"

Feather thought uneasily about why she'd gotten drunk. She asked, "Was this sea monster reported to be especially large?"

"They're all large to a man in a fishing boat. Why?"

"You don't fight sea monsters, do you?"

The king leaned toward her. His words were half solemn confession, half boyish mischief. "Actually, I get seasick. I like my monsters land-bound." He gave her a conspiratorial wink just as the door opened and Dektrieb, arms full, backed through.

In the presence of the servant Feather forced herself to stop staring at Sene. He had no right to be so charming. Perhaps he couldn't help it. Perhaps he was born that way. Then why hadn't he passed the trait on to his son? *Stop it,* Feather told herself desperately. *Chasa is a nice boy.*

Who wants to marry a boy?

Sene washed up, and Dektrieb departed, towel draped over one arm.

The king said, "It might be the two-mile bridge. I hope not. We'll need that road at harvest."

Out of the corner of her eye Feather watched his hands as he deftly quartered the green-skinned melon with a silver knife. Strong hands.

"Bridge?" she repeated, looking up. To her relief, her head no longer ached.

"A serious enough problem to call Jeyn away at this hour. If that's the problem. I'm only speculating. Have you seen Ivey?"

The door swung against the wall with a solid thunk, the noise a painful distraction. Feather uncovered her ears as Jeyn hurried up to the table.

"We've more than a sea monster to worry about," the princess announced.

"Not the bridge," Sene commented to Feather. To his daughter he said, "Tell me."

"Phantom cats. A pair."

The succinct words left Feather voiceless with dread. Sene asked, "Where?"

"Forty miles east of Bren. They were seen following a herd of gazelle westward, but—"

"But," Sene agreed. He used a spoon to scoop a juicy crescent of pulp from the melon, then raised it to his lips. "Where's Chasa?"

Jeyn said, "I'll worry about Chasa and his monster. You'll need help with the phantom cats."

"I'll take Ivey."

Jeyn sat down at the table. Her sardonic expression made her look suddenly very like her father. "He'll be thrilled."

"These were sweeter last year," Sene said. He swallowed one mouthful of melon and dug out a second.

"That stretch of cool weather," Jeyn reminded him. "Why Ivey?"

Sene's smile showed his dimples, but his eyes caught and held his daughter's with undisguised speculation. "He's available."

"I've noticed that."

"I noticed you noticing at dinner last night."

Feather's pulse hammered in her throat. "You can't kill phantom cats."

"Why not?" Sene's eyebrows rose. "I have done it before."

"But you're the king."

"Exactly."

Feather knew she sounded a fool. She couldn't help herself. "Raisal needs you."

"Raisal has Jeyn. And you." He quickly cleaned the last of the melon from its rind and got to his feet. "Who made the sighting?" he asked Jeyn.

"Felistinon's troop. They were going to try to turn the gazelle herd south."

"At this time of year? That won't be easy." He paused in the doorway. "Send someone after Ivey. Have him meet me at the stable."

"You'll watch out for him?" Jeyn seemed more annoyed than concerned. "He's not much of a horseman."

"He'll be fine," Sene promised cheerily as he left.

As the sound of his firm tread retreated, Feather turned angrily on the princess. "Why didn't you send Chasa after the phantom cats?"

"There's the sea monster, don't forget." Jeyn sounded distracted.

The princess picked a bell up off the table and rang it, then got up and paced. When Dektrieb appeared, she met him at the door and gave him swift, low-voiced orders. After he was gone, she turned and met Feather's eyes.

"Chasa's on his way to the border. Dad better not find out about this."

"What?" Feather shook her dully aching head. "Why?"

"He left me a message about somebody needing to do something useful for once. I was going to send Aage after him anyway. Those two need to talk." As if in response to her words, a sweet-smelling puff of smoke materialized by the terrace. "Aage! There you are!"

Feather coughed. In all her years of living with Jenil she'd never gotten used to the magical fog the Dreamers brought with them when they traveled through the web of power.

"Why can't you use the door?" she snapped.

Aage ignored her. He stepped up to the princess and waved a square of parchment under her nose. "He wrote this?"

"That's what I said in my note."

"He can't just ride up to a band of Abstainers and start a conversation!"

"I hope he's got something more subtle in mind."

Chasa was not subtle. Feather kept her opinion to herself. Brave, impetuous, sincere, but not subtle. Who did he think he was going to impress with a stunt like this?

Oh.

"I have to stop him," Aage said.

"You most certainly do," Jeyn agreed. "Find him and get him home. Dad'll be furious if he gets himself killed."

Aage nodded. "I'll find him. The sea monster?"

Jeyn's fingers drummed on the stone railing. "I'll take care of it. It's been a couple of years, but I haven't forgotten my training. Chasa's crew does most of the work anyway. Don't worry."

"I'll worry." Aage brushed his lips across the princess's forehead. "Be careful, love." He puffed off, leaving the scent of apple blossoms behind.

Feather stood. "You're going to kill a monster?"

"I haven't got much choice. That leaves you in charge of the kingdom," she added, and walked back into the house before Feather could protest.

Feather sat back down. She wasn't sure whether she should be more annoyed at Shapers or Dreamers or monsters. She settled on being furious with all of them.

CHAPTER 28

"You couldn't listen, could you?" Aage muttered under his breath.

Below his vantage point, the largest band of Abstainers he had ever seen occupied the top and sides of a low rise, its grass cropped short or flattened by several days of intensive grazing. A stream, the border between Sitrine and Rhenlan, meandered along the foot of the hill. This far into the summer, it didn't provide much of a barrier between the two kingdoms. In fact, its shallow water was barely sufficient to supply the band and its horses.

Once, the hill had been the center of a Rhenlan village. The stump of a broad chimney marked the site of a smithy or pottery. Scattered timbers and a few tumbled piles of stone were all that remained of the rest of the buildings, save one. Aage remembered the half-fallen ruin as a Brownmother house, renowned for the skill of the healers trained within its walls. Now, after years of vacancy, it gave succor once more—to Chasa.

In defiance of every argument Aage could muster, not to mention plain common sense, the prince had gone through with his plan to locate one of the bands of Abstainers that roamed the borderlands. Undeterred by the abnormal orderliness of the band's camp, he had crept into the village under cover of darkness and taken possession of the upper story of the house. When dawn broke, he called to the nearest Abstainer and requested a conference with their leader.

They had tried to kill him, of course. Abstainers did that. Chasa, who was nine times a fool but not stupid, had chosen his refuge for its defensibility and didn't even have to kill any of his attackers in order to protect himself. Late in the morning, his determination was rewarded. The Abstainer leader stood below his perch and spoke with him. Though it had been years since Aage had last seen him, the man's square jaw and heavy brow, framed by a tangled mass of red hair, was unmistakable: Soen, brother to Queen Gallia of Rhenlan.

Aage hoped that Chasa was happy to have stumbled on such a choice tidbit of information. Soen, the most powerful Shaper to have gone Abstainer in the last thirty years, was still alive. Furthermore, as the afternoon wore on he demonstrated an unusual ability to maintain control over the mad men and women who lived with him. He never conversed with Chasa for more than a few minutes at a time. As soon as he lost interest, the rest of the band resumed their assault on the prince. Still, the fact that Soen could restrain their impulse to destroy, even if only for short periods, made Aage distinctly uneasy. Sene would have to be told.

As soon, that is, as Aage could devise a way to extricate Chasa from his fortress.

"It's very simple," the king explained patiently. "I haven't lost an assistant yet."

"What if the horse can't outrun them?"

"The horse will outrun them. We're only talking about a few hundred yards. The horse will be as frightened as you are."

"I doubt that." Ivey squirmed unhappily in the saddle. He hadn't enjoyed the several days they'd spent riding from Raisal. "What if he runs away with me?"

"Just point him in the right direction. I'll do the rest."

Ivey shut up. There was no arguing with Sene's easy confidence. Of course he was confident. He'd slain monsters all his life, taught his son the same trade. Chasa had survived the experience. Ivey wanted to feel reassured, but didn't. The sun was shining in a crystal blue sky, the herd of gazelle browsed peacefully a mile downwind of them, yet Ivey couldn't enjoy the beautiful day. The phantom cats hidden somewhere in the brush and tall grass wouldn't leave his thoughts.

Sene glanced over at him. "Don't be ashamed of your fear. It's the proper response. They're monsters, after all."

"I'm more annoyed than ashamed," Ivey admitted. "After all the stories I've told about these beasts, your plan shouldn't surprise me. I understand that the magic will draw them to any of the Children, no matter how much other game is available."

The leather of the saddle creaked beneath him as he shifted once more. He'd never liked saddles. A good riding pad was just as comfortable. But Sene had insisted he would appreciate the stirrups before their hunt was over.

"A story's no substitute for personal experience," Sene said. "You'll find more meaning in your songs after tonight's work."

"I'll be grateful later."

Sene pointed in the direction of the gazelles. "We'll wait at the foot of that rise. The cats will hunt again at dusk. Once they've made their first kill, move in and attract their attention. The herd shouldn't drift much before then. You'll have a good run toward me, upwind and no obstacles."

The king nudged his horse with his heels and they started toward the position he'd chosen. Over his shoulder he added kindly, "Believe me, you won't be so nervous next time."

"Next time?" Ivey's voice, usually an obedient instrument, rose unsteadily.

Sene's grin was actually enthusiastic. "I'm sure you'll hunt often with Chasa. It's all part of the routine for a member of the ruling family."

Surprise almost overcame Ivey's fear. "What?"

The king's eyes narrowed. "I thought you'd noticed my daughter's intentions. No?"

Ivey found he was glad of the stirrups as his mind reeled. "What . . . uh . . . yes. I mean, we've talked. A few times. But I'd never presume to interfere with your choice of who she—"

"She interfered with that already. Don't you like her?"

"Of course I like her! She's lovely. Smart. Funny."

"Likes your singing."

"Likes my singing." *I could be happy with her,* Ivey thought with another burst of surprise. "But we hardly know each other!"

"Well, get on with it," the king ordered. "And let me know your decision, lad."

"Before or after I'm attacked by the phantom cat?" Ivey wanted to know.

Sene laughed. "It's not the phantom cat you have to worry about. Just trust me, and ride as hard as you can."

"Yes, Sire. If you say so, Sire."

Dael shaded his eyes with one hand against the westering sun. Gods and mothers, what a mess.

He had been with one of the border patrols when they found signs of an Abstainer band in the area. The hunt had lasted two days. When they knew they were close, Dael and one of the guards, a young woman named Janakol, went ahead to scout out the area. From the trail the band left, he had expected a large group, perhaps a match in numbers to the dozen people in the guard troop.

Now, the ruddy afternoon light revealed at least four times that many Abstainers, all well-armed, milling about a camp that showed inexplicable signs of order.

Dael and Janakol circled the encampment at a safe distance. The dry ground revealed little, until they approached the Sitrinian side of the border. Janakol, a few steps in front of him, held up her hand in warning.

"Company, Captain."

A single horse, wearing saddle, bridle, and a set of hobbles, grazed in the sheltered hollow. Dael didn't have to approach the animal to know they were in even more serious trouble than he'd realized. The familiar Sitrinian colors on the horse's tack were bad enough. The unmistakable insignia on the saddle cloth, used only by members of the royal house, was worse.

Janakol glanced at Dael and whispered, "One of their patrols, after the same thing we are?"

Dael chose not to correct her. "Could be. Keep alert."

They found a good vantage point on a grass-shrouded hill in Sitrinian territory. Less than twenty yards from the border, but a Sitrinian hill nonetheless. Dael watched a commotion begin in the camp, and guessed that they might not have to worry about a guard patrol objecting to their act of trespass. Even from this distance, he could make a good guess at the identity of the fair-haired man who'd somehow gotten himself trapped on top of the only portion of a building still standing on top of the Abstainer's hill.

Chasa, son and heir to Sene of Sitrine.

Janakol gripped Dael's forearm. "Captain! Is that who I think it is?"

For a moment, Dael heart sank. If Janakol recognized the prince, the rest of the troop would, too. Then he realized that she was pointing not at Chasa, but at the large man who stood at the foot of the building. His bellowing voice, if not his actual words, carried across the gully over the chatter and curses of his excited followers. Dael had never heard another voice like it—and had hoped he would never hear it again.

"Soen," he breathed.

"I thought he was dead!"

Mad Soen. That would be bound to arouse Hion's interest. As for Chasa—assuming Dael could get him away from the Abstainers, then what? Hold him captive, for the crime of entering Rhenlan territory? If Dael did that, Damon would be ecstatic. He might even make some twisted claim about the prince being an advance scout for an invasion. Everyone knew how heavily the Sitrinians patrol their borders. Suspicion of Sitrine was Damon's favorite excuse to add to Rhenlan's guard. Would he goad King Sene into declaring war to get his son back? It was very possible that people were going to die because one idiot had strayed over a border that nobody cared about ten years ago.

Unless I interfere.

Dael motioned Janakol to withdraw. The situation wasn't beyond saving. Not yet. According to Nocca, two members of the guard troop were part of Damon's spy corps. The rest were simply loyal guards. It would not occur to any of them to carry tales back to Edian, unless Dael did something unequivocally treasonous. He was not ready to confront them with the challenge of choosing between him and the king. Jordy was beginning to plant seeds across the kingdom that might, in time, prepare the way for an uprising—but not yet.

The very idea of defying Shapers was difficult for many to grasp. King's guards were no different than other Keepers. Dael hoped that when the choice was clear and the decision unavoidable, the groundwork laid by Nocca would ensure that the majority of Rhenlan's guards would refuse to fight an unjust battle against their fellow Keepers. At least, that was the plan. It would have a greater likelihood of success if Dael were there to set an example for the rest. He couldn't afford to displease Hion, or Damon, and risk losing his position in the guard.

He didn't know why he was worried about taking Chasa prisoner. He had to get him away from the Abstainers first.

Once out of sight of the Abstainer camp, he touched Janakol's shoulder. The band of Abstainers was so large that, even without the complicating factor of Chasa's presence, they would have had nothing to fear from a single troop of Rhenlan guards. However, the troop might be able to cause the diversion he needed to extricate Chasa from his impossible position.

"Now what, Captain?" she asked, voice low.

"I'm not sure. Odds of four to one, at least. Not good."

"Especially not if that's really Soen." She shuddered, the twitch of her shoulders obvious even in the deepening twilight. "Stones, a Shaper Abstainer! Do you suppose there's a troop or two of Sitrinian guards nearby, to go with that horse we saw?"

"It's possible." Dael looked over Janakol's shoulder. The setting sun cast their long shadows toward a patch of scrub forest, about a quarter mile behind the Sitrinian border. A flicker of movement, an uneven patch of blackness darker than the oncoming night, warned him that someone lay hidden at the foot of the trees. "But I wouldn't count on it. We need reinforcements."

"We might have to ride halfway to Edian to find anyone."

"If that's what it takes. I don't want that many Abstainers still at large when winter comes. We'll send two guards to find the nearest patrol and spread the alarm." He named Damon's spies. If others in the troop suspected favoritism, so be it. At least those two would be out of his way.

"The rest of us will follow the band. Maybe they'll split up, and we'll have a chance to pick them off in smaller groups." He waved Janakol in the direction of the waiting troop. "Go. I want them on the road right away."

"What about you, sir?"

"I'm going to circle the camp again. As soon as I'm sure they're not moving any farther tonight, I'll head back. Tell the corporal to set sentries, but no watch fires. We don't want to risk them noticing us."

With a nod, Janakol set off through the tall grass. As soon as she was gone, Dael crept back up the hill, then veered south.

By the time full dark had fallen, Dael was sure that only one other person, not an entire Sitrinian guard troop, lurked with him on the outskirts of the Abstainer camp. Dael approached the watcher as directly as he dared. The gods knew he didn't want to frighten him off, but he didn't have all night to waste, either.

Keyn's waning disk rose over the grassland. The light was not bright enough to reveal Dael, and a breeze sighed through the grass, so the man could not have heard him coming. Even so, he lifted his head at Dael's soundless approach, and stared so directly at him that Dael gave up and rose from the concealing grass.

"You're Dael, aren't you?" The man's silver-blond hair

was pulled back from a high forehead, secured by a head-band and a single, intricate braid at the nape of his neck. His embroidered black robe hid everything else about him. "Do you know who I am?"

"Only a wizard comes weaponless to face Abstainers. You're Aage."

The wizard continued to stare at him. "What do you want?"

"I'm guessing I want the same thing you do. Prince Chasa out of Rhenlan."

"You can't be Captain Dael. Not talking like that."

Dael moved. The next instant he had Aage on the ground, a knife at his throat. "Do you still doubt I'm Dael?"

"No." If there was a flicker of emotion in the wizard's ice-blue eyes, it was annoyance, not fear. Dael stepped back, and Aage got to his feet. "Forgive me if I suspect your motives. Your masters are no friends to Sitrine. Why would you betray them by helping me?"

"I have my reasons."

"I'd like to hear them."

Dael put away the knife and planted his fists on his hips. "Look, let's start over. There's a band of Abstainers on the other side of that hill. They're holding your prince captive. You're here to rescue him, but you need help."

"What makes you say that?"

"If you don't need help, then what are you waiting for?" He studied the wizard's sharp, disapproving features. "Or does Sitrine's prince have a reason to be on Rhenlan's side of the border?"

"Youthful indiscretion."

If the situation wasn't so serious, Dael would almost have thought that the man was making a joke. Dreamers! "Do you need my help, or not?"

"What do you know about Dreamer magic?"

"Only what my Redmother taught me. The power bends within you, and can be bent against anything that has magic of its own." Dael paused. "But that can't be right. You knew I was here, and I have no magic in me."

The wizard managed to look haughtily down his straight nose at Dael, despite their being the same height. "The web of power permeates the whole world. I can send my senses through it. I knew you were there, just as I know how many people are in your troop of guards, and know that Chasa is beginning to curse the impulse that brought him here."

"You know so much. Can't you just go into the Abstainer camp and put everyone to sleep? Or make the prince invisible so that he can walk out?"

"The power doesn't bend that way. If it did, we wouldn't be standing here, would we?"

An idea teased at the edge of Dael's mind. "You're magic's no good against people, even Abstainers."

"As much as they deny it, they are still Children of the Rock."

"I don't have enough guards to fight them. Not without help." What help was a wizard? The only thing Dael knew about Aage was that he defended villages against wind demons, and he could travel in an instant, via magic, from one place to another. "You move things. All Dreamers do. Yourselves, and your clothes. Jenil moves her healing supplies."

"Inanimate things, yes. If I can move it with my body, I can move it with magic. Living things, only if they are imbued with power."

Dael's inspiration wavered. "You can't bend the power and move every sword, bow, and knife out of the Abstainer camp?"

"Not unless I go there and physically take them out of the hands of their owners."

"Could you?"

"With the element of surprise on my side? I might disarm four or five people, on opposite sides of the camp, before the alarm was raised."

"Not enough. I can't attack without a bigger diversion than that." Diversion. Distraction. It all came down to tactics. "You can't fight twenty Abstainers single-handed. But you fight wind demons, and beat them. Control them."

318

"To an extent," Aage agreed. "I don't see how that helps. There's no wind demon here."

"It helps if it works both ways." Dael controlled his impatience. Dreamers weren't supposed to think like guards. Dreamers weren't supposed to think at all, if this one was any example of the breed. "If you can summon monsters as well as banish them."

"You're mad," Aage said.

Dael did not refute the statement. It had a certain element of truth in it, especially tonight. "Give me a diversion. Give me a monster. Arrange a disturbance. Your prince can make his escape, and I'll be too busy to take him prisoner to Edian."

"You call a monster a disturbance?"

"Nothing a trained Shaper can't handle, right? Just give me time to get my guards into position."

He left Aage standing in the Keyn-dappled shadows of the gully, and ran to alert the patrol.

Chapter 29

The phantom cats appeared side by side within the gazelle herd as the sun touched the horizon. Terrified animals stampeded in all directions. Sene remained astride his horse until he saw Ivey begin his desperate run back toward the ambush site. Then he dismounted, drew his sword, and slipped into the space he'd already cleared in the bushes near the base of the slope.

Ivey's horse pounded closer. Sene flexed his sword arm only once. The weapon was a part of him. They were long past needing any formal reacquaintance before a fight. An odd, greenish glow that had nothing to do with the fading sunlight brightened the edges of the blade.

Sene's horse raised its head, nostrils flaring. Two gazelles, panic-stricken, bounded down the slope toward them. The horse bolted. Ivey flew over the crest of the hill, one hand twined in his horse's mane, knees clamped vise-like around the animal's body as he forced it toward Sene's hiding place.

The phantom cats were only a few leaps behind Ivey's horse. They sensed the power in the sword. The one nearest leapt sideways, and barely evaded Sene's gutting thrust. But Sene anticipated that sensitivity and followed through with another stroke. The monster spat and howled, its wound spurting iridescent blood. Sene gave a furious yell and flourished the sword. Both beasts hissed. One backed off a few feet while the leading cat faced the sword. The trick to fighting a phantom cat was holding its attention. If allowed to disengage, it could vanish and the hunt would have to begin again.

The cat facing Sene crouched, snarled, and sprang. Sene, anticipating the creature yet again, timed his move and drove the sword deep behind its skull. Momentum carried the heavy body past him. Sene pivoted and kept his grip on his sword as the dead cat crashed to the ground. The second cat sprang forward, great body arching through the air. Sene braced himself, brought the sword up in a shining arc.

The phantom cat screamed, and disappeared.

The sound lingered for a moment on the evening air, an echo blended with a faint film of smoke. Sene slashed down at the sweet vapor, furious that one of the monsters had gotten away. He sniffed, then scratched his bald spot. Odd. Phantom cats didn't normally smell of cinnamon.

Chasa slumped against the rough stone of the wall. "Where," he muttered to the darkness, "is Aage? You think he'd at least pop in to say, 'I told you so.' I would, if I was a Dreamer. That's about all Dreamers are good for. Popping in and out and giving advice which no one ever listens to."

All right. He should have listened. Aage had warned him that he was going to get in trouble. Still, Chasa hadn't expected to run into Soen, of all people! Aage might appear again. The wizard had dogged him often enough these past few days, when Chasa didn't want to see him. Maybe that was it. If Chasa convinced himself he didn't want to see Aage, he would show up.

I don't want to see him. I don't need a wizard. Aage couldn't get him out of this, anyway. Wizards were useless in practical situations.

A piercing shriek shocked the night into momentary silence. Chasa threw himself to his barricade, sword in hand. Below him, the Abstainer camp erupted into chaos as a wedge of horsemen galloped into its midst. The leader, a tall man with wide shoulders, wore Rhenlan's sapphire and sky blue.

Aage popped into existence at the foot of Chasa's building, the puff of smoke blue-tinted by Keyn-light. "Don't stand there like an idiot! Hurry!"

Chasa pointed after the horsemen. "Who was that?"

"Not an idiot."

"Aage!"

"Dael, captain of Hion's guard. He agrees with me that you shouldn't have come to Rhenlan."

Sounds like an "I told you so" to me. "What's happened?"

"Phantom cat."

The shriek came again, answered by panicked neighs. Chasa scrambled out of the ruined house, sword ready in his hand.

"Where?"

"In the gully." Aage pointed across the camp, then vanished.

Chasa ran down the hill. A few scattered Abstainers fought sword-wielding guards, but most had already disappeared into the night, following their horses in mindless stampede. The rest of the troop was already at the gully, weapons in hand. Chasa shouldered his way into the ragged line, but the guards on either side hardly noticed his arrival. They were too busy witnessing a guard's nightmare made real.

Chasa paused at the top of the short slope, slack-jawed with disbelief. The captain of Rhenlan's guard was holding the phantom cat at bay with a demonstration of the finest swordsmanship in three kingdoms. The cat shrieked its frustration and sprang to the right. Dael moved with it, blocking its path. Virulent yellow light sparkled unnaturally in its fur, flashed in the depths of glowing eyes attuned to the pale glimmer of moonshine.

Why didn't the creature disappear? A large part of what made phantom cats deadly was their tendency to transport magically from one place to another. They typically materialized in the midst of a flock of animals—or gathering of people—grabbed their victim, and vanished, all in the space of a few heartbeats. Chasa couldn't understand why this one hadn't moved behind Dael and finished him off. For that matter, the watching guards or fleeing horses should have attracted the monster. They were easier prey than Dael. Dael couldn't have accidentally wounded it, however admirable his skill and reflexes. He lacked the specialized training and he lacked the proper sort of blade.

White teeth gleamed in the shimmering, fur-tufted face as the cat took the offensive and leapt forward. Dael's sword hissed through the air. The flurry of blows was daunting in its speed and savagery, a defense and counterattack that would have slaughtered three or four mortal assailants. The phantom cat merely paused, enraged at being delayed but completely uninjured. The Keeper's sword slid off its fur without effect.

Chasa skidded down the slope. Dust and pebbles flew from beneath his boots. At the sound, the cat whirled. Chasa tossed his belt and empty scabbard aside. Dael shouted defiance at the back of the monster, and, undeterred by his previous failures, slashed at its hindquarters.

The cat's shriek held a new note of fury as the first stroke of Chasa's specially forged blade traced a narrow gash down its shoulder.

He yelled, "I'll take care of it!" to the oncoming guard captain.

Dael hesitated, then circled wide around the cat, which had begun sputtering and snarling. The onlookers at the edge of the gully called encouragement. Somehow the captain made his words carry through the noise.

"How do you do that?" he demanded as another cut darkened the gleaming fur.

"Magic sword," Chasa panted. He dodged a claw and aimed again for the special spot behind the cat's head. "Dragon powder in the steel."

He thrust forward and down. The point of the sword entered between the two correct vertebrae, penetrating deeply under the force he put behind it. The cat died in mid-howl. The guards cheered. Dael, sword still raised, said conversationally, "This is your chance. Aage is waiting across the border. Go through me."

Chasa stopped in the act of jerking his sword free of the fading corpse to gape at the captain. Lightning flashed from the floor of the gully behind Dael up into the black, cloudless sky. Chasa staggered under the crack of sound. The captain sprawled forward. Another bolt, and another, shook the gully. Half blinded by the flashes, ears ringing, Chasa wrenched his sword loose and ran.

By the time Ivey returned on foot, leading the two white-eyed and trembling horses, Sene had removed the only valuable part of the rapidly decomposing corpse. He coiled the detached tail, its shimmer undimmed, into his belt pouch, then retrieved a cloth from his saddlebag and wiped the blood from his sword.

Ivey peered at the messy, gray-brown fur on the ground, then at Sene.

"You're fast," the minstrel said.

"Plenty of practice."

"Now I am ashamed of my fear."

Sene finished cleaning his blade. "Stones, man, why?"

"I was afraid because I doubted you," the minstrel said simply. "I apologize, Majesty. It won't happen again."

Sene made an impatient noise. "Don't exaggerate. Monsters deserve a certain respect. So do I. Though I hope not for the same reasons." He took his horse's reins and replaced his sword in its scabbard. "Besides, we lost one of them."

The younger man grimaced. There was still more admiration in his eyes than Sene liked to see, but at least the momentary blind devotion was gone. Sene couldn't abide blind devotion. "What do we do now, Your Majesty?"

Sene swung into the saddle. "I'm hungry. Let's find someplace to make camp."

"What about the other cat?"

Sene had been considering that. "We'll go home and wait for another sighting." And he would have a conversation with his wizard. "But first we eat."

Grasses brushed against his trouser legs as Chasa climbed out of the narrow ravine. The wizard did not react to his arrival. Aage stood quietly, arms at his side, Keyn-light lending his light hair a silvery cast. His closed eyes and a tiny frown gave the only hint that he was concentrating. Another crack and rumble of thunder rolled over them from the direction of the Abstainer camp.

Chasa stopped beside the oblivious wizard. "You won't hear me, but thank you."

"I hear you." Aage blinked and turned his head. "Are you all right?"

"Fine, now."

"Do you know who that was?"

"Dael, the captain of the Rhenlan guard? Or Soen, Hion's brother-in-law?"

"I can feel Soen. Not a bending of the power, an aberration. I don't like it."

"His band has scattered. Gods willing, Dael's troop will hunt them down and finish them, Soen included."

"What do you think of Dael?"

Chasa gazed toward the border. "He would have been within the law to take me prisoner, but he didn't. He let me leave."

"To prevent open battle between our kingdoms." Aage also looked toward the sounds of the chaos he'd help create. "I hate to admit it, but this little excursion of yours may have been a good idea after all."

"Because of what we learned about the Abstainers?"

"That, too. But your father will be much more interested in what I have to tell him about Dael."

"A good woman. Though she can't cook."

"Now, Herri." Jordy smiled as he set his mug on the porch beside him. Atade's innkeeper would have said something more colorful in her own defense, had she been present. But one of the major factors in the decade-long rivalry between the two best cooks he'd ever known was that Dimin and Herri had never actually met. Jordy willingly carried their feud back and forth along his trade route, but didn't repeat the insults they uttered word for word. "Dimin's cooking has nothing to do with her place as senior Brownmother of Atade. It's as Brownmother that she's going to get that town organized."

"They did listen to you, then?"

"Most did. Some are skeptical. Several of their families have had young people taken by the guard, though never with as much violence as here."

"Where else did you stop?"

"Hillcrest. They lost an entire herd of cattle. Requisitioning, the corporal called it. Their Brownmother agreed at the time, until I told her I'd seen just such a herd in the fields belonging to the king's brother Ledo, south of Fairdock. The members of the royal court are gathering power and enriching themselves at the expense of the rest of us."

"I take it Hillcrest listened to you, too."

"Aye. They have a smith who knows how to use a sword as well as make them. He'll be taking on a few extra apprentices as soon as the harvest is in."

"Apprentices in more than metalwork."

"It's what's needed."

"Well, you're certainly accomplishing all we could have hoped."

"All?" Jordy snorted his disagreement. "I've hardly had time to talk to half of the people who should hear what's been happening in the world."

"Enough bad news." Herri put his hands on his knees and pushed himself to his feet. "You should be getting home to Cyril and the children, and I've got to put away those kegs."

Jordy stood with him. "How are things here? Has Driss finally regained her strength?"

"Ah, Driss." Herri coughed uncomfortably. "She died, this nineday past."

"She was getting better!"

"For a while. It was sudden. She died in her sleep. The twins are doing fine, though," he added with determined cheerfulness. "And your daughter led the Remembering perfectly. Everyone was satisfied. She's a good girl."

They walked slowly across the inn yard to the wagon. "Making any friends?"

"Not yet. Iris is a shy one. Not unfriendly, but skittish,

if you know what I mean."

"Aye."

"There she is," Herri commented, with a nod.

Jordy turned away from the wagon to look in the direction his friend indicated. The girl was walking briskly up the path from the river, her reddish hair gleaming in the sunlight. She slowed as she became aware of them, and Jordy scowled. She was still so hesitant. Why? Was it suspicion, or fear? He didn't know what had happened to her at Soza, or before, and therefore he couldn't be sure how to give her what she needed. If he could give her what she needed.

"Do you see much of her?" he asked Herri.

"She comes down to the river every day, to learn memories from Canis or one of the other grandparents. They all like her. Say she's pleasant and respectful, and knows her Redmother lore." The innkeeper pushed the tailboard of the wagon back into place, and held it while Jordy fastened the latches. "She's not giving your family any trouble, is she?"

"No. The girls are very fond of her."

"That's reassuring," Herri agreed. "Pepper wouldn't accept her if she was shirking any of her duties, would she?"

Jordy had to smile. "Not Pepper." He raised his voice, and called, "Iris!"

She came across the square, her expression watchful.

Herri said, "Well, I'll be getting back to my work. When are you leaving again?"

"The day after tomorrow."

"Going south?"

"Aye." He belatedly heard the brusqueness of his reply, and gave Herri a wry smile before his friend was swallowed up by the cool shadows within the inn's wide doorway.

Iris came to a stop in front of Stockings. "Hello, Jordy."

Jordy gave a last tug to the tailgate, then walked toward his horse's head. "You've been working hard." He put his hand up to take Stockings's lead rope. "I hear you're making yourself known all over Broadford."

"As a Redmother must."

"Good girl. Ride back with me?"

The hesitation, faint as it was, threatened Jordy's resolution to maintain a pleasant demeanor with the girl. She said, "Yes, thank you," at last, just before he could repeat himself more sharply than would have been wise.

He waited until she had settled herself on the driver's seat before clucking his tongue at Stockings. As soon as the horse was moving he swung up beside her. "Everything well at home?"

"Yes, sir."

"Not too much for you, is it? Gardening, and working with Cyril, on top of hours spent down here?"

"No, sir."

He leaned against the backrest and rubbed one hand across his sweat-grimed neck. He was tired. That, he told himself, was why he felt so exasperated. The brief self-analysis did not stop him from saying, "A conversation shouldn't be this one-sided, lassie."

"I'm sorry." She shot him a nervous glance out of the corner of her eye. "Maybe I'm just out of practice."

The remark had a ring of normalcy to it. Jordy's hopes rose a fraction. "Oh?"

"Cyril doesn't ask much, in the way of conversation." Finally she looked fully at him. Ready, he felt sure, to measure his response and prepare her defenses.

"Pepper and Matti talk, but hardly ever listen, is that it?"

"Hardly ever."

"You come into the village every day."

A fleeting smile made her face very pretty. "Where other people talk, and I listen."

"Then it's no wonder you're forgotten how to have a quiet chat," he agreed. "We'll practice now."

"Yes, sir."

He sighed. "To start with, I'll have no more of that. Respect can be overdone, you know."

Her gaze dropped. "I'm sorry."

"And stop being sorry!" His vehemence had the advantage of reattracting her attention. Its disadvantage was that he immediately felt guilty for trying to push the child beyond her limits. "Never mind, lass. Enjoy your ride in peace."

The wagon creaked under them as Stockings turned onto the east road. Jordy watched her long shadow ripple over the rutted dirt ahead and resigned himself to an uncomfortably silent trip home. Then Iris startled him with a quiet, "Did Tob stop at Kessit's this morning?"

"Aye." He kept his voice casual. "They're fond of him, and he's promised to tell them when we hear anything about Pross."

"Have you?"

"The guard has grown too large," he said bitterly. "With all the newcomers they've brought in since spring, no one remembers one woodworker's son. At least no one who'll take a moment to talk to a mere carter."

"But you won't stop trying."

He looked down at her. "How can I? The boy's place is here, with his family."

"Your place is on the road." She lifted her head, eyes narrowing. "It can't be very efficient, your coming back here so often. If you'd gone directly from Atade into Dherrica, and then down south—"

"Sometimes I do," he interrupted her. "But not this year." He handed the reins to her and stepped over the back of the seat without waiting to see if she would protest the sudden responsibility. He trusted Stockings on this particular stretch of road. Nothing would happen, whether the girl knew how to drive or not. He stood behind her, balancing against the sway of the wagon. "Is there anything you'd like me to bring you next trip home?"

After a short, thoughtful silence Iris said, "Almonds."

"Eh?"

"For Fall Festival. There's a bread I'd like to make. We used to have it in Edian when I was a girl. I remember almonds." She licked her lips, eyes unfocused, in much the way Herri or Dimin looked when they were recalling a recipe. "Also saffron. Honey, of course. I'd like to see if I

329

can put together a version for our Festival."

She said "our," Jordy thought happily. "I'll find some almonds and saffron for you. Any spices, or other ingredients Cyril doesn't have?"

"No, I don't think so." For once she offered him an unhesitant, friendly smile. "This will be fun. I love that bread."

"I'm looking forward to it already."

They rode on in silence. But for the first time since Jenil had dragged the scruffy girl into his house, the quiet was companionable.

CHAPTER 30

Feather glanced at the king and was rewarded by a conspiratorial wink. She smiled back, then looked away. Chasa was saying something about supplies, but all she could hear was the rapid flutter of her heart. *Stop that,* she chided herself. Sene was going to be her father-in-law someday. This was a King's Council, discussing important business. She ought to have some respect.

Not that the Court of Sitrine was ever formal. Pleased by the distracting thought, Feather examined the familiar, comfortable dining room. Candles had been lit against the grayness of the afternoon. Their glow reflected off the silver tray in the center of the table which still held a few dark slices of date bread. The pitcher of fruit juice, refilled twice since lunch, occupied its own stand behind Jeyn. The princess, who sat near the middle of the table opposite Feather, was watching her brother.

Chasa tapped the map draped across the end of the table between himself and Ivey, and continued his complaint about shifting channels in the river north of Dundas. Ivey was dividing his time between staring moodily out at the late summer storm and staring moodily at Jeyn. Beyond them, the terrace windows were streaked with salt spray and rain. Every few minutes, a gust of wind rattled the door.

Sene announced, "That's decided then." He had contributed little to the discussion of what to do about reports of a band of Abstainers that was raiding coastal villages, an admirable demonstration of patience, considering that his son had finally evolved precisely the plan he'd suggested at the start. "Stop at all three villages, unless the weather turns against you. You can take Ivey with you."

This time, Feather mentally braced herself before looking at Sene. He sat with both elbows on the table, fingers laced together before him. She couldn't help but glance at Chasa and compare the two men. Despite a strong family resemblance, Chasa was, at best, a pale imitation of his father. The thought troubled her.

"Your Majesty, with all due respect, I must refuse." Ivey's stubborn voice drew all eyes, including Feather's, to him. She liked the minstrel. He had a memory for tales, and a knack for telling them that would make a Redmother proud. He was good-natured and kind. Therefore, the dangerous glint in his bright blue eyes was more than a little alarming. His glance lingered on Jeyn, who blushed, then concentrated on Sene.

"Nothing's decided," he told the king. "I want you to know that. Nothing. And I'm not going monster hunting again."

"We were discussing Abstainers," Sene said mildly.

"It doesn't matter," Ivey persisted. "I'm not going on another hunt. I'm not dragging back here to wait around until some other emergency crops up, either."

Sene leaned forward, gaze intent on the younger man. "You are in my service, are you not?"

"Aye, that I am. As a messenger, or to gather information. As eyes and ears and even voice for you. I should be on the road, Majesty."

"To serve me, you must serve the best interests of the Children of the Rock. At this moment, you can best serve me by helping to defend the Children against our enemies." He added his most winning dimpled smile. "For a few more ninedays, at least. You leave with Chasa tomorrow."

Ivey gestured toward the windows. The storm obligingly howled louder. "The summer is almost over! You've had no word of Pirse's movements or Palle's activities for ninedays now."

"The roads will still be there waiting for you," Sene said. "Chasa needs your help. Travel with him. Deal with these Abstainers. When you've finished, Chasa will drop you on the north coast of Rhenlan, and you can resume your travels."

"I—" Chasa began, but closed his mouth when Sene flicked his glance his way. Jeyn, wisely, kept out of the confrontation altogether.

Ivey shook his curls behind his shoulders and set his jaw firmly, then he pushed his chair back and stomped to the door. The heavy wood slammed shut behind him.

"I'm glad we understand one another," Sene said to the closed door. He absently rubbed at his forehead. "I am going to the library for some peace and quiet. Chasa, gather your supplies. You two," he added to Jeyn and Feather, "will have to fend for yourselves."

Chasa followed his father from the room, pausing long enough to make sheep eyes at Feather in passing. She turned her back on him and, as soon as the door closed again, asked Jeyn, "Have you seduced him yet?"

Jeyn's fair skin flushed bright red. Her eyes strayed toward the door before she looked directly at Feather. "Who?"

"Ivey. Curly hair. Dherrican accent." She pointed. "He went that way."

Jeyn fidgeted with the long strands of her amber necklace. "Why would I want to seduce Ivey?"

"Because you're not good at being coy." Feather crossed her arms. "Because you talk about him when he's not here, and insisted that your father describe every move he made, every word he said while the two of them were away. You tease him and flirt with him and take almost as good care of him as you do Aage. Besides, Sene's decided you're going to marry a minstrel instead of a builder. He says the minstrel's worth more to him than the builder, anyway. I think you should get on with it before Ivey dies of embarrassment."

"You and my father have discussed me and—" Jeyn's eyes widened in dismay.

Feather cut the princess off before she could start a tirade. "The way you and your father discuss me and Chasa."

The princess sighed. "Matchmaking. This house is full of matchmaking."

"It's all the Dreamers' fault," Feather replied. "Sene says so."

"Sene says too much," Jeyn complained. Her eyes strayed back to the door. She stood. "Wish me luck."

The servant in the hall told Jeyn that Ivey was bathing. She knocked on the door of his room anyway.

"Are you dressed?" she called, then turned the knob and entered.

He stood in front of the copper wash basin, wearing trousers and a towel over his bare shoulders. His hair lay in damp ringlets on top of the towel. "What if I'd said no?"

She pulled the door closed and smiled at him. "I probably would have come in anyway." Then she stopped her teasing. "I was worried about you. You're upset. How can I help?"

He rubbed idly at his hair with the end of the towel. "I wish you could, Princess."

"Sit down," she instructed. "That's an order." He continued to loom over her, water dripping on the carpet between them. She changed to a cajoling smile. "Please?"

With a faint smile he sat gracefully on the edge of the chair. "There. Is this better?"

"Much. I didn't ask my father to keep you—available, you know."

"Aye." His blush covered his entire torso, an intriguing sight for Jeyn. "If you were anyone else—"

"But I'm a Shaper."

"You're a pretty girl with a concerned father."

"Who's a king."

"Who's a king," he agreed. "And you're a Shaper. And Shapers . . ." He waved the subject away. "I need to travel. It's part of what I am. I need to know what Palle is doing, and where Pirse is, and there are things going on in Rhenlan—"

"There are Keepers planning to overthrow their Shaper rulers," she interrupted him. "My father, my Shaper father, doesn't see any other course for the Keepers of Rhenlan. All

Shapers aren't greedy and irresponsible, you know."

"I know that!" He leaned forward. "I wouldn't work for your father if I didn't admire him. That doesn't trouble me."

"Then what does?"

"You. Me. Us. Dreamers." He touched her chin with just the tips of his fingers, then quickly put his hand back in his lap. "I never thought I'd care for someone favored by the gods."

"It isn't much of a favor." Her voice rose. "Yes, the gods selected my family. For all the celebration and awe, what it comes down to is that I've got to make Dreamer babies. That scares people away—people I could be close to. I don't want it to scare you away. Besides, it touches us all, Ivey."

He pulled back a little. "It does, I suppose. I haven't been thinking about the consequences of this prophecy nonsense."

She did not want him to go all moody on her again. With a teasing smile, she made a show of examining his bare torso. "You've gotten a bit more muscle, but you're still too thin. That's because you don't eat." At her careful scrutiny he straightened slightly and tossed his hair off of his shoulder. She refused to be distracted. "You haven't eaten today, have you?"

"You're altogether too maternal, lass. No, I didn't eat."

"Because you were too busy working up the courage to yell at a king."

"Foolish of me." He leaned closer to her once more. "Especially when I could have been kissing a princess instead."

"You could still kiss the princess," she suggested softly. When he didn't move, she reached up, slipped her hand behind his neck, and pulled him toward her. "Do I have to do everything around here?"

He didn't answer. He did kiss her.

Pirse tied his horse's halter rope to the upper rail of the

yard fence, well away from Doron's garden. He tugged self-consciously at the hem of his tunic, which bore stains and inelegantly-mended tears, evidence of his summer's work. He really should have replaced it in Dundas. He would have, if an unexpected guard patrol had not forced him to divert to the west. Still, the diversion had led him here, a couple of ninedays earlier than he usually arrived. Better to come shabby and early to the Fall Festival, than not at all. Or so he hoped Doron would see the matter.

The scent of chicken and sweet basil greeted him as he stepped into the house. The sight of the familiar room and its furnishings, the one place in all Dherrica that he could think of as home, combined with the appetizing aroma of supper to bring a heartfelt smile to his face. He said a cheery, "Guess who?" then stopped.

Voice, expression, thought itself froze as his clever, beautiful, strong-willed dyer-woman turned away from the steaming pot to face him. Her face glowed with more than the heat of the fire. The severity of its lines was gone, soft-ened, a subtle shift in proportion of flesh over bone. Her eyes were bright with good health and flashing anger. Pirse hardly noticed her fury. What caught and rooted him stu-pidly in place was the high, rounded, unmistakable bulge that distorted the once-smooth lines of her blouse. She threw the wooden spoon she held in her hand at him, and he didn't even try to duck.

"You lying, conceited, vowless excuse for a man! Guess now, is it? Well, I've no time for your foolishness, and less time for your fantasies. Get out!"

Pirse reeled back a step from the verbal assault. "Doron, what are you saying? What happened?" He couldn't take his eyes off her belly. "What have you done? With whom?" He closed his eyes with pain. Fool, to have come to think of this place as his home. "Or will you tell me it's no business of mine?"

"You were there. Or will you pretend that more recent companions overshadow any memory of yourself in my bed?"

The lie hurt more than the thought that she'd taken another lover. "I can't have fathered that child!"

"Not only a liar but a coward as well." She rested a protective, possessive hand on her expanded abdomen. "Calling her impossible doesn't still her kicking. Deny her if you will. Your words mean nothing. They never have."

"Shapers and Keepers aren't fertile together." He backed to the door, his fists balled against the desperate, possessive anger that threatened to overpower him.

"That would only be relevant," she snapped, "if one of us were a Shaper."

He heard the conviction of her words. The full implication of her fury left him gaping at her. The pain in her voice and face touched his heart. Doron would not lie. Of that one fact, at least, he could be sure. "Of course I'm a Shaper. I'm Pirse, son of Dea, who was daughter of—"

"This proves otherwise, doesn't it? Now leave me alone."

"Doron." He pushed his fingers through his hair, searching frantically for inspiration. Could she be a Shaper? Some daughter of a lost family? As precious as Shaper bloodlines had become since the plague, it was highly unlikely. Not to mention unattractive, considering how she despised Shapers as a group. "There must be an explanation!"

"Not from your lips. I'll not believe another word you say. You, with your fine sword and dragon ears. Where is the real prince, I wonder? In hiding in the wild somewhere, is my guess, and you his messenger. You carry the dragon ears into Dundas because he can't risk the road. Or do you find his camp and steal them while his back is turned? You tell us the Dreamers need dragon ears for their magic and medicine. Is that just another piece of clever misdirection? Or are the dragon ears real enough, but you merely pretend to serve the prince, then sell the ears to the highest bidder instead? What would he say if he knew you used his name to win yourself willing bed partners the length of the country?"

"It's not true! Doron, you're the only one. And you didn't sleep with me because you thought me a prince."

"The only fool," she replied bitterly, "to fall for your stories. Aye, I believed you." Her proud chin lifted. "Well, fool or no, this is my house. You're not welcome here." She turned her back on him and resumed her work at the hearth.

He stood rooted where he was, staring at her, his heart sinking. Whatever he said now, she wouldn't believe him. Everything that had grown between them, the shared experiences, the friendship—aye, and the love—was ruined. But how? How?

His horse nickered inquisitively when Pirse wandered outside to stand at its head. He absently patted the warm neck, then untied the animal and led it out onto the road. Turning right, they proceeded uphill for a quarter mile until they came to a gate in the stone fence of a pasture, empty and silent. The sun disappeared behind the next range of mountains. Pirse loosened the animal's saddle girth and left it to graze. A short distance up the hill, he sat down, shifting a bit from side to side until he was as comfortable as the rocky soil would allow.

He had never been taught how to meditate. Not formally. Still, even in Dherrica some stories trickled down. Pirse felt around the stubbly grass until he came up with a pebble. He held it in his hand, a flat-sided chunk of basalt, an ordinary gray rock. How did the saying go in Sitrine? Rock and pool. Unchangeable stone, yielding water. He tried to imagine the stone resting in a pool of still water instead of his palm. He imagined himself as still as water, strong as stone. Yet rock could also be brittle, fragile, and water a force against which no one could prevail. Rock and pool. Pirse concentrated on the basic symbols of life, in the hope that there was something instinctively calming in the imagery.

He made himself as impervious as the rock, as motionless as the surface of water in the still evening air, and tried to juggle his confusion and pain into sense within the still place made by the calming exercise. Somehow, something which he had taken for a fact was not. But which thing? He didn't doubt Doron. What else was there? He couldn't doubt his own identity. He was a Shaper. The flaw had to lie in the truncated education he had received regarding the stories of the Children of the Rock. Perhaps it was his memory, his inadequate Shaper's memory, that was at fault. His mother had forbidden many of the traditional stories at the same time she'd banished Morb from the court. He had thought, in the rebellion of adolescence, that it was because they embarrassed the family. His mother had told him it was because the stories were nonsense, outdated fantasies that she refused to restore when she'd become queen.

The court of Sitrine, where he had trained as a youth, was full of tales, but he had listened to his mother's advice to ignore everything but the practicalities of monster-slaying. She had wanted her heir to believe in nothing more than the right of Shapers to rule Keepers. Magic and religion and Dreamers' tales held no interest for Dea.

Magic was not a mere product of imagination. It was real. Perhaps not in Bronle, but he'd seen it often enough in the wilds beyond the capital city, in the monsters he slew. He still shuddered at the memory of its touch on the one occasion he'd needed a Greenmother's healing. The magic users, the Dreamers, were real, too. Banished from the Dherrican court, scoffed at in Rhenlan, still, a few of them survived. Their existence, their peculiar gifts, demanded explanation, explanations faithfully repeated century after century, from one edge of the world to the other.

How could inaccuracy have crept in? Dreamers came from specific, god-chosen Shaper and Keeper unions. The present generation of Dreamers was to have been produced by the Shapers and Keepers of his mother's generation. The gods were, according to all the stories, extremely precise in their dealings with the Children of the Rock.

So why was Doron pregnant?

His concentration broke when someone placed a large,

warm hand on the top of his head. Pirse's eyes flew open. A scent of iris drifted down around him, alien aroma in the late summer air. Before him, the first stars had come out in the east. To his right loomed a figure in a heavy black robe. A woman's voice said, "This had better be important, boy."

Pirse ducked uncomfortably away from the hand and got stiffly to his feet, still clutching the stone. "Greenmother Savyea? What are you doing here?"

She clicked her teeth with her tongue in disapproval. "Why do you pray to the gods if you don't expect an answer?"

"Pray to . . ." He stared at her in confusion while she tapped an impatient foot in the dry grass. "Are you saying I called you here?"

"I said nothing of the kind. I said the gods sent me. That doesn't happen very often." She studied him from head to toe. "You look healthy enough. What were you praying for?"

Nearby, his horse could be heard munching at the grass. The windows of houses in Juniper Ridge were sparks of glowing yellow sprinkled down the mountainside. "Understanding. I was searching for understanding, I suppose. A reason."

"For what, boy?"

"I've fathered a child. I think. I must have."

Her blank expression shifted at once to bright happiness. "That's wonderful! When is the exciting day?"

"Day?"

"When the child will be born. You do remember the approximate date of conception, I trust?"

"But the mother is a Keeper!" He gestured back toward the village. "Doron."

"Of course she is." Savyea patted him fondly once more, this time on the shoulder. "You seem confused. Perhaps I'd better have a word with her. Why don't you join us?" With that she vanished, leaving another burst of spring scent behind her. The warmth of her hand on his shoulder lingered for a few heartbeats after the hand had gone.

Pirse half ran, half slid down the road to Doron's house.

Pebbles dislodged by his boots clattered ahead of him and continued down into the village after he'd left the road to vault the fence into Doron's yard. This time he did not hesitate at the door. He strode in and went directly to Savyea. "I'm not confused. It was Spring Festival. That doesn't make it possible."

Doron stood resolutely in front of the Greenmother through his tumultuous entrance. "It seems that, like everything else, this is Palle's fault."

He took a quick gulp of air. "Palle?"

"Just listen."

Savyea remained unperturbed. "As I was saying, Aage's prophecy is not widely known among Keepers. Or anyone else in Dherrica, I suppose. Your mother never told you, did she? Or allowed Sene to speak of it?"

"Aage?" Pirse echoed. "Mother? Sene?"

"Shh." Doron nudged him forcibly with her elbow. She was angry still, but it no longer seemed directed at him. That was an improvement, even if he remained as confused as ever. He kept still and listened.

"The gods spoke to Aage nearly twenty years ago. At that time your uncle was hardly the only one at fault. If his father—your grandfather, boy—had been more insistent, perhaps things might have been different. But Farren was directing the last stages of the hunt for the fire bears. That, and the ravages of the plague and the fighting with the horse people, distracted him. Hion had already inherited the throne in Rhenlan and decreed that Shapers who owed allegiance to him were exempt from the old vows. When Dea's Keeper betrothed died in the hunt, and Palle's met her mysterious accident, the king their father did nothing, despite Morb's protests. Morb was court wizard in Bronle in those days," Savyea added for Doron's benefit. "He tried again after Farren died and Dea became Queen. She was more interested in producing an heir, and so married your father. After you were born, Morb suggested it was still not too late for Dea to find a proper Keeper husband."

341

"Persistent wizard," Doron muttered, not without approval.

"I've heard some of this," Pirse said. "That argument was the final straw that got Morb banished."

"Personally, I was rather relieved when Aage learned that we could stop bothering with the present rulers and wait for their children to produce the next generation of Dreamers. I think it was the hardship of the plague more than anything else which distorted the priorities of Hion and Dea and their peers. You children—you, Pirse, and Chasa and Jeyn and Vray and a half dozen near cousins, I believe—are more level-headed. And there are still enough Shapers to reproduce another generation of Shapers without your aid." Savyea adjusted her robe with a complacent smile. "Healthy Dreamer babies. With the gods' blessings we might hope for several from each couple—and of course you'll have the gods' blessings, since they were rather insistent that your families be the ones to give us more Dreamers."

Doron's eyes narrowed. "Several?"

"Couples?" Pirse wanted to know. "Just what guarantee is there that my generation is going to be any more cooperative than my mother's was?"

Savyea looked meaningfully at Doron's abdomen. Pirse felt himself blush up to the ears, and Doron laughed.

"The power of the gods bends as it will," Savyea continued, and looked again at Doron. "All any of us, Dreamer or Shaper or Keeper, can do is respond as we are able. You're all old enough now. You'll be making lots of babies before we know it."

Pirse was still puzzled, but not especially alarmed, when the black-robed Dreamer disappeared in a whiff of cherry blossoms. He gingerly stepped up to Doron. "Do you understand any of this?"

"Aye." Doron heaved a gusty sigh and leaned back against the table. "Make babies. It really is all Greenmothers ever talk about. First it was several. Now it's lots. I haven't even had the one yet."

"I really didn't know," Pirse said quietly.

"That's why I blame Palle. Farren may have banished Morb, but your uncle's the one who suggested that Dea restrict the teachings of the Redmothers. Were you listening to Savyea? She as much as said that Palle wasn't content with refusing to wed a Keeper. He arranged to eliminate the possibility altogether."

Pirse frowned. "That is what she implied, isn't it?"

"I hate Shapers," Doron said fervently. Then she touched his shoulder, a gentle caress of her fingers, and his arms encircled her. She tilted her head and regarded him. "Present company excepted, most times."

"Thank you." He held her close, happy when she clung to him as fiercely as he did her. He resisted the urge to make love to her for a few moments longer. He had something he had to say. "We'll be having an announcement for the gathering, lass."

She stayed still and stubbornly silent in the circle of his arms.

He shook her a little. "Won't we? Or must you make everything harder than it has to be?"

She looked at him. "Duty or love, Pirse of Dherrica?"

He smiled at the question. "Since when are you a romantic, Doron of Juniper Ridge?"

"Answer my question."

"Both."

"Good."

"And if I ask you the same question?"

She buried her head in his tunic, but he heard her muffled, "Both," and knew better than to push for details. He swung her up in his arms. She yelped as her feet left the floor. He carried her toward the bed. "Pirse!"

"Hush," he ordered. "I want to find how much the—lass, is it?—is going to get in our way."

"Lass it is," she announced as she began pulling off his tunic. "And not much, knowing us."

"Good."

"Is it too late for supper?" Ivey asked plaintively.

"This is the king's house." Jeyn pulled on her second slipper. "The king is always hungry. Therefore it is never too late for supper."

"Good. I worked up an appetite."

"I hope so."

"Aren't you hungry, lass?" He found a clean tunic in the chest at the foot of his bed, and pulled it over his now-dry hair.

"I'm the king's daughter."

He glanced back at the rumpled bed. "I've been thinking about that."

"Let's go to the dining room. Someone will notice us if we sit at the table and look pitiful enough."

The rain had stopped, so they cut around the outside of the house on the terrace, hand in hand. Jeyn turned the corner first, then jerked Ivey back into the shadows.

To her relief, he didn't argue, but whispered, "What?"

"There's someone there," she whispered back.

He bit her ear. "I guessed that. Who?"

"My father."

"Let's leave." He tried to pull her away, but she stood on his foot.

"He's with someone."

"Who?" he repeated, then added in a light-hearted way, "Do I sound like an owl?"

"Yes. Feather."

"Oh."

Together they peered around the corner. Sene had just picked Feather up, his hands around her tiny waist, and settled her on the stone railing across from the dining room doors. He leaned against the pillar next to her, arms crossed over his broad chest. She smiled worshipfully into his face, and he beamed benignly back.

Ivey drew Jeyn back around the corner. His expression was distinctly puzzled. "Does he know he's doing that?"

"Doing what?" she temporized, although she knew exactly what he meant. She'd been watching it most of the summer.

"I know what we've been doing. Is that what they're doing?"

"I don't think so, exactly. At least, I hope not. She's supposed to marry my brother." She sighed. "But she's in love with my father."

Ivey looked back around the corner. The quiet voices of the couple were audible, although Jeyn couldn't make out any words. Ivey turned back to her. "Sene? He's too old."

"I don't think Feather's noticed. She avoids Chasa, and the way Dad dotes on her isn't helping any."

"Does he know what he's doing?" Ivey repeated.

Jeyn shook her head. "For the sake of peace in this family, I hope not. I really hope not." She took his hand again and turned them back the way they'd come. "Let's take the hallway."

"I think that's a fine idea," he agreed.

CHAPTER 31

From horizon to horizon, only one speck moved against the prevailing pattern of the gray-green waves. A hint of dark coastline hugged the southern rim of the visible world, as unobtrusive as the few birds floating on the wind. Only the ship, tacking hard to port, its wake a jagged curve of white foam, and the huge mound of water that rose up beneath its keel, interrupted the otherwise monotonous scene.

The sea had been growing more choppy as the day progressed. Restless waves reflected the agitated clouds that scudded overhead. The fitful wind strengthened, blowing the tops off the waves and spattering drops of water against the ship.

It was just after they'd seen the first flash of lightning against the dark clouds on the northern horizon that the sea monster had come.

Chasa saw it as a challenge. Ivey insisted that minstrel lore defined it as a sea dragon. Chasa, launching his harpoon toward the sensitive gill-slit, didn't waste breath replying.

After that, the battle became a blur to Chasa's senses. The captain and crew of his ship performed as heroically as always, carrying him close enough for the attack, evading the monster's attempts at retaliation. Ivey handed him two harpoons, one after the other. Both bounced harmlessly off the thick scales of the monster's body. On the next pass, Chasa passed his sword to Ivey. To his credit, the minstrel grasped the sword without hesitation, although he flinched at the tingle of magic against his palms.

The dragon's mighty tail whipped overhead, sending two seamen sprawling and threatening the mast. Ivey hacked halfway through it with his first blow. The monster's head surged out of the water, jaws wide, its roar slamming against Chasa's chest like a physical blow. Then it disappeared, taking its entire length below the waves. Ivey leaped to one side of the ship, Chasa to the other. A great mound of water rose beneath them, marking the precise location of the returning monster's head.

At Chasa's signal, the captain shouted instructions to his men. The ship slid backward. Chasa clambered over the rail, hooked a line in place, and leaned into his shoulder harness, feet braced against the side of the hull. Ivey balanced the sword in both hands, aiming at the dark green shape that grew larger and larger beneath them.

A child could have stood upright within the gaping mouth. The beast emitted a desperate scream as the minstrel pierced its right eye with the sword. Then its cry choked off, as Chasa's harpoon buried half its length into the monster's gill slit. The oarsmen backed them nimbly out of range of the spout of yellowish, faintly smoking blood that erupted from the triple nostrils. Chasa accepted Ivey's helping hand and pulled himself back on deck.

They rushed to the bow, water dripping from their clothes. The rest of the sea monster's body floated to the surface, over fifty feet of scaled muscle, tapering from the broad base of the head to a tail no thicker than a common snake's.

Chasa grinned at the look of annoyance on the Dherrican's face. "You get used to being wet."

"I never planned to become an apprentice hero. First phantom cats, then weapons training, now this. The whole summer, gone. I can't decide whether to blame your father or your sister. Or you."

"I promised I wouldn't do it again," Chasa muttered. Despite Jeyn's best efforts, their father had found out about his foray into Rhenlan. The king had listened to his and Aage's report about the Abstainers and Soen and Rhenlan's captain of the guard with his usual keen attention. Later, in private, he'd vented his disapproval of the escapade with such vehemence that Chasa's ears burned just thinking about it. "Besides, it's not my fault that it's been a busy summer for monsters."

Bare feet scuffled on planking behind them as the seamen prepared to raise the sail.

"They've kept you running from one end of Sitrine to the other," Ivey agreed. "Too bad you have to wait for a report before you can act."

"Aage can locate monsters the moment they appear—that is, if he had the time for daily searches. I look forward to the day Mojil or Forrit comes of age."

"Your Dreamer cousins?"

"Second cousins. No, third. I don't know them very well."

"Because of their Dreamer training, I suppose."

Chasa shrugged. "The Greenmothers visit them now and then, but apparently there's not much they can do in the way of training until their magic comes to them. So it's not that they're so busy, just that they live near Bren, and I don't get down there very often."

"It should come soon, shouldn't it?"

"The girl's thirteen, the boy's eleven. Aage says it's not just a matter of physical maturity. They have to be ready in every way to bend the power before their gifts will be revealed."

Ivey said, "I can't imagine waiting so long to know exactly what my life's work would be. I started training as a musician when I was seven."

"It would be unsettling, wouldn't it? Knowing that you'll have this amazing power, but not knowing what form it will take."

The ship steered past several of the floating harpoons, close enough that one of the men reached down to retrieve them from the troubled surface without much difficulty. The harpoons, like Chasa's sword, were the result of Aage's mastery of the art of making magic weapons. For over sixty years, he had overseen the forging of all of Sitrine's monster-slaying blades. Most followed the traditional pattern used by generations of Shapers—the killing edge permeated with dragon powder and the weapon as a whole magically attuned to a single user. Sene carried such a sword, as did Hion of Rhenlan and Pirse of Dherrica.

However, toward the end of the long battle with the fire bears, Aage had moved beyond tradition. As the death toll among the Shapers mounted, Aage had located a few exceptional Keepers with the strength and reflexes to control the power-filled weapons. In addition, he discovered that, if he infused a blade with the minimum amount of dragon powder necessary to harm monsters, he could render it safe for use by as many as ten people. The magically weak weapons were useless against the large dragons of Dherrica, but they proved acceptable against fire bears and ideal for hunting sea monsters.

The men and women who crewed Chasa's ship were chosen not just for their sailing skills, but because they could tolerate the bending of power that surrounded the specially forged harpoon heads and Chasa's dragon sword. A few had even learned to wield them. Ivey, to Sene's delight, proved receptive to Aage's magical imprinting. He would probably never develop the swordsmanship needed to defeat a phantom cat, but hacking at a sea dragon required no finesse, only perseverance.

Ivey moved out of the way as they pulled alongside the monster's corpse. Chasa snagged his sword out of its eye, then stretched forward to detach one of its gills.

"Not much smaller than a dragon's ears." Chasa resumed his education of the reluctant minstrel. "Aage prepares most of them for Jenil to use in her healing. He says all the monsters have to bend power to a certain extent, just to exist."

With the aid of a large hook, Chasa rolled the body in the water so that he could reach the other gill, then laid it on top of the first on the deck. Chasa pushed the now faintly shimmering body away with the hook, then took a dry cloth out of the storage locker forward of the mast and began to clean his sword.

"Being healed by magic's unpleasant. Our bodies aren't designed to have power bent through them. Without that," he indicated the sea monster's gills with a flick of his sword, "no one could survive any extensive power-bending healing."

The captain approached Chasa. "We've retrieved all the weapons, Your Highness."

"Very well. Set course for port."

"Aye, sir."

Chasa took one last look at the monster. All of its magic had dissipated, leaving it a peculiar mass of seemingly unrelated blobs of flesh. As he watched, what had been the tail jerked and vanished beneath the surface of the water, snatched by some scavenger fish glad of an easy meal.

Ivey stood at his shoulder. "You've given me another story to sing about—as soon as I'm back on the road."

Rain clouds loomed closer from the north. Chasa and Ivey went below out of the freshening wind before the storm arrived.

After the leaves began to turn, just after Fall Festival, there was the Horse Fair. There had been an annual Horse Fair in Edian for generations of Dreamers. Once, the horse people had been part of it. According to the Redmothers, the horse people had started it, long before Edian itself had existed. At the northeast corner of the lake, near the center of the best grazing land in the three kingdoms, horse traders and horse admirers gathered to buy, sell, and talk about horses.

Dael rode along the line of, and spoke briefly to, his guards at their posts. After this first inspection of the day he could get some breakfast. Once, he had enjoyed being at the fair. The easy duty of policing visitors and making sure the events went smoothly had been something to look forward to. The fair signaled the end of summer for him more than the Festival. Some of the people who arrived for the Fall Festival, especially the minstrels and entertainers of various sorts, stayed for the fair, some stayed until midwinter, and some simply stayed through until spring. A few outstayed their welcome, and had to be escorted out of town, but most contributed to a more colorful Edian. Dael still anticipated the post-Fair festivities. He enjoyed the parties with the entertainers, and the company of the pretty girls visiting from the countryside. But the fair itself, the animals and the skills they demonstrated, no longer interested him.

The queen's pavilions occupied their customary choice location, near the show rings and convenient to the watering troughs. Dael gave the complex a cursory glance. Queen Gallia brought her entire staff up each year, and needed no help from the guard. He saw several horses being exercised in the smaller ring, the thud of hooves clear in the still morning air. There was a dry smell of straw and sawdust. In the next row of stables a wisp of smoke from a cook fire spiraled lazily skyward.

The road into Edian was still empty. Dael urged his horse to a canter, in a hurry to be away. He was feeling very much alone today. The Fair was full of reminders of the royal family, and of the past. He didn't have time for melancholy anymore. He had a full day ahead of him, starting with breakfast at the Lakeside Inn. A breakfast planned since the beginning of the summer, although he no longer looked forward to the meeting.

Dael handed his reins to the inn's stable boy and crossed the yard. The familiar horse was standing next to the wall. He mounted the steps and walked into the cool interior of the inn's main room. A trio of merchants sat by the hearth, engrossed in conversation. He identified them as regular visitors to Edian, still blissfully ignorant of the unease growing among the local business leaders. They were of no concern to Dael this morning.

The man Dael had come to meet was seated at a table near the large, diamond-paned window that overlooked the lake.

"Dael," the carter said in greeting.

"You arrived last night?" Dael asked as he took a seat opposite Jordy.

"Aye."

A pretty serving girl, smiling familiarly, said, "The usual,

Dael?" then disappeared into the kitchen before Dael could do more than nod his agreement.

"You're well known, I see."

Dael smirked and reached across the table to snare a slice of bread from the carter's full plate. Jordy, his mouth full, merely raised his eyebrows.

"I've been working," Dael explained. "Where's Tob? He's usually the one to filch from your plate."

"Back at the market," Jordy said after he swallowed, "with the wagon. Probably still asleep. We came in very late."

"I have some news." Dael wanted to have it said at once. "I located that boy from your village."

Jordy put his fork down. "Pross. Well?"

"He was sent to the Dherrican border. An outpost on the Galla, fifty miles up from the sea."

"Can you get him away from there? Reassign him to a troop nearer home, at least."

"He's dead, Jordy."

The blunt statement drained the color from the man's face. Jordy lowered his eyes for just a moment, his jaw set. He looked up again to ask, "What happened?"

"The details aren't really necessary."

"His family will think so. Yours would."

Dael accepted the rebuke, tasting bitterness. "He and another boy were practicing swordplay. Pross dropped his shield. The other boy tried to stop his swing, lost control. His blade went through Pross's thigh. He bled to death."

There was more Dael could have said. He'd been thinking about it for days, ever since receiving the report of the accident. If he'd been the man training them it wouldn't have happened. If they'd had a Brownmother at that outpost, the boy might have lived. It was all so useless!

Jordy sighed. "It's not what I hoped to bring back to Broadford, but at least we know. I'll tell his parents, and our Redmother."

"Thank you, Jordy. I am sorry."

"Nothing you could have done." The carter picked up his fork, then stabbed it into a hunk of potato and pushed the plate away from him.

The serving girl chose that moment to reappear, a laden tray in her hands. She set a plate heaped with biscuits in front of Dael, and put the dish of ham gravy to one side. At his left she placed a pot of steaming tea and a cup.

"I'd rather have a brandy," he muttered.

"Nonsense," she replied, patting his head. "Eat your breakfast."

Dael watched her bustle over to another pair of early guests. He sighed. He was hungry. The news, dismal as it was, was old to him. He picked up a biscuit. "I'm making slow progress with the townspeople here."

The carter accepted the change of subject. "They're content. Edian reaps more benefits than troubles from the state of things. What about the guard?"

"Some I'm sure still follow their vows. Others enjoy the power Damon offers to those who serve him well. I have to be careful who I trust. Damon has spies in the guard, in the court, in Edian, and in the rest of Rhenlan as well. I hope you're careful who you talk to."

"I am that," Jordy agreed dourly. "There are one or two in any village who will be tempted by greed. I've been speaking only to those I know well, and respect."

"And?"

"It's going well. Better than I thought it would," he admitted grudgingly. "Thanks to the prince, as a matter of fact. He's pushing, laddie. Pushing everywhere. As I expect you're aware."

"The conscriptions, you mean?"

"And the extra taxing, as your corporals will have it. Stealing, I call it."

"So do I, Jordy," Dael reminded him. "None of those troops are sent by me. There's no longer a single king's guard in Rhenlan, although Damon doesn't know I've noticed that. There are some who report to Damon directly. I know who they are, or who most of them are."

Jordy's grouchiness was replaced by worry. "This is dangerous for you."

"I know. I keep friendly with Damon's favorites. Just as I'm still on the best of terms with Damon. I think I've identified his chief informer. A stableman named Palim."

"Watch him, lad. Watch all of them."

"Every minute," Dael agreed.

Jordy looked out over the lake. Dael concentrated on eating, using the tea to wash down half a gravy-soaked biscuit at a time. His mother would have nagged him to chew his food. The thought of her cheered him somewhat. He popped the last biscuit into his mouth whole. Gravy leaked out of the corner of his mouth, and he ducked his head to catch the warm liquid on the back of his wrist.

"You should chew your food," Jordy commented.

Dael started guiltily. "I'm in a hurry." The excuse had never worked at home, but it was all he could think of.

"A wife would feed you properly. Keep you out of inns, on a sensible schedule," the carter suggested.

"Not for me."

Jordy tilted his head toward the serving girl, busy behind the bar. "You don't lack for interested suitors."

"They're interested. I'm not. The only one I ever cared for is long gone."

The carter, thank the gods, made no answer to that. He stood and stretched. "I'm leaving for home first thing tomorrow. I've done all I can for this year. The winter will keep me in Broadford."

"You've planted the seeds," Dael assured him. "We'll see what the spring brings."

"Look for me before Spring Festival, if the weather is mild." With a wave, he left.

Dael leaned back in his chair. More biscuits? He wasn't sure whether or not to look forward to their next talk. At least he wouldn't have to bear sad tidings again. He hoped.

"Just because I'm Dherrican doesn't mean I like the cold," Ivey grumbled as he shrugged a light cloak across his shoulders. Mist floated on the still surface of the water between the shore and the ship, tendrils stretching up to seep across the sand where they'd made camp. Overhead, a few lonely gulls circled the ship, complaining bitterly, white bodies barely visible against a pewter sky.

Chasa looked up at them. "Don't blame me. Weather is Aage's responsibility, and he's not here."

Ivey rummaged through his pack. "There's a heavier shirt in here somewhere."

As Ivey added shoes to the pile of odds and ends beside him, Chasa said, "You've acquired a whole new wardrobe. Having your help is expensive."

"Expensive?" Ivey regarded him skeptically. "Passage on that weather-beaten excuse for a ship and a few new personal items isn't much compensation for my fearless company in battle."

Chasa snorted. Unlike their battle with the sea monster, yesterday's encounter had been nothing like a real fight. They'd found the reported Abstainers, but the band of dangerous marauders had turned out to be five thoroughly insane old people in a leaky fishing boat. He'd killed three with his javelins before they could draw alongside, then leaped across the gap between the rails, sword in hand, and dispatched the other two with more mercy than Abstainers deserved. Ivey had watched the entire episode from the boat. It had not been a battle. It had been an extermination. It was all that could be done when Abstainers started preying on settled folk, but Chasa had never learned to like doing it.

Now the task was finished. They had anchored on the coast west of Cross Cove, only a few day's overland travel from Edian. Ivey was eager to resume his usual life.

Chasa was not.

He dreaded Raisal. He didn't want to walk back into that house, into a farcical situation which everyone else pretended not to be aware of. No, not everyone else. But the one person who counted insisted on ignoring it. Ignoring him.

Someone else was ignoring the problem, too. Chasa forced back the surge of anger that rose within him. No. He was not going to think about Dad.

355

A long-fingered, callused hand dropped onto his shoulder. "Let's have breakfast," Ivey suggested. "We need to talk."

Chasa followed him to the campfire. The aroma of fresh fish and brown biscuits caused his stomach to rumble. The ship's cook deftly slid hot breaded fish and the round biscuits from the pans onto wooden plates, which he handed to Chasa and the minstrel. Nodding his thanks, Chasa silently followed Ivey away from the fire to a flat-topped rock near the high tide line.

Ivey attacked the food with enthusiasm. Between mouthfuls, he said, "I thought you'd be hungry."

Chasa lifted his gaze. "I thought you wanted to talk."

Ivey popped one more piece of biscuit into his mouth, then licked his fingers. "About the girl," he said.

"Which one?"

"Not mine." Ivey leaned forward on the rock, plate balanced on his knees. "Nothing to talk about. We're going to enjoy married life, though she hasn't asked me yet." He smiled. "Keepers need convincing about everything. The convincing can be quite pleasant. Take your girl, for example."

A heavy pause fell between them. Finally Chasa said, "Was that a joke?"

Ivey didn't move. "It was advice. From an almost-married man much your elder."

"Four years isn't much," Chasa corrected him.

"More experienced, then. With Keeper women. I've been watching you and Feather. Your behavior makes no sense to me. Are you betrothed, or aren't you?"

"Good question." Chasa picked the coating off a piece of fish, the grease warm and slippery on his fingertips. "She doesn't remember me."

"What's that got to do with it? Feather doesn't need to remember some child she once played with. She needs to get to know the man you are now. If you want her, that is."

"Of course I want her!"

Ivey sat back. "Why?"

"Another good question." Chasa looked out over the gray water, still fidgeting with the fish. "She's concise. Funny. She makes Dad laugh." *He wasn't going to think about Dad.*

Chasa forced his mind back to the list of Feather's good points. "She's beautiful. She'll be a strong consort, someone who'll help Jeyn and me run the kingdom someday. The staff all like her. Jeyn likes her." *Dad likes her. Stop thinking about Dad!*

"That's all very rational," Ivey said with dry approval. "A woman with attributes like that deserves to be recommended for Brownmother training."

"She already is a Brownmother."

"Yes—but are any of those reasons to marry?"

"I like her. I love her!"

Ivey nodded. "Actually, I noticed."

"She doesn't."

"Well, you never show her!"

"How can I? She doesn't like me."

"She doesn't know you."

The words jolted him. She didn't know him, didn't remember him. That was the whole problem. "So what am I supposed to do?"

"Go get her," Ivey advised. "A lass likes to be courted."

"Is that what you did with Jeyn?"

Ivey's smile was reminiscent. "No, lad. She got me." He fingered the pale blue material of his cloak. "She appealed to a sense of luxury I didn't know I had. Think of something that'll appeal to your Feather."

Chasa gazed into the mist obscuring the landscape. *Something to appeal to Feather.*

What could he give her his father couldn't?

357

CHAPTER 32

Vray straightened with a sigh from the washtub. Several strands of damp hair fell in front of her nose. She pushed them aside with the back of her forearm, wiping the sweat from her face in the process. The day was cool, but the hard work had warmed her.

"Pepper, you can go down to the village after we finish this."

The mornings had started to bring frost. There was no telling how much longer they'd be able to use the clotheslines strung across the yard. Vray didn't think that clothes dried in a wash house or before the hearth had quite the same quality as those dried in the fresh air. She was determined to get everyone's warm clothing washed and ready for use before the snow arrived.

"How much longer?" Pepper insisted.

"Never, if you don't take that pile of skirts up to our room and bring me Matti's tunic."

Pepper gathered up the clean clothes, each motion slow and grudging. "I don't know where it is."

"Look for it."

"But—"

"Go!"

Vray removed the last of the bedclothes from the water and carried them to the wringer, water dripping on the wooden floor. The wet coolness chilled her feet. The sheet fell from the wringer onto the top of the now-full basket, which she then lifted and carried out to the line.

Pepper wandered out onto the porch, waving a scrap of blue. "This one?"

"That one."

"What should I do with it?"

Vray gritted her teeth. "Put it in the washtub!" They had

358

been repeating this scene once a nineday since she'd taken over the family washing. Laundry was one chore Pepper simply hated. It would have been faster—and easier—to do the work without her, but Jordy had been firm about Pepper's having to help.

Pepper drifted back toward the house. "Then can I go?"

"Yes, then you can go."

A few seconds later Pepper tore down the hill. Vray watched her go, wishing she could join her. It had been a bright morning but the afternoon was growing cold. Heavy clouds hung overhead, dull and threatening. The gloomy skies didn't help Vray's loneliness. How Cyril could sit for hours at her loom, isolated from even trivial conversation, was incomprehensible.

"Later," Vray promised herself. "I'll go see Canis." She draped the first sheet over the line. No wind. That was convenient, at least.

As she finished, a man's voice called, "Anyone home?"

Vray stepped away from the laundry to peer toward the road. The familiar voice didn't belong to anyone in the village, which frightened her for a moment. The man who rode up the path on a black horse had curly brown hair, tied back off his neck. The leather-encased neck of a guitar was visible over his shoulder. His eyes lit with a smile when he saw her by the wash line.

"Hello! Remember me?" he asked as he dismounted.

"Ivey. Hello." Vray looked at the minstrel's travel-stained shirt and cloak, and at the bulky pack slung tied to the saddle horn, her mind still on washing. If he'd come to stay, she would end up doing his laundry, too.

"Where is everyone?"

"The girls are off playing. Cyril's inside."

He stopped a respectable distance from the clean clothing on the line, and put his pack down beside him. She tried not to look dismayed, but his widening smile proved she'd betrayed herself somehow.

"Don't worry. I'm not staying. Just wanted to see how you are."

She stepped away from him. "Cold." The word sounded angry, and she wasn't. At the Spring Festival, the minstrel had shown that he was concerned about her welfare, though she didn't know why. She wanted to accept him as a friend. She certainly didn't need another enemy. "Other than that, I'm fine, thank you."

"You're looking much better."

She tugged at her wet skirt. "I look like a dishrag."

He laughed. "Laundry does that to people."

He looked around the empty yard. Then his eyes met hers. "I'm here on business for the king of Sitrine. Any messages?"

Vray stared at him. The king. In Raisal. She had purposefully stopped thinking about kingdoms and their rulers years ago. "Messages? From me?"

"To King Sene."

A chill unrelated to the weather prickled her skin. "He knows about me?"

"I think he knows everything," Ivey said lightly. "I try to keep him informed."

Vray folded her arms tightly across her chest. "I think you should leave now," she told the suddenly dangerous-seeming man. Any man working for a king could be dangerous. She'd lived long enough in Hion's court to learn that much before she was sent away. She'd learned quite a lot about all three kingdoms, considering she'd been fourteen and not in the king's favor.

Ivey spread his hands. The gesture of harmless appeal made her all the more nervous. "What did I say?"

"Is Sene going to tell my brother where I am?"

"Certainly not!" Was his outrage real? Or simply an example of his storyteller's art? "He doesn't like your brother. You're safe here. As safe as you can be anywhere in Rhenlan. This is where the Dreamers want you to be."

Vray's head began to ache. How had her nice, quiet afternoon of backbreaking work gone awry? *Think, girl,* she chided herself. She hadn't been thinking about survival lately. It was time to resume that habit.

"I have no news for any king," she told him, stiff with caution.

"Well, the king has a message for you."

Vray hugged herself tightly. When she remained silent, the minstrel went on, "He asks that you begin to consider your choices. You're safe and where the Dreamers want you, but is it where you want to be?" A teasing smile brightened his face. "I think I remembered all of it, Redmother."

She wished she could put him and everything he'd said out of her mind, but that was a luxury lost to Redmothers. Besides, something in his words was too uncomfortable for her to ignore.

"Choices?"

Ivey said, "What would you like to do?"

Keep away from my brother, she thought bleakly. Ivey probably knew that already. After all, he was a messenger for Sene of Sitrine, who knows everything.

"I don't know," she admitted softly.

He accepted her statement without censure. "How much have you heard about what's gone on in the world in the last three years?"

"We never discussed policy in the scullery at Soza. I don't know anything."

"You've got an opportunity here to find out what you missed."

"From you?"

"You don't need me. You're a carter's daughter. He must hear all sorts of news, meet with all sorts of fascinating people, in the course of a summer."

She shrugged. "To hear his neighbors talk, he does."

The minstrel took a step back to pat his horse's neck.

"Jordy," he said in his light, conversational way, "is the most well-traveled, well-informed man in the three kingdoms. Excepting myself, of course."

"Of course." She peered into his face. "Minstrel, what are we talking about? What do you—what does Sene—expect from me?"

"Just remember, Jordy's horse and cart go everywhere."

Pepper, followed by a herd of children, came racing up the road from the village. Somebody spotted Ivey and called out his name. Shouts of delight at the prospect of songs and stories shattered the stillness of the afternoon.

"Looks like you're going to be busy," Vray said. "And I'd better get back to work."

"Think about it," he challenged her as the crowd of children surrounded him. Amid noisy questions and requests, Ivey mounted his horse, pulling the youngest of the children up behind him. He set off, followed by the rest of the crowd.

Vray watched them go, wishing she didn't remember every word he'd spoken. As for thinking about his words, she would. Eventually. When she was ready. Today she wasn't ready. She turned and hurried back into the wash house. The prospect of housework and solitude—and, later, Redmother tales for squabbling little girls, and Cyril's mercifully unquestioning silence—seemed no longer a burden, but a haven.

Chasa yawned as he followed his father through the house. His father had wakened him with the announcement that he wanted to get to the practice yard in the cool of the day. Chasa agreed, in theory, but wished the king hadn't persuaded him to get out of bed quite so early. His ship had just gotten in the night before, and he wasn't rested yet. He hardly noticed when they turned to take a short cut through the reception room. He did notice that they were suddenly surrounded by a great many busy people. Alert at last, he looked around the big room. From all the activity, he guessed today was one of Raisal's gathering days. In addition to holding midsummer and winter gatherings like smaller towns, Raisal's larger population required additional days for vow-taking. Chasa edged toward the wall behind his father, trying to weave between the tables which a small horde of servants were setting up without getting in the way.

"No, put that over there!" Feather's impatient demand

echoed slightly against the hardwood floor of the reception hall. "The Redmother has to stand where everyone can see her, and she'll want the bowl within reach. What do you expect her to do, stand on a chair?"

The chastised servant hastily transferred the large bowl he was carrying to the table Feather indicated.

Sene beamed at the chaos. "Coming along nicely," he called to Feather.

She had to step around a servant in order to locate them. "Are you here to help?"

"No, ma'am, just passing through," the king replied. "You seem to have the gathering well organized."

"I'll stay," Chasa volunteered.

His father turned his head, puzzled. "I thought we were going to weapons practice together."

"Dad," Chasa said, trying not to be annoyed. "I'd rather help Feather."

"She'll be here all afternoon," Sene coaxed with his best persuasive smile. "I enjoy working out with you, son."

Chasa noticed Feather watching them. Actually, she was watching Sene, and melting slightly from the effects of his father's charm, even though it wasn't directed at her. Chasa clenched his teeth. The noise of many people moving lots of furniture into position around the large room made any thought of a serious conversation impossible.

"I'll be out soon. Really."

"Suit yourself." Sene continued along the relatively uncluttered side of the hall, directing his devastating smile at Feather. "I knew you'd come in handy. You're a good Brownmother. I can tell." He waved his arm toward the busy workers. "All the servants are terrified of you."

She grinned, showing her teeth. "I do my best."

Sene laughed as he went out the other end of the hall. Chasa moved a stack of chairs closer to one of the tables. Dektrieb came by at once, frowned, and moved the chairs back again. Chasa sighed and looked around. So much for being helpful. He found himself facing the middle of the room, where Feather stood, hands on hips, as three people wrestled with a newly cleaned tapestry that didn't want to get back up on the wall.

While she was distracted he slipped up behind her. A fragrance of lemon soap hung around her. Her black hair, which she usually wore loose, was trying to escape from being tied at the back of her neck. Bending close to her ear, Chasa whispered, "I have to talk to you."

She spun to face him.

"I'm busy," she hissed back at him.

"I know. But this is important."

She turned her back on him. "Go bash something in the practice yard, Highness."

The only thing he wanted to bash was his father. And maybe Jenil. To Feather, he said, "That can wait. This is important."

"The gathering is important. It's tomorrow." A cook chose that moment to appear and head directly for Feather. Chasa waited stubbornly while the two women discussed the menu. Feather ignored his presence. The cook glanced at him curiously and rather uneasily once or twice, and finished her questions as quickly as she could. He supposed he was frowning thunderously at the poor woman. Or maybe she just didn't know what to make of his presence. When Jeyn organized the gatherings and Festivals, he'd happily run off to kill sea monsters rather than take part in any of the planning. Planning was harder work than killing monsters.

Especially planning how to court a wife.

After the cook was gone, Feather started to walk away. Chasa followed. Ivey had said to go get her. He intended to. But to get her, he first had to get her alone. The side door that led to the garden was propped open to allow fresh air into the crowded hall. She reached the opening, then whirled on him again. He took another step forward. She had no choice but to back out into the garden.

The air was still cool, the sky a sharp blue. The garden plants were bright with color, and the scents of many flowers mingled with birdsong and the thrumming of insect wings. It was as romantic a setting as he could have chosen.

This might be his only chance. His father was too adept at grabbing any romantic moment for himself.

"I've been thinking," he began.

"Good for you."

That did it. "Sometimes I wonder why I want to marry you!"

"So do I!" she shot back. "Why not forget the whole thing and leave me in peace?"

"Because you're not in peace! My leaving you alone wouldn't help."

"Tormenting me will?"

"I'm just trying to talk to you!" Belatedly, Chasa turned and glared at the gaping servants. Dektrieb shooed everyone back to work, and Chasa pulled the door closed.

"I don't want to listen to you!"

"I know!" Chasa spun back to confront her. "And I know why!"

She blinked. "What are you talking about?"

"You don't remember. But I do."

"Remember what?"

"First, I don't think you remember what you said the night that you got drunk."

She flushed. "I talked while I was I drunk? All I remember is being sick. And the pretty colors of the wineglasses against the tablecloth." Screwing her face in a frown, she continued, "And Dektrieb. He was angry. And there was someone else. That was you?"

"It was me. We had a conversation."

"I'm not responsible for anything I said while I was drunk."

"Yes, you are."

"Fine. I apologize. Can we go in now?"

"Not until you listen to me. You told me you don't like to hear my voice. I think my voice has gotten deeper, more attractive, since we were children, but maybe not." He tried his own charming smile on her. It didn't inspire her to run away. In fact, she seemed to be listening.

Encouraged by her attention, he continued, "Jenil took

your memories because they were making you very sick. She and Dad thought you might go crazy. I didn't think so. I thought you were stronger than that, that you'd grow out of the nightmares. But who listens to a child? They didn't listen to either of us, and so you lost your memories. Then I lost you, because they took you away. To Garden Vale. They wouldn't let me come visit you, either."

"A prince from Sitrine would hardly have been welcome in Rhenlan."

"I still wanted to come. You were my best friend, Feather."

"I don't remember!"

"I know!" His voice rose again, years of frustration pouring out. "But I do! We were friends, more than friends! We did everything together! The betrothal was our idea! I'm a Shaper. When a Shaper falls in love he stays in love! Child, adult, it doesn't matter. I love you! Let me give you back your memories. Our memories!"

Her mouth dropped open. "Uh . . ." No other sound came from her for several long seconds. She blinked suspiciously liquid eyes, closed her mouth, and swallowed, her throat working. In a small voice, she asked, "You love me?"

"Yes," he insisted. "Even if you are the meanest, most bad-tempered person I've ever met." That sounded a bit harsh, so he added, "But then I haven't spent much time in Dherrica. Ivey says their women are worse."

Thank the gods, she laughed. It was slightly shaky, but it was a good-humored reaction. After she caught her breath, she said, "I've been wondering how long you people were going to let me get away with it."

"With what?"

"Being a brat. Now," she continued, "what do you mean, you'll give me my memories?"

"I was there," he repeated. "Part of your childhood. I also heard a lot about what happened in your village. Jeyn remembers, too. And Aage. When you were little, you really liked him. I remember it used to surprise him."

Curiosity lit her eyes. "I used to surprise the wizard?"

"By crawling into his lap and asking for stories. You weren't afraid of him. You and Jeyn were the only children in Raisal who didn't run away when they saw him coming."

"Run away from Aage?" Feather was bemused. "Why? He's the best-looking man in Raisal."

"I'll ignore that," Chasa said dryly. To his delight, it made her blush again. "Children don't notice sexuality. All they see is his frown."

Behind them the door opened. Feather reluctantly looked away from him. "Yes, Dektrieb?"

"I'm sorry to interrupt." The depth of sincerity in the man's voice added to Chasa's sense of triumph. He didn't mind the interruption now. Feather had finally responded to him as a person. It was the start he needed. He stepped aside graciously to allow his betrothed to go back to her work. Dektrieb nodded politely, and Chasa hoped his answering grin didn't look as idiotic as it felt.

They'd made a start!

He sobered again at once. Now, for the next step.

Chapter 33

The target dummy swayed close as the guards on the wall
heaved on the line. Sene ducked under the heavy wooden
arm, caught his balance, and swung. His sword whacked
against the padding with a satisfying thunk. He jumped
back, lowering his sword.

"Enough!" he called to the corporal in charge of the practice yard.

The girl grinned down at him. "So soon, Your Majesty?"

"Yes, so soon," he growled, and pulled off his helmet to
aim a mock glare at the pretty youngster. She laughed.

"Not bad, Dad."

Sene tossed his helmet to one of the nearby guards, then
turned. Chasa was watching him from the entrance gate.

"How long have you been there?" Sene asked.

"Not long."

His son was still dressed in a quilted vest over a white
shirt, tucked into a pair of cream trousers. Sene shrugged
out of his padding, feeling all the more sweaty and grimy
next to his son's elegance, and walked toward the gate.

"Thought you were going to join me."

"Something came up. Dad, I need to talk with you."

"Excellent." He took Chasa's arm and escorted him out
of the yard. "I've been meaning to talk to you, too."

Chasa gingerly extricated his sleeve from Sene's grip.
"You need a bath, Dad."

"You didn't come down here to tell me that. Never
mind. We'll talk in the bathhouse."

Chasa followed him past the stables to the stone bathhouse. A servant stoked the fire higher, then began to draw
water for the king's bath.

Sene stripped off his clothes and tossed them into a
corner. "It's about Feather, son. I notice that you two

aren't exactly getting along."

Chasa remained standing near the doorway. "Oh, really?"

"Yes. You know how Jeyn felt about the marriage I'd arranged with Daav. He's a good man, and a good friend. But he's my friend. She was right to decide not to marry him. I was pushing her to do something I wanted. She was wise enough to know what she wanted."

"Are you saying I don't have to marry Feather?"

Sene paused before moving toward the tub of hot water. This was difficult for him to say, but he'd been giving it a lot of thought.

"No, you don't. Not if you don't want to. I'm very fond of the girl, but that shouldn't affect your decisions on such an important matter."

His son took several steps toward him. He did not look relieved, which was what Sene had been expecting. In fact, he looked angry.

Chasa met his gaze firmly. "I want to marry her. I want you to leave her alone. That's what I came here to talk to you about."

"What?"

"I want her. I've wanted to marry her since we were children. You sent her away. I never wanted her sent away. I never thought it was a good idea, what you and Jenil did to her memories. You know why she doesn't come near me? The sound of my voice frightens her, that's why."

"What do you mean, doesn't come near you?"

"You wouldn't have noticed." Anger, and hard sarcasm, roughened the boy's voice. "Every time I try to come near her, you get in the way! If you want her for yourself, fine. Let's get it out in the open."

"For myself!" Sene sputtered. "What are you talking about? She's a child! A baby! My foster daughter, by the gods!"

"You don't treat her like a child."

"I treat her exactly as I do you and Jeyn. I enjoy her company. She makes me laugh. My behavior toward her is beyond reproach! The way I express my affection—"

"The way you express your affection," Chasa interrupted him, "has made her fall in love with you."

"Nonsense!"

"Truth. The question is, are you in love with her?"

Sene remembered the bath behind him, and belatedly sat down in the tub. Warm water was supposed to be soothing. His whirling mind needed soothing. He looked at Chasa through the rising steam. The boy was furious. He'd never seen his son furious before. Or jealous. This was jealousy! If it hadn't been such an unthinkable situation, he might have been amused.

It was unthinkable. Feather was clever, a bright, stimulating person to share conversation with. He liked her skepticism, and her intelligent questions, and her acid wit. He'd begun to think she was too much for Chasa to handle. But love her for himself?

"Nonsense," he repeated aloud. "I love her, yes. But, in love? No."

Chasa bent toward him, bracing his hands against the edge of the heavy cedarwood tub. "Are you sure? Are you sure you aren't seeing Mother in her?"

"Jeyana?"

"That was our mother," the boy returned impatiently.

"Feather doesn't have a thing in common with Jeyana!"

"That's not what you used to say."

"Your mother," Sene stated with growing anger of his own, "was a tall, willowy, mature, silver-haired beauty. Does that describe Feather?"

"In looks, no. But that's not what attracts you, is it?"

"Nothing attracts me!"

"Then why do you spend every free minute with my betrothed?"

"Because you don't!"

"Because you're always there first!"

Sene opened his mouth to shout again, then shut it abruptly. "Am I?"

"Yes."

370

Grandmother taught him to recognize the truth, to remember that he could be in error. She insisted he accept defeat with dignity. If necessary. This time, it was necessary.

"She is like your mother," Sene admitted quietly. "I didn't see it. But you're right. Jeyana was a difficult woman, and I loved her for it. Feather is very like her."

More like her than Chasa and Jeyn were. Loneliness flooded him. Jeyn could tease as her mother once did, but her wit never cut. His son, however, might have more of Jeyana's inner strength than Sene had guessed. Chasa hadn't shown it often. Sene was glad to find it there.

"Do you want her?" Chasa asked. "If you do, we'll be rivals. I'm not going to back down for your sake. All I ask is that you give me a fair chance with her. Give me some time alone with her. If she chooses you without ever knowing me, it's not fair to any of us."

"I notice you don't mention duty, or the Dreamer prophecy."

"That's your concern, not mine. I love her! You taught me the old saying about Shapers, that once we give our heart it's forever. I fell in love with her when I was six."

"You waited a long time."

"Too long to give up without a fight."

Sene forced his muscles to relax, to present as unthreatening a demeanor as he could. Easy, considering his present position. "I'm not your rival, son."

The boy's eyes narrowed. "Are you certain about that?"

"Yes. I'm certain. Feather's your betrothed, as long as she wants it, too. That's between the two of you. I apologize for getting in the way. It really was unintentional. I'll stop, now that you've brought the matter to my attention."

Slowly, Chasa straightened and smiled. "Good." He started to turn to the door.

"Good luck," Sene called after him.

Chasa grinned over his shoulder. "I'll need it."

After the boy was gone, Sene smiled to himself. Ah, well. His son was used to killing sea monsters. One mean young woman shouldn't give him too much trouble.

One special young woman. Sene rested his head against the edge of the tub, and his smile faded.

Special. But not his.

"There! The last sleeve is in," Vray said brightly. "Now I can start the interesting part."

Clack, clack, clack. The steady beat of the loom was the only noise in the house. Cyril showed no response to Vray's comment, but Vray was used to that by now. She held the shirt up, knowing that the motion would attract the woman's attention.

"I was thinking of green fern leaves across the yoke. Pepper should look good in green, shouldn't she?"

Cyril turned her head. Her eyes flicked over the garment with what Vray read as pleased approval, before she went back to her own work. The cloth on the loom was an intricate pattern of cream and blue, reminding Vray of birds and water.

She set Pepper's new shirt aside for a moment and bent down to rummage in her sewing basket for the medium-size embroidery hoop. Pulling it out, she rested it on her lap and chose a skein of pale green thread and her favorite needle. She settled back in the chair and wriggled her shoulders. The sewing had seemed to go fast, but the slight ache in her muscles reminded her she'd been at this all morning. She slipped cloth between the wooden circles, tightened the one on top, then looked at Cyril again. Her foster mother was surprisingly good company, despite never speaking, or hardly even looking at her. On second thought, perhaps that was precisely why she was good to be with. Vray enjoyed the peace, and appreciated having no demands made on her. No demands, but plenty of expectations. A morning spent working beside Cyril was satisfying. Expectations were encouraging as demands never were.

Or suggestions. Or choices. In the days that had passed since her conversation with the minstrel, the idea of having choices kept cropping up in her thoughts. She was glad he'd only spent one night in the village. She'd heard from Herri that the minstrel was heading for his home village in Dherrica. She hoped he made it before the winter settled in—and once there that he'd be snowed in until spring. If he couldn't report to Sene of Sitrine, he couldn't deliver any more messages. She didn't want to hear from kings. She was comfortable where she was.

It was especially comfortable with the house quiet. The weather was threatening snow, so she'd made sure the girls were warmly dressed before letting them go outside to play. They wouldn't be back until supper. A whole day without children arguing, questioning, pestering, and playing underfoot!

Vray sighed. A combination of contentment and boredom suddenly made her wish she had someone adult to talk to. She studied Cyril. The woman's shiny black braid fell to the center of her back. Her expression was closed and enigmatic, but alert with the concentration needed for her weaving. Someone to talk to, even if not someone to carry on lively conversation with. Cyril had limitations, certainly. Yet somehow she gave the impression of listening, although Vray could never be sure whether she was actually paying attention. Still, Pepper and Matti always came to her for help and comfort. Vray was her daughter, too. Or so Jordy insisted. She should act like one. Whine? Complain? Get into a fight with Pepper and Matti? She chuckled, and watched Cyril carefully for a response. She saw none. Very little made the Keeper woman react.

Vray rubbed her palms together. She wanted her mommy's attention. She was seventeen, not seven. What problems did seventeen-year-olds bring to mothers? Boys, of course. There was one in the village trying to court her. But Lim was certainly no problem, although he wanted to be. She grinned. The boy was so inexperienced he didn't know the meaning of the word "problem."

"There was a guardsman in Edian," she said suddenly. "I was in love with him before my family sent me away."

Cyril had reached the end of one section of the pattern. The loom fell silent, and she reached for the next color.

Vray folded her hands in her lap, embroidery abandoned. "Handsome. More than handsome. I was eleven when I decided I wanted him. I didn't know quite what I wanted him for, but I was willing to learn. Only trouble was, he wasn't willing to teach me. Kept thinking of me as a little girl just because he'd known me all my life. I was flat-chested and skinny, which didn't help. He likes girls—" She held her hands out a good twelve inches in front of her chest,

"—ample. Cows."

Cyril did not seem to notice the gesture. However, she was busy sorting thread, and the continued silence of the loom was enough encouragement for Vray to continue.

"He liked lots of girls, all the time. Different girls. Every girl in Edian. I'm not exaggerating! Of course they liked him, too. The most handsome man in Rhenlan, with eyes the color of a midsummer sky at dusk, hair like ripe wheat, but smooth and flowing, shoulders wide as a door, narrow waist, strong thighs, and in between . . ." She thought of several possible descriptions, all of which Dael had blushed over when she'd tried the words on him. She decided she wanted Cyril's attention, not her disapproval, and left those words unspoken. "Charming. The things he would say to flatter a girl! Meant them when he said them, too. Whichever girl he was with he loved the most. I always hated the way they'd smile at him on the street, and the way he'd smile back. All I wanted was for him to smile at me like that.

"So I set about seducing him. It would have worked eventually, I know it. He was weakening, but I ran out of time. There was this inn he liked. Spent many off-duty nights there. One night, just before I was sent away, I put on a new dress and followed him there. It had an ample bodice, cut to reveal assets I really didn't have." She shook her head at the memory. Her maid had nearly fainted at the sight of her.

"He looked. He laughed, but he did look. Then he dragged me home. Again. He was always doing that. I followed him back to the inn, and upstairs to a room. He was with a girl, of course. I stood and watched for a while. I think he knew I was there and let me stay. Sort of thing he'd do to try and prove a point. I dumped a pitcher of ale over them. The girl was furious, I think more over the ruined bedclothes than out of embarrassment. What did she care about me? I was just a skinny child. He cared. He blushed all over. Such lovely pink flesh.

"He also got very angry. Made me clean up the mess and pay for the ale, while they went off to a different room. They locked the door that time. And after all he'd done over the years to further my education!" Vray sniffed, still affronted by that locked door.

The loom began to move steadily once more. Cyril watched her hands, then the shuttle, then scanned up along the cloth. Her expression had not changed, and her walnut-brown skin betrayed no hint of embarrassment.

Vray threaded her needle. "Of course, that was years ago," she finished softly. "He's probably fat and the father of three children by now. He really was too old for me, I suppose."

She would never believe that. She would never believe he could get fat, either. But it had been years ago. Even if he never changed, she had.

Well, she had talked. Even if she hadn't entertained Cyril, she had enjoyed telling the story. Dael thought she should have been ashamed of her behavior that night, but she still thought it was funny. It was Cyril's loss that she couldn't appreciate it.

Vray pictured the bed, the girl's hair soaked with pungent dark ale, and the livid shock on Dael's face, the image fresh and vivid in her mind's eye. She grinned. It was one of her fondest memories. She'd enjoyed it then, and she enjoyed it now.

Looking out the window she noticed that it had begun to snow, and wondered if it was too late to start baking a pie for dinner.

375

"You left it till the last minute, didn't you?"

Tob, plodding along beside the wagon, looked up at the friendly hail. Their neighbor surveyed them from the other side of his stone fence. Jordy, walking a couple yards in front of Tob at Stockings's head, called back, "Have you nothing better to do than watch the road for us, then?"

"Don't tell me Herri didn't give you a piece of his mind."

"I didn't hear any complaints about the goods we brought."

"You were lucky."

Jordy turned and walked backwards for a few paces, exchanging a smile and a rueful glance at the sky with Tob. "Aye," he admitted.

Their neighbor laughed and waved them on before returning his attention to the fence he was mending. Tob took one hand out of his pocket long enough to pull his cloak snug at the neck. The snowflakes that drifted down from the iron gray sky were growing fatter and more frequent. It would be wonderful to get home and stay home. He hoped they never had such an arduous summer again.

Treating Broadford as the hub of a wheel and the other villages they visited as the tips of its spokes had served a purpose. Jordy'd managed to complete all of his pickups and deliveries and still return home frequently enough to at least begin to build a relationship with the newest member of the family. Stockings probably hadn't even noticed the many extra miles she'd walked. Tob hadn't much enjoyed the many nights of rough camping in miserable weather, nights which in a normal year they'd have spent safe and dry in some village inn, even at the cost of one or two days' delay. His father's only real worry had been this final trip. Snow would have immobilized the wagon.

The bushes along the left edge of the road were brown and bare of leaves. Stockings swung through the opening in the hedge, lowering her head as she leaned into the harness to pull the wagon up the final slope into the yard. A dusting of snow clung to the roofs of the buildings, dim patches of white in the fading light. A gust of wind blew cold, damp flakes against his cheek. They were very lucky, all right!

Jordy threw open the stable doors. A delighted Matti leapt out of a pile of straw, dropped the kitten she'd been playing with, and squealed, "Daddy!" Pepper's head appeared at the window of the goat shed, and a moment later she was pelting up the hill. The two children managed, just barely, to keep out from under foot as Tob and Jordy maneuvered Stockings and the wagon into the dry security of the stable.

Ignoring his younger sisters, Tob began unloading what little remained in the wagon, mostly spices and the durable thread his mother used in her weaving. Jumping to the ground, he gathered up a few empty sacks from the tailboard and started around the front of the wagon to put them away.

Someone entered the stable from the yard. Tob stared. Billowing hair, bright eyes, slender neck. Her cloak lay carelessly across her shoulders, open in front to reveal a single lightweight calf-length tunic of pale green. The tunic slid across her soft, gentle curves as she moved. She smelled of wood smoke and cinnamon and sweat—a woman's sweat. She was beautiful.

She was Iris.

Tob tripped over one of the shafts in front of the wagon and dropped most of the sacks. Iris shook her head as she passed him. "Careful, Tobble," she chided kindly. "You must really be tired."

"Hello," Tob replied inanely.

His father, who was inspecting Stockings's hooves, looked up at him sharply. Iris didn't notice.

"Pepper," she said, resting one hand on top of the eight-year-old's head. "I think Mama wants you. Supper's almost ready and she's put the dishes on the sideboard."

"I better go," Pepper agreed. Matti ran out after her.

Jordy smiled pleasantly at Iris, showing none of the reactions to her appearance that were afflicting Tob. "Look at yourself, my girl. Summer dress, flushed face, flour on your hands—you and Cyril are baking."

Iris's light laugh made Tob's chest ache. His chest and other parts of his body. "All right, it's obvious. Now, guess what we're baking?"

"Spiral rolls," Jordy guessed at once.

"Apple pie. I'd better go back. Is there anything I can take with me?"

Jordy bent and picked up another of the big mare's hooves. "The box of spices. Cyril will be glad to see that. Tob, show her which it is."

Tob hurriedly wiped his damp palms on his trousers and joined Iris at the back of the wagon. She returned his smile absently. "This one?" she said, indicating a moderate-sized crate with the toe of her slipper.

"You're joking?" The inappropriateness of her choice was enough to startle him out of his bemusement. He picked up the correct, much smaller box and placed it in her hands. "This is all one family needs for a year."

"Oh, of course. Thank you."

He stood, staring after her as she slipped out of the stable. He continued to stare, his mind full of vague and disturbing thoughts, until his father's voice said, "Tob."

"Yes, Dad?"

"Come here."

Jordy had nearly completed grooming Stockings. Tob accepted the cloth his father handed him and began rubbing the animal's deep brown coat. They worked for several minutes on opposite sides of the mare.

"Dad," Tob said at last.

"Aye."

"Iris has changed."

"Has she?"

"Yes. You saw her. She's so . . . pretty."

"She's always been pretty, lad." Jordy stepped back to examine Stockings with a critical eye.

"Not that pretty."

"She's not as thin as she was." The admission was made absently as Jordy roused Stockings from her doze and led her into her stall. The horse stuck her nose into an empty feed rack. Guiltily, Tob clambered up into the loft and dropped a couple of generous forkfuls of hay into place. When he returned to the floor, he found his father studying the general disarray around the wagon.

"Sorry, Dad. It'll just take me a minute to finish."

Jordy regarded him with a rather odd expression. "I think our Iris is not so much prettier than she's been all summer, as healthier. Less upset than she was at first, certainly. She's come to trust us, lad. To have confidence in her life here. But that trust may still be fragile. If you care for her, go gently." He paused, then retrieved his cloak from the top of the feed bin and swung it over his shoulder. "I'll see you in the house."

Tob leaned weakly against the side of the wagon after his father had gone. Care for her? Of course he cared for her. Didn't he? As a family member? She needed someone to look after her. She used to need someone. Obviously, she had changed. She was beautiful. No, Dad was right. Her face hadn't really changed. It was more than that. Something inside her.

He shivered and looked down at his hands. Or, he wondered with an insight he didn't really want, was the change inside him?

CHAPTER 34

Vray stood in the darkness in her corner of the attic. "Not again."

Where had she left it this time? She would never have guessed a year ago how difficult it would be to keep track of a cloak. A year ago she hadn't owned a cloak. She had shivered through cold weather at Soza wrapped in a blanket that didn't leave her shoulders for ninedays at a time. If you never parted with something, you could hardly lose it. It was too easy, too tempting, to forget all that. Her present abundance was making her careless. She had warm skirts and blouses, and a long, sleeveless, quilted tunic, one of Cyril's peculiar yet practical designs. Jordy had brought the hooded woolen cloak, dyed a rich rust brown, all the way from southern Dherrica just for her. She faced the increasingly colder mornings well dressed and content.

Her trouble was that the cold mornings had been giving way to mild afternoons, a warm streak that she appreciated for as long as it would last. Vray had paused in the act of unlacing her blouse, suddenly conscious of the missing cloak. She'd worn it on her morning visit to Canis to learn more of Broadford's history. She'd worn it back, too. It had rained just before midday and she remembered adjusting her hood against the cold drops that were washing away the first snowfall. She'd worn it out to the stable after lunch. Tob had been mending harness and she had wanted to listen to his travel tales while she worked on her embroidery.

In the privacy of her curtained alcove Vray made a face. She saw the cloak clearly in her memory, draped over the side of the wagon. If the sun hadn't come out to warm the later afternoon she wouldn't have forgotten it. She had two choices: retrieve it now, or face the morning chill without it.

Even without it she'd be better dressed than she'd been at Soza. A quick dash across the yard would do her no harm in the morning.

Vray sat on the edge of her bed. "I'm spoiled," she admitted aloud. "I don't care. There's nothing wrong with appreciating comfort."

She pulled on her boots and retrieved her quilted half-jacket from the end of the bed. Let Tob tease her about devoting too much of her memory to Redmother business and leaving nothing for herself. Pepper said he was always insufferable after a summer spent adventuring with the carter. If the little ones could ignore him, so could she.

She descended the ladder to the main room. The banked fire revealed shadows and emptiness. Tob was no longer at the table where she'd last seen him. A glimmer of lamplight peeked out from under the curtain blocking the entrance to Cyril and Jordy's room. Relieved to be unobserved, Vray tiptoed to the front door and slipped outside.

Under the overcast sky the night was very dark. The yellow light that leaked around the edges of the stable door seemed all the brighter in comparison with the blackness of the other farm buildings. Vray ran lightly across the yard. With luck it would only be the carter making his final check on the animals. She really didn't want to face Tob's teasing tonight.

The stable door moved noiselessly under her hand. Once inside she heard Jordy talking to someone at the far end of the aisle between the stalls. Stones! Tob wouldn't hold his tongue just because he was with his father. Vray quickly ducked between the wagon and the partition that separated it from the storeroom. She'd just have to grab the cloak and slip out again without being seen.

Her hand closed on soft wool just where she'd left it. From the end of the aisle a voice answered Jordy. Vray hesitated, startled. The voice did not belong to Tob.

"You can't blame Sitrine."

"Sene is a proper king." The calm tenor voice of the blacksmith, Lannal, was unmistakable. Vray abandoned the cloak and dropped to one knee in the shadows behind the wagon. Bending further, she peered through the spokes of the front wheels.

She'd been correct in guessing that Tob was in the stable with his father. It had simply never occurred to her that they would not be alone. Lannal sat on the oat bin, his thick forearms crossed over his chest. Beside him Herri occupied Jordy's three-legged stool. Jordy himself was cross-legged on the floor, his back resting against the door to Stockings's stall. A familiar pair of boots dangled at the upper edge of Vray's field of vision, revealing Tob's location, perched at the edge of the hay loft.

"Still," Jordy said. "I expected stronger feelings. Damon's greed is a threat to everyone. I thought I could make that clear."

"They agree he's a danger to us," Tob's voice floated down reasonably. "And to Dherrica. But they're also sure that King Sene will never support us against Damon. They're both Shapers, after all."

Jordy's face twisted sourly. "I asked no one in Sitrine what they thought their Shapers would do. I asked them, Keeper to Keeper, what they could do to help us. They've forgotten how to think for themselves. They depend entirely on their rulers."

"We all did," Herri said quietly, "before the plague."

"Leave Sitrine for now," Lannal suggested. "I understand the people of Dherrica are a little less complacent."

"Aye. But they've too many problems of their own to bother with Rhenlan's affairs. Many in Dherrica say they've had enough of kings, though."

Vray's face went hot with an equal mixture of anger and betrayal. How dare he? A Keeper's place was to keep, not to concern himself with Shaper affairs! She'd known Jordy to be outspoken in his criticisms. She'd heard it for herself, and heard more from neighbors and friends over the summer. Justifiably critical, considering her father's mishandling of the kingdom and his gross mishandling of his son the prince. But it wasn't his fault! Vray had wanted to shout that at the carter several times, when she'd overheard his opinions of Hion's muddled rule. She wanted to stand up and shout it now.

Instead, she firmly pressed her lips together, reminding herself that Jordy also lacked traditional respect for the Dreamers. Of course, just because he considered the Dreamers ineffectual didn't mean he should try to work his own weather magic. Not that he would consider it. Jordy had no real respect for magic, either. Whatever the shortcomings of the Shapers of Rhenlan, a Keeper like Jordy wasn't justified in making arrangements to replace their authority with something of his own devising! No respect for any tradition, that was the trouble with him. Just like Damon.

The abrupt comparison chilled her. Her brother was a terrible person, totally selfish, spoiled, intent on reshaping the world to rules only he understood. Tradition was a joke to Damon. He laughed through recitations of vows, stories of Redmothers. He said he didn't need reasons, or vows. She hadn't seen it before, but Jordy had exactly the same attitudes. Jordy, who she had foolishly thought she might trust.

Herri said, "Now what happens?"

"Many guards will be home by now, for the winter. When Tob and I travel our route next summer we'll learn how many are as dissatisfied as their families are. Meanwhile, each village must think of its own defense. We know what even a dozen unopposed intruders can do."

Herri nodded grimly. Lannal said, "Kessit has been making bows all summer. We know you've horses to train, Jordy, but if you can spare the time, you won't want for pupils of the two-legged variety."

"I'll make the time. Only a few at once, mind. The youngsters must see this as an apprenticeship like any other."

"They understand," Herri said.

So did Vray. They weren't talking about deer hunting, either. They intended to teach young Keepers how to kill!

She should stand up and tell Jordy, tell them all, that killing Shapers was not such an easy thing. *We are born to dragon hunting, you fool! Show us weapons and we will use them—on you!*

Easy to say, if she could force her locked muscles to obey. Too many years in Soza. Too much practice at putting self-preservation before honor. Soon, she promised herself. Jordy didn't know what she was. She knew what he was, now. She didn't have the strength yet, but it would come back to her. It had to.

Forget choices, Sene. I have none. I have to protect Rhenlan from two madmen, now!

The blacksmith got to his feet, tilting his head back to look at Tob. "We were all sorry to hear about Pross. I know you'll miss him."

A light shower of hay accompanied Tob as he dropped down into the aisle. "It wasn't really a surprise. I always knew he wasn't a killer."

"None of us should be killers," Herri said. "Not of each other. We are all Children of the Rock."

Vray shrank back in the shadows against the rough boards of the partition. Tob opened the stable door as the men said their good nights. A gust of wind stirred the bottom of Herri's long coat, carrying with it a few flakes of snow. The innkeeper and the smith left together, Tob following them out into the yard.

"I'll close up, lad," Jordy called after his son. He shut the door. Vray held her breath. What else did he have to do? The animals were quiet, and he held the only lit lamp in his hand. He took a few steps toward the wagon. "Iris?"

She straightened slowly. Sometime over the course of the summer she had forgotten what it was like to want to avoid meeting another person's eyes. Now the desire returned, as enticing as it had ever been at Soza. If she didn't meet their eyes nothing they said, nothing they did, would truly touch her. She kept her head up, resisting the urge with an effort that made her temples throb. "Yes, sir?"

His blue eyes were unreadable. "You stayed to listen. Why?"

"I didn't know you knew I was here."

"That's not good enough."

She stroked the cloth of her troublesome cloak. "I didn't expect to discover a conspiracy against the king in a carter's stable." She hated the nervous rasp that was her voice.

The corner of his mouth lifted in a grudging smile. "I should hope not. A conspiracy will hardly succeed if its participants are predictable." The smile faded as quickly as it had appeared. "You weren't meant to hear any of our talk, lass."

"Perhaps I didn't," she answered, very quietly.

Puzzled, he said, "Do be sensible, Iris. Of course you overheard. I'm not angry with you. How do you think Tob first got involved? I just want to be sure you understand that it must not be spoken of outside the family."

She came out from behind the wagon. Jordy waited until she had wrapped her cloak around her before opening the door. "Oh, it won't be."

"That's a good girl." He shielded the lamp in the crook of his arm as they hurried toward the house. The night had grown very cold. Snow swirled around them, tickling Vray's face and the back of her hands with feather-light touches. Jordy put his hand on her elbow to guide her around a snow-whitened patch of ice. She had trouble keeping herself from shaking off his touch. She recalled Soza once more, and the many unwanted hands she hadn't shaken off then.

They reached the porch. Jordy extinguished the lamp, and Vray shook the snow off her cloak. Inside, the house was quiet. Conspiracy in a carter's stable. What could she do about it? What should she do? The only thing she knew for certain was that she must not arouse the carter's suspicions by seeming critical in any way.

"You're doing what you feel you must," she said.

"Aye." Jordy sat down on the chest next to the door to remove his boots. "What I have to do."

Vray's boots were only slightly damp. She wiped them on the mat next to the door. "I understand. Good night, Jordy."

His voice followed her as she climbed the ladder. "Good night, lass."

The first nineday of really cold weather forced Tob indoors. He wanted to be outside, chasing around the fields and back lanes with his friends, exploring the changes that came with the arrival of snow. However, he couldn't do any of that, because over the course of the summer he'd outgrown his winter clothes. Again. For the third year in a row, he went to pull on his lined trousers and couldn't get them around his hips. For the third year in a row, he couldn't close his winter jacket properly. As for his boots, one look and he knew there was no point in even trying to pull them on. For the third year in a row, Jordy was sympathetic and offered him the use of any of his spare clothes. That was a very unsatisfactory solution to the problem. Tob's wrists protruded from the sleeves of his dad's old jacket, and the left boot leaked. Jordy worked hard and wore clothes until he'd worn them out. Tob was able to get around the yard well enough to do his chores, but he wasn't able to enjoy himself.

In previous years he hadn't minded so much. He enjoyed sitting in his parents' room with Cyril, watching his new clothes take shape. He had clear memories of the time before Pepper was born, of sleeping in their big double bed, playing on the floor as his mother worked on her loom, the irregular vibrations passing through the wood floor to become part of his games, of curling up in Jordy's lap in the deep chair in front of the fire to be sung to sleep. It was a nice room. He also liked helping with the sewing. Cyril made the measurements, cut the cloth, and did the finer detail work. But Tob helped with everything else. His efforts gave pleasure to his mother, and got his new clothes finished twice as fast.

Having Iris work with them ruined everything. For one thing, she talked, to him and to Cyril. He couldn't complain about her sewing. After he'd done one sleeve of his jacket and she the other he couldn't tell the work apart. But she made him uncomfortable. For the first time in his life, he had a problem that he hesitated to bring to his dad. He just wasn't ready for the feelings she evoked.

At last the project was finished. One evening, Jordy brought the new boots up from Broadford, and the next morning Tob dressed himself from head to toe in his new things. Jordy eyed him over breakfast.

"We need more firewood brought up from the river," he observed.

"I'll do it," Tob answered with real enthusiasm.

Jordy nodded. "Take the two-wheeled cart."

While he was harnessing Stockings he heard voices in the yard. Several of his friends from the village, or so he guessed from the laughter and playful shouts.

"Good morning, Jordy." That was Lim, a tall, skinny boy as old as Pross. Tob buckled another buckle. He missed Pross. Pross would have been able to answer his questions.

"You're making an early start today," he heard his father say.

"We're going sliding," Lim replied.

"The weather is perfect," Heather added.

Grinning to himself, Tob took Stockings's lead rope. "Walk on," he ordered the horse. It was too late to get out of fetching the wood. If Lim and the others wanted his company, they'd just have to come help him.

As he and Stockings emerged from the barn he had to close his eyes against the sudden glare of sunlight on snow. He heard Lim say, "We were wondering if Iris could come with us?"

"I've no objection," Jordy said. "You'll have to ask her. Just don't track in any snow."

Tob stopped, until Stockings's momentum dragged him on again. Iris? They were asking for Iris? He didn't want his friends coming around bothering Iris. Maybe during the summer they'd become her friends, too. He hadn't thought of that. Well, there was nothing wrong with Iris having friends. Friends like Heather. But why did Lim have to come visit?

By the time he blinked the sunshine and confusion out of his eyes, the half dozen young people were crowded on the porch, Lim closest to the door. Tob told Stockings, "Whoa," then waved at Heather, who was the only one to turn in his direction.

Iris pulled open the door. "Hello, Lim," she said brightly. Why did she have to sound so pleased?

"We're going sliding." Lim cleared his throat. "It's a lot of fun. I think you'd like it. We all think so."

"Yes, come with us," someone else said.

Looking as nervous as she always did when she was asked to make a decision, she said, "I'm not sure. I've got work to do."

"Your father said you could," Lim encouraged her.

Jordy, standing with one booted foot propped on the end of the porch, said nothing. Iris's expression shifted in a way Tob couldn't interpret. She said, "All right. I haven't been sliding in years. I'll go change clothes."

The door closed. Lim turned, saw Tob, and smiled at him in a perfectly friendly way. "Are you busy?" he called. "Or can you come, too?"

Tob, not feeling the least bit friendly, grumbled, "I've got to get firewood."

"You can do that later. Can't he, Jordy? Before the wind picks up and makes it too cold for sliding this afternoon. We'll be happy to get down off the hill then. We'll even help you, if you like."

"It's up to you, lad," Jordy said.

"I've already harnessed the horse," Tob complained. He didn't want to be complaining. He knew they were only being reasonable. A morning of sliding, perhaps one of Herri's big hot lunches at the inn, then willing hands helping him load wood many times faster than he could do it alone, should have combined to form a delightful prospect for the day. Maybe he was missing Pross more than he knew. Pross loved winter days.

Was that all that was bothering him? If so, what did Pross have to do with the way Lim smiled at Iris?

"We'll take her with us," Heather said, pointing at Stockings.

"Sure," Lim agreed. "It'll save time. We won't have to stop for her later."

Tob was running out of objections. He looked to his dad for help, but all Jordy said was, "You'll have to bring her feedbag, water, and a blanket or two. I'll not have her taking sick."

Iris came out of the house. Tob found himself swept along by the general consensus, loading supplies for the horse, bringing up the rear as they all trooped out of the yard together. Once on the main road they took turns riding in the cart. Iris talked with Lim and the others, and tossed her remarkable red hair over one shoulder or the other whenever it got in her face. Tob refused to stare at her. He joked with Heather, determined to enjoy himself. After all, he could see Iris any day. They ate their meals together, and did chores side by side. That such close proximity had been making him miserable for days was irrelevant. He could have far more of her attention than anyone else could hope to win. She was his Iris, not theirs.

Now all he had to do was figure out what he wanted to do with her.

CHAPTER 35

"You're pregnant!"

His sister brushed past him and dumped her armload of firewood into the box against the wall before pushing her hood back from her face and favoring him with an exasperated stare. "Hello, Ivey. How are you?"

"Hello, Ivey? How can you stand there and say 'Hello, Ivey' looking like . . . looking like . . ."

"Looking like a pregnant woman?" Doron finished his sentence for him. "When did you get in?"

"A few hours ago. I came straight up to the house and took a nap." Ivey refused to be distracted. "Never mind me. What about you? I didn't even know you were seriously interested in anyone." Belatedly he jumped forward and helped her remove her cloak, a host of vague worries vying for his attention. "You look huge. When is the baby due? Are you getting enough rest? You might have told me you were taking a new husband."

"Ivey, lad, stop hovering." As soon as he stepped out of the way, she pulled a bench clear of the table and sat with a tired sigh. It was actually easier for him to hover now since he didn't have to look up to do it. "Aye, I might have told you something, if you were ever here. If there'd been anything to tell."

He sat next to her on the bench. "I spent most of last winter here. You might have told me then what you were planning."

"It wasn't planned."

The words were briefly meaningless. "How can you take a man to your bed on a night you're fertile and not plan for the outcome?"

"Neither of us knew I could be fertile with him."

This made even less sense. Ivey mentally reviewed the

male population of Juniper Ridge. "Who are we talking about, lass?"

"Who's the only man I've been that close to since Betajj died?" she countered. "The prince, you great idiot. Pirse."

"A Shaper of the royal line! Gods!" Ivey devoted a few timeless seconds to considering his reaction. He felt the storyteller's need to find just the right words to express himself. As a minstrel he'd sung and told any number of dramatic tales and never wanted for the proper turn of phrase. It was, he discovered, much different being personally involved. At last he settled for a plain but sincere, "I'm going to kill him."

"You are not. He meant no harm."

"He was irresponsible."

"He didn't know."

"Of course he knew! All the royal courts have known for twenty years that the princes and princesses were to fulfill the vows left incomplete by their parents. It's been part of my duty to spread the story."

Doron glared at him. "You knew?"

"Aye, of course!"

She rapped her knuckles lightly on the side of his head. "You might have mentioned it to me."

"I've told the tale a thousand times!"

"Never in Juniper Ridge."

His sister's accusation forced him to pause and swallow his indignation. "I didn't?"

"We never hear any of your fine tales. How many Festivals do you spend at home? You're out and about in more important villages." She reached out again. Ivey flinched, but she tousled his curls affectionately this time. "Never mind. I can't really fault you. You've said often enough you come home to rest, not to sing."

He grabbed her hand and firmly buried his anxieties. "That's because you don't like my singing."

"Who can blame me? A rutting ram has a smoother voice."

"There are some who'd argue with you."

"Shows the low standards of the company you keep."

Ivey gave her hand a squeeze and released her. "Perhaps it does." Shapers. That was who she meant. It was true he spent much of his time in the company of the ruling elite in Sitrine, and with lesser members of the Rhenlan court. It was also true he'd neglected Dherrica. Everyone was neglecting Dherrica.

"Does he know now?" he asked after a moment.

"Aye. He was here not a nineday ago."

"And left again."

"That wizard, Aage, came to fetch him," she responded with a shrug. "He's wanted in Sitrine."

Frustration set Ivey's teeth on edge. As if there wasn't enough to worry about! What could be happening in Sitrine that required the presence of Pirse of Dherrica? He thought of phantom cats, and sea monsters, and Abstainers, and wondered what Jeyn was doing. At least Sene would be pleased. He'd been waiting, hoping, for Aage's prophecy to be fulfilled. That it was Pirse who'd been first to father a Dreamer, rather than Chasa or Jeyn, would not trouble the king of Sitrine. At least someone had succeeded.

Succeeded. Aye, with Ivey's sister.

I'm still going to kill him.

Vray held one of the new black robes up to the lantern light, examined the red embroidery on neck, sleeves, and hem, and decided she was pleased. She had better be. Midwinter had arrived far too fast and she had run out of time. She'd spent the last two ninedays on the work. It made her fingers and eyes tired just thinking about all the stitching. She hoped Mankin liked it. She had begun training the girl near the end of summer and was going to surprise her apprentice with her first robe at the ceremony tonight. She'd used one of Cyril's designs instead of the traditional circle-and-square pattern of Edian. On Mankin's gown, the moons' phases in stem and satin stitches formed a flowing pattern that could be unique to Broadford's Redmothers from now on. Cyril had woven her a pair of wide red and black belts to match the embroidery. It would look very proper, she decided, and folded the robe once again before placing it on the table.

She glanced from the black mound of cloth to the crackling fire in the hearth, past Pepper at the table, to the window, restless to be away from the house. Outside, the iron gray day was turning quickly into night. She was glad she had an excuse to spend the evening away from Jordy. He'd been gone for a nineday, traveling to neighboring villages, but the carter was due back tonight. Nine days spent spreading his poison to other Keepers. The less she saw of him, the better.

"At least it's stopped snowing," she murmured gratefully. Earlier in the day she'd been afraid the ceremony would have to be canceled because of the weather. Fortunately, the heavy clouds had held more threat than actual snow. No more than a dusting had fallen. She wasn't looking forward to the walk, though it wasn't that far to the village, and not at all windy. She could wear lots of layers under and over her robe. Herri's inn would be snug and warm and she'd have a wonderful time. After the ceremony.

She didn't know why she was nervous. She knew the ceremony. She chewed on a knuckle and watched Pepper as the girl carefully wrapped and placed the half dozen loaves of cinnamon bread she'd made herself into a big basket. One of Pepper's young friends was taking her vows, and Pepper was sending a present for the party afterward.

Vray's contribution would be to not make any mistakes. There were only a few words she had to say. Still, she'd never taken any Keepers' vows before. If any of the children should stumble over the words. . . .

She shook her head, banishing the worrisome thoughts. The children would have their parents to help them. No one would mind if she had to ask for help. Which she wouldn't. After tonight, she would know what to expect for the midsummer ceremony. There was nothing to be nervous about.

The door opened, letting in cold air along with Tob and

a load of firewood. "Hello," he called as he dumped his burden in the bin near the hearth. He stripped off his gloves and held his hands out to the fire. "Brrr."

Vray looked at his boots and where he was standing. "You're dripping on the rug and I'm not going to clean it."

He gave her a put-upon look but retreated to the rag rug near the door. Vray got up to pour the boy some warm cider. While he was pulling off his boots, Cyril and Matti came out of the other room. Cyril went to the fire to check the stew pot and Matti climbed into Vray's lap.

The room was comfortably warm, the air rich with the smell of cooking vegetables and an underlying aroma of cinnamon and yeast, illuminated by fire and lantern light. Tob's cheeks, toes, and fingers still tingled with cold but the cider had begun to warm his insides. He sat in silence, wishing the girls would go away, glad they didn't, wanting to talk to Iris, but not sure what to say.

It was Matti who broke the silence. "I want a story, please."

Iris stroked her hair. "A story? Now?"

"You won't be here when we go to bed," Pepper pointed out and sat down at the table. "So we should have a story now."

"Oh, it's 'we', is it?" Iris laughed. "Stories in the middle of the day. I'm not sure it's proper. What do you think, Tob?"

He looked up from his cider. "I'd like a story, please."

Iris looked thoughtful. He liked it when she looked thoughtful. The way her eyes narrowed made her look a little bit like a cat.

"Let's see. Do you know about the time the Abstainers tried to steal the horses from the big horse fair in Edian? Not just any Abstainers, either, but a band led by the queen's brother, Soen."

"Edian?" Pepper was looking suspicious.

"Is this going to be about *him?*" Matti demanded. "You're always telling stories about him."

Iris squeezed Matti's waist. "I know," Iris said patiently. "I'm from Edian. It's not my fault if the town's hero is the captain of the guard, and Redmothers there learn lots and lots of stories about Dael. This is a very exciting story. You like exciting stories, remember?"

"Other towns have heroes," Pepper pointed out. "You're Broadford's Redmother now. Tell an exciting story about Broadford."

"Does Broadford have heroes?" Matti wondered.

"There's Dad," Tob spoke up. "I've heard Herri tell lots of stories about him."

"Daddy saved Jenk from drowning when the river flooded," Pepper said. "That was heroic. Wasn't it, Iris?"

Iris was silent for a few seconds before she said, "Yes."

Tob wondered why she looked annoyed. Maybe she didn't like anybody being brave but her Dael. Dael just sounded like a guard performing his duty, as far as Tob was concerned. He wasn't all that special. Tob knew, because he'd met this famous Dael a couple of times. Tob remembered the aftermath of the Abstainer fight in the lake country three summers before. He and Jordy had shared camp that night with Dael's guards. He remembered noticing stains of dried blood on the captain's tunic. Dael killed people. Maybe Iris liked to remember him because he was tall and handsome. Maybe she ignored the man's violent nature just because he did brave things. What would she do if Tob told her he knew him? That Dad saw him when they were in Edian? Maybe she'd want Tob to take a message to him. Would she want to see him?

Tob studied Iris, angry and suspicious, suddenly afraid she'd go away. He should tell her she belonged in Broadford. This new fear was worse than thinking about her with Lim. At least Lim was here. At least he could compare himself to Lim. He spoke up. "I don't want to hear about Edian, Iris. Tell us the sort of Redmother tale you teach Mankin."

"All right," she agreed. "Perhaps I'll give you the short version of the story about how Greenmother Coria saved an island in the northern sea from a volcano."

"What's a volcano?" Matti asked.

"A mountain that burns," Iris said. "It's something I've re—" She faltered, then started again. "It's a very long story. It's got dragons and a couple of princes and a fisher folk flotilla caught in a great wave and Coria putting wild animals to sleep so they could be brought safely to the mainland. It took me weeks to learn the tale. But Mankin," she smiled proudly, "recited it back to me after I'd told it to her only once. The girl has the best memory of anyone I've ever met. Redmother Vissa started training my memory when I was your age, Matti, before I even took my vows, and I still couldn't have remembered such a long tale all at once at Mankin's age."

"If it's a long tale you'd better start it," Pepper said. "Supper'll be ready soon. Then you'll have to go."

Iris nodded. "You're right. The short version of Coria and Heelm Island. Centuries of centuries ago . . ."

Tob leaned forward to listen, happy to hear a new tale. And happy to have Iris's mind away from Edian and Captain Dael.

"Is everybody here?" Herri yelled from behind the bar.

Canis, sitting at a table near the wall on the other side of the inn's common room, called back, "Ask Iris."

Vray lifted the skirt of her robe and stepped up onto a chair. As soon as Herri noticed her, she nodded.

His bellowed, "Quiet!" brought all conversation in the room to a halt. The people present looked expectantly between the innkeeper and Vray. Herri continued, "I hereby declare this the official midwinter gathering of Broadford. Redmother, take charge."

Friendly, smiling faces turned toward Vray. She relaxed and smiled back. She wasn't really nervous now. It was only a gathering. Unlike the Festivals, which were filled with as much feasting and celebration as a day would hold and attended by every member of the community, the gatherings called at midwinter and midsummer were smaller, more personal affairs. Everyone who had come to the inn tonight had a specific reason to be there. Last summer had seen a completely different gathering of people, and next summer would attract yet another group. The entire ceremony would take less than an hour.

"We gather in support and approval of six vow-takers," Vray began. "We are not witnesses. A vow may be spoken, but it is made not with our friends or family. A vow exists within us, where only the gods may truly see our sincerity. We are not judges. A vow may be broken according to one person's understanding, yet still be honored in the mind of another. Truth is complex, and only the gods know our intentions. We gather to welcome these people to the responsibilities they choose today. Only the gods know where their vows will lead them."

She located the six children seated here and there in the common room with their families, and addressed her next words to them. "For some of you, today's may be the only vow you ever take." She looked at ten-year-old Mankin. "Or it may be one of several. But each time you vow, remember this—you vow for your entire life. Remember this, too." She put warmth and reassurance into her voice for the six-year-olds. "We know how you're feeling. We've been where you are now. All of us. All the way back to the Firstmother." Her training held her voice steady, but tears already glistened in the eyes of several of the parents. From the direction of the bar she heard a suspicious sniff.

"Oriel?" she said gently to the brown-haired boy seated nearest the hearth. "You go first."

The six-year-old, with his father's assistance, imitated Vray and stood on his chair. He hitched up his pants, scratched at his nose for a moment, then clasped his hands behind his back and closed his eyes. "My name is Oriel. My family has shown me what it means to be a Keeper. I know the nine gifts of the gods to their children. They are animals and plants and water to give us strength. The air above and earth below, our place to live. Intelligence," he pronounced the word carefully, "so we can think and plan. The bending of power which brings us magic." He paused, face screwed up in thought.

A helpful childish whisper prompted from somewhere in the room, "That's seven."

"I know," Oriel said. "And our bodies. And our love, so that there will always be more Children of the Rock. I vow to keep these gifts. I vow to keep my body healthy with the right use—"

"Proper use," his mother prompted.

"—proper use of the gifts of plants and animals and water and air and earth. I vow that I'll be a helper in my family and my village by thinking and loving. And I don't have to vow anything about magic," he concluded, opening his eyes, "because my parents are Keepers and so am I." His round face was flushed with pride and relief and, hopefully, his first inspired understanding of the words he had said. "And I vow to do whatever I'm supposed to do to help everybody else keep their vows. Because we are all Children of the Rock."

"Well done, Oriel," his father said.

The common room erupted with hand clapping and slapping of tables, shouts of approval and good wishes. Oriel, grinning, plopped down in his chair. As soon as the clamor died down a bit, Vray picked out the next vow taker.

After each of the six-year-olds had recited their Keeper's vows, Mankin made her commitment to become a Redmother. As she received the gathering's congratulations, Vray sighed, glad the ceremonial part of the evening was over. She smiled fondly at the people, all of them now moving toward the food tables and warmth of the hearth. Some noticed her and smiled back.

Oriel's father called out, "Why are you still perched up there, Iris? Come have some mulled wine."

"How lovely," Vray answered. She stepped down just as the door from the kitchen opened and a laughing young man stepped through, a tray perched on his muscular arm. She stared, hardly able to draw breath, totally disoriented as he moved forward, his attention on the food.

Candlelight shown on his silky black hair, caught the sparkle of his eyes. Vray saw his broad shoulders, and the confident grace with which he moved, and did not recognize a thing about him except the green and saffron embroidery on the neck of his tunic. Embroidery she'd done for Tobble. Her little brother Tobble.

She blinked, and Tob became Tob once more. Only— Vray took a deep breath and stumbled a few steps into the crowd. She was grateful Tob hadn't noticed her. Tob, who was always underfoot lately. She took a seat, and accepted a cup of warm wine from Oriel's father.

Her eyes went back to the young man who stood beside Herri, laughing merrily at one of the innkeeper's jokes. She still hardly knew him. No, she didn't know him at all. He'd grown. He'd more than grown. Tob wasn't a child any more. What happened to the boy she'd walked here with tonight? She covered her mouth to hide an embarrassed smile, and tried to forget the confused tingling of her body, tingling warmth that would not go away, despite her realization of who she was looking at.

Don't be a fool, she chided herself. *We all stop being children sooner or later.* Vray put down the wine cup and hugged herself closely, as memories of Soza returned. She looked away from Tob and into the fire blazing in the wide hearth.

Some just lose their childhood sooner than others.

CHAPTER 36

When Pirse showed up in Raisal in the middle of autumn, the only member of the royal household who didn't seem to be surprised was Sene. At first, Feather took it for one more demonstration of Sene's knack for knowing everything about everything. During the ninedays that followed, however, she learned that Sene had welcomed Pirse as if he'd been expecting him because he was. Before Aage's departure for one of his visits with Morb, Sene had asked the wizard to find Pirse and send him to Sitrine. With his usual supreme confidence, it never occurred to Sene that the Dherrican prince would fail to answer his summons.

Feather hardly noticed Pirse's arrival. She had too many other things to worry about. A few ninedays earlier, without warning, the king had taken her aside and revealed that he was aware of her less-than-daughterly feelings for him. He'd given her a long, serious lecture about how he wasn't offended, and understood that her reaction to him was rooted in a perfectly natural desire to express her gratitude for his protection. He also made his wishes clear. Whatever its harmless source, the attraction had to stop. He did not evict her from the royal residence, or banish her from future council meetings, even after she told him that she did not want to change the way she felt. He'd been kind, but as immovable as stone. From that day on, it was as if a wall had been erected between them. Subtle as the change was, perhaps even undetectable to anyone else, day by day Feather struggled with the hard reality. Sene was no longer part of her life.

Chasa, however, was always there. Even after Pirse appeared on their doorstep, Chasa made a point of drawing Feather into all of his conversations with the Dherrican prince. There was, not surprisingly, a lot of conversation. When they were young, Pirse had learned monster-slaying with Chasa and Jeyn. The three shared fond memories of their adolescent adventures. Feather began to understand some of Chasa's anger with Jenil. If the Greenmother had not whisked her away to Garden Vale, she would have been a full member of this inner circle, a participant in the daily activities and grand schemes that even now, years later, reduced Pirse, Chasa, and Jeyn to breathless laughter as they described the incidents to Feather. Instead, her only memories of those years involved tapestries and Brownmother training.

The next time Jenil showed her face in Raisal, Feather would have a few things to say to her.

Most of the conferences with Pirse, however, concerned the present rather than the past. Sene quizzed him for hours on the state of affairs in Dherrica. On other days, the discussion centered on Rhenlan. Pirse had not been observing events as closely as Sene had, but he knew about the unrest among the Keepers—and he had heard of Captain Dael.

"A fine swordsman," Pirse said over supper on the day after mid-winter. "He takes his vows seriously, too, by all accounts. More seriously than Hion and Damon take theirs. He could do it."

"A Keeper, learn to slay dragons?" Jeyn asked. They were dining in the king's audience hall for the sake of its wide hearth. Feather did not think the day had been particularly cold—not compared to what was usual in Garden Vale at this time of year—but with the setting of the sun enough of a chill crept into the air to make her willing to take the seat closest to the fire. Jeyn sat to her right at the long, linen-covered table, her brother across from her and Pirse, in turn, to Chasa's right, across from Feather. Sene occupied the head of the table, between his children. For the moment, the king was concentrating on using a piece of crusty bread to mop up the last of his fish chowder. However, the tilt of his head assured Feather that he was listening to every word his children and their guest were saying.

"What about you, Feather?" Chasa asked. "What do you think?"

401

Feather silently thanked the gods that her memory retained the content of conversations even when she was not consciously paying attention. "We all know the Redmother stories. Shapers are traditionally the monster slayers because Keepers have enough to keep them busy with their herds and crops."

"There's more to it than that," Jeyn argued.

"Personality, mostly," Chasa replied. "Dael has the self-discipline, and if you'd seen him against that phantom cat you'd know he's fast enough."

Sene swallowed his last mouthful of bread and followed it with some wine. "Rhenlan needs a monster slayer. If not this winter, then the next. That's Aage's prediction, and I believe him."

"Dragons in the western coastal villages?" Pirse shook his head. "I respect the foresight of the wizard Aage, but that seems unlikely to me. Most dragons attack in spring and summer. By Fall Festival, the danger is past."

Chasa took an apple tart from the platter in the center of the table. "What happens? Do dragons disappear, the way phantom cats do?"

"No. It's just rare to find one moving about in winter," Pirse explained. "They hate the storms that blow up along the coast. Too much wind, awkward for flying."

"Awkward for sailing too," Chasa returned. "That doesn't stop fisher folk from going out, if they're hungry enough."

The door to the hall jerked open, the motion too abrupt to come from the hand of a servant. Since only members of the royal staff were allowed this far into the building without escort, Feather expected to see one of the king's guards, or perhaps a messenger. Therefore she didn't recognize the man in the mud-splashed trousers, damp brown hair flattened against his skull, until he was halfway down the length of the room.

Pirse knew him, though. He jumped up and away from the table.

"Ivey, what are you . . ." Jeyn began.

Ivey reached the end of the table. "By your leave, Your Majesty," he said. Not waiting for Sene's response, he hauled back his fist, and punched the still-retreating Pirse in the eye.

Pirse staggered against the wall and into a needlework stand, which toppled over with a clatter. Chasa leapt belatedly to his feet. Sene bellowed, "Ivey!"

". . . doing?" Jeyn concluded in the sudden silence.

"That's for irresponsibility," the minstrel announced, ignoring the rest of them as he advanced toward Pirse. "The next one's for abandonment. Then I'm going to—"

Pirse, one hand cupped over the injured eye, yelled, "We're going to be married!"

Ivey paused. "When?"

"At Spring Festival."

"She didn't mention it."

"Did you ask?"

"Ivey," Sene said. "Sit down."

"My sister! He took advantage—"

"Sit!"

Ivey stalked to Pirse's chair and sat.

Chasa said, "Rock and Pool, Ivey, what's the matter with you? Pirse is involved with your sister."

A muscle bunched on the side of Ivey's jaw. "Yes."

"With her consent."

"Yes."

"Well, then. It's not as though she's a child."

"I'd rather she were," the minstrel said in a tight voice. "She's been hurt once already by his family. He played on her sympathy while she was still mourning Betajj—"

Pirse pushed himself away from the wall. "I did nothing of the kind!"

"You're the last thing she needs."

"Obviously the gods feel he's precisely what she needs," Sene told Ivey. "They honor your family."

Feather tried to disguise her snort of disbelief as a cough. Chasa eyed her suspiciously, then said, "The honor isn't in Keeper marrying Shaper. It's in parenting Dreamers."

"A Dreamer." Sene's eyes widened as he regarded Pirse.

"A baby? You never mentioned the two of you were having a baby!"

The prince lowered his hand from his face. "Aye. We are."

"When?"

"Any time. I told you I have to leave in the morning. That's why."

The king turned on Ivey. "Have you learned nothing from your years at this court? You should be congratulating him! Thanking him!"

Ivey shook a few wet curls out of his eyes and glared at Pirse. The prince accepted the scrutiny, but there was a defiant glint in his unswollen eye. Feather heard the lilt of the mountains in their voices as they spoke, though they seemed unaware of those echoes of kinship.

"She knows you'll be back before spring?" Ivey asked.

"Not exactly. She doesn't like me traveling the mountain roads in winter."

"So you're going to surprise her."

"Better surprised," Pirse said curtly, "than worrying."

"You might've considered that before you left her alone."

"She's safe at home."

"Is that marriage? A baby coming and you not there to see it?"

"I'll be there!"

"For how long?"

"I can't spend my life in Juniper Ridge, though don't think the thought hasn't tempted me. Are the demands of marriage more important than my vows?"

"I never said—"

"When you marry, will you stop traveling from village to village with your songs and tales?"

Ivey folded his arms across his chest. "Now that's just daft. I could no more stop at home . . . I'd ask my lass to come with me if . . ." He stopped again, and stabbed a finger toward Pirse. "We aren't discussing me. We're discussing Doron."

"My wife."

"My sister."

Feather had had enough. "Who is better off in Juniper Ridge." Startled, they both looked around. "Well away from either of you."

Jeyn hid a smile behind her hand. The king pushed his chair back and stood. "I can see we're not going to accomplish anything else useful until you two have cooled down. Pirse, put something on that eye before it swells shut. Chasa, come with me. I want to speak to Captain Prester about rigging a ship for winter seas. If the land dragons are going to change their habits, we may soon have trouble with sea dragons as well. Ivey, go change your clothes, you're wet. I don't expect to see you again until you're ready to be a coherent, useful, member of this council."

Three voices murmured, "Yes, Sire."

"I'm glad we understand one another," Sene said.

Pirse, gingerly touching the puffiness around his eye, departed at once. Ivey, still rather flustered, slipped out far more quietly than he'd arrived. Sene made certain each had gone his separate way before he left as well. Chasa shoveled the last bite of tart into his mouth and followed his father.

Feather glared at the last remaining Shaper in the room, torn between suspicion, disbelief, and a whole new level of admiration. "Your father couldn't have planned that, could he?"

Jeyn seemed honestly surprised. "Planned what?"

"The future ruler of Dherrica marrying your minstrel's sister."

"It was chance that they fell in love. Dad can't arrange that."

"Much as he might want to."

Jeyn chose to ignore that uncomfortable remark. "If anyone's responsible, it's Aage. He brought them together."

"You can't deny it's convenient. You marry Ivey, his sister marries Pirse. Instant alliance between two ruling houses."

Jeyn tried to turn the subject away from herself. "Pirse has no throne."

"And you're not married yet."

"No. Dad couldn't have foreseen Doron marrying

405

Pirse." Jeyn eyed the last of her wine and made a face. "What about Rhenlan? Who marries into that family?"

"Don't look at me. The King's already chosen my husband, remember?"

"Pity you don't have any sisters or cousins."

"There are," Feather said with a heartfelt shudder, "some advantages to being an orphan."

Jeyn left Feather and Dektrieb fussing over the broken support bar on the tapestry stand that Pirse had knocked to the floor, and hurried through the house to the minstrel's room.

The room did not actually belong to Ivey. It was one of several guest rooms on the west side of the building, used by a variety of visitors during the course of the year. However, Ivey somehow managed to time his arrivals and departures to coincide with periods when the room was available for his use. He did not leave personal belongings behind when he went away, as Aage did. The wizard, despite his frequent travels, made no secret of the fact that he considered the royal residence of Sitrine his true home, and he treated his quarters there with a proprietary air. Ivey, however, had always claimed that the road was a minstrel's only home.

Now Jeyn knew better. Ivey the ever-restless had roots, after all, with his sister in far-off Juniper Ridge.

He let her in, his expression grim. He had already changed into dry clothing. "Don't say it. I know. That was stupid."

"A little late to be losing your temper about it, at least."

"Right. The damage is done and the problem's far away. It's not even my problem."

Jeyn came further into the room and sat down in the chair near the fireplace. "Pirse has been talking about Doron since he arrived. He says she's stubborn and opinionated and too self-sufficient for her own good. He loves her very much."

"If he loves her, why isn't he with her?"

"Because she doesn't want him to be! That's what Pirse says, at least. What did Doron tell you about Pirse?"

"Nothing. I didn't stay around long enough for a talk."

"Ran off in a righteous rage, did you?"

"Aye." His blush covered his entire torso. "If it was anyone else—"

"What have you got against Pirse?"

"It's his family."

"I admit that Dad has a low opinion of Palle, as he had of Dea and Farren before her—but Pirse has proved himself time and again. You've brought us the reports yourself! He keeps his Shaper vows."

"It's not the lad. It's the family. The other members of the family."

"Ivey, what are you talking about?"

"Palle."

"When did Palle ever have anything to do with Doron? Pirse says she's never been to Bronle, and Palle's spent his whole life at the castle, or on the estates of other Shapers."

"She was married."

"Yes, Pirse mentioned that."

"Did he tell you how Betajj died?"

"No. Pirse doesn't know. He says Doron doesn't speak of it."

"Betajj died in Bronle. He was a merchant, making his final delivery of goods for the season."

"Just a minute!" Jeyn said. "Is this the same merchant you mentioned to Dad a few years ago? The one who disappeared under mysterious circumstances?"

"Aye."

"Stones, Ivey! You said you were investigating the matter because it seemed suspicious, not because it involved your family!"

"It was suspicious—and still is! The fact that Doron is my sister means nothing, except of course that I may never have heard about it otherwise. Palle is too clever not to cover his trail."

"Palle again." Jeyn leaned forward, elbows on her knees.

"You've learned something. Why didn't you tell Dad?"

"I intend to." Ivey combed his fingers through his damp hair, and his expression relaxed into a wry smile. "I only started putting the pieces together on this last trip. When I got to Juniper Ridge, other things pushed it out of my mind."

"You've been negligent long enough, minstrel," Jeyn said, in her best imitation of Sene's sonorous tones. "What have you learned?"

Ivey smiled in appreciation of her mimicry, but the good humor quickly faded from his face. "It was a boating accident on the river. To make matters worse, no word was sent to Juniper Ridge. Doron had to worry for six long months, until I found out from an innkeeper friend, and took the news to her myself."

"If no one bothered to contact her, who led the Remembering?"

"There was none. The Shapers of Dherrica no longer let us train Redmothers. All of our traditions are dying."

"If Pirse were king, he'd set things right."

"I know that," Ivey snapped. "I just wish he would have left my sister out of it."

"Aage sent him to Juniper Ridge. To Doron specifically. The Dreamers wanted them to be together. To have babies." She hesitated, considering what she had heard, and what she knew of Pirse and his continuing exile from a throne that, in justice, should have been his. "To help each other, perhaps. To heal each other?"

Ivey scowled. "That would be like them, wouldn't it?"

"They are healers—and it seems to have worked."

"They're also baby mad."

"You've been helping them. You brought Vray to that Rhenlan village."

"That's different. Doron is my family!"

"That doesn't exempt her from doing the will of the gods."

"Aage's prophecy." Ivey sat down on his bed and matched Jeyn's elbows-on-knees posture. "I've been reciting it in every village and town for as long as I've been a minstrel. I just never expected it to apply to Doron."

"We all want to protect the people we love. I'm protective of my brother, too." She smiled, teasing once more. "Don't worry about Doron. From the sound of it, she can handle Pirse. No one forced them into bed together, you know."

"Aye, I imagine not," he growled. "She's bigger than he is."

"Is she?"

"Bigger than most. Betajj had an inch or two on her, though."

"What else do you know about Betajj? How could Palle have anything to do with his death?"

"I'm certain that he ordered it—but I have no proof. Worse, I still don't know why. I don't know if Palle hoped to gain something by Betajj's death, or if it was all a tragic mistake." Ivey dropped his head into his hands for a moment, then straightened and sat back in his chair. Fatigue from his long journey, mingled with old grief, deepened the lines around his nose and mouth. "It's been over four years. You don't know what it's like in Dherrica, Princess. Secrets and lies, wherever you turn."

"Because of Pirse's exile?"

"That's part of it, of course, but Dherrica had problems even before Dea died. The guard was captained by a decent man, and many of them were devoted to Pirse. Over the years, though, Bronle had split into factions, some more loyal to Palle than to the throne."

"When Palle became king, the factions should have united behind him."

"They did—for a time. Palle's greatest weakness is that he doesn't inspire loyalty, he buys it. Half the Shaper families, and more Keeper merchants than I like to admit, no longer bother to do what's right if they can get away with doing what's convenient."

A shiver raised the hairs on Jeyn's arms. "Has the entire kingdom forgotten its vows?"

"Most of the villages are still all right. It's Bronle that's in danger. Bronle, where Betajj died. As I said, I can't prove that Palle was involved. Those who know the truth are either loyal to Palle, or too afraid of him to speak out. All I have to go on are the rumors of rumors."

Jeyn rubbed her hands up and down her arms. "Tell me the tale, minstrel."

"My sister Doron is a dyer. Betajj was taking the dyed cloth to market, his last trip of the season. He traveled from Juniper Ridge to Dundas by wagon. In Dundas, he and three other merchants boarded a river barge for the voyage down to Bronle. He made the same trip three or four times a summer, every year.

"They reached the outskirts of Bronle at dusk. Betajj and another man wanted to camp where they were for the night, and continue to the market landing at first light. The other two merchants and the barge owner voted to finish the voyage in the dark. Less than half a mile before they reached the wharves, the barge capsized."

"Capsized? Don't you mean foundered?"

"Capsized. Like a wood chip in a millstream."

Jeyn stared at him. "I may have lived in Sitrine most of my life, minstrel, but I've been to other lands more than once. Chasa and I visited Pirse and Emlie when we were young. I remember traveling the river between Bronle and Dundas. A Dherrican river barge is as steady as a house."

"Aye."

"Was there a storm?"

Ivey shook his head.

"Was the barge poorly laden? Was the river running too low? Too high?"

The minstrel rejected each of her suggestions, then cut in before she came up with ideas even more outrageously unlikely. "I've asked all those questions, and more, these four years past. Instead of answers, I find more questions. Of all the people aboard, only Betajj drowned. Of all the cargo aboard, only Betajj's goods were lost without a trace."

"They sank?"

410

"The river at that point is less than ten feet deep. At dawn, the other merchants retrieved their cargo from the bottom, or found it washed up on shore at the next bend in the river." Ivey's mouth twisted with grim humor. "Don't scowl so, Your Highness. You won't make sense of my tale until you've heard it through to the end."

"Then tell me! Or are you saving the best part for my father?"

"I wish I were. From a hint here, a fragment of overheard conversation there, I've pieced together a few more details. The barge owner was not well known in Dundas. He traveled that stretch of the river for only that one summer. The next spring, a new man came up from Bronle, and he'd never seen or heard of the other one. The merchant who voted with Betajj to spend the last night outside of Bronle was a Dundas man, and friend to Betajj. The other two were strangers. I traced one of them this past summer. He's become one of Palle's favorites at court. On the night of the accident, and the morning after, guards and bystanders helped retrieve cargo. A few of those bystanders had never been seen in Bronle before, and haven't been seen there since."

"Have they been seen elsewhere?" Jeyn guessed.

"Aye."

"Working for Palle?"

Ivey flipped his hair back over his shoulders with a casual flick of his head. "That, Your Highness, is what I need to discover next."

"How?"

"I have no idea."

"Then it's definitely time go talk to my father."

CHAPTER 37

Damon rode into Bronle as the winter night fell, under gray clouds heavy with snow. A bitter wind whispered through the narrow streets of the capital and dug at the cracks and crevices of the soot-grimed stone buildings. Here and there, the yellow glow of candles or a glimmer of ruddy light from a hearth fire leaked around the edge of a shutter or under a door. For the most part, however, Damon and his escort climbed the hill to the castle through a bleak dusk unrelieved by the least sign of life from the inhabitants of the town.

When they reached the castle gates, a muffled voice hailed them from the darkness atop the wall. One of the guards at Damon's back identified himself, and the gate swung open in a chorus of creaks and rattles. The noise grated on Damon's ears, but his horse barely flinched, and moved forward readily at the touch of Damon's heels on its flanks.

Damon dismounted in the courtyard and handed his reins to his spokesman. The other guard stayed close at his heels. Damon vaguely recognized the Dherrican guard corporal who led them into the castle from his previous visits. Fortunately, she knew her job and walked ahead of them in silence, saving him the trouble of trying to remember her name. They reached the guest rooms at the same time as a harried pair of servants who, at a brusque nod from the corporal, scurried inside ahead of them.

The corporal waited in the corridor while Damon and his guard entered their quarters. The servants laid and lit fires in the sitting room and bed chambers, then continued to bustle about for several minutes. Damon threw his cloak over the back of a chair and ignored them. As long as lamps were lit when he needed them, food placed on the table when he was hungry, and his chamber pot emptied whenever he used it, he cared nothing for the details of how the tasks were accomplished. He was a Shaper, heir to the throne of Rhenlan, with far more important concerns to occupy his mind.

Dinner arrived, platters and bowls and baskets and jugs, in the arms of three more servants. Palle hurried through the door in their wake. "Dear cousin! It is a pleasure to see you again!"

"And you, cousin."

In truth, Damon saw little to please him, and less to respect, in the self-proclaimed King of Dherrica. Palle wore his thin, brown hair long and tied back from his face, in the fashion of a guard, but the conceit ended there. The rounded torso, the hint of a double chin, and the shortness of breath with which he greeted Damon suggested that he devoted most of his time to enjoying the privileges of his position, and none to such tedious matters as swordsmanship, or any other physical exercise.

Damon had no illusions about his own skill with a blade, and no interest in improving it, either. Warrior kings like Hion, or the over-active Sene of Sitrine, were relics of the past. A king did not have to take up a sword with his own hands. That's what guards were for. Damon knew the strengths and limitations of those who served him as intimately as his mother knew the traits of each horse she so carefully raised and trained. Captain Dael was his sword, keen-edged, strong, designed for public displays of heroism and the committing of mighty deeds. Palim was his dagger, just as deadly, and suited to the quick, silent thrust. Like any weapon, they demanded strength in the hand that wielded them. For that reason, he would never allow himself to sink into the self-indulgent softness that had trapped Palle.

Palle prattled on about inconsequentials—the weather, last autumn's harvest—while the servants set the table and finished making the room comfortable. As far as the servants, and everyone else in Bronle, were concerned, Damon was the younger son of a minor Shaper family with holdings somewhere near the Rhenlan border. In Rhenlan, the only person who knew of his secret visits to the king of Dherrica was the invaluable Palim. Dael would have been worried for his safety. After all, the princess of Dherrica had died during her visit to the court of Rhenlan. Hion would not be concerned for his safety, because it was clear that Palle offered no threat. The man couldn't even capture his own nephew, despite numerous opportunities provided by Pirse's regular appearances throughout the kingdom. Hion would have objected only because he would want to be in charge of their dealings with Dherrica, and Damon had no intention of permitting that. Palle belonged to him, not to his father.

Damon's guard stepped into the corridor after the last of the servants and closed the door behind him, leaving Damon alone with Palle. The king said, "I understand the need for discretion, my lad, but don't you think you're taking it a bit too far?" He cast a disdainful glance around the sitting room. "Especially at this time of year. It takes hours to get the chill out of these rooms."

"You are too considerate, Your Majesty." Damon seated himself at the table and took a sip of wine. He had no intention of ever giving Palle advance warning of his arrival. Even now, his guards, both Rhenlaners who had grown up close enough to the border that they could pass as Dherricans, were taking advantage of their surprise arrival to gather all the latest news and gossip from the stables and guard barracks. If Palle had time to prepare for his visits, who knew what he might do? At the least, he might give away the fact that his young visitor was someone more important than a lowly cousin. At the worst, with time to plan he might get some inconvenient ideas, and that Damon could not allow.

"How fares your father, and the beautiful Queen Gallia? They are well, I trust?"

"Never better," Damon replied. He had spent a tedious afternoon with his mother at her beloved Horse Fair. Long enough to flatter her with praise of her herds, and confirm her continued disinterest in the business of running the kingdom. As for Hion, although he hid it well, his weakness grew with each passing season. The fact of Hion's illness, however, was a secret that Damon had shared with no one, not even Palim. He most certainly would not mention it to Palle.

"And what of your family, Your Majesty? What news of the prince?"

A grimace crossed Palle's face. "Really, Prince Damon, I do not think it proper that you share your respected title with my lawless nephew. Pirse gave up all status and position with his cowardly attack on my dear sister Dea."

"If there is any truth in the tales that reach Rhenlan, many Dherricans consider Pirse more hero than coward."

"The misplaced gratitude of ignorant sheep herders. Those mountain villages are so isolated, the people are impressed by any idiot who can lift a sword without chopping off his own hand."

"Too isolated to be reached by normal guard patrols, I gather."

"The royal guard protects every town and village in my kingdom, no matter how small or how distant from Bronle!"

"I never meant to imply otherwise. And of course they can't protect the villagers from Pirse, because the villagers refuse to recognize him as a danger."

"Exactly! On top of that, it's too easy for one man to elude a troop of guards, especially in the winter. When he comes north in the spring, away from the aid of his village dupes, we'll have a better chance to catch up with him."

"So you said last year—and the year before that, and the year before that."

"Pirse is a clever, dangerous opponent. Trust me, my dear Damon. You would not find it an easy matter to deal with him, were you in my position."

"Of course not, Your Majesty. I meant no criticism. However, my offer of assistance stands. Say the word, and I can send a dozen troops of guards to aid in your next hunt for your nephew."

"That won't be necessary."

"Well, at least you may rest assured that if I ever find that Pirse has set foot outside of Dherrica, by my vow, he will be hunted down and killed like the lawless Abstainer he is."

"Abstainer he may be, but I would prefer him captured, not killed." Palle passed his hand over his high forehead, wiping away a sheen of sweat that was not caused by the young fire on the hearth. "When a ruling Shaper commits such a heinous crime, he should be judged before the law readers and his own people."

"Not that it is even an issue," Damon said. "Your border patrols will never permit Pirse to enter Rhenlan."

"Exactly."

Palle refilled Damon's wine glass and deftly turned the conversation away from the troublesome Pirse. Damon allowed himself to be distracted, at least for the moment. He would not argue with Palle about the competence of his border guards or the inaccessibility of Dherrica's mountain villages. Damon knew, even if Palle didn't, that if Palle were king in more than name he could have inspired the Keepers of Dherrica to locate and capture Pirse within the first half-year after Dea's death. Even without the cooperation of the outlying villages, Palle's guardsmen should have been loyal enough, and competent enough, to catch up with Pirse at least once in the past almost-four years.

Instead, for some reason that Damon did not yet completely understand, Pirse remained free. Rumor said that he protected villagers against Abstainers during the harsh mountain winters, which could explain his popularity among the Keepers. Damon had heard nothing to suggest that Pirse did not spend all of his time within the borders of Dherrica, but it didn't hurt to raise the suspicion in Palle's mind.

Every spring, Palle said that he was going to bring Pirse to justice, and every spring he allowed the fugitive prince to slip through his nets. Why? Perhaps Palle had less control over his guard troops than he liked to pretend. Did they fail to obey Palle's orders to capture the prince—or did they refuse? The other possibility was that Pirse's continued freedom had something to do with his role as dragon slayer. Damon knew all the tales about dragons and the deadly danger they represented, and believed about half of them. Rhenlan, however, was rarely visited by dragons. Damon had never seen one. Yet they seemed important to Palle, important enough that he let Pirse live, even though that weakened his authority as king. Did Palle know more than he was telling Damon?

Damon leaned his elbows on the table, and turned the conversation to the subject of dragons.

"You're daft," Doron insisted.

"I'm not arguing, am I?" Pirse replied patiently.

She gave him credit for the patience. Everything else he had done appalled her. "What if there'd been an early blizzard? You of all people should know better than to risk the high roads so soon after midwinter—and the pass from Larch Valley at that!"

Because he was sitting behind her on the bed, she couldn't see his face. His fingers continued to knead the back of her neck. "I had to be here."

"Then you should have come earlier."

"Well, it's done. I'm here. Don't get yourself in a dither."

"I do not dither."

She intended to say more. Instead, she had to inhale with the beginning of another contraction.

"Don't push yet," warned the Brownmother who sat at the foot of the bed.

Doron nodded, panting a little, lost in the contradiction of having to try to relax her muscles while the very center of her body insisted otherwise. Finally, the incredible tension eased and the contraction faded away.

"All right?" Pirse murmured in her ear.

"I'd rather be dyeing wool." Lifting skeins of wet wool in and out of vats never tired her as much as the last few hours had done.

"You're doing fine," Brownmother Seildon said with a smile for Pirse. "One more like that and I think we'll be ready to get to work."

"Good," Pirse said. "The sooner we finish, the sooner we can all have something to eat. I know I'm getting hungry."

"Well, I'm not," Doron snapped. His patience she could live with. His determination to be cheerful was another matter.

"Of course not," the Brownmother agreed. "Dinner should be the last thing on your mind, Your Highness."

"Sorry."

Deprived of one reason to be annoyed, Doron transferred her attention to the woman who had arrived with Pirse. Brownmother Seildon was pleasant enough to look at, perhaps older than herself, certainly plumper and much shorter. In the warmth of the house she'd removed her black robes long enough to shed several layers of woolen tunics and trousers. Then she'd resumed her robes, rolled up her sleeves, convinced a still-astounded Doron to allow herself to be examined, and sent Pirse to bring in extra firewood with the pronouncement that the baby would be born before the day was out. Doron had fumed quietly for an hour as Seildon and Pirse bustled about, moving her bed, foraging in her cupboard, and generally disregarding her venomous glares. She had almost worked herself up to throwing them both out, falling snow or no falling snow, when she felt her water break. She must have made some sound of surprise, because Seildon took one look at her and ordered her to bed.

After that she lost her desire to be alone. Seildon's confidence and obvious experience were rather comforting. She fixed a hot drink for Doron that dulled the labor pains to manageable aches. Pirse obeyed the instructions she gave him immediately and without question. He'd spoken to Doron of Raisal and Rhenlan and the fact that Brown and Redmothers were still relatively common there. Still, she had never expected to meet one. She certainly hadn't expected him to bring a Brownmother directly from Garden Vale, a student of Greenmother Jenil, just to midwife her. Juniper Ridge had several women skilled in midwifing. She'd intended to call one of them. What if they thought she didn't trust them?

"That's another thing," she complained aloud. "If you'd come a day later, you would have missed the birth in spite of everything. What would have been the use of your foolishness then?"

Although she'd meant the words for Pirse, Seildon was the one to reply. "Call the journey dangerous, but not foolish. Even if we had been delayed, I don't believe it would have made a difference. The child would have waited for us."

"Indeed?" Pirse sounded skeptical, which delighted Doron.

Seildon remained unperturbed. "Indeed. The gods speak to Dreamers, you know."

Another contraction swept through Doron, gripping her body as tightly as the confusion that gripped her mind. She kept forgetting this child would not be like her. Or like Pirse. Trying to forget. She didn't know how to raise a Dreamer child! Pirse said there was nothing to worry about, that children were children, but Doron had heard enough tales to know that Dreamer children required special training. Bending of power, they called it. Dreamers had to be taught the laws of magic. Pirse said such training was years away. Far off it might be, but the moment was there, waiting for her, for this child she had yet to meet. This child, who was presently doing her best to burst into the world.

"Are you comfortable?" Seildon asked. Doron looked up in disbelief, only to discover that the Brownmother was looking past her, at Pirse. "You have to be braced to support her."

Pirse shifted very slightly behind her. "I'm ready."

"Good. With the next contraction, Doron, you push."

The contraction began an instant later. Doron lost track

of everything except the demands of her body. At some point Seildon shifted from the bed to the floor, and knelt close between Doron's legs, offering encouragement. Doron wasn't sure whether the encouragement was for her or for Pirse or for the baby. It didn't matter. Nothing mattered except the need of the baby to be free.

Doron was able to rest for a moment after the head emerged. She relaxed her crushing grip on Pirse's hands. He bent his head to peer at her face, and gently brushed a few damp strands of hair from her forehead.

Another flurry of activity and it was over. Seildon lay the naked baby on her stomach and draped a blanket over them both while they waited for the afterbirth.

"Her eyes," Doron whispered. "She's looking at me."

"An alert, healthy daughter," Seildon confirmed. "You should be very proud of yourselves."

Pirse reached over Doron's shoulder to touch a tiny fist. "Should she be so small?"

"She is not small," the Brownmother said firmly. "She's a perfectly normal-sized baby."

"Oh."

Seildon set the prince to work clearing away the soiled bedclothes and straightening up while she made Doron comfortable. As soon as she and the baby were clean and dry—admittedly a temporary state for her daughter—Doron snuggled the baby to her breast and contentedly closed her eyes.

The faint glow from the embers of the banked fire provided the only illumination in the sleeping loft. On the bed, a mound of blankets muffled the outlines of the sleepers. The black-robed figure materialized next to the fireplace. Cedar-scented smoke mixed unobtrusively with the other odors of the hearth. Leaning forward soundlessly, Morb peered at the tiny face beneath its cap of black hair. The mother, lying on her side with one arm crooked protectively over her infant, slept on. Behind her, the blanket moved. Morb straightened and disappeared.

Outside, a row of three black-hooded figures leaned with various degrees of patience against the yard fence. The row became four. Sheyn and Keyn floated high above the tree-tops; their light sparkled on the snow. Aage's teeth flashed in a quick, appreciative grin. "She's going to be a beauty," he told the other wizard.

Jenil buried her hands in her sleeves. "You might give the child a decade or two to grow up."

"They should move to a warmer part of the world." Morb shifted from one sandal-clad foot to the other. "Wherever the child is trained, it won't do to have her snowbound here half the year."

"Be honest," Jenil said. "It's the Prince's mobility you're worried about."

"The dragons aren't going to stop coming," Morb warned.

Savyea glanced over at him. "You should have worn boots, dear."

"Too uncomfortable," Morb grouched back.

"Parenthood won't make the Prince give up monster-slaying," Aage said. "According to Sene, if anything, a wife and family will make him more diligent."

"More aware of the needs of this village, certainly," Jenil said. "No harm in widening his perspective."

They contemplated the silent house and its unsuspecting occupants for a long moment.

Savyea spoke, voice warm with approval. "They named her Emlie."

"I'm glad," Jenil agreed.

"Well, time we all got back to work," Morb said.

One by one, the cloaked shapes, black as their double shadows, winked out of sight.

CHAPTER 38

Snow squeaked beneath Vray's boots as she emerged from the river path onto the village square. The thinly clouded sky was bright, almost as white as the layer of snow that blanketed the landscape. The cloth cover of a mattress propped against an upended table was a conspicuous splash of color in the center of the square. A short distance to Vray's right, at the edge of the square in front of the smithy, Jordy and his three archer apprentices stood in a loose line, facing the mattress.

Vray paused. She had spent an entire morning trying to establish a chronological order for some of old Canis's ramblings, and she longed for the comforting silence of lunch with Cyril. It was not the least bit amusing to find her route blocked by the makeshift archery range Jordy had set up just after the midwinter gathering.

Today's archery lesson seemed to be taking longer than usual. The only safe course would be to go around behind Jordy and his pupils. That would require exchanging at least a minimal greeting with the carter. Vray's seething dissatisfaction intensified at the thought. She had managed to avoid him for nearly a nineday, mostly by making herself aware of his plans and then arranging to be elsewhere herself. So far he'd ignored her absences from meals, but she couldn't guess how long such permissiveness would continue. Tob and Pepper were already annoyed with her, and Matti regarded her with wide, troubled eyes when she came down for her late breakfasts. Neither girl had asked for a bedtime story for the past three nights. Cyril, as always, seemed oblivious to the people around her.

The rest of the village, as far as Vray knew, was equally unaware of any tension in the carter's household. That would change, however, instantly and irretrievably, if she

422

snubbed Jordy publicly. She didn't want to become the focus of village attention. She wasn't ready to be any kind of center of attention. It would serve no purpose.

To her left, the gate to the inn yard squeaked lightly as it swung open. Herri smiled when he saw her, the sleeves of his sweater pushed up past his elbows and the ever-present apron protecting his thick gray trousers.

"Iris." His breath misted and drifted upward in the cold air. "You've been busy these days. How's Canis?"

"Verbose," she replied, then smiled to blunt the edge of bitterness that had crept into the single word. "Getting information from an untrained source is difficult."

She found herself moving with Herri in the direction of the archery class. As they drew near, Jordy's voice became audible, offering Lim instructions for his next shot. A corner of Vray's memory noted the advice, compared it with similar lessons she'd heard long ago, and acknowledged the carter's expertise. Most of her attention, however, was on Lim and the other young people, and her continued nagging unhappiness with what they were doing.

This particular lesson at least seemed nearly over. Fifteen-year-old Heather and her elder sister Haant were unstringing their bows even as they listened to Jordy. Lim pulled the last arrow from the quiver at his back and took aim at the defenseless mattress sixty paces away. When the arrow left the string, she could not resist turning her head with the rest to watch its flight. Old straw dribbled from the new rip in the mattress cover as the arrow buried itself next to a dozen others near the center of the target. Vray fleetingly, trivially, wondered who had donated the mattress and if they had entertained any unrealistic hope of reclaiming the poor thing when Jordy and his apprentices were finished with it.

"Well done, lad. All of you can retrieve your arrows." Haant and Heather started for the target. Lim caught Vray's eye and grinned proudly as he unstrung his bow.

Jordy nodded to her. "Hello, Iris."

"Hello. Excuse me, Herri." She answered Lim's unspoken invitation to approach and said, "That was very nice shooting."

The young man fumbled his bow into its soft cloth cover. "Oh, we've all been working really hard."

"Is that a family bow?" she asked. "It seems just right for you."

"No. Kessit made it this summer." He pulled back the cover again and Vray could clearly see the newness of the wood. "But it's mine to keep now. Jordy helped me choose it. He gave all of us several to choose from."

Lim led her to the door of the smithy. Just inside a dozen or more bows rested against one wall. Vray hardly saw them. Behind her Herri's voice was saying, ". . . should go to Long Pine while the weather's still predictable."

"I'd be gone two ninedays, maybe three," Jordy answered. "I've only just started training that colt from Garden Vale. If I break my schedule now—"

"Take him with you."

"Haant still isn't sure which one she likes best," Lim continued, distracting Vray. "Jordy wants her to try the heavier pull when we go hunting."

Vray spun toward him more abruptly than she'd intended. "Hunting?"

Outside, Herri said, "They need you, Jordy. A little practical advice, a few suggestions to get them moving in the right direction might make all the difference."

"Jordy knows where there's an old buck—where there's usually an old buck—bedded down in the forest to the east of here. He says it's time we tried our skills on a moving target. Heather's done some spear fishing, so she's not too excited. But Haant and I have never actually killed an animal, except with snares and box traps."

Vray nodded politely, all the while concentrating on the conversation taking place outside. Jordy's reply drifted to her ears, a hint of rueful exasperation in the words. "The idea is for each community to organize its own defense. They don't need my interference."

"No, but they do need encouragement. People trust you, man."

The idea appeared in Vray's mind complete and inarguable, as abruptly as a Dreamer might materialize out of thin air. She reached out to pick up a bow perhaps five feet in length. "When are you going?" she asked Lim.

"This afternoon. Now. Why, would you like to come and watch?" He sounded hopeful.

"I'd like to come and join you."

Lim looked surprised, then pleased. "You already know how to shoot?"

"I'll show you."

They went out into the pale daylight. Herri was gone, the inn gate just closing behind him. Heather and Haant had returned to Jordy's side and were watching as he made adjustments to the fletching on an arrow. He looked up. "Lim, I want you to see this."

Lim moved somewhat guiltily to join the girls. Vray said, "Jordy? I'd like to go hunting, too."

His hands on the arrow grew still. "I'm pleased to see you take an interest, but you haven't done any of the preliminary work the others have."

"I didn't want to waste your time," she lied easily. "I already know how to shoot."

She kept her face passive as he studied first her, then the bow in her hand. Then he handed the arrow to Heather, reached into his pocket, and produced a coil of gut which he offered to Vray. "String your bow," he instructed her crisply. "Let's see just how much you know."

She took her place in the center of the area of trampled snow and faced the target, grateful for the absence of wind. Her hands were already cold enough with excitement. Curiously, she experienced no hesitation as she handled the bow and considered what she was about to do. Her last lessons with Dael were as clear as though they had happened a few days rather than a few lifetimes ago. The string Jordy had given her was already looped at one end. She slipped it into place, then braced the bow against her boot and strung it carefully, testing the tension as Dael had taught her. Jordy indicated his approval by silently handing her an arrow from Haant's quiver. Vray accepted it and looked out across the glimmering white square to the mattress.

How long since she had raised a bow? Four years? Nearly that. She did remember what to do. She was Redmother trained, after all. Even if she had been more interested in spending time with Dael than in the lessons, he'd made her learn, and she'd done her best to please him. The question was how much her muscles remembered. The best technique in the world wouldn't help her if her hand shook. Perhaps she should have chosen a smaller bow, one with less pull. She wasn't going to need much range. No, but she did need power. Dael had taught her that, too. A few pounds pull might make the difference between a grazing wound and a killing penetration.

She chose a spot on the target and aimed at it with her mind's eye, the bow still held at her side. Dael said that the mind was everything, that the body only followed the procedures already rehearsed for it in thought. She remembered his instructions and mentally measured her target and its physical relationship to her, its size and distance and relative location. The exercise took only a moment. When she felt she could reach out with her eyes closed and find the spot she had chosen, she put her arrow to the string. She raised the bow slowly. It felt wrong. No, it wasn't the bow. Her arms were too long. She suddenly felt ungainly, unfamiliar with her own body. This was not the body which had learned archery, was it? She was taller, stronger, her shape subtly different, her center of gravity off. She would need practice to adjust.

Hesitantly, she completed aiming and let fly, pretending Dael was in his usual place behind her, and she was trying to coax a pleased smile from the guard captain.

She missed the spot she aimed for.

Lim said, "Nice shot."

"You're pulling to the left," Jordy said. "Try another."

Vray gave him a frosty nod of agreement. She needed to

be proficient enough to convince Jordy that she could safely accompany the group. With each shot, her confidence improved. After putting ten arrows into various spots on the target, she received the carter's thoughtful nod of approval.

"All right, lass, you know what you're doing. Fetch the arrows back for Haant, then find yourself a quiver in the smithy. We'll be leaving in five minutes."

In less time than that, with Lim's help, Vray was ready and the five of them set out down the wide road that led to the ford. A few hundred yards short of the river Jordy led them onto a smaller path that snaked into an area of scrub forest and marsh, unused by anyone for farming or pasturage. As they walked, Jordy described the terrain they would be hunting across, what they could expect of the deer when they found it, and reviewed the strategy they'd be using. From his questions to the others Vray gathered that, in several days' lessons, they'd used moving targets ingeniously rigged by the carter on ropes between trees. Not as sophisticated a method as the training Vray had received, but it was sufficient to give them practical understanding of how to lead a target.

Only one of the technicalities of the hunt interested Vray, and she gave only the barest minimum of attention to the preliminaries. She had experienced an enlightenment. Anything unconnected with that was irrelevant. She didn't notice where they were walking, responding with surface courtesy to Lim's eager smiles. When they halted after a quarter of an hour for final instructions and to string their bows, Vray positioned herself as far from Jordy as she could without being obvious about it.

She was rewarded. Jordy took one end of the line, from which he intended to flush the buck. Vray and the apprentices were to walk parallel with him in a widely spaced shoulder-to-shoulder formation to diminish the chance of accident. Vray found herself in exactly the position she'd maneuvered for, at the other end of the line, far to Jordy's left.

The group proceeded forward without speaking, bows in

hand, arrows nocked, alert for the first glimpse of movement ahead. Vray lagged one subtle pace behind Heather, immediately to her right. From there, her view of the carter was perfect.

Carter turned killer. He dared too much! She had been struggling with that one thought for days now. By the Rock, he was a Keeper! Bad enough that he presumed to criticize Shaper behavior. Given the circumstances, she might forgive that. Worse was this attempt to prepare his neighbors to defy the king's guards. Even that she might have ignored. She hadn't forgotten the night of the Spring Festival, the harsh laughter of the invaders, the burning of the trees. But Jordy's influence extended beyond his own village, and that she could not ignore. His ideas, his schemes, followed to their conclusions, would threaten all of Rhenlan. Pond and pool, this was her country! Hers and her brother's and her father's, to shape as they saw fit. To shape and to protect.

The situation was clear to her, as clear as still water. More clear than anything had been since she'd begun to lose herself at Soza during her first long, wretched winter there. She had a duty to protect her people, to eliminate danger.

The carter had become a danger.

Ahead lay a frozen stream screened by thickets of bushes and tall, dead reeds. Just beyond was a steep bank. If the deer was where Jordy said it was, it would burst out of cover somewhere between Lim and Jordy and flee in the only direction not blocked by threatening people, up the bank. Bows crept upward along the line. Vray flexed her fingers once, then carefully relaxed every muscle. Her eyes never left the beige figure of the carter. Brown boots, darker brown trousers, sleeveless tunic woven in tans and grays, worn over the lighter tan of an old work shirt, short sandy hair unkempt from ducking beneath tree branches. His bow was also brown, wood dark with age, taller than he was. She drew forth the image she held in her memory, the image of him competing in the archery contest at the Spring Festival. She pictured the stance he would take, the position he would hold for a second or two, bow raised, left arm out-stretched, back turned toward her. She kept that image clear in her mind's eye, aiming carefully at that back as it would look when it turned toward her in reality. She clothed the image in beige and put snow in the background. It became one with the flesh and blood man stepping cautiously through the brush. She felt the connection snap into place. The distance, the spatial relationship between herself and her target was there, palpable, an invisible thread to guide her arrow. She wouldn't miss.

The deer burst out of cover midway between Jordy and Lim and half a dozen paces in front of their line, scattering snow and dead leaves in every direction. Haant gave a startled squeak, but raised her bow as quickly as the rest of the apprentices and Jordy raised theirs. Vray moved in unison with them. The only difference was that her arrow was not pointing toward the bounding animal.

Not bounding, floating. The buck seemed to be taking its leaps at an unnaturally slow pace. No one and nothing moved, breath hung as clouds in the winter air, and the echo of Haant's small, excited cry drew out into a faint wail. Everything was slowed, nothing moved—and images whirled behind Vray's eyes, between her and the beige back of her target. Balls of bright cloth tossed themselves around her while the silence of Cyril's mourning rang in her head and she saw Tob's sad comforting of Matti and Pepper's grieving as if it was already recorded in her memory. She saw the Spring Festival clearly, heard Jordy claim her place in the village, in his family. She felt the warmth of the stable and saw Jordy's hands, so competently and carefully grooming the stupid horse he declared to detest. Carter, archer, juggler, father, husband, friend, conspirator, catalyst, stubborn fool. Not a monster. A man.

All the images conjured by memory and imagination screamed that what she did was wrong. She felt tears welling and refused to shed them—her vision had to stay clear. She felt the urge to tremble and denied it, found within her the stillness of a Pool ritual. A man, not a monster, the words repeated themselves. Men are not monsters. Men can be reasoned with. Could Damon be reasoned with? Wasn't Damon danger enough to this land? Could she kill a man because his views were inconvenient?

Damon could. I'm Damon's sister. I could kill this man. But I won't.

Vray shifted her aim. No more than a few inches, but it was enough. She released the arrow, almost falling to her knees as the tension left her. She didn't bother to follow its flight with her eyes. She didn't care whether it struck the deer or not. Her eyes remained on Jordy. She heard the shhh and thwock of the arrows and the thrashing fall of the big animal. There were cries of elation and surprise from the apprentices, a rushing forward of the other young people toward the kill. Vray didn't move. The deer didn't matter. Neither did the fact that the apprentices were one step closer to being trained archers, a potentially deadly threat to the next troop of king's guards that rode into Broadford.

The only thing that mattered was Jordy, very much alive, who turned a measured smile on her and said, "Well done, lass."

All she could think of to say was, "Thanks, Dad," before she unstrung her bow and ran blindly back toward the village.

As soon as they returned to the square, Jordy put Lim in charge of storing away the class's bows and arrows. Herri came out of the inn to supervise the butchering of the kill. With everyone profitably occupied, Jordy left his apprentices to their work and set out for home as fast as his legs would carry him.

He found her where he expected her to be, in the stable. She had a brush in each hand, and was slowly stroking them across Stockings's already immaculate back. The horse, typically, was fast asleep. Iris wasn't paying any attention to what she was doing. Her expression was one of aching melancholy. Jordy paused in the doorway. He had to have a talk with the girl. Her behavior had been getting stranger and stranger. He'd intended to insist upon an explanation. But did she have to look so sad?

He waited to be noticed. He walked toward the horse, making no special effort to step quietly through the loose straw on the stable floor, but still the girl did not look up. He finally sighed and said, "Iris."

She jumped. Her greenish eyes turned on him. "Jordy." She said his name oddly. Guiltily?

"Let's have a talk, lassie." He gestured for her to come out from behind the horse. She complied slowly, setting down the brushes one at time on the shelf above Stockings's head. He pointed toward the feed bin. "Sit down, m'girl."

To his bewilderment, she sniffled, and a tear spilled down her cheek as she moved to obey. She wiped it brusquely away. Sitting, she stared past him. This was nothing like the defiance that he'd coped with from his other children. When Tob misbehaved he stomped and sulked. Pepper's temper expressed itself in red-faced screaming fits that reminded Jordy uncomfortably of his own childhood behavior. Matti, still the baby, liked to wheedle and whine. None of their bad moods lasted for long. Iris's inexplicable moodiness had been going on for several ninedays now. Enough was enough. He'd thought she was coming out of it when she'd asked to accompany the hunters. What had gone wrong?

"You did well today." He offered the comment experimentally.

In reply she hid her face in her hands. A muffled, "No I didn't!" came out surrounded by a sob. "Jordy, I'm sorry!"

He cautiously took a seat beside her. Perhaps this was typical of teenage daughters. He thought of Pepper's tantrums magnified several times, and shuddered inwardly. Putting an arm over her shoulder, he said, "There now, it's all right."

Her entire body shook, but she did not answer.

"You've nothing to be sorry for. I was quite proud of you this afternoon. I'm sure your friends. . . ."

He didn't get to finish the sentence. Her sobs became a wail of despair, and she suddenly twisted toward him and buried her head against his shoulder. The force of her movement almost knocked them off the feed bin. Jordy braced himself and helplessly hugged her back.

"What is it? What's the matter? Iris, you've got to tell me what's wrong. I can't help you if I don't understand what's troubling you. Iris?"

"Daddy!"

"Yes, lass." He patted her back and rocked her as best he could on the uneven seat. "I'm here. Tell me."

"I called you 'Dad'! It just came out. I couldn't help it! And I couldn't—" Her words broke off into more sobbing while Jordy listened with total incomprehension. This was a confession of a problem? He hadn't known what to expect when he and Cyril took Iris into their family. Parents worried about irresponsible behavior, about sickness. With a child like Iris, he'd been concerned that she wouldn't fit in with the other young people in Broadford. She had become popular, though, and no one could ask for a more conscientious Redmother for the village—or a finer daughter.

"Iris, I don't understand. I'm your father. You can call me whatever name you like best."

She pulled violently away from him, and some of her sorrow seemed to shift to anger. "No! I wish you were. I wish I'd been born here, raised here. But I'm only fooling myself to think that!"

His own quick temper flared in response. Now it began to make sense. Soza, and the family that had abandoned her there, still stood between them. "You're here now! The past doesn't matter. No one pretends you didn't have another father, a woman who gave birth to you. Parents who abandoned you! They sent you away because you disobeyed them. It's tragic, I know, but it's over. It wasn't your fault. We love you, Iris!"

"I know all that!" she cried. "I love you, too."

"Then what are we yelling about?" he demanded. "Have you been moping all this time because you don't think you

432

have the right to love us? Don't you remember the Spring Festival? You belong here now."

"I wish I did."

"You do!" Jordy declared as firmly as he knew how. She quieted ever so slightly in the face of his determination. "The only one who can take you away from us is you yourself." A frightening thought knocked the anger out of him. "Is that it? Are you thinking of returning to that other family? Do you want to go back to Edian?"

Her shocked, "No!" woke the horse. Stockings snorted irritably and stamped one foot on the dirt floor. Jordy was thankful for the distraction. Iris glanced toward the disgruntled animal as well, and a hint of amusement broke through her distress.

"Don't mind her," Jordy said gruffly.

"Well, it is her home."

"I'm glad you see that." She faced him, her anguished expression relaxing, ever so slightly, under the force of his words. "It's her home, but she doesn't mind sharing it with us. That's what it means to be family. We'll never send you away, Iris. I only mentioned Edian because you've been so unhappy and restless. But if that's not what you want, we won't speak of it again."

Her voice was a whisper. "Thank you."

"Good. Now, we know that you don't want to leave, and you know how much we care for you. Has anything else been bothering you?"

She wiped the back of one hand across her damp face, pushed some loose hair behind one ear, then tugged at her rumpled clothing. At least her general air of despair was gone. She seemed to be carefully searching for just the right words. Perhaps she hadn't actually known why she was upset until he'd confronted her. The thought that he'd done the right thing gave him a warm sense of relief.

When she finally spoke, her voice was hesitant, as if she had to figure out her thoughts before she could speak them. "I've been very confused. Torn. Not knowing who to be loyal to, not knowing who to be, really. I think I made my choice today. Making choices frightens me. I know which family I love. I can't forget my other life, I shouldn't, and that's what hurts. It's just taken me a while to see that what they'd want of me isn't relevant right now."

"What others want of you is never important. Always make your own decisions, lass."

"It was making my own decisions that got me in trouble in the first place!"

The complaint sounded more like the spirited young woman he suspected she was. "That may be. But just because your family over-reacted and sent you away, doesn't mean that the decisions themselves were wrong." He stood up and offered her his hand. "Are you hungry? Cyril will have supper ready by now."

To his great satisfaction, she smiled. "I'd better go help her," she said. She put her hand in his and got up.

"Wash your face first," he instructed.

"Yes, Dad."

CHAPTER 39

On Festival morning, only a few wisps of high clouds interrupted the otherwise endless blue of the sky over Raisal. Aage had successfully banished the rain of a few days before, providing the perfect weather the king expected. Feather could recall more than a few rainy Spring Festivals in Garden Vale. Now she realized why the east wind had risen with such regularity a day or two before Festival to carry clouds out of Sitrine. She was surprised Jenil hadn't given Aage or Sene a good talking-to about having some consideration for their neighbors. Then again, maybe she had. Both wizard and king were very good at humbly accepting a scolding, then going right ahead and doing what they wanted anyway.

"Who was supposed to bring the garlands?" Feather called out to Dektrieb as he passed.

The harried servant paused, a long ladder balanced on his shoulder. "A boy from Cheinil's shop. They promised to send him at midmorning."

"He's late," Feather complained loudly. Dektrieb, wisely, resumed crossing the lawn. Following his progress with her eyes, Feather saw that at least the kitchen pavilion was up. Smoke emerged from vents at either end of the structure. She hoped that was a sign of function, not disaster.

"Do we know if all the supplies arrived this morning?" she asked.

Beside her, Jeyn toyed with a ribbon streamer she'd picked out of a bush half an hour ago. "Hmmm?"

"Cooking supplies. Food," Feather enunciated clearly. "Did everything come in from the market?"

Jeyn wound the ribbon through her fingers and bestowed a fond smile on Feather. "I'm sure it did. Stop worrying. Everything will be fine."

435

"How would you know? All you're doing is thinking about Ivey! You're not being any help at all!"

Jeyn smoothed the ribbon with a wistful smile.

Feather considered killing her. "How can you stand there looking so—so mushy! And beautiful," she added truthfully.

"You're beautiful, too. It's your day, Feather. Everything's beautiful today."

"If it's my day, why am I doing all the work?"

"I had to talk to the law readers yesterday, and the day before. I dealt with that delegation about taxes late last night, too," Jeyn pointed out.

"And what do you mean, everything is beautiful?" Feather went on as if Jeyn hadn't spoken. She pointed at a section of lawn full of upended tables and frantic servants. "Do you call that beautiful?"

"Yes."

"I'm going to be sick. Go away, Jeyn."

Jeyn drifted away, still smiling.

Behind Feather, a masculine voice laughed. "My sister is in love," Chasa said.

"I never would have guessed."

He kissed Feather on the cheek. "We're twins, you know. Twins do everything alike."

"At least you don't look mushy."

"You wouldn't let me."

Chasa walked past her and gazed critically up at the half-decorated platform. "Are you sure it will be finished in time?"

"In time for what?" she asked with as much innocence as she could muster.

"Not for the announcements," he shot back. "Today I'm not interested in whatever's happened to anybody else. I want us to be up there together. Almost like when we were little."

He was doing it again. All winter, Chasa had done nothing but fill her head with stories. Her days had been monopolized by the prince, until she became so used to his company that even his voice didn't bother her the way it had at first.

Obliging him, she rose to the bait. "All right, what did we do to the Festival platform when we were little?"

It was his turn to look innocent, his big brown eyes wide. "Why, nothing, Feather. We weren't always in trouble."

"Just most of the time."

"The Festival I was thinking about was the one just after you turned five. The fall after Dad brought you home. He stood up on the platform to formally introduce you to the people as his daughter. You were shy, and didn't want to go up beside him. So I held your hand and we went up together." His smile was radiant and more than a little smug. "Everyone said we looked so cute."

"I bet they did," Feather replied, teeth clenched.

Sure enough, her betrothed continued, "You're still cute."

"I've heard that before, Your Highness."

"And never liked it."

"And never will."

A servant ran toward them. She acknowledged Chasa with a quick, "Good morning, Your Highness," then turned to Feather. "A boy is coming up the road with a cart full of flowers."

"Send him right over." The servant ran off and Chasa began to back away. Feather caught his sleeve. "Oh, no. You just stand right there. If your twin is going to be useless, you can work in her place."

Vray pulled the brush through her hair a final time. Considering the dampness of the day, it was the best she could do. She turned on the low stool beside her bed. "All right, who's next?"

"Me! Me!" Pepper and Matti clamored simultaneously. Pepper, older and quicker, reached her first.

"I'd like a single braid, please. With this ribbon. Make sure it doesn't come loose."

Matti pushed in beside her. "What about my buttons?

Can't you do my buttons first?"

"One at a time," Vray replied. She took Pepper by the shoulders and turned her to face the other way. Swiftly, she fastened the fancy tunic Matti had chosen to wear. The ladder from the main room creaked and Tob poked his head up through the floor.

"Almost ready?" he asked.

"Yes. Matti, go to your brother. Pepper, I'll get this started, then I'm sure Mama can finish it for you."

"But I want you to do it!"

Tob leaned far enough into the room to finish helping Matti. He made faces at her as he worked, causing her to giggle at the novelty of being nose to nose with her big brother. "Mama knows how to braid," he told Pepper. "Iris and I promised to be early to help Canis with the Festival decorations."

"We could help, too," Pepper insisted.

"You're too little," Tob said, then told Matti, "All done."

"We are not," Pepper said.

Vray tried a soothing tone. "You'll be there soon enough. There'll be plenty to do on a rainy day like this."

"But we want to come with you," Matti said.

Tob tapped her on the nose. "We want to be with our friends."

"You want to be with each other." Pepper, blunt as always, twisted around to glare at Vray, pulling her half-finished braid out of reach. "Tob never plays with us anymore. When he's not doing his chores he's following you to the village, and we have to stay here. It's not fair!"

Vray pressed her lips down on the threatening smile. "Tob and I like to talk. It's grown-up talk. You wouldn't be interested. Maybe it's not fair, but that's the way it is."

"How do you know I wouldn't be interested?" Pepper challenged. "I can talk about anything Tob can talk about."

"Talk yes, make sense, no," Tob muttered.

Matti snatched the opportunity. "Pepper, Tob's picking on you."

So much for a graceful exit, Vray thought. She said,

"Time to go," and quickly moved to the ladder.

Vray nudged Tob's shoulder firmly. He took the hint and whisked out of sight, clearing a path for her own escape. In the main room, Cyril was still cooking. Jordy sat off to the side of the hearth in his stocking feet, a cloth across his lap, polishing a boot. He looked up as Tob and Vray hurried toward the door.

"We've got to go, Dad," Tob announced.

"The girls are dressed," Vray added. "Pepper still needs help with her hair."

"What were they arguing about this time?" Jordy asked mildly.

Some subtle magic came to parents, Vray decided. That was the only explanation for Jordy's ability to be so consistently aware of his children's activities. She'd never noticed it in her own parents. Thinking back, there was very little they had done that was parental—not as she'd come to understand the term. She said, "They're feeling left out."

Tob followed her example. "I told Pepper they're too little to come to the inn now. She didn't like being reminded."

Pepper came scrambling down the ladder. Jordy said, "More tact next time, lad. Off with you now."

Gratefully, Vray ducked outside behind Tob. For the moment, the overcast sky was producing no more than a fine mist. They drew up their hoods and hurried down the hill, watching their footing on slick stones and mud.

Once on the main road, they fell into step with one another. Tob twined his fingers with Vray's. She squeezed his hand fondly.

"It is not fondness," she announced aloud.

Tob smiled his impish smile at her. He smiled at almost everything she did. That in itself alternately amused and terrified her. "What isn't fondness? Holding hands?"

She set their linked hands swinging. "That. This. Everything our very perceptive little sister was complaining about. We have been ignoring them. We do spend all our time together."

"Why not? Who else would we spend time with?"

"Our little sisters," Vray repeated. "We're family."

"Not physically." Tob's voice had deepened over the winter. It was difficult to think of him any longer as a boy. "You're a Redmother. You know the rules. I'm your adopted brother. I can love you if I want. If we both want."

He was still young enough to blush. She held his hand more tightly still. What she felt wasn't fondness. Desire, yes. He was a very attractive young man. There. She'd admitted it. The boy she'd met only a year ago—the boy who'd offered her kittens when she cried—had grown in more than size. Today was Spring Festival, a day for joy, celebration. For what seemed like the hundredth time she mentally reviewed the positions of the moons as far as her body's cycle was concerned. Even if Ivey was right, and she was destined by Dreamer prophecy to take a Keeper husband, she was not fertile today. There was no reason not to resume having sex.

Resume the practice of sex. Sex as she'd known it at Soza? No. There was no danger of that. This was Tob. She didn't fear him. Didn't fear anyone in Broadford.

Of course she didn't fear Tob. He was eager, but totally inexperienced. Whatever happened would happen her way, or not at all.

"I love you," she informed him. "As a brother."

"I love you more than Lim does," he returned.

She pulled her hand away from his and whacked him on the shoulder. "Will you stop talking about Lim?"

"He spent a whole summer impressing you. I worry."

"You had the whole winter."

"He's older than me."

"But not as handsome." She groaned at the smug expression her remark produced.

"That's true." He caught her hand again. "Let's hurry. I want to get this day over with."

His comment wasn't what she'd expected. "Why? I thought you love Spring Festival day."

The smile he gave her was mature to the point of being

440

unnerving. "I'm hoping I'll love Festival night more."

By midmorning the work was complete, and people began to arrive at the royal estate from Raisal and the surrounding countryside. Fruits and cheeses and cool drinks were served from the kitchen pavilion, and children's games began in the large paddock. The real festivities, the feast and announcements, would not begin until noon. For the moment, Feather's time was her own. She allowed Chasa to lead her to one of the tables set below the terrace, where Jeyn was standing, a platter and pitcher and several glasses in front of her.

"About time you dragged her away from there," Jeyn greeted her brother.

"She gets enthusiastic," Chasa replied. He reached for the pitcher and poured lemonade for each of them.

"You know, you two do look a little bit alike," Feather conceded as they sat down around the small table.

Jeyn and Chasa exchanged identical glances. "No!" they exclaimed in unison.

Feather laughed. Although she and Jeyn were dressed as Brownmothers and Chasa wore the house colors, the stronger connection lay between the tall, fair-haired, dark-eyed brother and sister. Feather felt a little excluded. She'd seen it happen before when the two of them got caught up in one another. They could share a mood or an emotion unique to them and leave the rest of the world outside. It had never affected her with the least bit of jealousy before. Lately, however, she'd been spending a lot of time with either one or the other twin. Alone with Jeyn, she felt herself a cherished sister. Alone with Chasa, she knew with absolute certainty that she was special to him. Now, watching them together, she found it hard to feel secure.

She sipped her lemonade and pushed the mood away. Lingering questions, however, remained in her mind. "I didn't even know people had twins. Before Savyea started getting so silly, that is, about everyone having lots of babies."

"It used to be rare," Jeyn agreed. "It was rare when we were born."

Chasa looked at his sister significantly. "We almost weren't born."

"Mother died from it," Jeyn concluded.

"I'm sorry about that," Feather said. "I shouldn't have raised the subject. Today is for celebrating beginnings, not endings."

"That's all right," Chasa said. "Actually, it was Aage's doing, in a way."

"Not Mother's dying," Jeyn hastened to add. "Our birth."

Feather couldn't resist that opening. Eyebrows rising, she said, "Really? But you look so much like Sene."

"Feather!" Chasa exclaimed.

"Not that, either," Jeyn said. "You see, Mother and Dad were infertile for a long time. Three or four years, and then when she did get pregnant she kept miscarrying. The fire bears were still everywhere, and even though the Dreamers were dying Dad knew he had to produce more Shapers, for the fighting if for nothing else."

"You're telling me Aage got your mother pregnant?" Feather asked. "Dreamers don't do that."

Chasa reached over to pat her hand. "I know it's confusing."

"Aage," Jeyn said, "has a library full of books."

"Books don't have anything to do with it, either," Feather protested.

"They do when they're filled with Dreamers' healing knowledge going back for generations and generations."

"What does healing have to do with having babies?"

"You're being difficult," Chasa complained.

"I'm always difficult," she reminded him. He just smiled.

Jeyn folded her arms. "You did ask."

"Sorry. Go on."

"Aage found methods for increasing fertility. Some work on men, some on women. Some require special herbs, others dragon powder and a Dreamer's power-bending. He found something that he believed would help Mother. An experiment." Jeyn tilted her head at her brother. "We're the result."

"The magic of it had nothing to do with Mother dying," Chasa took up the tale. "Aage and Dad and Aunt Mara have all said that, and we believe them. She simply wasn't strong enough."

"She was strong," Jeyn said, "in many ways. Just not for childbirth."

"The methods are effective," Chasa continued. "After we were born, Savyea came and spent half a year with Aage, going over what he'd found and adapting it with her practical healing experience. She's been using the knowledge ever since. Ivey tells us that twins have been born in many villages in the past ten years."

At the mention of the minstrel's name, Jeyn's expression softened.

"She's got that over-cooked turnip look on her face," Feather warned Chasa. "Can we leave?"

"Yes." He took her hand and pulled her to her feet. To his sister he said, "I love you dearly, but I can't take that look."

"Then don't look in a mirror, brother."

Chapter 40

At the last Spring Festival, her dress had been white. Today Feather would wear saffron and scarlet, the strong, gaudy colors of the royal family of Sitrine, colors that actually suited her better than last spring's more delicate dress. She and Jeyn had spent the Festival morning dressed in elegantly-cut black gowns, the tight-fitted sleeves heavily embroidered in gold and bronze threads, amber and topaz beads sewn into the pattern—Jeyn's idea of proper Brownmother robes. Feather went in to her room to change for the afternoon's event as the senior Redmother began listening to the community announcements. Having accepted her part in the scheme of things, Feather didn't feel any more need than Chasa to hear anyone else's news today.

She'd felt Chasa's eyes on her as she left the pavilion to come indoors, and suspected he was afraid she might be planning to run away. She almost turned back to tell him that she had already tried running and knew it didn't work. Why repeat mistakes? She'd made her decision and she'd go through with it. She supposed having an urge to reassure the prince was a good sign. Besides, this was what Sene wanted, why he'd brought her from the shelter of Garden Vale's Brownmother house in the first place.

She missed Sene. He had been busy all winter, running the kingdom or going off to kill monsters in Chasa's place. Perhaps after she did this one thing to please him, he'd stop being so distant. Now that she knew Chasa, it didn't seem quite so terrible an ordeal as it had when she first arrived. She would just get it over with—fulfill her vow and make the best of it.

Determined or not, she still spent a few minutes having one last cry alone in her room. The weeping didn't last long, which was another good sign. Just a few tears, more from nerves than a broken heart. Once that was over with, she washed her face, made sure the wreath of flowers on her head was tilted at a saucy angle, and walked purposefully from her room.

Chasa was waiting outside the door, leaning against the wall, his arms crossed with studied casualness. "Very pretty dress," he said.

Feather looked up at the prince. "It's getting harder to get away from you all the time."

He moved closer, and put his hands on her shoulders as he smiled down into her eyes. "After today, it'll be harder still."

Mixed emotions tightened Feather's throat. She managed to keep her voice light as she answered, "I had hoped to marry someone a bit closer to my own size. But I suppose it's asking too much to try and find a miniature version of you at this late date."

His smile showed dimples remarkably like Sene's. "We could ask Aage to shrink me."

She shook her head at the suggestion. "Wouldn't be worth all the trouble to have your clothes altered. And the sea monsters would just laugh at you." Not that that would stop him. Chasa would go out to fight the monsters if he was two feet tall and had to use a twig as a harpoon. Like his father, and his sister—like everyone Feather had met since coming to live in Sitrine—Chasa let nothing stand in the way of keeping his vows.

"It'd be an easier way of killing them, watching them laugh themselves to death." His smile disappeared, and his hands tightened on her shoulders. "You're sure you want to go through with this?"

"Yes." She stamped on his foot to get him to move. The gesture gave her a great deal of satisfaction and, although she doubted she could do much damage, it was quicker than politely asking to be let go. He yelped and jumped back, releasing her. When she smiled at him, he returned it. She and Chasa had developed an understanding lately. Chasa let her bully him, but only so far, and always with a glint in his eyes to tell her he knew exactly what she was up to.

"What about you?" she asked. "Do you want to go through with it? Limp through life with me?"

"I'll limp. But you'll have an aching neck, little one." He put his hand on the back of her neck and rubbed gently. It felt rather nice. "They've finished the announcements. We'd better not keep everyone waiting."

Perhaps I should kiss him, she thought, *to see if I like it or not.* No. There was no time. She'd just have to leave that experiment until after the wedding.

Laughing and breathless, Vray collapsed in the corner of the landing. She pulled her knees up to her chin as Oriel led his team down the stairs.

"The wood shed. Come on!" he yelled, voice shrill with excitement.

Vray watched the group hurtle down the inn stairs. She had been an illusive quarry in the elaborate game of hide and seek/treasure hunt which was occupying the full attention of the village children. Only when caught by three of a team's children was she required to reveal the next clue. She was having just as much fun as the youngsters.

The noise of the children faded, leaving her in an island of temporary peace and solitude. Not that the stairwell was silent, with most of the population of the village crowded into the inn. Rain changed the character of a Festival day. Vray found few similarities between this day and the Spring Festival she'd celebrated in Broadford one year before. Today she had actually enjoyed telling the Story of Beginnings. She had looked around the packed common room and recognized every face. Sitting on the landing, as she was now, she could locate many of the villagers by the sounds of their voices that drifted up to her from the conversations in the common room, or down from the guest rooms, where one group was quilting, another carving, another arguing about something to do with chickens. She intended to join the quilters when her part in the game was over. Unless it was time to eat again by then.

I'm very comfortable here, she thought abruptly. *I suppose that means it's time to leave.*

Sobering, she rested her chin on her knees. That was an odd idea. Or was it? This was her home. Family, friends, a useful future were all available to her here. Tob certainly seemed to think so. Her cheeks warmed slightly. She had to make a decision about him. She remembered what Ivey had said. Where was the minstrel celebrating Spring Festival this year? In Sitrine? Not Broadford, unfortunately for her. She would have welcomed a few words with Ivey. Words she saw now they should have had on his last visit. What had he said about needing to learn of events in the king-doms? About sending a message to King Sene? She was Redmother of a moderately-sized village in Rhenlan. Broad-ford's welfare was her responsibility.

One of her responsibilities.

"There she is!" Matti squealed from the top of the stair-case.

Vray sprang up and threw herself down the stairs. An-other team to evade. She'd never hear the end of it from the others if she allowed her sister's group to catch her too easily. She squeezed round the bar and through the kitchen, leaving shouts of encouragement and laughter in her wake. She skidded on wet straw outside the kitchen door, turned left, and darted through Oriel and his group as they emerged from the wood shed in search of their next quarry.

Vray cut across to the stable. She wanted to give the chil-dren a good, long chase. That was half the fun of the game. Right now, a good game was her contribution to the success of this Festival.

She would give other matters some serious consider-ation—later.

The yard in front of the inn was crowded. Jordy cast a critical eye over the lines that supported the area's canvas roof. With so many people passing through the open-sided tent all day, it was always possible that someone might acci-dentally loosen an important connection. Jordy's inspection revealed no flaws. Rain dripped from the still-taut edges of the ribbon-hung expanse of canvas, its patter a steady accompaniment to the chattering conversations within.

Jordy gave his wife's waist a light squeeze. They sat side by side on one of the benches backed against the stable wall. He hadn't seen Pepper and Matti since supper, but he wasn't worried about them. There were singers in the main room of the inn and Canis was upstairs, making scrap dolls for the younger children. His daughters would be with one or the other, unless they had found a quiet corner and gone to sleep.

Belatedly he corrected himself. His youngest daughters were inside the inn somewhere. His adopted daughter, like Tob and every other young adult in the village, was present in the yard. After the clouds lifted somewhat in midafternoon and the downpour slacked off enough to tempt people out of doors, Herri and Kessit had strewn the wet ground in the yard with a thick layer of hay and sawdust, and the dancing had begun.

As the musicians struck up a new tune, Kessit edged past a knot of gossiping parents and sat down next to Jordy. "It's been a better Festival than last year, despite the rain," the woodcarver said.

"Aye. Herri will complain of the state of the inn when it's over, but you can tell he's enjoying himself."

"Loves being indispensable, does our Herri."

Jordy studied his neighbor's face. "How's Jaea?"

"Sad," Kessit answered. "Still, we had to come. She said she won't let last year's bad memories destroy the meaning of the Festival for her. She's true to her vows."

Jordy nodded. "A strong woman."

"I miss the boy," Kessit said. After an awkward pause, he changed the subject. "You must be pleased with your year's work."

"Eh?"

With a nod of his head, Kessit indicated the dancing young people. "The girl's doing well. Last spring we didn't see her dancing at the Festival. Seemed afraid of her own shadow, remember? When she wasn't speaking as a Redmother that is."

Jordy stole a glance at Cyril. His wife's eyes were on the embroidery in her lap, her expression serene. His attention returned to the dancers. "Iris is stronger than she looks. We've given her the security, the support, that any child needs. That's all. The rest she's done for herself."

"Mordi's boy, Lim, likes her. I think he'd more than like her if it wasn't for Tob."

Jordy looked at him sharply. "What do you mean?"

"They're about to become rivals for a girl's affections. It's the last thing I expected, considering the difference in their ages. Lim's nearly nineteen. Time for him to think about a wife. I'm sure he's hoping that Tob's first infatuation won't last long, and that after it's over Iris will want a young man closer to her own age."

"I knew Iris and Tob were growing close this winter," Jordy said. "I should have seen that Lim was getting involved, as well. Thanks for telling me."

"Not that there's much you can do about it." Kessit got up with a rueful smile. "I wouldn't be in your place, carter. Lim and Tob aren't the only boys she'll attract. A real beauty, graceful as a princess. Maybe we can hope she'll make her choice and marry soon."

The woodworker's words hung in the air after he'd gone. Jordy drew his arm away from Cyril and leaned forward, resting his elbows on his knees. The dance concluded with a burst of laughter and applause. Iris imperiously gestured several couples to form a line, and placed herself and Tob at the head. Graceful as a princess. Her red hair had grown a great deal in the past year. She wore it loose for the Festival, a luxurious cloud which, with her greenish eyes, gave her a striking appearance.

He sat up so abruptly that Cyril put her embroidery down and turned toward him with concern.

"It's all right. No one else will see it," he murmured, the reassurance as much for himself as for her. He replaced his arm around his wife's waist. As the shock lessened, a cold anger grew within him. He was going to have a serious talk with Jenil. "This is Iris," the Greenmother had said. Naturally he'd accepted the name without question. The oddities in the girl's personality and attitudes he'd attributed to Soza.

The time had come to stop fooling himself. He'd seen a face and hair like hers only once, when he was a youth on his first visit to Edian. He'd managed to forget that day in the courtyard of King Hion's castle. There wasn't much he cared to remember of the life he'd led before wedding Cyril. But there was no point in denying this particular memory. Iris's resemblance to her mother was remarkable.

Her mother, Gallia, wife of Hion. Her mother, Queen of Rhenlan.

Oh, yes. Jenil had some explaining to do.

"You've only been here a few days, why do you have to go?" Jeyn pouted and tried to look pleading. Ivey kept packing his bag. She tugged on his sleeve. "Look at me when I'm being petulant."

He laughed and grabbed her around the waist. "You've been taking Feather lessons, love. I'm not sure I like it."

"She's a bad influence on me."

"Yes, she is."

Jeyn pressed herself against him. "Then stay in Raisal as a counter to her bad effect."

"I'll be back." He kissed her, then let her go.

Outside, the last of the Festival celebrants had begun to disperse. A burst of laughter carried from the field to the house on the still evening air, and the staccato drumming of hoof beats announced the departure of one of their more affluent guests. By any measure, this year's Festival had been a huge success. They had sent out word of Chasa and Feather's marriage ninedays ago, and every village in Sitrine had sent a representative, if not an entire delegation, to witness the royal wedding. Greenmother Jenil came, too, but either Chasa forgot that he intended to have words with her, or he never tore his eyes away from his new bride long enough to notice the Dreamer's presence. Jenil spent most of the day in Sene's company, to their evident mutual satisfaction. Jeyn watched her father throughout the day, but saw no hint that he felt anything other than joy at the marriage of his son and his ward. Jeyn's only disappointment in the entire day was that Aage had to leave immediately after the ceremony, to go help Morb.

That is, it was the only disappointment, until now. Jeyn sat on the bed beside Ivey's pack. She was tempted to dump the contents out, or pull him down beside her, but folded her hands in her lap instead. She was used to the way the minstrel intermittently entered and left the king's household. He'd been doing it for years. However, that was before he'd become so important to her. Last summer, she'd gotten used to his being more in than out of Raisal. She had hoped that pattern would continue this summer. Yes, the minstrel's life was on the road, where he could attend to his singing and his duties as courier and spy. All very well and good, but she did not like the idea that her lover would be gone for a whole season or more. She was lonely already.

"Let me go with you," she said suddenly.

"Jeyn!"

The idea seemed to surprise Ivey as much as it had her. She smiled slowly, even as Ivey frowned. Of course. Why not?

"You told me once that when you had a lass you'd take her on the road with you."

He looked shocked. "I didn't mean you!"

Jeyn gestured around the bedroom. "If I'm not your lass we'd better have a talk about the rent."

He scratched his chin. "Would I be able to afford it, Highness?"

"No."

"Then I suppose you're my lass."

"I know I am. I love you, Ivey." She'd murmured it often enough while they'd been making love, but she had never said it, just said it, to him before. She held her breath.

He colored, looked pained, relieved, and finally gave her

451

a delighted smile. His bright blue eyes answered her even before he said the words. "And I love you, Jeyn of Raisal. What do you think we should do about it?"

"You're going to make love songs."

"I've done that already."

"And marry me."

He went back to rubbing his chin. "Very likely," he agreed. "But, then what?"

"You'll take me with you on the road. Feather can do almost everything I do around here. Besides, it's time Chasa learned how to do more than bring home magical body parts and chase Abstainers. Take me with you."

"That I will not."

"I have a horse. Several horses. You wouldn't have to walk with that old pony of yours."

"I like to walk."

"Please, Ivey?"

"It wouldn't be safe, Princess. Your father's not the only man in the three kingdoms who's interested in other people's business. Damon has plenty of spies of his own. You might be recognized. What if you were caught in Rhenlan? Have you forgotten Prince Pirse's sister? Princesses don't do well in Damon's company. He could use your intrusion as an excuse to start a war with your father—or force an alliance by marrying you himself. Either way, you'd make too valuable a hostage. It'd be no better if you were found in Dherrica. No, you're staying right here, where you're safe. I'll be back soon. I promise. I have work to do for your father. So do you. Right?"

Slowly, Jeyn nodded. "All right. Still, I wish I could be with you. Maybe someday?"

"I hope so. Through Sitrine, at least. That would be nice. But it's Rhenlan and Dherrica for me now."

"All right, go alone. Just don't get too lonely. I know your reputation, Ivey of Juniper Ridge." Jeyn waved a finger at him. "I'd better not hear any new stories about you. To think I used to enjoy hearing about your singing pretty village girls into bed!"

"That was before I knew you. I'll come home to you, love."

"Soon?"

"Soon. We'll discuss getting married then, all right?"

"Fall Festival?" she suggested. "Think how happy that would make Dad and Aage and Jenil."

He looked thoughtfully at her for a moment. His vows called him to the road, where he had long served the Children of the Rock by serving Sene of Sitrine. Jeyn worked toward the same goals, but the vows she lived by were not the same as his. "Is that what this is about? You want to please the Dreamers?"

She stroked a finger across his collarbone. "No. I want to please you. I'll miss you, minstrel."

"I'll miss you, Princess." They kissed again. Ivey ran his hands down her back, memorizing the shape of her body, the taste of her mouth, the smell of her skin. Marriage wouldn't change their vows. She would always be a ruling Shaper, he a traveling minstrel. Duty would keep them apart more often than it brought them together.

They would simply have to make the most of the time they had.

He turned and moved his pack from the bed to the floor. "I have to get an early start."

Jeyn lay down on the bed, and opened her arms wide. "In the morning," she agreed. "After we've said a proper good-bye."

The stable smelled of used straw and damp horse hair. The horses themselves were gone, removed one by one as their tired owners reluctantly decided to go home.

They spread blankets in the hay loft, well away from the opening in the floor. Exploration began with gentle touches, fingertips tracing a jaw or trailing along an arm. He, the virgin, showed no hesitation. Coaching, probably. Who would he have gone to? Herri? Kessit? For herself, she was quickly lost in the novelty of a leisurely seduction. No one had ever undressed her gently. No one had ever asked her permission before reverently cupping her breasts. No one had ever paused to express interest in her reactions. No one had ever approached her in love rather than in lust.

Still, he was only fifteen and it was his first time. The moment he entered her his restraint cracked, then crumpled. With a groan he thrust once, twice, eyelids fluttering shut as the spasms took him. She raised her hips to meet him, holding him with her legs, caressing his back with her fingers. She marveled at the absence of pain.

He hung above her, arms beginning to quiver. Blinking his eyes back into focus he whispered, "Iris?"

"Come here." Awkwardly he complied, helping her shift their bodies until they lay side by side, still coupled, legs entwined. He stroked her shoulder, sending a shiver down her spine. She squirmed closer against him. If this was desire, it wasn't frightening. So many of the tales that filled her memory made sense now. Lust produced only a specialized form of violence. Desire—desire could mold lives, change the policies of entire kingdoms.

"I think that was a little too fast," he murmured. "I was selfish. I didn't do anything for you."

She pulled the dark head close and kissed him. "Don't say that, Tob. Never think it again." Her intensity alarmed him and he tried to lift himself on one elbow. Vray caressed his face, soothing him. She would not allow fear to intrude. Not for either of them.

"Just stay," she said more calmly. "You don't really think we're finished, do you?"

Tob subsided onto the blanket, as understanding and then appreciation put a mischievous gleam into his eye. "Ah. Now it comes. The truth revealed at last. Not so reluctant as you thought you were, eh? Or is it just my irresistibility?"

"Utterly irresistible," she agreed. Then her hand snaked down and danced along his ribcage.

He jerked back with a gasp of shock. "That's not fair!"

Vray rolled onto her knees but didn't follow up her advantage. When Tob saw he was safe from further tickling, he slowly unrolled from his defensive position.

"Let's start over," she suggested. "From the beginning. As we did before."

He knelt in front of her. "Only more so?"

"Only more so," she breathed.

CHAPTER 41

Jordy left the house well before dawn. The rain had ended during the night, but the sky was still obscured by clouds. He led Stockings down the hill out of the yard, depending on feel rather than sight to keep to the path. The eastward road was an avenue of darkness between darker, looming walls of faintly rustling vegetation. Jordy continued to walk until the road passed out of the small woods and the river became audible on his right. Then he mounted, and with the growing light, urged the horse to pick up her pace.

He had so much to say to Jenil that he couldn't decide where to begin. What had the woman been thinking of? Whose interests had she thought to serve, bringing the princess to Broadford? Family troubles, Ivey had said. Jordy's anger grew as he remembered the minstrel's casual familiarity with the girl's story. He must have been quite pleased with his cleverness. Fooling a gullible village with his tale. The girl's Redmother training, oh, aye, he understood that, now! Her service to Broadford had been founded on lies. Perhaps she'd never actually spoken falsely, but she hadn't spoken the truth, either. She'd misled them all.

Perhaps what troubled him most was the lack of purpose. Broadford hadn't benefited. They'd gained a Redmother they couldn't keep. What had the girl learned? Some embroidery? Some gardening? He kept returning to the same question: What had Jenil been thinking of to bring the girl to him?

He reached Garden Vale at midmorning. The residents were out and about, removing decorations and tidying up after the previous day's Festival. At the Brownmother house he was greeted with concern, under the natural assumption that he'd come for a healer. Two of the more experienced healers offered to return with him to Broadford at once, since the Greenmother herself was unavailable. She had gone to Sitrine and wasn't expected back for a nineday or more.

Jordy didn't lose his temper. He made the women understand that no one was ill, that he had other business with the Greenmother. He left the only message he could, that he wanted to speak with her and that if she would ask at any of the major markets of summer she'd be able to find him. The Brownmothers suggested he rest a while and have something to eat, but he declined. He watered Stockings at a public trough and turned at once for home.

Toward midday the clouds began to break, allowing patches of sunlight to dapple the river and fields. The breeze decreased fitfully, losing its chill. The change for the better in the weather did not improve his mood. He was faced with a decision he did not want to make. If he could see through the girl's deception, others would. She no longer kept to herself as she once had. All it would take would be a single traveler passing through who had known her in Edian. How had Ivey phrased it? The girl had been banished because she was an inconvenience. When word reached the royal court that she was no longer confined to the life they'd chosen for her, retribution was sure to follow. Broadford didn't need another visit from the king's guard.

No foresight, Jordy raged inwardly. That was the trouble with the Greenmother and the rest of her kind! No thought to the consequences of their actions. How many lives had Jenil irrevocably ruined this time?

Jordy did not go directly home. As they passed the foot of their lane, Stockings turned her head to look, but he anticipated her with a stern, "Walk on, m'girl," and she didn't pause. He rode her all the way to the entrance to the square, where he dismounted. He had to think before he spoke to Herri. The innkeeper had a right to know, but the knowledge itself could endanger him. Then there was Canis. The princess had turned to her for advice more than once. Canis would be deeply hurt to learn that everything she thought she knew about their Iris, beginning with her name, was a lie.

He turned to the left and led Stockings along the eastern edge of the square. The mare lowered her head, content to amble behind him and lick at the ground in a desultory search for a few blades of new grass. Fifteen or twenty of the older children were just completing the clean up of the inn yard. He saw the girl at once, folding an awning with Tob. Jordy watched them with growing unease. The girl's face shone with happiness. All of the young people seemed to be enjoying their work together, but this was something else. He saw Tob gather the folded bundle into his arms, his gaze never leaving her face. Her hand touched his forearm, a gesture of graceful familiarity. Tob bent toward her, confident, serene, giddy. The kiss was sweet and intimate. A few of the others glanced at them tolerantly before resuming their work.

Jordy stopped and leaned against the nearest tree, shaken. He'd seen it coming. It hadn't worried him before. He'd entertained the indulgent notion that they might have a future together. Now that was impossible.

Herri came out of the stable, saw him, and waved. Others turned in his direction, including Tob and the girl. Jordy had no choice but to walk over to the inn, Stockings trailing behind him.

"Where'd you go, Dad?" Tob said as soon as he drew near.

"Wanted to avoid the hard work," Herri observed.

"Like everyone else's parents," was Heather's tart comment. Her friends laughed appreciatively. The girl, now holding Tob's hand, smiled too.

"I had to go to Garden Vale," Jordy said.

"At least it turned out to be a pleasant day," Herri said.

The rest of the young people went back to their own conversations. They had no interest in carting business. Herri turned his head, saw two boys having trouble with dismantling the largest roasting spit, and hurried away to help. Only Jordy's children stood expectantly before him.

His children. Tob was his height now, perhaps an inch taller, and certainly outweighed him. He looked at the girl and his resolve faded. Was she still his child? His frightened Iris, now fully blossomed into a young woman. What were her hopes and dreams? In the last year she'd revealed so many fine qualities. He'd accepted her before he knew what kind of person she was. He couldn't back out of that commitment now. Whoever else she was, she was his daughter. His mouth tightened. He wouldn't deny her just because it was convenient.

A worry line formed between her eyebrows. "Is something wrong?"

"I have a lot to do," he explained lamely. "We really should be on the road tomorrow."

"That's something we wanted to talk to you about." Tob was brimming with more than newfound maturity. Something else had sparked his enthusiasm. "It's really between you and Iris, but I want you to know I think it's a great idea."

"What idea?" Jordy asked, perplexed.

Iris lifted her chin. Diffidence no longer interfered with her ability to express herself. "I've been thinking about my Redmother duties. I've gathered just about all of the village family memories, and taught them to Mankin. I've instructed her to learn Tagg's family on her own as part of her training. So I'll really have no urgent duties here until Fall Festival."

"True," Jordy agreed cautiously.

"I should know more stories. I never completed my training in Edian. I learned that every town and village has its own unique tales, but I didn't learn many of the tales themselves. I think I should. To properly fulfill my vows, I need to learn about the rest of the world."

Jordy made no comment. As a young princess, she must have studied Rhenlan and its neighbors. Which vows had prompted this renewal of interest? Redmother responsibility? Or something else entirely?

"I'd like to travel with you and Tob," she continued. "See life in Dherrica, hear the stories of Sitrine for myself."

"She could help us too, Dad," Tob put in eagerly. "Just

last summer you were saying how much you were looking forward to Pepper getting old enough to come with us. You said having another person to run errands would give you more time for the bartering."

"Yes, I'll help in whatever way I can," the girl said.

"I'm sure you will. " Jordy examined the suggestion for drawbacks. It was a good idea, better than Tob could know. Jordy's only doubts involved her motivation. Still, whatever her reasons, it was a valid request. She was old enough to decide how to improve herself. He'd been searching for a way to avoid attracting Damon's attention to Broadford. This was a temporary solution at best. In the fall they'd be tactically and physically right back where they'd started. But it was a solution.

"So she can come?" Tob asked.

"You want to see the world," Jordy said to her. "All right, lass. Ride with us."

Perhaps she would see a few things she didn't expect.

"I really should be going."

Doron measured another spoonful of ocher powder into her vat before looking toward her husband. He was seated on her tall stool, feet hooked on the rungs, Emlie in his lap. The baby stared raptly into her father's face while he alternately grimaced, stuck out his tongue, and crossed his eyes. Neither of them showed any inclination to interrupt the game.

"You've been saying that for four days," Doron observed.

"Well, I mean it." He held his large hand briefly over Emlie's eyes, then whisked it away, answering her start of surprise with a wide smile. Gurgling, she smiled back.

"Because spring is here and the dragons will be returning," Doron said, indulging him. She was well aware that he really couldn't remain in Juniper Ridge much longer. She supposed she should be urging him to get back to his work. It wasn't as if she needed him for anything. Emlie was a good baby. Pirse had already built a playpen for her in the corner of the dye shop and Doron knew she would continue to adapt her work habits to her baby's changing needs.

"It's not just the dragons," Pirse said, interrupting her thoughts. "I've been considering what to do about Palle."

Doron turned abruptly back to the dye vat. "I want you to stay away from him."

"He's ruining Dherrica."

"You do more than enough for Dherrica. You slay all the monsters that need slaying, you've forced the Abstainer bands to withdraw—"

"Only from this area. It's not enough, lassie. If I want to make a difference, I need access to the resources of the royal treasury, and full command of the guard. I need to be king."

"If you go to Bronle, he'll kill you."

"Aye. But perhaps I don't have to go to Bronle."

His speculative tone drew her unwillingly away from the soothing slosh of the dye vat. She came to stand in front of him, wiping her hands on her apron. "If I've heard it once from you, I've heard it a thousand times. You can't be king until you answer your uncle's rightful challenge."

"Aye." He picked up Emlie and held her against his shoulder. "That's his advantage. According to the evidence, I killed his sister. I owe him a life."

Doron's blood froze. She stepped forward and snatched Emlie out of his arms. "He can't have her."

"Of course not." A hurt expression crossed his face. "Besides, what use would Palle have for a Dreamer child?"

"Well then, what are you on about?" Doron snapped. Emlie's little face twisted into a frown, and she began a whimpered protest. Doron forced herself to relax and cuddle the baby gently until Emlie quieted once more.

Pirse got up and guided Doron to her rocking chair. Once she was settled there, he seemed to lose a bit of his serenity. He paced several times between her and the window, then finally dragged the stool close to her and perched on it, hands resting on his knees. "If I went to the law readers now, that would be their verdict. I owe Palle a life. A Shaper life. It's my life he'd prefer."

"Because he knows that you didn't kill Dea. If you can ever prove that, the throne is yours, not his. Especially because he probably killed her himself."

He shook his head. "What proof? I've dug and puzzled for years, talked with the wizards and Ivey and Captain Cratt's daughter. None of them can tell me how Dea really died. I doubt we'll ever know. What's important now is that I owe Dherrica an acceptable heir to my mother's throne. If I can't be king myself, I can still answer Palle's claim against me without actually having to face him. All I have to do is father a Shaper child."

"Father a Shaper . . ." As his meaning became clear, Doron's worry evaporated in a flash of indignation. "With a Shaper lass, I suppose?"

Pirse's chin jutted forward defensively. "That is the accepted procedure, aye."

"I don't suppose I have anything to say in the matter?"

"It's not as if there were a lot of options available!"

"Oh, aye, such a terrible choice," Doron mocked him. "Having to take another wife."

"I said nothing about a wife."

"What do you call it then? Bedding a woman, starting a family?"

"It's exactly what law readers demand in such cases!"

"It's not automatic, man! I've heard of other repayments that might be offered and accepted."

"I've tried to find proof that I didn't kill my mother. I can't. I can't let Palle remain king, either. I owe Dherrica a life."

"And what of the life Dherrica owes me!" Doron cried. "Where was your precious Shaper law when Betajj died?"

"Doron." He leaned toward her, picked up her hand and held it between his. Emlie squirmed in Doron's arms, craning her head to watch their faces. "That's just one more example of why I must reclaim the throne. Dherrica deserves law readers and Redmothers and a thousand things Palle will never permit."

"Rot," Doron said succinctly. "Sitrinian ideas. You spend too much time listening to their precious king."

"And your brother," he admitted. "Ivey knows how much Dherrica has lost. They've both given me some things to think about. Important things."

Doron pulled her hand away from him. "Like pretty Shaper lasses?"

"Aye. Kamara is pretty." He straightened and folded his arms over his chest. "Does that really matter?"

"It matters that you're not only considering this, you've already chosen the woman! An old friend from the court, I suppose."

"You'd rather I assault an unwilling stranger?" Pirse flared back at her.

Emlie started to cry. Doron, distracted, lifted the hem of her blouse and put the baby to her breast. The familiar, soothing routine of nursing calmed her as much as it did the baby. She looked up, and found Pirse watching them. His anger, too, had gone. Resignation, and a deep sadness, darkened his eyes and turned down the corners of his mouth.

"Oh, be off with you," Doron said, her voice low. "You'll do what you think you must. I can't stop you."

"You could understand me."

She understood all too well. He could not deny his Shaper's vows. To be truthful, she would probably throw him out of her house if he did. As painful as their fragmented relationship was, she cherished every devoted, earnest, honest, insufferably conscientious bone in his body.

She swallowed the ache in her throat. "Just see that you come back."

In two long-legged strides he was kneeling beside her again. He wrapped his arms around her and kissed her, Emlie gently enfolded between them. Doron closed her eyes when he pulled back, and didn't open them until she heard the sound of the gate and his footsteps trudging up the hill.

"You have to come back." Privacy freed the words she had never said in his presence. "Please, Pirse. I love you."

About the Authors

Marguerite Krause and Susan Sizemore have been friends since their days writing and editing for a Star Trek fanzine. In fact, they met through writing. Marguerite was Susan's first editor and publisher . . . long ago in a galaxy far far away.

When they decided to give up fan writing to try their luck in the world of professional publishing it seemed only natural to collaborate on a fantasy novel together. The results are *Moons' Dreaming* and *Moons' Dancing*.

Susan has been published in the romance and dark fantasy fields, both in paperback and by electronic publishers. She has won the Romance Writers of America's Golden Heart award. Susan is the proud mother of a spoiled mutt with a remarkable resemblance to the ancient Egyptian god Anubis.

Marguerite has become a freelance editor, and her fantasy novel, *Blind Vision*, was published by Speculation Press, in August, 2000. Marguerite is married, and the mother of two brilliant, award-winning children . . . who are both finally in college!